Elizabeth Kostova graduated from Yale and holds an MFA from the University of Michigan, where she won the Hopwood Award for the Novel-in-Progress for *The Historian.*

Also by Elizabeth Kostova

The Historian

The Swan Thieves

A novel

Elizabeth Kostova

sphere

SPHERE

First published in Great Britain in 2010 by Little, Brown
This paperback edition published in 2010 by Sphere
Reprinted 2010 (four times), 2011

All characters and events in this publication, other than those clearly in the public domain, are fictitious and any resemblance to real persons, living or dead, is purely coincidental.

A CIP catalogue record for this book
is available from the British Library.

ISBN 978-0-7515-4142-7

Printed and bound in Great Britain by
Clays Ltd, St Ives plc

Sphere
An imprint of
Little, Brown Book Group
100 Victoria Embankment
London EC4Y 0DY

An Hachette UK Company
www.hachette.co.uk

www.littlebrown.co.uk

For my mother
la bonne mère

You would hardly believe how difficult it is to place a figure alone on a canvas, and to concentrate all the interest on this single and universal figure and still keep it living and real.

—Édouard Manet, 1880

The Swan Thieves

Outside the village there is a fire ring, blackening the thawing snow. Next to the fire ring is a basket that has sat there for months and is beginning to weather to the color of ash. There are benches where the old men huddle to warm their hands—too cold even for that now, too close to twilight, too dreary. This is not Paris. The air smells of smoke and night sky; there is a hopeless amber sinking beyond the woods, almost a sunset. The dark is coming down so quickly that someone has already lit a lantern in the window of the house nearest the deserted fire. It is January or February, or perhaps a grim March, 1895—the year will be marked in rough black numbers against the shadows in one corner. The roofs of the village are slate, stained with melting snow, which slides off them in heaps. Some of the lanes are walled, others open to the fields and muddy gardens. The doors to the houses are closed, the scent of cooking rising above the chimneys.

Only one person is astir in all this desolation—a woman in heavy traveling clothes walking down a lane toward the last huddle of dwellings. Someone is lighting a lantern there, too, bending over the flame, a human form but indistinct in the distant window. The woman in the lane carries herself with dignity, and she isn't wearing the shabby apron and wooden sabots of the village. Her cloak and long skirts stand out against the violet snow. Her hood is edged with fur that hides all but the white curve of her cheek. The hem of her dress has a geometric border of pale blue. She is walking away with a bundle in her arms, something wrapped tightly, as if against the cold. The trees hold their branches numbly toward the sky; they frame the road. Someone has left a red cloth on the bench in front of the house at the end of the lane—a shawl, perhaps, or a small tablecloth, the only spot of bright color. The woman shields her bundle with her arms, with her gloved hands, turning her back on the center of the village as quickly as possible. Her boots click on a patch of ice in the road. Her breath shows pale against the gathering dark. She draws herself together, close, protective, hurrying. Is she leaving the village or hastening toward one of the houses in the last row?

Even the one person watching doesn't know the answer, nor does he care. He has worked most of the afternoon, stroking in the walls of the lanes, positioning the stark trees, measuring the road, waiting for the ten minutes of winter sunset. The woman is an intruder, but he puts her in, too, quickly, noting the details of her clothes, using the failing daylight to brush in the silhouette of her hood, the way she bends forward to stay warm or to hide her bundle. A beautiful surprise, whoever she is. She is the missing note, the movement he needed to fill that central stretch of road with its dirt-pocked snow. He has long since retreated, working now just inside his window—he is old and his limbs ache if he paints out of doors in the cold for more than a quarter of an hour—so he can only imagine her quick breath, her step on the road, the crunch of snow under her sharp boot heel. He is aging, ill, but for a moment he wishes she would turn and look straight at him. He pictures her hair as dark and soft, her lips vermilion, her eyes large and wary.

But she does not turn, and he finds he is glad. He needs her as she is, needs her moving away from him into the snowy tunnel of his canvas, needs the straight form of her back and heavy skirts with their elegant border, her arm cradling the wrapped object. She is a real woman and she is in a hurry, but now she is also fixed forever. Now she is frozen in her haste. She is a real woman and now she is a painting.

CHAPTER 1

Marlow

I got the call about Robert Oliver in April 1999, less than a week after he'd pulled a knife in the nineteenth-century collection at the National Gallery. It was a Tuesday, one of those terrible mornings that sometimes come to the Washington area when spring has already been flowery and even hot—ruinous hail and heavy skies, with rumbles of thunder in the suddenly cold air. It was also, by coincidence, exactly a week after the massacre at Columbine High School in Littleton, Colorado; I was still thinking obsessively about that event, as I imagined every psychiatrist in the country must have been. My office seemed full of those young people with their sawed-off shotguns, their demonic resentment. How had we failed them and—even more—their innocent victims? The violent weather and the country's gloom seemed to me fused that morning.

When my phone rang, the voice on the other end was that of a friend and colleague, Dr. John Garcia. John is a fine man—and a fine psychiatrist—with whom I went to school long ago and who takes me out for lunch now and then at the restaurant of his choice, seldom allowing me to pay. He does emergency intake and inpatient care in one of Washington's biggest hospitals and, like me, also sees private patients.

John was telling me now that he wanted to transfer a patient to me, to put him in my care, and I could hear the eagerness in his voice. "This guy could be a difficult case. I don't know what you'll make of him, but I'd prefer for him to be under your care at Goldengrove. Apparently he's an artist, a successful one—he got himself arrested last week, then brought to us. He doesn't talk much and doesn't like us much, here. His name is Robert Oliver."

"I've heard of him, but I don't really know his work," I admitted. "Landscapes and portraits—I think he was on the cover of *ARTnews* a couple of years ago. What did he do to get arrested?" I turned to the window and stood, watching hail fall like expensive white gravel over the walled back lawn and a battered magnolia. The grass was already very green, and for a second there was watery sunlight over everything, then a fresh burst of hail.

"He tried to attack a painting in the National Gallery. With a knife."

"A painting? Not a person?"

"Well, apparently there was no one else in the room at that moment, but a guard came in and saw him lunging for a painting."

"Did he put up a fight?" I watched hail sowing itself in the bright grass.

"Yes. He eventually dropped the knife on the floor, but then he grabbed the guard and shook him up pretty badly. He's a big man. Then he stopped and let himself just be led away, for some reason. The museum is trying to decide whether or not to press assault charges. I think they're going to drop, but he took a big risk."

I studied the backyard again. "National Gallery paintings are federal property, right?"

"Right."

"What kind of knife was it?"

"Just a pocketknife. Nothing dramatic, but he could have done a lot of damage. He was very excited, thought he was on a heroic mission, and then broke down at the station, said he hadn't slept in days, even cried a little. They brought him over to the psych ER, and I admitted him." I could hear John waiting for my answer.

"How old is this guy?"

"He's young—well, forty-three, but that sounds young to me these days, you know?" I knew, and laughed. Turning fifty just two years before had shocked us both, and we'd covered it by celebrating with several friends who were in the same situation.

"He had a couple of other things on him, too—a sketchbook and a packet of old letters. He won't let anyone else touch them."

"So what do you want me to do for him?" I found myself leaning against the desk to rest; I'd come to the end of a long morning, and I was hungry.

"Just take him," John said.

But the habits of caution run deep in our profession. "Why? Are you trying to give me additional headaches?"

"Oh, come on." I could hear John smiling. "I've never known you to turn a patient away, Dr. Dedication, and this one should be worth your while."

"Because I'm a painter?"

He hesitated only a beat. "Frankly, yes. I don't pretend to understand artists, but I think you'll get this guy. I told you he doesn't talk much, and when I say he doesn't talk much, I mean I've gotten maybe three sentences out of him. I think he's switching into depression, in spite of the meds we started him on. He also shows anger and has periods of agitation. I'm worried about him."

I considered the tree, the emerald lawn, the scattered melting hailstones, again the tree. It stood a little to the left of center, in the window, and the darkness of the day had given its mauve and white buds a brightness they didn't have when the sun shone. "What do you have him on?"

John ran through the list: a mood stabilizer, an antianxiety drug, and an antidepressant, all at good doses. I picked up a pen and pad from my desk.

"Diagnosis?"

John told me, and I wasn't surprised. "Fortunately for us, he signed a release of information in the ER while he was still talking. We've also just gotten copies of records from a psychiatrist in North Carolina he saw about two years ago. Apparently the last time he saw anybody."

"Does he have significant anxiety?"

"Well, he won't talk about it, but I think he shows it. And this isn't his first round of meds, according to the file. In fact, he arrived here with some Klonopin in a two-year-old bottle in his jacket. It probably wasn't doing him much good without a mood stabilizer on board. We finally got hold of the wife in North Carolina—ex-wife, actually—and she told us some more about his past treatments."

"Suicidal?"

"Possibly. It's hard to do a proper assessment, since he won't talk. He hasn't attempted anything here. He's more like enraged. It's like keeping a bear in a cage—a silent bear. But with this kind of presentation, I don't want to just release him. He's got to stay somewhere for a while, have someone figure out what's really going on, and his meds will need fine-tuning. He did sign in voluntarily, and I bet he'll go pretty willingly at this point. He doesn't like it here."

"So you think I can get him to talk?" It was our old joke, and John rose obligingly to it.

"Marlow, you could get a stone to talk."

"Thanks for the compliment. And thanks especially for messing up my lunch break. Does he have insurance?"

"Some. The social worker is on that."

"All right—have him brought out to Goldengrove. Tomorrow at two, with the files. I'll check him in."

We hung up, and I stood there wondering if I could squeeze in five minutes of sketching while I ate, which I like to do when my schedule is heavy; I still had a one thirty, a two o'clock, a three o'clock, a four o'clock, and then a meeting at five o'clock. And tomorrow I would put in a ten-hour day at Goldengrove, the private residential center where I'd worked for the previous twelve years. Now I needed my soup, my salad, and the pencil under my fingers for a few minutes.

I thought, too, of something I had forgotten about for a long time, although I used to remember it often. When I was twenty-one, freshly graduated from Columbia (which had filled me with history and English as well as science) and headed already for medical school at the University of Virginia, my parents volunteered enough money to help me go with my roommate to Italy and Greece for a month. It was my first time out of the United States. I was electrified by paintings in Italian churches and monasteries, by the architecture of Florence and Siena. On the Greek island of Páros, which produces the most perfect, translucent marble in the world, I found myself alone in a local archaeological museum.

This museum had only one statue of value, which stood in a room by itself. Herself: she was a Nike, about five feet tall, in battered pieces, with no head or arms, and with scars on her back where she'd once sprouted wings, red stains on the marble from her long entombment in the island earth. You could still see her masterful carving, the draperies like an eddy of water over her body. They had reattached one of her little feet. I was alone in the room, sketching her, when the guard came in for a moment to shout, "Close soon!" After he left, I packed up my drawing kit, and then—without any thought of the consequences—I approached the Nike one last time and bent to kiss her foot. The guard was on me in a second, roaring, actually collaring me. I've never been thrown out of a bar, but that day I was thrown out of a one-guard museum.

I picked up the phone and called John back, caught him still in his office.

"What was the painting?"

"What?"

"The painting that your patient—Mr. Oliver—attacked."

John laughed. "You know, I wouldn't have thought of asking that, but it was included in the police report. It's called *Leda*. A Greek myth, I guess. At least that's what comes to mind. The report said it was a painting of a naked woman."

"One of Zeus's conquests," I said. "He came to her in the form of a swan. Who painted it?"

"Oh, come on—you're making this feel like Art History 125. Which I almost failed, by the way. I don't know who painted it and I doubt the arresting officer did either."

"All right. Get back to work. Have a good day, John," I said, trying to uncrick my neck and hold the receiver at the same time.

"And you, my friend."

CHAPTER 2

Marlow

Already I have the urge to begin this history over again by insisting that it is a private one. And not only private but subject to my imagination as much as to the facts. It has taken me ten years to sort through my notes on this case, and through my thoughts as well; I confess I originally considered writing something about Robert Oliver for one of the psychiatric journals I most admire and where I've published before, but who can publish what might eventually prove to be professional compromise? We live in an era of talk shows and gargantuan indiscretion, but our profession is particularly rigid in its silences—careful, legal, responsible. At its best. Of course, there are cases when wisdom rather than rules must prevail; every doctor knows such emergencies. I've taken the precaution of changing all the names associated with this story, including my own, with the exception of one first name so common, but also so beautiful to me now, that I see no harm in retaining the original.

I wasn't raised around the medical profession: my parents were both ministers—in fact, my mother was the first female minister in their smallish sect, and I was eleven when she was ordained. We lived in the oldest structure in our town in Connecticut, a low-roofed maroon clapboard house with a front yard like an English cemetery, where arborvitae, yews, weeping willows, and other funereal trees competed for space around the slate walk to the front door.

Every afternoon at three fifteen, I walked up to that house from school, dragging my knapsack full of books and crumbs, baseballs and colored pencils. My mother opened the door, usually in her blue skirt and sweater, later sometimes in her black suit and white dog collar if she'd been visiting the sick, the elderly, the shut-in, the newly penitent. I was a grumbling child, a child with bad posture and a chronic sense that life was disappointingly not what it had promised to be; she was a strict mother—strict, upright, cheerful, and affectionate. When she saw my early gift for drawing and sculpting, she encouraged it with quiet certainty day after day, never inflating her praise and yet never allowing me to doubt my own efforts. We could not have been more different, I think, from the moment I was born, and we loved each other fiercely.

It's odd, but although my mother died rather young, or perhaps because she did, I have found myself in middle age becoming more and more like her. For years, I was not so much single as unmarried, although I finally rectified that situation. The women I've loved are (or were) all something like I was as a child—moody, perverse, interesting. Around them, I have become more and more like my mother. My wife is not an exception to this pattern, but we suit each other.

Partly in response to those once-loved women and my wife, and partly, I have no doubt, in response to a profession that displays to me daily the underside of the mind—the misery of its environmental molding, its genetic vagaries—I've retrained myself since childhood into a kind of diligent goodwill toward life. Life and I became friends some years ago—not the sort of exciting friendship I longed for as a child, but a kindly truce, a pleasure in coming home every day to my apartment on Kalorama Road. I have a moment now and then—as I peel an orange and take it from kitchen counter to table—when I feel almost a pang of contentment, perhaps at that raw color.

I have achieved this only in adulthood. Children are assumed to enjoy little things, but actually I remember dreaming only big as a child, and then the narrowing of that dream from one interest to another, and then the channeling of all my dreams into biology and chemistry and the goal of medical school, and finally the revelation of the infinitesimal episodes of life, their neurons and helices and revolving atoms. I first learned to draw really well, in fact, from those tiniest shapes and shades in my biology labs, not from anything as large as mountains, people, or bowls of fruit.

Now when I dream big, it's for my patients, that they may eventually feel that ordinary cheerfulness of kitchen and orange, of putting their feet up in front of a television documentary, or the even bigger pleasures I imagine for them of holding down a job, coming home sane to their families, seeing the realities of a room instead of a terrible panorama of faces. For myself, I have learned to dream small—a leaf, a new paintbrush, the flesh of an orange, and the details of my wife's beauty, a glistening at the corners of her eyes, the soft hair of her arms in our living room's lamplight when she sits reading.

I said I wasn't raised around the medical profession, but perhaps it isn't so strange that I should have chosen the branch of it I did. My mother and father were not at all scientific, although their personal discipline, transmitted to me along with my oatmeal and clean socks with the intensity parents pour through an only child, stood me in good stead through the rigors of college biology and the worse rigors of med school—the rigor mortis of nights spent entirely in study and memorization, the relative relief of later sleepless nights hurrying around on hospital rotations.

I had dreamed of being an artist, too, but when the time came for me to select my life's work, I chose medicine, and I knew from the beginning it would be psychiatry, which for me was both a healing profession and the ultimate science of human experience; in fact, I'd also applied to art schools after college, and to my pleasure had been accepted at two rather good ones. I'd like to be able to say it was an agonized decision, that the artist in me rebelled against medicine. In reality, I felt that I could not make a serious enough social contribution as a painter, and I secretly dreaded the drift and struggle to make a living that that way of life might entail. Psychiatry would be a direct path to serving a suffering world while I would continue to paint on my own, and it would be enough, I thought, to know I could have been a career artist.

My parents reflected deeply on my choice of specialty, as I could tell when I mentioned it to them in one of our weekend telephone conversations. There was a pause on their end while they digested what I had laid out for myself and why I might have selected it. Then my mother observed calmly that *everyone* needs someone to talk to, which was her way of quite rightly connecting their ministry and mine, and my father observed that there are many ways to drive out demons.

Actually, my father does not believe in demons; they don't figure in his modern and progressive calling. He likes to refer sarcastically to them, even now in his very old age, and to read about them, shaking his head, in the works of early New England preachers such as Jonathan Edwards, or in those of the medieval theologians who also fascinate him. He is like a reader of horror fiction: he reads them because they upset him. When he refers to "demons" and "hellfire" and "sin," he means these things ironically, with a disgusted fascination; the parishioners who still come to his study in our old house (he will never fully retire) receive instead a profoundly forgiving picture of their own torments. He concedes that although he deals in souls and I deal in diagnoses, environmental factors, behavioral outcomes, DNA, we are striving for the same end: the end of misery.

After my mother became a minister as well, our household was a busy one, and I found plenty of time to escape on my own, shaking off my occasional malaise with the distraction of books and explorations in the park at the end of our street, where I sat reading under a tree, or sketching scenes of mountains and deserts I had certainly never seen myself. The books I liked best were either adventures at sea or adventures in invention and research. I found as many children's biographies as I could—on Thomas Edison, Alexander Graham Bell, Eli Whitney, and others—and later discovered the adventure of medical research: that of Jonas Salk and polio, for example. I was not an energetic child, but I dreamed about doing something courageous. I dreamed of saving lives, of stepping forward at the right moment with some lifesaving revelation. Even now, I never read an article in a scientific journal without a version of that feeling: the thrill of vicarious discovery and the twinge of envy for the discoverer.

I can't say that this desire to be a saver of lives was the great theme of my childhood, although, as it turns out, that would make a neat story. In fact, I had no vocation, and those biographies for children had become a memory by the time I was in high school, where I did my homework well but without unusual enthusiasm, read extra Dickens and Melville with considerably more pleasure, took art classes, ran cross-country with no distinction, and lost my virginity with a sigh of relief my junior year to a more experienced girl, a senior, who told me she'd always liked the back of my head in class.

My parents did rise to some distinction themselves in our

town, defending and successfully rehabilitating a homeless man who'd wandered in from Boston to take up shelter in our parks. They traveled to the local prison to give talks together, and they prevented a house nearly as old as ours (1691—ours was 1686) from being torn down for a supermarket lot. They came to my track meets and chaperoned my proms and invited my friends for ecumenical pizza parties and officiated at the memorial services of their friends who died young. There were no funerals in their creed, no propped-open coffins, no bodies to pray over, so that I didn't touch a cadaver until medical school and I didn't see a dead person I knew personally until I was holding my mother's hand—her perfectly limp, still-warm hand.

But years before my mother died, and while I was still in school, I made the friend I mentioned before, who gave me the greatest case of my career, if we're going to relent and put it that way. John Garcia was one of several male friends from my twenties—college friends with whom I studied for biology quizzes and history exams or threw a football around on Saturday afternoons, and who are now balding, other men I knew in medical school by their quick steps and flying white jackets in labs and lectures or later in the throes of awkward patient interactions. We were all getting a little gray by the time of John's phone call, a little sloped around the middle or else valiantly leaner in our attempts to combat sloping—I was already grateful to myself for my lifelong running habit, which had kept me more or less lean, even strong. And to fate for the fact that my hair was still thick and as much brown as silver, and that women still glanced my way on the street. But I was indisputably one of them, my cohort of middle-aged friends.

So when John called to ask me his favor that Tuesday, of course I said yes. When he told me about Robert Oliver, I was interested, but I was also interested in my lunch, my chance to stretch my legs and shake off the morning. We are never really alert to our destinies, are we? That's how my father would put it, in his study in Connecticut. And by the end of the day, when my meeting was over and the hail had changed to a fine drizzle and the squirrels were running along the backyard wall and leaping over the urns, I had almost stopped thinking about John's call.

Later, after I'd walked quickly home from my office and shaken out my coat in my own foyer—this was before I was married, so no one greeted me at the door and there was no sweet-smelling blouse from the workday slung over the foot of the bed—after I'd left the streaming umbrella to dry and washed my hands and made a salmon sandwich on toast and gone into my studio to pick up the paintbrush—then, with the thin, smooth wood between my fingers, I remembered my patient-to-be, a painter who had brandished a knife instead. I put on my favorite music, the Franck Violin Sonata in A Major, and forgot about him on purpose. The day had been long and a little empty, until I began to fill it with color. But the next day always comes, unless we actually die, and the next day I met Robert Oliver.

Chapter 3

Marlow

He stood by the window of his new room, looking out of it, hands dangling at his sides. He turned as I came in. My new patient was an inch or two over six feet, powerfully built, and when he faced you head-on he stooped a little, like a charging bull. His arms and shoulders were full of barely restrained strength, his expression dogged, self-assertive. His skin was lined, tanned; his hair was almost black and very thick, touched with silver, breaking in waves off his head, and it stood out farther on one side than the other, as if he rumpled it often. He was dressed in baggy pants of olive corduroy, a yellow cotton shirt, and a corduroy jacket with patches on the elbows. He wore heavy brown leather shoes.

Robert's clothes were stained with oil paint, smudges of alizarin, cerulean, yellow ocher—colors vivid against that determined drabness. He had paint under his fingernails. He stood restlessly, shifting from foot to foot or crossing his arms, exposing the elbow patches. Two different women later told me that Robert Oliver was the most graceful man they had ever met, which makes me wonder what women notice that I don't. On the windowsill behind him lay a packet of fragile-looking papers; I thought these must be the "old letters" John Garcia had referred to. As I came toward him, Robert glanced directly at me—this was not the last time I was to feel that we were in the ring together—and his eyes were momentarily bright and expressive, a deep gold-green, and rather bloodshot. Then his face closed angrily; he turned his head away.

I introduced myself and offered my hand. "How are you feeling today, Mr. Oliver?"

After a moment he shook hands firmly in return but said nothing and seemed to slip into languor and resentment, folding his arms and leaning against the windowsill.

"Welcome to Goldengrove. I'm glad to have the chance to meet you."

He met my gaze but still said nothing.

I sat down in the armchair in the corner and watched him for a few minutes before speaking again. "I read your file from Dr. Garcia's office just now. I understand you had a very difficult day last week, and that's what brought you to the hospital."

At this he gave a curious smile and spoke for the first time. "Yes," he said. "I had a difficult day."

I had achieved my first goal: he was talking. I composed myself so I wouldn't show any pleasure or surprise.

"Do you remember what happened?"

He still looked directly at me, but his face registered no emotion. It was a strange face, just balanced between the rough and the elegant, a face of striking bone structure, the nose long but also broad. "A little."

"Would you care to tell me about it? I'm here to help you, first by listening."

He said nothing.

I repeated, "Would you like to tell me a little about it?" Still he was silent, so I tried another tack. "Did you know that what you attempted to do the other day was reported in the papers? I didn't see the article myself, at the time, but someone's just given me a clipping. You made page four."

He looked away.

I persisted. "The headline was something like this—'Artist Attacks Painting in National Gallery.'"

He laughed suddenly, a surprisingly sweet sound. "That's accurate, in a way. But I didn't touch it."

"The guard seized you first, right?"

He nodded.

"And you fought back. Did you resent being pulled away from the painting?"

This time a new expression came over his face: it was grim, and he bit the corner of his lip. "Yes."

"It was a painting of a woman, wasn't it? How did you feel when you attacked her?" I asked as suddenly as I could. "What made you feel like doing that?"

His response was equally sudden. He shook himself, as if trying to throw off the mild tranquilizer he was still on, and squared his shoulders. He seemed even more commanding in that moment, and I saw that he could have been quite intimidating if violent.

"I did it for her."

"For the woman herself? Did you want to protect her?"

He was silent.

I tried again. "Do you mean you felt she somehow wanted to be attacked?"

He looked down then and sighed as if it hurt him even to exhale. "No. You don't understand. I wasn't attacking her. I did it for the woman I loved."

"For someone else? Your wife?"

"You can think whatever you like."

I kept my gaze fixed on him. "Did you feel you were doing it for your wife? Your ex-wife?"

"You can talk with her," he said, as if he didn't care one way or the other. "You can even talk with Mary if you want.

You can look at the pictures if you want. I don't care. You can talk to anybody you want."

"Who is Mary?" I asked. It was not his ex-wife's name. I waited a little, but he was silent. "Are the pictures you mentioned pictures of her? Or do you mean the painting at the National Gallery?"

He stood in utter silence before me, gazing somewhere over my head.

I waited; I can wait like a rock when I need to. After three or four minutes, I observed placidly, "You know, I'm a painter myself." I don't often comment about myself, of course, and certainly not in an initial session, but I thought it was worth the small risk.

He flashed me a look that could have been either interest or contempt, and then he lay down on the bed, stretched out full length on his back with his shoes on the bedspread and his arms behind his head, gazing upward as if at open sky.

"I am sure only something very difficult could have compelled you to attack a painting." That was another risk, but it, too, seemed worth taking.

He closed his eyes and rolled away from me, as if preparing for a nap. I waited. Then, observing that he wasn't going to speak further, I stood up. "Mr. Oliver, I am here whenever you need me. And you are here so that we can care for you and help you get well again. Please feel free to have the nurse call me. I'll come see you again soon. You can ask for me if you'd simply like a little company—there's no need to talk more until you're ready."

I couldn't have known how thoroughly he would take me at my word. When I visited the next day, the nurse said he hadn't spoken to her all morning, although he had eaten a little breakfast and seemed calm. His silence wasn't reserved for the nurses; he didn't speak to me either—not that day or the next, nor for the following twelve months. During this period his ex-wife did not visit him; in fact, he had no visitors. He continued to display many of the symptoms of clinical depression, with periods of silent agitation and perhaps anxiety.

During most of the time he was with me, I never seriously considered releasing Robert from my care, partly because I could never be completely sure whether or not he was a possible risk to himself and others, and partly because of a feeling of my own that evolved a little at a time and to which I'll admit gradually; I've already confessed that I have my reasons for considering this a private story. In those first weeks, I continued treating him with the mood stabilizer John had started him on, and I also continued the antidepressant.

His one previous psychiatric report, which John had sent me, indicated a serious recurrent mood disorder and a trial of lithium—Robert had apparently refused the drug after a few months of treatment, saying it exhausted him. But the report also described a patient frequently functional, holding down a teaching job at a small college, pursuing his artwork, and trying to engage with family and colleagues. I called his former psychiatrist myself, but the fellow was busy and told me little, except to admit that after a certain point he had found Oliver an unmotivated patient. Robert had seen a psychiatrist mainly at his wife's request and had stopped his visits before he and his wife had separated more than a year before. Robert had not had any long-term psychotherapy, nor had he been previously hospitalized. The doctor hadn't even been aware that Robert no longer lived in Greenhill.

Robert now took his medication without protest, in the same resigned way in which he ate—an unusual sign of cooperation in a patient so defiant as to hew to a vow of silence. He ate sparingly, also without apparent interest, and kept himself rigorously clean despite his depression. He did not interact with the other patients in any way, but he did take supervised daily walks inside and outside and sometimes sat in the bigger of the lounges, occupying a chair in a sunny corner.

In his periods of agitation, which at first occurred every day or two, he paced his room, fists clenched, body trembling visibly, face working. I watched him carefully and had my staff do the same. One morning he cracked the mirror in his bathroom with the butt of his fist, although he didn't injure himself. Sometimes he sat on the edge of his bed with his head in his hands, jumping up every few minutes to look out the window, then settling again into that attitude of despair. When he was not agitated, he was listless.

The only thing that seemed to interest Robert Oliver was his package of old letters, which he kept close to him and frequently opened and read. Often, when I visited him, he had a letter in front of him. And once during the first weeks, I observed before he folded the letter up and put it back into its faded envelope that the pages were covered with regular, elegant handwriting in brown ink. "I've noticed you're often reading the same thing—these letters. Are they antiques?"

He closed his hand over the package and turned away, his face as full of misery as any I'd seen in my years of treating patients. No, I could not discharge him, even if he had stretches of calm that lasted several days. Some mornings I invited him to talk to me—with no result—and some I simply sat with him. Every weekday I asked him how he was doing, and Monday through Friday he looked away from me and out the nearby window.

All this behavior presented a vivid picture of torment, but how could I know what had been the trigger for his breakdown when I couldn't discuss it with him? It occurred to me, among other ideas, that he might be suffering from post-traumatic stress disorder in addition to his basic diagnosis; but, if so, what had the trauma been? Or could his own breakdown and arrest in the museum have traumatized him this much by themselves? There was no evidence of a past tragedy in the few records I had at my command, although likely his split with his wife would have been upsetting. I tried gently, whenever it seemed the right moment, to prompt him toward conversation. His silence held, and so did his obsessive and private rereading. One morning I asked him whether he would consider allowing me to look at his letters, in confidence, since they clearly meant a great deal to him. "I promise I wouldn't keep them, of course, or if you let me borrow them, I could have copies made and return them safely to you."

He turned toward me then, and I saw something like curiosity on his face, but he soon grew sullen and brooding again. He collected the letters carefully, without meeting my gaze anymore, and turned away from me on his bed. After a moment, I had no choice but to leave the room.

Chapter 4

Marlow

Entering Robert's room during his second week with us, I observed that he had been drawing in his sketchbook. The drawing was a simple image of a woman's head in three-quarter profile, with curly dark hair roughed in. I recognized at once his extreme facility and expressiveness; these qualities leapt off the page. It's easy to say what makes a sketch weak but harder to explain the coherence and internal vigor that bring it to life. Oliver's drawings were alive, beyond alive. When I asked him whether he was sketching from imagination or drawing a real person, he ignored me more pointedly than ever, closing the book and putting it away. The next time I visited, he was pacing the room, and I could see him clenching and unclenching his jaw.

Watching, I felt anew that it wouldn't be safe to release him unless we could ascertain that he would not become violent again from the stimulus of his everyday life. I didn't even know what that life consisted of; the Goldengrove secretary had done a preliminary search for me, but we couldn't track down any place of employment for him in the Washington area. Did he have the means to stay home and paint all day? He wasn't listed in the DC telephone directory, and the address John Garcia had received from the police had turned out to be that of Robert's ex-wife in North Carolina. He was angry, depressed, approaching real fame, apparently homeless. The episode with the sketchbook had made me hopeful, but the hostility that followed it was deeper than ever.

His sheer skill on paper intrigued me, as did the fact that he had a genuine reputation; although I usually avoided unnecessary research on the Web, I looked him up. Robert held an MFA from one of New York's premier arts programs and had taught there briefly, as well as at Greenhill College and a college in New York State. He had placed second in the National Portrait Gallery's annual competition, received a couple of national fellowships and residencies, and had solo shows in New York, Chicago, and Greenhill. His work had indeed appeared on the cover of several well-known art magazines. There were a few images from his sales over the years—portraits and landscapes, including two untitled portraits of a dark-haired woman like the one he'd been sketching in his room. They owed something, I thought, to Impressionist tradition.

I found no artist's statements or interviews; Robert himself was as silent on the internet, I thought, as he was in my presence. It seemed to me that his work might be a worthwhile channel of communication, and I provided him with plenty of good paper, charcoal, pencils, and pens, which I brought from home myself. He used these to continue his drawings of the woman's head when he wasn't rereading his letters. He began to prop up the drawings here and there, and when I left some tape in his room, he fastened them to the walls in a chaotic gallery. As I've said, his draftsmanship was extraordinary; I read in it both long training and an enormous natural gift, which I was later to see in his paintings. He soon varied his sketches of the woman's profile to full-face; I could observe her fine features and large dark eyes. Sometimes she smiled, and sometimes she seemed angry; anger predominated. Naturally, I conjectured that the image might be an expression of his silent rage, and I also speculated about some possible confusion of gender identity within the patient, although I couldn't get him to respond even nonverbally to questions on this topic.

When Robert Oliver had resided at Goldengrove for more than two weeks without speaking, I had the idea of outfitting his room as a studio. I had to get special permission from the center for my experiment, and to put a few security measures in place: it was a risk, granted, but Robert had shown full responsibility when using his pencils and other drawing supplies. I considered equipping a corner of the OT Room instead. However, Robert was unlikely to paint in front of other people, I thought, in this situation. I arranged his room myself while he was on one of his walks, and I was there to observe his reaction when he returned.

The room was a sunny one, and a single, and I'd moved the bed to one side to make space for a large easel. I had stocked the shelves with oil paints, watercolors, gesso, rags, jars of brushes, mineral spirits and oil medium, a wooden palette and palette scrapers; some of these items I brought from my own supplies at home, so that they were not new and would give the feel of a working studio. I stacked one wall with empty stretched canvases of varying sizes and provided a block of watercolor paper.

Finally, I sat down in my customary chair in the corner to observe him as he came back in. At the sight of all the equipment I'd put there, he stopped short, clearly startled. Then an expression of fury crossed his face. He started toward me, his fists clenched, and I stayed seated, as calmly as I could, without speaking. I thought for a moment that he would actually say something, or perhaps even hit me, but he seemed to think better of both urges. His body relaxed a little; he turned away and began to examine the new supplies. He felt the watercolor paper, studied the construction of the easel, glanced at the tubes of oil paints. At last he wheeled around and glared at me again, this time as if he wanted to ask me something but couldn't bring himself to do it. I wondered, not for the first time, if he had somehow become unable, rather than simply unwilling, to speak.

"I hope you'll enjoy these items," I said as placidly as possible.

He looked at me, his face dark. I left the room without trying to speak to him again.

Two days later, I found him painting with deep absorption on a first canvas, which he had apparently prepared for that purpose overnight. He did not acknowledge my presence, but he allowed me to observe him and to study the picture, which was a portrait. I examined it with the greatest interest; I'm first and foremost a portrait painter myself, although I also love landscape, and the fact that my long work hours prevent me from painting from live models on a regular basis is a source of sorrow to me. I work with photographs when I have to, although that runs against my natural purism. It's better than nothing, and I always learn from the exercise.

But Robert, as far as I knew, had painted his new canvas without even a photograph to refer to, and it radiated startling life. It showed the usual head of a woman—now, of course, in color—in the same traditionalist style as his drawings. She had an extraordinarily real face, with dark eyes that looked directly out of the canvas—a confident yet thoughtful gaze. Her hair was curly and dark, with some chestnut lights in it; she had a fine nose, a square chin with a dimple on the right side, an amused, sensuous mouth. Her forehead was high and white, and what little I could see of her clothing was green, with a yellow ruffle around a deep V of neckline, a curve of skin. Today she looked almost happy, as if it pleased her to be appearing in color at last. It's strange for me to think of this now, but at that moment and for months afterward, I had no idea who she was.

That was a Wednesday, and on Friday, when I went to see Robert, the room was empty; he had apparently gone out for his walk. The portrait of the dark-haired lady stood on the easel—nearly finished, I thought—magnificent. On the chair where I usually sat lay an envelope addressed to me in loose script. Inside it I found Robert's antique letters. I drew one out and held it in my hand for a long minute. The paper looked very old, and the elegantly handwritten lines I could see on the outer side were in French, to my surprise. I suddenly felt how far I might have to travel to know the man who had entrusted them to me.

CHAPTER 5

Marlow

I hadn't intended at first to take the letters off the Goldengrove property, but at the end of the day I put them in my briefcase. On Saturday morning I called my friend Zoe, who teaches French literature at Georgetown University. Zoe is one of the women I dated when I first came to Washington years ago, and we've remained good friends, especially since I didn't feel strongly enough about her to regret her terminating our relationship. She made excellent occasional company to a play or a concert, and I think she felt the same about me.

The phone rang twice before she answered. "Marlow?" Her voice was businesslike, as always, but also affectionate. "How nice that you called. I was thinking about you the other week."

"Why didn't you call me, then?" I asked.

"Grading papers," she said. "I haven't called anyone."

"I forgive you, in that case," I replied sarcastically, since that's our custom. "I'm glad you're done with the papers, because I have a possible project for you."

"Oh, Marlow." I could hear her doing something in her kitchen as she talked to me; her kitchen dates from just after the Revolutionary War and is the size of my hall closet. "Marlow, I don't need any projects. I'm writing a book, as you know from paying at least a little attention these last three years."

"I know, dear," I said. "But this is something you'll like,

exactly your period—I think—and I want you to see it. Come over this afternoon and I'll ask you out to dinner."

"It must be worth a lot to you," she said. "I can't do dinner, but I'll come over at five—I'm going to Dupont Circle after that."

"You have a date," I said approvingly. I was a little shocked to realize how long it had been since I'd had anything like a date. How had so much time slipped by me?

"You bet I do," Zoe said.

We sat in my living room, unfolding the letters Robert had carried on him even during his attack at the museum. Zoe's coffee was cooling off; she hadn't even started it. She'd aged a little since I'd last seen her, in some way that made her olive skin look weary and her hair dry. But her eyes were narrow and bright, as always, and I remembered that I must be aging in her sight, too. "Where did you get these?" she asked.

"A cousin sent them to me."

"A French cousin?" She looked skeptical. "Do you have French roots I don't know about?"

"Not particularly." I hadn't planned this well. "I guess she got them at an antique shop or someplace and thought they would interest me because I like to read history."

She was scanning the first one now, with gentle hands and a keen glance. "Are they all from eighteen seventy-seven through seventy-nine?"

"I don't know. I haven't looked through them thoroughly. I was afraid to because they're so fragile, and what I saw, I couldn't understand much of."

She opened another. "It would take me some time to read them properly, because of the handwriting, but they seem to be letters from a woman to her uncle, and vice versa, as you've already figured out, and some of them are about painting and drawing. Maybe that's why your cousin thought they'd interest you."

"Maybe." I tried not to peer over her shoulder.

"Let me take one that's in better condition and translate it for you. You're right—that might be fun. But I don't think I can do them all—it's incredibly time-consuming, you know, and I have to get on with my book right away."

"I will pay you generously, to be blunt."

"Oh." She thought this over. "Well, that would be welcome, I have to say. Let me give one or two a try first."

We worked out a fee and I thanked her. "But just do them all," I said. "Please. Send me the translation by regular mail, not electronically. You can send them a couple at a time, as you get to them." I couldn't bring myself to explain that I wanted to receive them as letters, real letters, so I didn't try. "And if you can work without the originals, let's walk to the corner and photocopy them, in case something happens. You can take the copies with you. Do you have time?"

"Ever-careful Marlow," she said. "Nothing will happen, but that's a good idea. Let me drink my coffee first and tell you all about my *affaire de coeur*."

"Don't you want to hear about mine?"

"Certainly, but there will be nothing to tell."

"That's true," I said, "so you go ahead."

When we parted at the office-supply store, she with the crisp photocopies and I with my letters—Robert's, actually—I went back home and thought about grilling a sandwich, drinking half a bottle of wine, and going to a movie by myself.

I set the letters on my coffee table, then refolded them along their worn lines and put them into the envelope, arranging them so they wouldn't knock against one another, with their fragile edges. I thought about the hands that had touched them, once upon a time, a woman's delicate hands and a man's—his would have been older, of course, if he'd been her uncle. Then Robert's big square hands, tanned and rather worn. Zoe's short, inquisitive ones. And my own.

I went to the living-room window, one of my favorite views: the street, lapped and laced with branches that have shaded it for decades, since long before I moved in, the old stoops of the brownstones on the other side, the ornate railings and balconies, blocks built in the 1880s. The evening was golden after days of rain; the pear trees had finished their bloom and were a rich green now. I gave up my idea of a movie. It was a perfect night to stay home in peace. I was working on a portrait from a photograph of my father, to send for his birthday—I could make some progress on that. I put on my Franck Violin Sonata and went into the kitchen for a cup of soup.

Chapter 6

Marlow

It had been more than a year, I was sorry to realize, since I'd actually entered the National Gallery of Art. The steps outside were overrun with schoolchildren; they swarmed around me in their drab uniforms, a Catholic school, or perhaps one of those public schools that require pleated navy and dull plaids in an effort to restore some long-lost order. Their faces were bright—the boys with mostly very short hair; some of the little girls with plastic bubbles on their braids—and their skin was a spectrum of lovely colors, from pale and pinkly freckled to ebony. For a moment I thought, *Democracy.* It was that old idealistic feeling I got from social studies class in my Connecticut grade school, from reading about George Washington Carver and Lincoln, an America with the dream of belonging to all Americans. We were moving together up the grand staircase toward a museum free of charge and, in theory, open to everyone, everyone and anyone, where these children could mingle with one another and me and the paintings without restraint.

Then the mirage cleared: the children were shoving each other and sticking gum in one another's hair, and their teachers were trying to keep the peace with only the resources of diplomacy. More important, I knew that most of DC's population would never make it into this museum, nor feel welcome here. I hung back and waited for the kids to go in ahead of me, since it was too late for me to thread my way through and beat them to the doors. That also gave me time to turn my face to the afternoon sun, which was warm, in the full flush of spring, and enjoy the green of the Mall. My three o'clock appointment (borderline personality disorder, a long struggle) had canceled, and for once I didn't have an appointment after that, so I'd left my office for the museum, free, released; I wouldn't have to go back to work at all that day.

Two women presided over the information desk; one was young, with a cap of dark, straight hair, and the other a retiree—a volunteer, I guessed, frail-looking under her frothy white curls. I chose the older for my question. "Good afternoon. I was wondering if you could help me locate a painting called *Leda*."

The woman glanced up and smiled; she might have been the younger docent's grandmother, and her eyes were a faded, nearly transparent blue. Her badge read MIRIAM.

"Certainly," she said.

The younger woman edged toward her and watched her find something on a computer screen. "Hit 'Title,'" she urged.

"Oh, I almost had it." Miriam sighed deeply, as if she'd known all along that her efforts were useless.

"Yeah, you've got it," the girl insisted, but she had to press a key or two herself before Miriam smiled.

"Ah, *Leda*. That's by Gilbert Thomas, French. It's in the nineteenth-century galleries, just before the Impressionists."

The girl looked at me for the first time. "That's the one that guy attacked last month. A lot of people have been asking about it. I mean—" She paused and tucked an obsidian strand back in place; I realized then that her hair was dyed black, so that it appeared carved, Asian, around her pale face and greenish eyes. "Well, not a lot, I guess, but several people have asked to see it."

I found myself staring at her, unexpectedly stirred. Her gaze was knowing as she stood there behind the counter, her body lean and flexible under a tight-zipped jacket, the smallest curve of hip showing between that and the top of a black skirt—that would be the maximum glimpse of abdominal skin permitted in this gallery full of nudes, I speculated. She might be an art student, working here in her spare time to get through school, a gifted printmaker or fashioner of jewelry, with those long, pale hands. I pictured her up against the counter, after hours, no underwear under that too-short skirt. She was just a kid; I looked away. She was a kid, and I was no catch, I knew—no aging Casanova.

"I was shocked to hear about that." Miriam shook her head. "I didn't know it was that painting, though."

"Well," I said, "I read about the incident, too—strange that someone would attack a painting, isn't it?"

"I don't know." The girl rubbed one hand along the edge of the information counter. She had a broad silver ring on her thumb. "We get all kinds of crazies in here."

"Sally," murmured her elder.

"Well, we do," said the girl defiantly. She looked me full in the face, as if daring me to be one of the lunatics to whom she'd just referred. I imagined discovering some sign that she found me attractive, inviting her for a cup of coffee, a preliminary flirtation, over which she would say things like *We get all kinds of crazies in here.* The image of the woman in Robert Oliver's drawings came into my mind—she was young, too, but also ageless, her face full of subtle knowledge and life. "The man who attacked that painting seems to have cooperated with the police, once he was arrested," I observed gently. "Maybe he wasn't that crazy."

The girl's eyes were hard, matter-of-fact. "Who would want to hurt a work of art? The guard told me afterward that it was a very close call for *Leda*."

"Thank you," I said, now an elderly and correct man with a gallery map in his hand.

Miriam took the map back for a moment and circled with a blue pen the room I wanted. Sally had drifted away already; the frisson had been only on my side.

But I had the whole afternoon to myself; with a feeling of lightness, I climbed the stairs to the tremendous marble rotunda at their summit and wandered among its gleaming, variegated pillars for a few minutes, stood in the middle, taking a deep breath.

Then a strange thing happened—the first of many times. I wondered if Robert had paused here, and I felt his presence, or perhaps simply tried to guess what his experience must have been—here, where he had preceded me. Had he known he was going to stab a painting, and known which painting? That might have sent him past the rotunda's glories in a rush, his hand already in his pocket. But if he hadn't known ahead of time, if something had incited him to it once he was in front of the painting, he might well have lingered in that forest of marble trunks, too, as would anyone with a sense of surroundings and a love of traditional forms.

In fact—I put my hands in my own pockets—even if his attack had been premeditated and he had felt confident in it, or savored the thought of the moment when he would draw out his knife and open it in his palm, he might still have stopped here for the pleasure of postponement. It was difficult, of course, for me to imagine wanting to damage a painting, but I was imagining Robert's urges, not my own. After another moment, I walked on, glad to leave that celestial, dim place and to be among paintings again, the long first galleries of the nineteenth-century collection.

To my relief, I found the area free of visitors, although there was not one but two guards there, as if the museum administration expected a second attack on the same painting at any moment. *Leda* drew me across the room at once. I'd resisted the temptation to check for it in books or on the internet before visiting today, and now I was glad—I could always read its history later, but the image was fresh for me, startling and real.

It was a large canvas, frankly Impressionist, although the details were somewhat more in evidence than they might have been in a Monet or a Pissarro or a Sisley, and it was about five by eight feet, dominated by two figures. The central figure was a mainly nude female form, lying on beautifully real grass. She was supine, in a classical attitude of despair and abandonment—or abandon?—her head with its burden of golden hair thrown back on the earth, a wisp of drapery caught over her middle and slipping off one leg, her shallow breasts bare, arms outspread. Her skin was numinously painted against the reality of that grass; it was too pale, translucent, like the sprout of a plant that has grown under a log. I thought at once of Manet's *Le déjeuner sur l'herbe,* although the figure of Leda was full of struggle, startled and epic—not calmly naked like Manet's prostitute, the skin cooler in tone, the brushwork looser.

The other figure in the painting was not human, although it was certainly a dominant character—a huge swan, hovering over her as if about to land on water, its wings beating backward to slow the speed of its assault. The swan's long wing feathers curved inward like talons, its gray-webbed feet almost touched the delicate skin of her belly, and its black-circled eye was as fierce as the gaze of a stallion. The sheer force of its flight toward her, caught on canvas, was astonishing, and this explained visually and psychologically the panic of the woman in the grass. The swan's tail curled under it, a pelvic thrust, as if to further aid its impulsive slowing. You could feel that the bird had burst over those vague thickets only a moment before, that it had come upon the sleeping form suddenly, and just as suddenly had veered to land on it in a paroxysm of desire.

Or had the swan been searching for her? I tried to remember the details of the story. The momentum of the great creature could have knocked her down, knocked her onto her back, perhaps, as she was rising from a nap en plein air. The swan needed no genitalia to make it masculine—that shadowed area under the tail was more than enough, as were the powerful head and beak as it bent its long neck toward her.

I wanted to touch her myself, to find her sleeping there, to push the creature forcefully away. When I stepped back to see the canvas as a whole, I felt Leda's fear, the way she had started up and fallen backward, the terror in her very hands as they dug into the earth—none of this had the voluptuous victimhood of the classical paintings that lined other galleries in this museum, the soft-porn Sabine women and Saint Catherines. I thought of the poem by Yeats I'd read several times over the years, but his Leda was a willing victim, too—"loosening thighs"—without many reactions of her own; I would have to find it again to be certain. Gilbert Thomas's Leda was a real woman, and she was really frightened. If I desired her, I thought, it was because she was real, and not because she had already been overpowered.

The plaque for the painting was all too succinct: "*Leda [Léda vainçue par le Cygne]*, 1879, purchased 1967. Gilbert Thomas, 1840–1890." Monsieur Thomas must have been a highly perceptive man, I thought, as well as an extraordinary painter, to put this sort of authentic emotion into the portrayal of a single moment. The rapidly worked feathers and the blurring of Leda's draperies recorded the advent of Impressionism, although it wasn't quite an Impressionist painting: the subject matter, to begin with, was the kind that the Impressionists had disdained—academic, a classical myth. What had made Robert

Oliver draw a knife with the idea of plunging it into this scene? Was he, I wondered again, suffering from an antisexual derangement, or a condemnation of his own sexuality? Or had this act of his, which could have damaged these painted figures beyond repair if he hadn't been caught in time, been some strange defense of the girl flung helplessly back under the swan? Had it been gallantry of a twisted, delusional sort? He might simply have disliked the eroticism of the work. But was it an erotic painting, exactly?

The longer I stood in front of it, the more it seemed to me to be a painting about power and violence. Staring at Leda, I didn't want so much to touch or defile her as to push away the huge feathered chest of the swan before it flew into her again. Was that what Robert Oliver had felt, pulling the knife out of his pocket? Or had he simply wanted to liberate her from the frame? I stood pondering this for some time, looking at Leda's hand digging into the grass, and then turned to the next work, also by Gilbert Thomas. Here, maybe, was an answer to my growing question, curiosity beyond any thought of Robert Oliver and his knife: *What sort of person had Thomas been?* I read the title—"*Self-portrait with Coins,* 1884"—and had just gotten an impression of firmly stroked-in black coat, black beard, smooth white shirt, when I felt a hand on my elbow.

I turned, not wholly surprised—I've lived in Washington for more than twenty years now, and it is rightly called a small town—but saw that I'd been mistaken. There was no one I recognized; someone had simply brushed against me by accident. In fact, there were now more than a few other people present: an elderly couple pointing out a painting to each other in low voices, a dark-suited man with a shiny forehead and long hair, some tourists speaking what was probably Italian.

The person nearest me, whom I'd thought I felt at my elbow, was a young woman—youngish, in any case. She was looking at *Leda* and had stationed herself directly in front of the painting as if she intended to stay there for a few minutes. She was tall and lean, almost my own height, standing with her arms crossed in front of her, dressed in blue jeans and a white cotton blouse, brown boots. Her hair was artificially dark red and quite long, hanging straight down her back; her profile—cheek, three-quarters—pure and smooth, with a light-brown eyebrow and long lashes, no makeup. When she bent her head, I saw that her hair had blond roots; she had reversed the usual procedure.

After a moment she stuck her hands in the back pockets of her jeans like a boy and leaned closer to the painting, studying something. I knew from the way she craned at the brushwork—can I be making this up, in retrospect?—that she was a painter herself. Only a painter would examine the surface from that angle, I thought, watching her turn and bend to take in the texture of the paint aslant, where the lighting hit it. I was struck by her concentration and stood there observing her as discreetly as I could. She stepped back, studying the whole again.

I felt that she stayed in front of *Leda* a moment too long, then another, and for some reason that was not a question of craft. She apparently sensed my gaze but didn't care about it much. Then, in fact, she walked away—no glance for me, no curiosity. She shrugged it off: a handsome tall girl used to being stared at. Perhaps, I thought, she wasn't a painter but a performer, or a teacher, hardened to the gaze of others, even enjoying it. I waited for a glimpse of her hands, hanging now at her sides as she turned to the Manet still life on the far wall; she seemed to peer with less concentration at his luminous wineglasses, his plums and grapes. My eyesight, although still keen, is not exactly what it once was; I couldn't see whether or not she had paint under her nails. And didn't care to step closer to her shrug to find out.

Suddenly she surprised me by turning all the way around and smiling in my direction, a bemused, noncommittal smile, but a smile nonetheless and one that even contained some conspiracy for a fellow close-to-the-picture gazer, a fellow lingerer in front of the view. Her face was an open one, made more alert by the absence of makeup, her lips pale, her eyes a color I couldn't figure out, her skin fair but also rosy next to the auburn hair; on her collarbone she wore a necklace of knotted leather strung with long ceramic beads that looked as if they could have had prayer parchments rolled up inside them. Her white cotton blouse showed possibly full breasts on an angular body. She held herself erect but not delicately, not so much like a dancer as like someone on a horse, exercising a grace that was partly caution. The old people were closing in on her, so that she had to edge away: Thomas, Manet, strange middle-aged man, farewell.

CHAPTER 7

Marlow

She really was leaving—the young woman with the beautiful smile—and I wondered whether I'd communicated anything to her without intending to; I would have liked to ask her about my hunch that she was a painter, too. There was a Renoir on the next wall, and she strode past it, unseeing—uncaring—and out of the room. This pleased me: I don't like Renoir either, with the exception of that canvas in the Phillips Collection, *Luncheon of the Boating Party*, where the people are almost eclipsed by sunlit grapes and bottles and glasses. I didn't trail her; noticing two young women in one day seemed to me tiresome, futile, without pleasure to the exact degree that it was without future or purpose.

This had all taken only a second or two, and I went directly back to the Thomas self-portrait, where the man with the greasy forehead was now in the way. When he moved, I stepped forward to look more closely myself. Again, a painting that verged on Impressionist, particularly in the casual handling of some of the background—dark curtains—but quite different from the daring and grace of *Leda*. A painter of diverse abilities, I thought—or maybe Thomas had changed his style in the 1880s, progressed in a new direction. This painting owed something to Rembrandt: the brooding expression and somber palette, perhaps also the unsparing auto-portrayal of the subject's red nose and fleshy cheeks, the descent of a previously handsome man into less-flattering age, even the dark velvet cap and jacket—smoking jacket, it might have been called: the Painter as Old Master and aristocrat, all in one.

The title of the self-portrait came from the foreground, where Thomas had folded his elbows on a bare wooden table piled with coins—large coins and worn ones, bronze, gold, tarnished silver—antiques of various shapes and sizes so skillfully painted that you could almost have picked them up one by one between your thumb and forefinger. I could see even the marvelous old writing on them, the characters of strange alphabets, the square holes, the knotted borders. Those coins were considerably better rendered than the image of Thomas himself; next to Manet's fruit and flowers, the painting was rather clumsy. Perhaps Thomas had cared deeply about money and not much about his own face. In any case, he had been striving for the look of the seventeenth century, turning his gaze two hundred years back, and I was staring at the nineteenth-century result, nearly a hundred and twenty years later.

There was one personal characteristic Thomas hadn't caught from all those smoky Rembrandt portraits, I thought: sincerity. He'd been harsh enough, apparently—or vain enough, or deluded enough—to paint a wily self-consciousness around his own eyes. That shrewdness was probably calculated to make the viewer uncomfortable, especially with the presence of the coins in the foreground. It was an interesting face, in any case. Had Thomas made a lot of money from his paintings, I wondered, or had he merely wanted to? Had he had some other sort of business, or a grand inheritance?

I didn't know the answers, of course, so I went on to the Manet still life, admiring, as the girl I'd noticed a few minutes before also probably had, the glass with its white wine pooling inside, the light on the dark-blue plums, the corner of a mirror. There was a little canvas by Pissarro I remembered liking, too;

I went into the next section of the gallery for a few minutes to see him and, while I was at it, his fellow Impressionists.

It had been years since I'd looked really deeply into an Impressionist painting; those endless retrospectives, with their accompanying tote bags, mugs, and notepaper, had put me off Impressionism. I remembered some of what I'd read in the past: the small group of the original Impressionists, including one woman—Berthe Morisot—who'd first banded together in 1874 to exhibit works in a style that the Paris Salon found too experimental for inclusion. We postmoderns take them for granted, or disdain them, or love them too easily. But they had been the radicals of their day, exploding traditions of brushwork, making subject matter of ordinary life, and bringing painting out of the studio and into the gardens, fields, and seascapes of France.

Now I saw with fresh appreciation the natural light, the soft, subtle color of a scene by Sisley: a woman in a long dress disappearing down the snowy tunnel of a village road. There was something touching and real, or touching because it was real, in the bleakness of the trees along the lane, some of which towered over a high wall. I thought of what an old friend of mine once said, that a painting has to have some mystery to it to be any good. I liked this glimpse of the woman, her slim back turned to me in the twilight, more intriguing to me than Monet's endless haystacks—I was walking along a row of three that showed various stages of daybreak on their pink and yellow slopes. I slipped my jacket on and prepared to leave. I believe in walking out of a museum before the paintings you've seen begin to run together. How else can you carry anything away with you in your mind's eye?

In the lobby downstairs, the black-haired girl had disappeared. Miriam was deep in consultation with a man her own age who seemed to be having trouble reading the museum maps. I walked by, poised to smile if she glanced up, but she didn't see me, so I had to postpone my greeting. Pushing out through the doors, I experienced that mingled relief and disappointment one feels on departure from a great museum—relief at being returned to the familiar, less intense, more manageable world, and disappointment at that world's lack of mystery. There was the ordinary street, without brushwork or the depth of oil on canvas. The traffic was roaring past in the usual Washington chaos, some driver trying to get over in front of another, a near miss, horns leaned on or punched. The trees were beautiful, though, heavy with blossoms or new green; I'm always struck by their beauty after the nondescript winter that seems to be the best the mid-Atlantic can muster.

I was thinking about a blend of colors that might express those bright-green and russet leaves against one another when I saw the girl again—the young woman who had been studying *Leda* ahead of me. She was standing at a bus stop. She looked very different now, not reflective or engaged but defiant, straight and tall, with a canvas bag over her shoulder. Her hair shone in the sun; I hadn't noticed before how much dark gold was mixed with the red. Her arms were folded across her white blouse, and her lips were pressed tightly together. I was seeing her profile again, and already I would have known it anywhere. Yes, she was self-sufficient, almost hostile, but for some reason the word "disconsolate" came to my mind. Perhaps it was just that she seemed thoroughly alone, even deliberately so, and she was of an age to have been standing there with a handsome young husband. I felt a pang, as if I'd seen an acquaintance from a distance without having time to stop and speak; I had a sense of sneaking away before she could notice me.

I went quickly down the steps, and she turned just as I reached the bottom. She saw me, half recognized me (the undistinguished fellow in a navy jacket, no tie). Why was I familiar to her? Was that what she was asking herself, not remembering me from our encounter inside? Then she smiled, as she had in the museum—a sympathetic, almost embarrassed smile. She was mine for a moment, an old friend after all. I gave what was probably a ridiculous half wave with one hand. *Strangers are strange to each other,* I thought. Well, I had been stranger than she. I could see the lines around her eyes when she smiled; she might be over thirty after all. I tried to stand tall and straight, like her, as I walked away.

Chapter 8

Marlow

I got up even earlier than usual the next morning, but not to paint; by seven I was at Goldengrove to use my office computer and have a cup of coffee before most of the day staff arrived. The art encyclopedia at home had revealed little more than I already knew about Gilbert Thomas, although my *Classical Handbook* gave me the story of Leda: She was a mortal woman ravished by Zeus, who visited her in the form of a swan. She had slept with her husband, Tyndareus, king of Sparta, on the same night. This explained her giving birth to two sets of twins at once, two immortal children and two mortal: Castor and Polydeuces (Pollux, the Roman version), and Clytemnestra and Helen, later held responsible for the troubles at Troy. Some versions of the myth, I learned, had Leda's children hatching from eggs, although they seemed to have gotten mixed up even in the shell, since Helen and Polydeuces, as children of Zeus, were divine, while Castor and Clytemnestra were doomed to mortality.

I had also looked up paintings of Leda and the Swan while I was at it and found quite a tradition, including a copy after a highly erotic Michelangelo, a Correggio, a copy after Leonardo in which the swan appeared to be a kind of household pet, and a Cézanne that showed the swan seizing an apparently unconcerned Leda by the wrist as if begging to be taken out for a walk. Gilbert Thomas had not made it into this august company, but I thought there might be something more on the web.

I should probably say again here that I don't like to resort to the internet, even now, and was less tolerant of it then—what will we someday do, I always wonder, without the pleasures of turning through books and stumbling on things we never meant to find? That happens during internet research, of course, but in a more limited way, to my mind. And how could anyone consent to give up that smell of open books, old or new? While I was searching my shelves for the myth of Leda, for example, I learned about a couple of other classical figures who don't enter this tale but whom I still think about from time to time. My wife tells me that this propensity to leaf through a volume instead of doing my research efficiently is one of the things that most dates me, but I've noticed that she handles books in the same way sometimes, looking through biographies and museum catalogs with a deep, aimless pleasure.

In any case, I don't claim to be expert at web searches, but that morning I did learn a little more about Gilbert Thomas in the depths of my office computer. He had been promising, at best, in the early years of his career, and was really known only for the *Leda* Robert had objected to and for the self-portrait I'd seen next to it. He had also been an acquaintance of many French artists of the day, including Manet; he and his brother, Armand, had jointly owned one of the earliest sale galleries in Paris, second or third in importance to that of the great Paul Durand-Ruel. An interesting figure, Thomas; his business had ultimately gone under and he had died in debt in 1890, after which his brother had sold off most of their remaining stock and retired. Gilbert had painted the landscape for *Leda* outdoors around 1879, at his retreat near Fécamp in Normandy, finishing it in a Paris studio. The painting had been displayed at the Salon of 1880, to acclaim; it had also drawn criticism for its erotic nature. This had been the first Thomas painting accepted to the Salon, although it had not been the last; the others were lost or undistinguished, and his reputation rested mainly on this masterwork, now on permanent exhibition at the National Gallery.

When I knew the residents had finished their breakfast, I went down the hall to Robert's room and knocked on the door, which was closed. Robert never answered, of course, so I always had to push it open a little at a time, calling in and trying not to surprise him at any possibly private moment. It was one of the things I found most inconvenient—embarrassing, even—about his silence. That morning was no exception, and I knocked and called and widened the door several times before stepping in.

He was drawing at the counter that served as a desk, his back to me, his easel currently empty. "Good morning, Robert." I had begun to call him by his first name, but politely, this last week or two, pretending that he had invited me to do so. "May I come in for a moment?"

I left the door ajar, as always, and stepped inside. He did not turn, although his hand slowed in its motions on the paper and I saw that he gripped the pencil harder; with him, I had to watch for any possible sign that might take the place of language.

"Thank you so much for the loan of the letters. I've brought back your originals." I laid the envelope gently on the chair where he'd left them for me, but he still didn't turn around.

"I have just a quick question for you," I began again, cheerfully. "How do you go about your research? I'm wondering—do you use the internet? Or do you spend a lot of time in libraries?"

The pencil stopped for a split second, and then he went on shading something in. I didn't allow myself to move close enough to see what he was drawing. His shoulders, in their old shirt, were forbidding. I could see the beginnings of a bald spot on the crown of his head; there was something touching about that place age had worn away already when the rest of him still seemed so vigorous. "Robert," I tried one more time, "do you do some research on the web for your paintings?"

This time the pencil did not swerve. For a moment I wanted him to turn and look at me. I imagined his expression as dark, his eyes wary. In the end, I was glad that he hadn't; I needed to be able to speak to his back, without being observed myself. "I do that, too, once in a while, although I prefer to use books."

Robert did not move, but I felt rather than saw something shift in him: Anger? Curiosity?

"Well, then, I guess that's it." I paused. "Have a good day. Let me know if I can do anything for you." I decided not to tell him that I was having his letters translated—if he could be silent, perhaps I would try a little of the same.

As I left the room, I glanced at the wall above his bed. He had taped up a new drawing, somewhat larger than the others—the dark-haired lady, somber, accusing, where she could watch over him even in his slumber.

On the following Monday, there was an envelope from Zoe waiting in my mailbox. Before opening it, I forced myself to eat my dinner; I washed my hands, made some tea, and sat down in the living room with a good lamp. Of course, the letters were likely to be mere domesticities, like most old letters, but Zoe had promised some passages about painting, and she had left in the French salutation, knowing I would like that.

October 6, 1877

Cher Monsieur:

Thank you for your kind note, which it falls to me to answer. We were very glad to see you last night. Your presence cheered my father-in-law, for one thing, and it has been difficult to make him laugh since he came to live with us. I believe he misses his own home, although for several years already it no longer contained the loving presence of his wife. He always says what a good brother you are to him. Yves sends you his best; he is relieved that you have returned to Paris. (Life is much improved with an uncle nearby, he says!) I am pleased to have met you myself at last. You will forgive me if I do not write at length, as I have much to attend to this morning. May you travel safely to the Loire and enjoy your stay there, and I trust that all your work will go well. I envy you the landscapes you will surely paint. And I shall read to my father-in-law the essays you left for us.

Respectfully,
Béatrice de Clerval Vignot

When I'd finished reading it, I sat trying to understand what Robert saw in this letter, what forced him to read it—and others—over and over in his solitary room. And why he had let me see them at all, if they were so precious to him.

CHAPTER 9

Marlow

We don't usually try to interview our patients' ex-spouses, but as I watched that striking face take shape on Robert Oliver's canvases from week to week without being able to get any explanation from him, I felt a kind of moral defeat. Besides, he had said himself that I could talk with Kate.

Robert's ex-wife still lived in Greenhill, and I had spoken with her once during his first days with us. On the phone, she'd had a soft voice, a tired-sounding one, made more tired by my news of his admission to Goldengrove, and there was the noise of children in the background, someone laughing. We had talked just long enough for her to confirm that she knew about the diagnosis he'd previously received and that their divorce had been finalized more than a year earlier. He had lived in Washington during much of that year, she said, and then she added that it was a difficult subject for her to discuss. If her husband—her ex-husband—was not in any actual danger and I had the papers from his psychiatrist in Greenhill, would I please excuse her from talking more?

When I called her a second time, therefore, I was violating both my usual policy and her request. I reluctantly took her number out of Robert's file. Was it right for me to do this? But then, would it be right not to? During my early-morning visit that day, Robert had seemed to me more starkly depressed, and when I'd asked him if he ever thought about the painting called

Leda, he had simply stared at me, as if too exhausted even to take offense at my absurd question. Some days he painted or sketched—always the lady's vivid face—and other days, like this one, he lay in bed with his jaw clenched, or sat in the armchair I usually used myself when I visited him, holding his letters and looking bleakly out the window. Once, when I came into his room, he opened his eyes, smiled at me for a moment and murmured something, as if seeing someone he loved, then leapt off the bed and briefly raised a fist in my direction. If nothing else, his wife might be able to tell me how he had reacted to his previous medications, and which had been most effective.

At five thirty, I dialled the number—Greenhill, in the western mountains of North Carolina; I'd heard of it from friends who spent summers there. When that same quiet voice answered, this time as if she had just been laughing about something with someone else, I was filled with wonder. I thought I could hear on the other end of the phone the lovely face Robert sketched day after day. Her voice quivered with joy for a moment. "Yes, hello?" it said.

"Mrs. Oliver, this is Dr. Marlow at Goldengrove Residential Center in Washington," I said. "We talked several weeks ago about Robert."

When she spoke again, the joy was gone and it had been replaced by a dull dread. "What is it? Is Robert all right?"

"There's nothing unusual to worry about, Mrs. Oliver. He's about the same." Now I could hear a child's voice laughing, too, and calling in the background, then a crash as if something had fallen to the floor nearby. "That's the problem, however. He does seem quite depressed still and fairly unstable. I want him in much better shape before I can consider discharging him. The most difficult thing is that he won't talk to me at all, or to anyone else."

"Ah," she said, and I heard for a second an irony that could have belonged to those radiant dark eyes, to that amused or angry mouth Robert was constantly sketching. "Well, he didn't talk with me much either, especially during the last year or two we were together. Wait—excuse me." It sounded as if she pulled away from the phone for a moment, and I heard her say, "Oscar? Kids? Go in the other room, please."

"While Robert was still talking, his first day here, he gave me permission to discuss his case with you." She was silent, but I persisted. "It would be very helpful for me to speak with you about how his condition manifested itself—for example, how he reacted to the earlier medications he was given, and some other issues."

"Doctor . . . Marlow?" she said slowly, and beyond the trembling of her voice I heard again the child noise, laughter, and a pounding, thumping sound. "I have my hands full, to say the least. I've already talked with the police and two psychiatrists. I have two children and no husband. Robert's mother and I are planning to pay some of his institutional bills when his insurance runs out—that's coming out of his inheritance and mine, mostly his, but I'm helping a little. As you probably know." I hadn't known. She seemed to be taking a deep breath. "If you want me to spend time talking about the disaster of my life, you'll just have to come down here yourself. And now I'm trying to make dinner. I'm sorry." That tremble was the sound of a woman unused to telling people to go to hell, a woman usually polite but cornered now by circumstance.

"I apologize," I said. "I'm sure your situation is a difficult one. I do need to help your husband, your former husband, if I possibly can. I'm his doctor and I'm responsible for his safety and well-being at the moment. I'll call you another day to see if there's an easier time for you to talk."

"If you must," she said. But then she added, "Good-bye," and hung up gently.

That evening I went home to my apartment and lay down on the sofa in my green-and-gold living room. It had been an exhausting day, beginning with Robert Oliver and his usual refusal to talk with me. His eyes had been bloodshot, almost desperate, and I wondered if I needed to put a night watch on him. Would I come in one morning to find he'd swallowed all his oil paints—my gifts to him—or cut his wrists somehow? Should I return him to John Garcia for a more secure hospital stay? I could call John and tell him this case wasn't right for me after all; I was spending too much time on it, with no real hope of results. We had cleared Robert of acute risk, but I still worried. I wondered if I could tell John, also, that something about the way I was behaving made me uneasy—the way my heart had jumped at the sound of Kate Oliver's voice on the phone. Had I been reluctant to call her or actually eager?

I felt too tired to fill my water bottle and go out for a run, my normal activity at this hour. Instead I lay there with eyes half closed, looking at the painting I'd done to hang over the fireplace. You shouldn't hang oils over a fireplace, of course, but I seldom lit a fire and the space had cried out for something when I'd first moved in. This was perhaps what it felt like to be Robert Oliver, or any patient depressed to the point of exhaustion; I slitted my eyes nearly shut and rolled my head listlessly, experimentally, on the arm of the sofa.

When I opened them, there was the painting again. As I've said, I like to paint portraits, but the oil over my fireplace is a landscape seen through a window. And I usually paint landscapes from life, especially out in Northern Virginia, where those blue hills in the distance are so tempting. This one is different, a fantasy inspired by some of Vuillard's canvases but also by memories of the view from my childhood bedroom in Connecticut: the green windowsill and frame all around the edges, the heavy treetops, the roofs of the old houses, the very tall white spire of the Congregational church rising out of the trees, the lavender and gold of the spring sunset. I had put everything I remembered into it, with rough strokes, everything except for the boy leaning out the window and soaking it all in.

I lay on the sofa, wondering, not for the first time, if I should have moved the church spire farther to the right; it really *had* been exactly in the center of my view from that boyhood window, just as I'd painted it, but the painting was too balanced that way, too symmetrical for comfort. Damn Robert Oliver—damn, most of all, his self-sabotaging refusal to speak. Why would anyone choose to be more of a victim when his own brain chemistry was hurting him enough? But that was always the question, the problem of how our chemistry shapes our will. He had once had two little children and a soft-voiced wife. He was still a man with a great facility in his eyes and fingers, a deftness with the brush that made something hurt in my head. Why wouldn't he talk to me?

When I was too hungry to lie there any longer, I got up and changed into my pajamas and opened a can of tomato soup, garnishing it with parsley and sour cream and cutting a big slice of bread to go with it. I read the paper and then part of a mystery novel, P. D. James, a really good one. I didn't go into my studio.

The next afternoon I phoned Mrs. Oliver once more just before I left work. This time she answered in a serious voice.

"Mrs. Oliver, this is Dr. Marlow, calling from Washington. Forgive me for disturbing you again." She was silent, so I went on. "This is unusual, I know, but it seems to me that we both care about your husband's condition, and I'm wondering if you would let me take you up on your offer." Silence, still. "I'd like to come to North Carolina to talk with you about him."

I heard a little intake of breath; she seemed to be startled and thinking very hard about this.

"I promise it wouldn't be for long," I said hurriedly. "Just a few hours of your time. I would stay with some old friends who have a house down there, and I would disturb you as little as possible. Our conversation would be completely confidential, and I would use it only in my treatment of your husband."

At last she spoke again. "I'm not sure what you think you would gain by this," she said almost kindly. "But if you care that much about Robert's condition, it's all right with me. I work until four every day, and then I have to get my children from school, so I'm not sure when we can talk." She paused. "I can figure something out, I guess. I told you before that it's not always easy for me to talk about him, so please don't expect too much."

"I understand," I said. My heart was leaping; it was a ridiculous feeling, but the fact that she had consented at all filled me with strange happiness.

"Are you going to tell Robert you're coming down?" she asked, as if this had just struck her. "Is he going to know I'm talking about him?"

"I usually do tell my patients—I might tell him later—and if there are things you don't ever want me to share with him, I'll keep your confidence about them, of course. We can discuss that carefully."

"When do you plan to visit?" Her voice was a little cold now, as if she already regretted having agreed.

"Perhaps early next week. Would you be able to talk with me on Monday or Tuesday?"

"I'll try to arrange something," she said again. "Call me tomorrow and I'll let you know."

It had been nearly two years since I'd taken time off, apart from the usual holidays—the last occasion had been a painting trip to Ireland organized by a local art school, from which I'd returned with canvases so dominated by bright green that I didn't quite believe in them after I got home. Now I pulled out my map collection and stocked my car with bottles of water and tapes of Mozart and my Franck Violin Sonata. It was about a nine-hour drive, I calculated. My staff was a little surprised by the short notice of my vacation. Probably for just that reason—poor Dr. Marlow; it's overwork—they didn't ask questions. I rescheduled my private patients as well. I left orders that Robert Oliver be watched more frequently while I was gone, and I went into his room on Friday to say goodbye. He had been drawing—the usual curly-headed woman, but also something new, a sort of garden bench with a high ornate back, surrounded by trees. His draftsmanship was remarkable, I thought, as I often did. His sketch pad and pencil had fallen onto the bed and he lay with head tipped back, staring up at the ceiling, his brow and jaw working, his hair standing crisply upright. He turned reddened eyes toward me when I came in.

"How are you today, Robert?" I asked, sitting down in the armchair. "You look tired." He returned his gaze to the ceiling. "I'm going to take a few days off," I said. "I'll be gone until Thursday or maybe even Friday. Road trip. If you need anything, you can ask one of the staff. Dr. Crown will be covering for me, too. I've told them to be right here for you if you need someone. One question—will you keep taking your medications on schedule?"

He cast an eloquent, almost reproachful glance at me. For

a moment, it shamed me. He was taking them; he had never shown any sign of resistance about that.

"Well, so long," I said. "I'll look forward to seeing your work when I get back." I rose and stood in the doorway; I lifted a hand in farewell. There is nothing harder, at moments, than talking to someone who has all the power of silence. This time, I felt a strange flash of power, too, which I quelled at once: *Good-bye. I am going to see your wife.*

At home that evening, I found a package of translations from Zoe in my mailbox; she had apparently made progress. I tucked them into my luggage, to read in Greenhill. They would be part of my vacation.

Chapter 10

Marlow

I've loved Virginia since my days at UVA, passed through it many times on my way to other places, gone out into its blue and green for rests and painting excursions and sometimes even a hike. I like the long reach of I-66 that puts the sprawl of the city behind you—although, as I write this, Washington has extended its tentacles clear to Front Royal; there are clusters of bedroom communities springing up like fungus all along the interstate and adjacent roads. On this trip, with the highways full of a midmorning quiet, I found myself forgetting about work before I had passed Manassas.

Sometimes when I've driven this way, in fact, I've stopped at Manassas National Battlefield, alone or once recently with my wife, swinging spontaneously onto the exit ramp. One ghostly September morning long before I met her, I paid my fee at the visitor center and walked across the field to stand where some of the worst fighting took place; the landscape that sloped away from me, down to an old stone farmhouse, was filled with mist. There was a single tree in the middle distance that seemed to cry out for me to walk out to it and take up a vigil beneath its branches, or to paint it from where I'd positioned myself. I stood there watching the mist thin out and wondering why people kill each other. There wasn't another living soul in sight. That is the sort of moment I both miss and shudder to think about, now that I'm married.

I pulled off the road near Roanoke and had breakfast in a diner. I'd glimpsed the sign for it on the highway, but when I reached its dreary facade, with four or five pickup trucks parked around it, I found I'd been there before on some previous excursion, perhaps a long-ago painting trip; I simply hadn't recognized the name. The waitress, unapologetically tired, gave me my coffee in silence, but she smiled when she brought the eggs and she pointed out the hot sauce on my table. Two big-armed men were talking in a corner about jobs—jobs they didn't have or hadn't been able to get—and two women who were all dressed up, not well, were just paying their bill. "I don't know what he thinks he wants," one of them concluded loudly to the other.

For a moment of near-hallucination in the midst of the steaming coffee, the reek of cigarette smoke, the dirty sunlight coming through the window at my elbow, I thought she meant *me*. I remembered my slow roll out of bed before dawn for this trip, the sense that I was breaking not only with my schedule but also with my professional code, the twinge of desire as I awoke and remembered the woman on Robert Oliver's canvases.

I hadn't been to Greenhill before, but it was easy enough to find once I'd made my way up to a long mountain pass—there was a city nestled in the valley below. Spring here was indeed somewhat behind what we had in Washington; the trees along the roads were freshly green, and there were dogwoods and azaleas still in bloom in the front yards I passed on the way into town, rhododendron with conical thick buds that had yet to burst. I skirted the edge of downtown—a hilltop studded with red tile roofs and miniature Gothic skyscrapers—and headed up a winding street that my friends had described to me on the phone: Rick Mountain Road, residential but hiding its small houses behind a screen of hemlocks, firs, and rhododendron, and of dogwoods in floating, meditative bloom. When I rolled down my window, I could smell mossy darkness, deeper than the approaching twilight.

Jan and Walter's house was just off a dirt drive, marked by one wooden sign: HADLEY COTTAGE. The Hadleys themselves were conveniently in Arizona, tending to their allergies; I was glad I wouldn't have to explain my errand in Greenhill to them in person. I got out of the car and stretched my legs, stiff. I certainly needed to spend more time running, but when and how to fit it in? Then I walked around to the backyard because it seemed to promise a view, and it delivered: there was a bench at the edge of the steep drop, an enormous vista—the distant buildings, a miniature of the town. I sat down, breathing in cool air and a sense that spring was rising up to me out of the pines. Why, I wondered, did the Hadleys live anywhere else even part of the year?

I thought of my harried commutes at home, the long drive out to Goldengrove through grueling suburban traffic. I could hear wind in pine boughs, a distant hushing sound that might be the interstate below, a sudden interruption of birdsong—what birds, I didn't know, although a cardinal flew out of the trees in the bluff just below the Hadleys' yard. Somewhere down in that town—I wasn't sure where, but I'd check the map this evening—was a woman with two children, a soft-voiced woman with her hands full, her heart broken. She lived down there in a house I couldn't yet picture, in a solitude that Robert Oliver had at least partly caused. I wondered if she would have anything to say to me. It would be a long way to drive just to have her change her mind about talking with her ex-husband's psychiatrist.

The house key was in its promised place, under a planter full of dirt, but the front door gave me some trouble until I pushed it hard with my hip. I brought in a couple of flyers for pizza that were lying on the porch, wiped my feet on the mat inside, and propped open the door to let out the smell of musty winter that greeted me. The living room was small and crowded—rag rugs and outdated furniture, rows of paperback novels and a gilded set of Dickens on the built-in shelves, the TV apparently locked away in a closet somewhere, the sofa lined with needlepoint cushions that felt faintly damp to the touch. I opened some windows and then the back door as well, and carried my suitcase upstairs.

There were two small bedrooms, one obviously the Hadleys' own; I took the second, which had twin beds with navy bedspreads and watercolors of mountain scenes on the walls, originals, not too bad. I opened the plaid curtains—they were slightly damp, too, uncomfortably alive under my fingertips—and propped up the windows. The whole house was shaded by spruces and other evergreens, but at least I could get it aired out before I had to sleep there. Walter had told me a fire might help, and I found logs already arranged in the fireplace downstairs. I saved them for evening. There was nothing in the elderly refrigerator except a few jars of olives and packages of yeast. I wasn't hungry yet; I would drive down later for some groceries, a newspaper, a local map. Tomorrow afternoon I might have time to explore the city itself.

I changed and went for a run up the mountain road, glad to shake off my car trip—glad, also, to shed my thoughts of Robert Oliver and the woman I would meet the next day. On my return I showered, grateful to find that hot water was available at the Hadleys' after all, then got out my easel and set it up in the backyard. There were similar houses on each side, screened by more spruces; those, too, seemed still deserted at this season. I hadn't expected a vacation, exactly, but as I rolled up my shirtsleeves and opened my watercolor box, I felt for a moment a sudden languid release from all the rest of my life. The evening light was beautiful, and I thought I would outdo those faded paintings in the guest room, perhaps leave a gift for Jan and Walter, a view of spring, their city down below, a small payment of rent.

In my twin guest bed that evening, I began to read the letters Zoe had sent.

October 14, 1877

Cher Monsieur:

Your note from Blois arrived this morning and brought pleasure, especially to your brother. In fact, I read it to Papa myself and described the sketch to him as fully as I could. Your sketch is lovely, although about that I dare to say very little, or you will understand what a beginner I am. I have also read him your recent article on the work of M. Courbet. He says he can see some of Courbet's paintings quite clearly in his mind's eye, and that your words recall them to him better than ever. Bless you for your kind attentions to us all. Yves sends fond greetings.

With regards,
Béatrice de Clerval Vignot

CHAPTER 11

Marlow

Mrs. Oliver's house, as it turned out the next morning, was nothing like what I'd pictured; I'd imagined it tall, white, stereotypically Southern and gracious, and instead it proved to be a large cedar-and-brick bungalow with hedges of boxwood and towering spruces in front. I got out of the car as gracefully as I could, putting on my wool sport coat and taking my briefcase with me. I'd dressed with care in the Hadleys' dingy little guest room, meticulously not thinking why I was doing it. There was indeed a porch, but it was small, and someone had left a pair of muddy canvas gardening gloves on the bench next to the door and a pile of miniature plastic gardening tools in a bucket—toys, I assumed. The front door was wooden, with a big, clean window; through it I could see the deserted living room, furniture, flowers. I rang the bell and stood there.

Nothing moved inside. After a few minutes I began to feel foolish because I could see so far into the house, as if I were spying. It was a comfortable, simple front room, decorated with quiet-colored sofas, lamps here and there on what looked like antique tables, a faded olive carpet, a smaller Oriental rug that might be a very fine one, vases of daffodils, a darkly polished cabinet with glass panes, and above all books—tall cases of them, although I couldn't read any titles from where I stood. I waited. I became aware of the birds in the trees around the house, calling or singing, taking off with a rush—crows, starlings, a blue jay. The morning had begun springlike and bright, but clouds were coming up, making the front porch cold, the light gray.

Then for the first time I felt hopeless. Mrs. Oliver had changed her mind. She was a private person and I was probably in the wrong. I'd driven nine hours, like a fool, and it served me right if she had decided to lock her door (I did not, of course, try the handle) and go somewhere else instead of talking with me. I might, I thought, have done the same in her place. I rang the doorbell a second time, hesitantly, vowing not to touch it again after this.

Finally I turned away, my briefcase hitting my knee, and started back down the slate steps, riding a surge of anger. I had a long trip ahead of me, with too much time to think. I'd already started the thinking, so that it took me a second to register the click and creak of the door behind me. I stopped, the hair rising on the back of my neck—why should that sound startle me so badly when I'd been waiting five minutes for it? In any case, I turned and saw her standing there, the door opening toward her, her hand still on the knob.

She was a pretty woman, a quick, alert-looking woman, but she was certainly not the muse who filled Robert's drawings and paintings at Goldengrove. Instead, I got a sudden impression of the seashore: sandy hair, fair skin starred with freckles of the sort that fade as their owner ages, ocean-blue eyes that met mine warily. For a moment I was frozen on the steps, and then I hurried up to her. Once I was close I realized that she was small, delicately built, and that she would come up to my shoulder and therefore up to Robert Oliver's breastbone. She opened the door a little wider and stepped out. "Are you Dr. Marlow?" she asked.

"Yes," I said. "Mrs. Oliver?"

She took my extended hand quietly. Her own hand was small, like the rest of her, and I expected her grip to be soft and childlike, but her fingers were very strong. If she was almost as small as a little girl, she was a strong little girl, even fierce. "Please come in," she said. She turned back to the house, and I followed her into that living room I'd been staring at. It was like walking onto a stage set, or perhaps like watching a play where the curtain is already up when you sit down in the audience, so that you've studied the scenery for a while before the actors come on. The house was deeply hushed. The books, as I came close, turned out to be mainly novels—two centuries of them—as well as some poetry and works of history.

Mrs. Oliver, a few steps ahead of me, wore blue jeans and a fitted, long-sleeved top of slate blue. She must, I thought, know the color of her own eyes well. Her body looked limber—not athletic but graceful, as if finding its outlines constantly through movement. There was something determined in her walk; it excluded any gesture that might have appeared forlorn. She motioned me to a sofa and sat on another one just across from mine. The living room made a bend there, and now I could see huge windows, floor-to-ceiling, with a view out over a broad lawn, beech trees, a giant holly, flowering dogwoods. It hadn't seemed so large from the driveway, but her property extended far over two open lots, verdant and tree-lined. Robert Oliver had once enjoyed this view. I set my briefcase at my feet and tried to compose myself.

Looking across the room, I saw that Mrs. Oliver was already fully collected, her hands clasped on the knee of her jeans. She wore childish canvas sneakers that might once have been navy. Her hair was thick, straight, cut with rough elegance to her shoulders, with so many tints of lion's mane and wheat and gold leaf that I would have found it hard to paint.

Her face was beautiful, too, with little makeup—soft lipstick, the finest lines around her eyes. She didn't smile; she was examining me gravely, poised on the edge of speaking. At last she said, "I'm sorry you had to wait. I almost changed my mind." She offered no apology for her doubts, and no further explanation.

"I don't blame you." I'd thought for a split second of more gallant statements, but they seemed useless in this situation.

"Yes." It was simple concurrence.

"Thank you for agreeing to see me, Mrs. Oliver. Here's my card, by the way." I handed it to her and then felt I had been too formal; she looked down.

"Can I get you some coffee, or a cup of tea?"

I considered refusing and then decided it was better manners, in this pleasant Southern room, to accept. "Thank you very much. If you have coffee already made, I'd gladly have a cup."

She rose and went out—that compact grace again. The kitchen wasn't far away; I could hear dishes clinking and drawers opening, and I glanced around the room while she was gone. There was no sign of Robert Oliver here, among the lamps with their flower-painted porcelain bases, unless the books were his. No trace here of oily paint rags, no posters from the new landscape artists. The art on the walls consisted of a blurred heirloom needlepoint and two old watercolors showing a marketplace in France or Italy. There were certainly no vivid portraits of a lady with curling dark hair, no paintings by Robert Oliver or any other contemporary artist. Perhaps the living room had never been his domain; it was often a wife's sphere anyway. Or perhaps she had erased every reminder of him on purpose.

Mrs. Oliver came back in carrying a wooden tray with two cups of coffee on it. The china was a delicate blackberry pattern;

there were tiny silver spoons, a silver cream-and-sugar service, all very elegant next to her blue jeans and faded sneakers. I noticed that she wore a necklace and earrings of gold set with tiny blue gems—sapphires or tourmaline. She put the tray on a table near me and handed me my coffee, then took her own cup to her sofa and sat down, deftly balancing it. The coffee was good, warming after the chill porch. She regarded me in silence, and I began to wonder if the wife was going to prove as laconic as the husband.

"Mrs. Oliver," I said as easily as I could, "I know this must be difficult for you and I want you to understand that I don't wish to force your confidence in any way. Your husband is proving to be a challenging patient, and as I said on the phone I'm worried about him."

"Ex-husband," she said, and I sensed something like a hint of humor, a gleam of laughter directed against me, or possibly against herself, as if she had said aloud, "I can be firm with you, too." I hadn't yet seen her smile; I didn't see it now.

"I want you to know that Robert isn't in any immediate danger. He hasn't attempted to harm anyone, including himself, since that day in the museum."

She nodded.

"He actually seems quite calm a lot of the time, but he goes through periods of anger and agitation, too. Silent agitation, I mean. I intend to keep him until I can assure myself that he's really safe and functional. As I said on the phone, my main problem in trying to assist him is that he won't talk."

She, too, was silent.

"By which I mean—he doesn't speak at all." I reminded myself that he had spoken once, to tell me that I could talk with the woman sitting across from me now.

Her eyebrows rose over her coffee cup; she took a sip. Those eyebrows were a darker sand than her hair, feathered as if painted by—I tried to think what portraitist they reminded me of, what number brush I would have used. Her forehead was broad and fine under the glinting wave of hair. "He hasn't spoken to you even once?"

"The first day," I admitted. "He acknowledged what he'd done in the museum and then he said I could talk with anyone I wanted to." I decided to omit—for now, at least—his having said that I could even talk with "Mary." I hoped Mrs. Oliver might eventually tell me whom he'd meant by that, and I hoped I wouldn't have to ask. "But he hasn't spoken since then. I'm sure you'll understand that talking is one of the only ways he can let go of what's troubling him, and one of the only ways we can figure out what triggers make his condition worse."

I looked hard at her, but she didn't help me with even a nod.

I tried to compensate with reasonable friendliness. "I can continue to manage his medications, but we can't work on much unless he'll talk, because I can't know exactly how the medications help him. I've sent him to both individual and group therapy, but he doesn't speak there either, and he's stopped going. If he won't talk, then I need to be able to talk to him myself with some sense of what might be troubling him."

"To provoke him?" she said bluntly. Her eyebrows were up again.

"No. To draw him out, to show him I understand his life, to some degree. It might help him start speaking again."

She seemed to think hard for a moment; she sat up straighter, raising the line of her small breasts under her shirt. "But how will you explain knowing in detail things about his life that he hasn't told you himself?"

It was such a good question, such a direct, keen question, that I put down my coffee and sat watching her. I hadn't expected to have to answer this right away; in fact, I'd been struggling with it myself. She'd caught me out in the course of five minutes' conversation.

"I'll be honest with you," I said, although I knew it sounded like a professional line. "I don't know yet how I'll explain that to him if he asks. But if he asks me, it will mean he's talking. Even if he's angry about it."

For the first time I saw her lips curve away from even teeth, the top front ones slightly too large and therefore very sweet. Then she pursed her mouth again. "Hmm," she said, almost a soft little song. "And will you bring my name into it?"

"That's up to you, Mrs. Oliver," I said. "We can talk about how to handle that, if you'd like."

She took up her coffee cup. "Yes," she said. "Maybe so. Let me think about that and we'll agree on something. Call me Kate, please." That small movement of her mouth, the look of a woman who had once smiled often and might learn to again. "For one thing, I try not to think of myself as Mrs. Oliver. I'm in the process of changing back to my maiden name, in fact. I decided just recently to do that."

"Kate, then—thank you," I said, glancing away before she did. "If you're comfortable with it, I'll take some notes, too, but only for my own use."

She seemed to ponder all this. Then she set her cup aside as if the time for business had come. I realized at that moment how extremely clean and neat the room was. She had the two children, whom she'd said were at school during the day. Their toys must have been elsewhere in the house. Her blackberry china was immaculate and apparently stored somewhere out of reach. This was a woman who managed prodigiously, and I hadn't even noticed that until now, perhaps because she made it look effortless. She folded her hands on her knee again. "All right. Please don't tell him I talked with you, at least not yet. I need to think about that. But I will be as open as I can. If I'm going to do this at all, I want the record to be complete."

It was my turn to feel surprised, and I thought I showed it in spite of myself. "I believe you'll be helping Robert, however you may feel about him at this point."

She dropped her eyes, so that her face aged suddenly, dimmed without their blue. I thought of the name of a color in my Crayola set from childhood: "Periwinkle." She glanced up again. "I don't know why, but I believe so, too. You know, I couldn't help Robert very much in the end. In fact, I didn't really want to, by then. That's the only thing I've truly regretted. I think that's why I've paid some of the residential bills. How long will you be here?"

"You mean this morning?"

"In general. I mean, I've reserved two mornings. We have until noon today, and again tomorrow." She spoke as dispassionately as if we'd been discussing checkout time at a hotel. "If necessary, I can take a third morning off, although it would be difficult. I'll have to double up some of my work assignments as it is. I already work at night sometimes to be freer for the children after school."

"I don't want to trespass on more of your time when you've been so generous," I said. I finished my coffee in two sips, set it aside, and took out my notepad. "Let's see how far we get this morning."

For the first time, I saw that her face was not merely guarded but sad, with its colors of ocean and beach. My heart twisted inside me—or my conscience? Was it my conscience? She looked directly at me. "I guess you want to know about the woman," she said. "The dark-haired woman—right?"

It threw me; I had planned to ease into Robert's story, to ask her a little at a time about his earliest symptoms. I saw from her face that she would not appreciate hedging on my part. "Yes."

She nodded. "Has he been painting her?"

"Yes, he has. Nearly every day. I noticed that she was the subject of one of his shows as well, and thought you might know something about her."

"I do—as much as I want to know. But I didn't think I would ever be telling a stranger about it." She leaned forward, and I saw her small body rise and fall. "You're used to hearing very private things?"

"Of course," I said. If my conscience had been a person at that moment, I might have strangled him.

October 17, 1877

Mon cher oncle:

I hope you will not mind my addressing you thus, as a true relative, which I am in spirit, at least, if not by blood. Papa bids me thank you for the package you sent in response to my note. We shall read the book aloud, with help from Yves on his evenings at home—he is also much intrigued. These lesser Italian masters have long been of interest to him, he says. I am going to my sister's house for three nights, where I stay to feast on her lovely children. I do not mind telling you they are my favorite models, in my own dabblings. And my sister is my most admired friend, so that I understand very well your brother's devotion to you. Papa says of you that because of your modesty no one knows that you are the bravest, truest man on earth. How many brothers speak so warmly of each other? Yves promises evenings will be all for reading to Papa while I am gone, and I shall pick up where he leaves off.

With warmest thanks for your kindness,

Béatrice Vignot

CHAPTER 12

Kate

I first saw her, the woman, at a highway rest area somewhere in Maryland. But I should tell you before that about when I first saw Robert, too. I met him in New York City in 1984, when I was twenty-four. I'd been working there for about two months, it was summer, and I was homesick for Michigan. I'd expected New York to be exciting, and it was exciting, but it was also tiring. I lived in Brooklyn, not Manhattan. I took three trains to work instead of strolling through Greenwich Village. At the end of the workday, hours as an editorial assistant at a medical journal, I was too tired to stroll anywhere anyway, and too worried about the cost to go to an interesting foreign movie. I was not meeting people quickly either.

The day I met Robert, I went after work to Lord & Taylor, which I knew would be too expensive, to get a birthday present for my mother. As soon as I was inside, away from the summer street, the perfumed air-conditioning hit me hard. Meeting the contemptuous gaze of mannequins in their bathing suits with the new high-cut leg, I wished I'd dressed better for work that morning. I wanted to get my mother a hat, something she would never get for herself, something lovely she might have worn as a young woman meeting my father at the Philadelphia Cricket Club for the first time. She might never wear it in Ann Arbor, but it would remind her of her youth, with its white gloves and feeling of stability, and it would remind her, too, of a daughter's love. I had thought the hat section would be on the first floor, near the silk scarves signed by famous designers I had barely heard of, near the upside-down disembodied legs with their long, smooth stockings. But there was some construction going on there, and a lady in a makeup smock told me to go upstairs to the temporary hat display.

I didn't want to venture farther into the store—my own legs were starting to feel bare and scratched, ugly because I hadn't worn hose to work that morning. But it was for my mother, so I went on up the escalator—always that little catch of breath as I stepped off safely at the top—and when I found the section I was glad to stand alone among the hat trees, each of which blossomed with pale or bright colors. There were sheer hats with silk flowers pinned to a grosgrain band, and navy straw and black straw, and a blue one with cherries and leaves. They were all a little gaudy, especially taken together, and I began to think this hadn't been a good idea for a birthday present after all, and then I saw a beautiful hat, a hat that was out of place there and just right for my mother. It was broad-brimmed, covered with a tight swirl of cream-colored organdy, and over the organdy was fastened a spray of different kinds of blue flowers, almost real flowers—chicory, larkspur, forget-me-nots. It was like a hat decorated in a field.

I took it down and stood holding it in both hands. Then I turned the paper tag over very carefully. The hat cost $59.99, more than I usually spent on groceries in a week. If I saved this amount only three times, I could take the bus home to Ann Arbor to see my mother. But when she opened it she might smile, might hold it very carefully and try it on in the hall mirror at home, smiling and smiling. I held the hat by its delicate edges, beaming with her. I felt sick to my stomach and my eyes were beginning to fill with tears, which was going to ruin the small amount of makeup I wore to work. I hoped no salesclerk would come around the hat tree and accost me. I was afraid that one word from someone else would make me buy it.

After a few minutes I put the hat back on its knob and turned toward the escalator, but I went to the wrong one, the up escalator again, and I had to back away as people came off it. I walked blindly to the down escalator on the other side and rode to the first floor, holding on with both hands. The railing wavered under my grip, and as I neared the bottom I felt very, very sick. I thought I might miss the step off, stumble. I bent over farther so that the surge through my stomach would recede, and then I did stumble. A man passing the bottom of the escalator turned and half caught me, quickly, and I threw up on his shoes.

So the first thing I knew about Robert was his shoes. They were pale-brown leather, heavy and a little clumsy, different from other people's, something an English guy might wear on a farm or for walking across the moors to the pub. I later learned that they actually *were* English, hand-sewn, very expensive, and they lasted about six years. He had two pairs at a time, changing them irregularly, and they had a broken-in, comfortable look without getting shabby. Apart from this, he paid no attention to his clothes, except that he had an interesting feel for their colors, and they tended to come and go, usually to and from flea markets, thrift shops, friends. "That sweatshirt? It's Jack's," he would say. "He left it in the bar last night. He doesn't care." And the sweatshirt would be with us until it disintegrated and became a rag for cleaning our house in Greenhill, or for wiping paintbrushes—we were married long enough, after all, for clothes to become rags. None of that mattered to Robert, because meanwhile Jack had the gloves or the scarf he'd left on Jack's sofa when they argued about pastels until two in the morning. Most of Robert's clothes had so much paint on them that they weren't likely to appeal to anyone but a fellow artist anyway. He was never careful about that, as some artists are.

But his shoes were his prize. He saved money for them, he saved them, he put mink oil on them even though he wouldn't eat chicken, he was careful not to get paint on them, he lined them up side by side at the foot of our bed next to a pile of his recently shed clothes. The only other expensive item in his life—besides oil paints—was normally his aftershave. But I later learned that, by strange coincidence, he had come into Lord & Taylor to buy a birthday present for his own mother. When I threw up on his shoes, he made an involuntary rude face, a kind of "Oh God, did you have to do that?" I thought at the time that he was merely disgusted by my vomit, not by where it had landed.

He pulled something white out of his pocket and started to wipe his toes, and I assumed he was ignoring my apologies. In the next second, though, he seized me by the shoulders. He was very tall. "Quick," he said, and his voice was quick, too, low and soothing in my ear. He hurried me through the most direct aisles, past a wave of perfume that made me clutch my stomach again, past mannequins holding tennis rackets, their collars turned jauntily toward their ears. I ducked, I tried to get away. Each new sight, all those things to buy, all those things that I couldn't afford and that my mother wouldn't enjoy, sent a new wave of illness through me. But the stranger who had me by one arm and one shoulder was strong. He was wearing a short-sleeved denim shirt and stained gray jeans, and when I tried to turn my bowed head, I got a glimpse of someone rough, of curly hair, unshaven chin. He had a kind of linseed smell that I recognized vaguely even through my nausea and that I might have found pleasant under other circumstances. I wondered if he was using my illness to abduct me, take my wallet, or worse—this was New York in the '80s, after all, and I didn't yet have my requisite mugging story to tell in Michigan.

But I was too utterly sick to ask him his intentions, and after a minute we burst out into the open air, or the relatively open air of the crowded sidewalk, and he seemed to try to steady me. "You're okay," he said. "You're going to be okay." As soon as he said it, I turned and threw up again, this time aiming far away from his shoes and into the corner of the entrance area, away from the shoes of the passing crowd as well. I began to cry. He let go of me while I threw up but kept rubbing my upper back with what felt like a big hand. I was somehow horrified by this, as if a strange man had made a pass at me on a subway car, but I was too feeble to resist. When I was done, he handed me a clean paper napkin from his pocket. "Okay, okay," he murmured. Finally I straightened and leaned against the side of the building. "Are you going to faint?" he said. I could see his face now. There was something sympathetic and matter-of-fact in it, direct, alert. He had large greenish-brown eyes. "Are you pregnant?" he said.

"Pregnant?" I gasped. I had one hand on the outside wall of Lord & Taylor. It felt tremendously solid and strong, a fortress. "What?"

"I'm only asking because my cousin's pregnant and she threw up in a store, too, just last week." He had stuck his hands in his back pockets as if we were chatting in a parking lot after a party.

"What?" I said stupidly. "No, of *course* I'm not pregnant." Then I began to feel hot and red with embarrassment, because I thought he might think I was revealing something about my sex life, which in truth was nonexistent at that point. I'd had exactly three relationships in college, and a short-lived one in the postcollege gloom of Ann Arbor, but so far New York had been a complete flop in this area—I was too busy, too tired, too shy, to keep an eye out for dates. I said hastily, "I just felt weird all of a sudden." Remembering my first huge retch onto his shoes—I couldn't bring myself to look at them—made me weak again, and I put both hands and my head against the wall.

"Wow, you really are sick," he said. "Do you want me to get you a drink of water? Do you want me to help you sit down somewhere?"

"No, no," I lied, moving my hand toward my mouth in case I had to try to cover it again. Not that covering it was going to help. "I have to get home. I have to get home right now."

"Yeah, you'd better lie down with a bowl," he observed. "Where do you live?"

"I don't tell strangers where I live," I said faintly.

"Oh, come on." He had begun to grin. His teeth were beautiful, his nose ugly, his eyes very warm. He looked just a few years older than I was. His dark hair stood up in crisp locks, like gnarled branches. "Do I look like I'm going to bite you? What's your subway line?"

People were pushing past us in droves, into the store, along the sidewalks, toward home, the end of the workday. "The . . . there . . . Brooklyn," I said weakly. "If you can maybe walk me in that direction, I'm fine. I'll be fine in a minute." I took a stumbling step and covered my mouth. I wondered later why I hadn't wanted a taxi. My habit of thrift was very strong, I guess, even in that situation.

"Oh, like hell you will," he said. "Try not to puke on my shoes again, and I'll get you to your station. Then you can let me know if there's someone you want me to call." He put one arm around me, propping me up, and we moved in a clumsy knot toward the subway entrance at the end of the block.

When we got there, I held on to the railing and tried to put out a hand, getting in everyone's way on the steps. "Okay, thanks. I'll just catch my train."

"Come on." He went ahead of me, shielding me from the fray, so that I could see only the back of his denim shirt. "Down the stairs."

I held on to the stranger's shoulder with one hand and the railing with the other.

"You want me to call someone? Your family? Roommates?"

I shook my head. I shook it two or three times, but I couldn't speak. I was about to vomit again, and then my humiliation would be complete. "All right, now." He was smiling again, exasperated, friendly. "Get onto that train."

And we got on together, into the horrible mass of people. We had to stand, and he held me from behind, not pressing himself against me, to my relief, but gripping me firmly with one big hand while he grasped a ceiling loop with the other. He swayed for both of us as the train rounded corners. At the first stop, someone got off and I sank into a seat. I thought that if I vomited again in that closed space, where my excretion would reach at least six other bodies, I would decide to stop living. I would go back to Michigan, because I was not made for the city—I was weaker than the rest of the seven million people there. I was a public vomiter. My biggest pleasure in leaving or dying would be never again seeing this towering young man with his denim shirt and the dark stain on his shoes.

CHAPTER 13

Kate

At my stop, I hardly knew where I was, but the gallant stranger got me out of the train and up to the surface before I threw up again—this time into a rain drain at the curb. I realized feebly that my aim was getting better each time, my choices more appropriate. "This way?" he asked when I was done, and I gestured down the street toward my apartment building, which was blessedly close. I believe I would have pointed the way even if I'd really thought he was going to cut my throat when we got there, and it was the same with opening the front door with my brass key, which he took out of my trembling hand, and with the elevator. "I'm all right now," I whispered.

"Which floor? What number?" he said, and when we arrived in the long, smelly, carpeted hall, he found my other key on the ring and opened the door to my apartment. "Hello!" he shouted. "Nobody around, I guess." I said nothing—I didn't have the strength or inclination to tell him that I lived alone. He would have figured it out immediately anyway, because my apartment was one room, with a tiny kitchen area half screened by cupboards. My bed doubled as a sofa, some pathetic old pillows from my childhood piled up on the bedspread, and the top of my dresser held dishes I couldn't fit in the kitchen. There was a threadbare Oriental on the floor, from my aunt's house in Ohio, and my desk was scattered with bills and sketches, with a coffee cup on top as a paperweight. I glanced around at all this as if I'd never seen my room before, and I was struck by its shabbiness. Having my own place was very important to me. In order to get one, I'd settled for a seedy building and a seedy landlord. The pipes above the sink were exposed, peeling paint—they wept steady tears of cold water that I had to soak up with a towel tucked behind them.

The stranger helped me in and lowered me to the edge of my bed-sofa. "Would you like a drink of water?"

"No, thank you," I groaned, watching him carefully. It was surreal, to have someone cross my threshold from the streets of New York. The only person who'd been there so far was my landlord, who'd come by once for two minutes to see why the oven wouldn't light and had shown me how to rattle the front of it with my foot. I didn't even know this man's name, and he was standing in the middle of my room, gazing around as if for something that would stop me from vomiting again. I tried not to breathe too deeply. "Could I just have a bowl from the kitchen, please?"

He brought me one, and a wet paper towel to clean my face as well, and I leaned back a little on the sofa. He had his hands on his hips, and I saw his bright eyes travel over my gallery: a black-and-white photograph of my parents talking together on our front porch, which I'd taken in high school; several of my recent drawings of milk cartons; and a poster of a mural by Diego Rivera—three men moving a block of stone, their reddish bodies bulging with effort. He studied this for a moment. I felt a stab of uncertainty. Was he ignoring my sketches? Some people would have said, "Oh, did you do these?" But he only stood staring at Rivera's Mexican workers, their grimacing faces and huge Aztec bodies. Then he turned back to me. "Well, are you all set?"

"Yes," I almost whispered, but something about the way he

was standing in the middle of my room, this stranger with his baggy pants and snaky brown hair, filled me with nausea again—or maybe it wasn't him—and I flew off the bed and dove for the bathroom. This time I vomited in the toilet, with the seat neatly up. It gave me a sense of safety and homecoming. I was finally throwing up in just the right place.

He came to the bathroom door, or near it, and I could hear his movements even though I couldn't look at him. "Do you want me to call an ambulance? I mean, do you think this is really serious? Maybe you have food poisoning. Or we could go get a taxi and just go to a hospital."

"No insurance," I said.

"Me neither." I heard him shifting his heavy shoes outside the bathroom.

"My mother doesn't know that," I added, wanting for some reason to tell him at least one thing about myself.

He laughed, the first time I ever heard Robert laugh. "Do you think mine does?" Looking sideways, I saw him laugh—he bared his teeth completely so that the corners of his mouth squared, wide open. His face was dazzling.

"Would she be upset?" I found a washcloth and cleaned my face, then rinsed hastily with mouthwash.

"Probably." I could almost hear his shrug. When I turned around, he helped me back to the bed without a word, as if we'd been doing this invalid thing for years. "Do you want me to stay for a while?"

I assumed this meant he had other places to be. "Oh, no—I'm really fine now. I'm all right. I think that was the last round."

"I didn't keep count," he told me, "but you can't have much left to throw up."

"I hope I don't give you some contagious thing."

"I never get sick," he said, and I believed it. "Well, I'm going to get going, if you're all right, but here's my name and number." He wrote it on the edge of a paper on my desk without asking whether I needed that paper for something else, and I told him my own name, awkwardly. "You can call me and tell me how you are tomorrow. Then I'll know you're really okay."

I nodded, on the verge of tears. I was so, so far from home, and my home was one woman taking out the garbage alone, a $180 bus ticket from here.

"All right, then," he said. "See you. Be sure you drink something."

I nodded and he smiled and was gone. I was amazed by how little hesitation there seemed to be in this stranger—he came in to help, then left without a fuss. I stood up and leaned against the desk to study his number. The handwriting was like him, a little rough but bold and firmly pressed into the page.

By the next morning, I felt almost well, so I called him. I was calling, I told myself, just to say thank you.

October 22, 1877

Mon cher oncle:

I am not your equal in assiduous correspondence, but I hasten to thank you for the thoughtful note, which arrived this morning and which I've shared with Papa. He sends you the message that a brother must visit somewhat more often in order to be counted as a family member at the dinner table; that is your scolding for the day, although it is a truly gentle and admiring one, and I pass it on to you in the same spirit, with a plea that you heed it for my sake, too. We are a little dull here, in this rain. I enjoyed the sketch very much—the child in the corner is delightful—you catch life so wonderfully that the rest of us can only hope to do as well . . . I returned from my sister's family with several sketches of my own. My eldest niece is now seven years old, and you would find her a model of the most engaging grace, I'm certain.

Warm regards,
Béatrice de Clerval Vignot

CHAPTER 14

Kate

Robert and I lived together in New York for almost five years. I still don't know where that time went. I read once that there's a good probability that everything that's ever happened is stored somewhere in the universe, one's personal history—all history, I guess—folded away in pockets and black holes of time and space. I hope those five years survive out there somewhere. I don't know if I'd want most of our time together saved, because some of it was awful at the end, but those years in New York . . . yes. They went by in a flash, I thought afterward, but while we were in New York together, I was sure things would always be that way, on and on, until something vaguely like an adult life took over. It was before I began to long for children or to want Robert to have a stable job. Every day seemed both just right and exciting, or potentially exciting.

Those five years happened because I did pick up the phone to call Robert the day after I stopped vomiting, and because I lingered long enough on the line for him to say that some of his friends were going to a play the next evening at their art school and I could go with them if I wanted. It wasn't exactly an invitation, but it was something like one, and it was also very close to the kind of offer I'd pictured filling my evenings in New York when I first moved there from Michigan. So I said yes, and of course the play was incomprehensible, a lot of art students reading from a script they tore up near the end and then decorating the faces of the people in the front row with white and green paint, a proceeding no one in the back rows could see very well. I was sitting there myself, aware of the back of Robert's head, which was in a row closer to the stage—he had apparently forgotten to save me a seat next to him.

Afterward, Robert's friends drifted away to a party, but he found me and we went to a bar near the theater, where we sat side by side on twirling stools. I had never been in a New York bar before. I remember there was an Irish fiddler playing into a microphone in the corner. We talked about the artists whose work we liked and why. I mentioned Matisse first. I still love his portraits of women because they're so quirky, and I don't apologize for it anymore, and I love his still lifes, full of swimming colors and fruit. But Robert discussed a lot of contemporary artists I'd never heard of. He was in his last year of art school, and in those days people were painting sofas and wrapping up buildings and conceptualizing everything and anything. I thought some of what he described sounded interesting and some of it sounded juvenile, but I didn't want to show my ignorance, so I listened while he went through a litany of works, movements, activities, points of view completely unfamiliar to me, all hotly contested in the studios where he worked and where his work was critiqued.

I watched the edge of Robert's face as he talked. It oscillated between ugly and handsome, his forehead jutting in almost a ledge over his eyes, his nose predatory, one lock of hair falling in a corkscrew on his temple. I thought he looked like a bird of prey, but every time this occurred to me, he smiled in such a childlike, happy way that I wondered what I'd been seeing the moment before. His apparent unawareness of himself was mesmerizing. I watched him rub his index finger next to his nose, then rub the end of his nose with a flattened palm as if it itched, then scratch his head the way you might scratch a dog—absently, kindly—or the way a big dog might scratch itself. His eyes were sometimes the color of my glass of stout and sometimes olive green, and he had an unnerving way of suddenly fixing me with them, as if he were sure I'd been listening all along but wanted to know my reaction to the last point he'd made and needed to know right away. His skin was a warm, soft color, as if it kept the sun even in November in Manhattan.

Robert was in a very good art school, one I'd heard about for years. *How had he gotten there?* I wondered. After college, he had bummed around, as he put it, for nearly four years before deciding to go back to school, and now that he was almost done with it, he still wondered whether it had been a waste of time, you know? My mind wandered a little from the contemporary painters whose work he was arguing over, mostly by himself. I found myself imagining him with his shirt off and more of that warm skin showing. Then he was talking about me, out of the blue, asking me what it was that I wanted from my own artwork. I hadn't thought he'd even noticed my sketches when he'd taken me home to let me throw up safely at my apartment. I said as much, with a smile—conscious that it was about time I smiled at him and glad I'd worn the one shirt I had that I knew matched the color of my eyes. I smiled, I demurred, I thought he'd never ask.

But he seemed unmoved by my attempt at charming modesty. "Sure, I noticed them," he told me flatly. "You're good. What are you doing about it?"

I sat staring at him. "I wish I knew," I said finally. "I came to New York to find out. I was suffocating in Michigan, partly because I didn't really know any other artists." He hadn't, I realized, even asked me where I was from, and he hadn't told me anything about his background either.

"Shouldn't a real artist be able to work anywhere? Do you need to know other artists in order to do good work?"

It stung, and it whipped me into a rare pique. "Apparently not, if your assessment of my work is correct."

For the first time, he seemed to see me completely. He turned and put one of his big unusual shoes—the one I'd vomited across, to judge by a fading stain—on the footrest of my stool. His eyes were edged with lines, old for his young face, and his wide mouth curled up in a chagrined smile. "I made you mad," he said with a kind of wonder.

I sat up straighter and took a sip of Guinness. "Well, yes. I've worked pretty hard on my own, even when there weren't art students for me to sit talking to in fancy bars." I wondered what had gotten into me. I was usually far too shy to snap at people like this. The bubbling stout, maybe, or his long monologue, or perhaps the sense that my little fit had caught his attention when all my polite listening had failed to. I had the feeling he was studying me carefully now—my hair, my freckles, my breasts, the fact that I hardly came up to his shoulder. He was smiling at me, and the warmth of his eyes with those premature wrinkles around them crept into my bloodstream. I had the feeling that it was that moment or never. I had to get and keep his full attention or it might never return. Otherwise, he would drift back into the vast city and I wouldn't hear from him again, he who had dozens of fellow art students to choose from. His solid thighs, his long legs in their eccentric trousers—pleated tweed this evening, with rubbed spots on the knees, surely a thrift-store purchase—kept him balanced in my direction on his bar stool, but he might lose interest at any moment and twirl back toward his drink.

I turned on him and looked him in the eye. "What I mean is, how dare you walk into my apartment and analyze my work without saying anything? At least you could have said you didn't like it."

His expression grew more serious, his eyes searching. Full-face, up close, he had lines in his forehead as well. "I'm sorry." I felt as if I'd struck a dog—the puzzled way his eyebrows worked on the problem of my annoyance. It was hard to believe that he'd been holding forth to himself about contemporary painters a few minutes before.

"I haven't had the luxury of art school," I added. "I work ten hours a day at a soporific editing job. Then I go home and draw or paint." This wasn't completely true, because I worked only eight hours, and often I went home exhausted and watched the news and sitcoms on the little television my great-aunt had bequeathed to me years before, or made phone calls, or lay on my bed-sofa in a stupor, or read. "And then I get up and go to work again the next day. On weekends I sometimes make it to a museum or paint in a park, or I draw inside if the weather is bad. Very glamorous. Does that qualify as an artist's life?" I put more sarcasm into the last question than I'd meant to, scaring myself. He was the only date I'd had in months and months, if you could even call this a date, and I was chewing him out.

"I'm sorry," he said again. "And I have to say I'm impressed." He glanced down at his hand on the edge of the bar and at mine, wrapped around my Guinness. Then we sat looking at each other, longer and longer, a staring contest. His eyes under their thick brows were—perhaps it was the color that held me. It was as if I'd never really seen another person's eyes before. I felt that if I could name their color, or the shade of the flecks in their depths, I would be able to look away. Finally he stirred. "Now what do we do?"

"Well," I said, and my boldness alarmed me because deep down I knew—I *knew*—that it was not me, that it was inspired entirely by Robert's presence and the way he was gazing into my face. "Well, I think this is where you invite me to come home and look at your etchings."

He began to laugh. His eyes lit up, and his generous, ugly, sensual mouth brimmed with laughter. He slapped his knee. "Exactly. Will you come home with me now and see my etchings?"

October 29, 1877

Mon cher oncle:

We have received your note this morning and will be delighted to welcome you at dinner. Papa hopes you will come early, with the papers to read to him.

In haste, your niece,
Béatrice de Clerval

Chapter 15

Kate

Robert lived in an apartment in the West Village with two other art students, who were both out when we arrived. Their bedroom doors were open, floors strewn with clothes and books like in dorm rooms. There was a Pollock poster in the untidy living room, a bottle of brandy on the counter in the kitchen, and dishes in the sink. Robert led me to his bedroom, which was also a mess. The bed was unmade, of course, and there was dirty laundry on the floor, but he had hung a couple of sweaters neatly over the back of the desk chair. There were piles of books—I was impressed to see that some of them were in French, art books and perhaps novels, and when I asked Robert about this, he said that his mother had come to the United States with his father after the war, that she was French and he had grown up bilingual.

The most striking thing, however, was that every surface was covered with drawings, watercolors, postcards of paintings. The walls were hung with what had to be Robert's own sketches—pencil, charcoal, sometimes the same model over and over, studies of arms, legs, noses, hands, hands everywhere. I had assumed that his room would be a shrine to modern painting, full of cubes and lines and Mondrian posters, but no—it was an ordinary workspace. He stood watching me. I knew enough to understand that his drawings were astounding, technically assured and yet also full of life and mystery and motion. "I'm trying to learn the body," he said soberly. "It's still very hard for me to draw. I don't care about anything else."

"You're a traditionalist," I said in surprise.

"Yes," he said shortly. "I actually don't care about concepts very much. Believe me, I'm taking a lot of shit for that at school, too."

"I thought—when you were talking at the bar about all those great contemporary artists, I thought you admired them."

He gave me a strange look. "I didn't mean to give you that impression."

We stood staring at each other. The apartment throbbed with silence, that off-season feeling of a deserted space at the heart of a busy night in the city. We could have been alone on Mars. There was a secret feeling to it, as if we had been playing hide-and-seek and no one knew where we were. I thought briefly of my mother, already long since asleep in the big bed that had once contained my father as well, the cat at her feet, the front door sensibly locked and checked twice, the clock ticking in the kitchen below her. I turned to Robert Oliver. "So what *do* you admire, then?"

"Honestly?" He raised his heavy eyebrows. "Hard work."

"You draw like an angel." It popped out of me, and I said it as my mother might have said it—and I meant it.

He seemed unexpectedly pleased, full of surprise at my words. "We don't hear that in critique very much. Actually, never."

"Nothing you've told me so far makes me want to go to art school," I noted. He hadn't asked me to sit down, so I wandered around once more, looking at the drawings. "I assume you paint, too?"

"Of course, but at school. Painting's the main thing, as far as I'm concerned." He lifted a couple of loose sheets from the desk. "These are a study for a model we've been working with in studio, a big oil on canvas. I had to fight to get that class. This guy, the model, has been very challenging for me. He's an old man, actually—incredible, tall, with white hair, kind of ropy muscles, but also deteriorating. Do you want something to drink?"

"I don't think so." I was beginning to wonder, in fact, exactly what I wanted from this encounter and whether I shouldn't go home. It was so late already that I was going to have to take a taxi to be safe when I got to my street in Brooklyn, and that would eat up any savings I'd set aside from the week. Perhaps Robert had a trust fund and wouldn't understand. I was wondering, also, where my pride was. Probably Robert Oliver cared mainly about himself and his paintings and had liked me because I'd been a good listener, at least at first. That was what my instinct told me, the prickling instinct girls develop about boys, women develop about men. "I think I'd better go. I'm going to need to catch a cab to get home."

He stood in front of me, in the middle of his untidy, windowless bedroom, imposing and yet somehow cowed, vulnerable, his hands hanging at his sides. He had to stoop a little to see into my face at all. "Before you go home, may I kiss you?"

I was shocked, not so much by his wanting to kiss me as by his asking, his inept delivery. I felt sudden pity for this man who looked like a conquering Hun and yet was asking me timidly for—I stepped forward and put my hands on his shoulders, which felt solid and trustworthy, the shoulders of an ox, a worker, reassuring. His face blurred to shadow in its closeness, his eyes a smudge of color in my nearest vision. Then he touched my lips with his firm ones. His mouth felt like his shoulders, warm and muscular, but hesitant, and he seemed to wait there for me for a second until I felt again something like compassion and kissed him back.

Suddenly he put his arms around me—the first time I felt his vastness, his whole huge, tall body—and almost picked me up, kissing me with unself-conscious passion. There was nothing timid about him after all. It was as if he simply did not know how not to be himself, and I felt his selfhood go down through me like lightning—I who doubted and second-guessed and analyzed every second of my own life. It was like drinking a potion when I hadn't known that potions existed: every drop of it, the whole elixir, went to the back of my head and deep into my rib cage, then shot to my feet. I had an urge to pull back and examine his eyes again, but it wasn't the urge of fear. It was more like a kind of wonder that someone could be so complicated and yet so simple, as it turned out. His hand moved to the small of my back and gathered me harder against him—he pressed me to him as if I were a package he'd been eagerly waiting for. He lifted me off my feet and literally held me in his arms.

I expected that after that there would be the click of the door closing, the smell and feel of a bed with unwashed sheets, where I would wonder if anyone else had lain under him there recently, the rummage for condoms in the bedside drawer—this period was the first panic of the AIDS epidemic—and my half-fearful, half-eager consent. But instead he kissed me once more and set me down on the floor. He held me against his sweater. "You are lovely," he said. He stood there stroking my hair. He took my head awkwardly in his hands and kissed my forehead. It was such a tender, domestic gesture that I felt a lump rise in my throat. Was this rejection? But he was putting big hands on my shoulders, caressing my neck. "I don't want you to feel rushed. Or me. Would you like to get together tomorrow night? We could go have dinner at this place I know in the Village. It's cheap and it's not noisy like the bar."

I was his, from that moment—he had me in his pocket. No one had ever not wanted me to feel rushed. I knew that when the time came, whether it was the next night, or the night after, or the next week, I would feel him stretch out above me not as an intruder but as a man I could fall in love with, or already had. That simplicity—how did he keep feeling it in the midst of my wariness? When he found me a cab, we kissed lingeringly on the street, which made my stomach lurch, and he laughed with what sounded like joy and hugged me, making the driver wait.

I didn't hear anything from him the next morning, although he'd promised to call me at work first thing, to give me directions to the restaurant. The euphoria drained slowly from my limbs as noon approached. His not sleeping with me had been an easy way to let me down, a kind way—he hadn't intended for us to have dinner after all. I had a long article on spinal-tap procedures to correct, and it faintly nauseated me, as if some of the sickness I'd felt when I'd first met Robert in the department store had returned, a mild relapse. I ate lunch at my desk. At four my phone rang, and I grabbed it. No one else but my mother had my direct work number, so I knew it could be only one of two people. It was Robert. "Sorry I couldn't call sooner," he said without further explanation. "Do you still want to go out tonight?"

That was the second evening of our five years in New York.

CHAPTER 16

Marlow

Kate rose from the sofa in her quiet living room and actually paced a little, as if I'd caught her in a cage. She walked to the windows and back, and I watched, feeling a sort of pity for her, for the position in which I'd placed her. She hadn't gotten close, in her story, to the things I most needed to know, but I didn't feel like pressing her at that moment.

It struck me what a good wife she would have made—must have been—a woman not unlike my mother in her uprightness, her organization and neat gestures of hospitality (it wasn't the first time I'd thought it), although she lacked my mother's good-natured confidence, her ironic sense of humor. Or perhaps whatever Kate's sense of humor was, it had been erased by her separation from her husband. A temporary lapse of happiness, I hoped. I had seen so many women emotionally knocked off their feet by a divorce. There were a few who did not recover, in the sense that they sank into permanent chronic bitterness or depression, especially if the divorce became linked to some previous trauma or to an underlying condition. But most women were remarkably strong, I'd always thought; those who healed themselves were full of a deeper life afterward. Intelligent Kate, with the light from the windows catching her smooth hair, would go on to something or someone else better and be content, and wise.

As I was thinking this, she turned to me. "You believe it really couldn't have been so bad," she said accusingly.

I felt myself gaping. "Not exactly," I told her. "But you're almost right. I'm sure it was bad, but I was thinking how strong a person you seem."

"So I'll get over it."

"I believe so."

She looked as if she might be about to reproach me, but then she said only "Well, you've seen a lot of patients, I guess, and you must know."

"I never feel I know anything about human beings, ultimately, but it's true that I've observed a lot of people." It was an admission I wouldn't have made to a patient.

She turned, her little collarbones catching the light. "And do you like people, Dr. Marlow, after observing so many?"

"Do you? You seem extremely observant yourself."

She broke into a laugh, the first I'd heard since I'd walked into her living room. "Let's not play games with each other. I'll show you Robert's office."

This surprised me considerably, on two counts: first, that he'd had an office, and second, that she was that generous in the midst of her grief. Perhaps it had doubled as a home studio. "Are you sure?"

"Yes," she said. "It's not much of a room, and I've started cleaning it out because I want to use the desk for a place to pay bills and organize my own papers. I still have to clean out his studio, too."

In this house with Robert, she had had neither an office nor a studio of her own, while he'd had both. Robert Oliver had taken up considerable space in her life, literally. I hoped she would show me the studio as well. "Thank you," I said.

"Oh, don't be too grateful," she rejoined. "His office is a mess. It's taken me a long time even to open the door to that room, but I feel better now that I've started sorting through it. You can look at anything you like. I'm saying that because I don't care about anything in there now. I really don't."

Kate stood and collected our cups, glancing back over her shoulder. "Come with me," she said. I followed her into a dining area as neat and restful as the living room—high-backed chairs grouped around a gleaming table. Again, the pictures were watercolors, this time of the mountains, and a couple of old bird prints, cardinals and blue jays, in the Audubon manner. No Robert Oliver paintings in here either. She led me momentarily into a sunny kitchen, where she deposited our cups in the sink, and then past the kitchen into a room not much bigger than a large closet. It was furnished, or rather completely crammed, with a desk and shelves and a chair. The desk was an antique, like most of Kate's furniture, a huge rolltop open to show pigeonholes stuffed with papers—a mess, as she'd promised.

Here, much more than in the living room, I felt Robert Oliver's presence, imagined his big hand shoving bills and receipts and unread articles into the desk sections. There were a couple of plastic bins on the floor, neatly labeled to receive various kinds of files, as if Kate had been sorting. There was no file cabinet in sight—nothing else would have fit in the room—although perhaps Kate had one tucked away somewhere else. "I hate this job," she said, again without further explanation. The bookshelves contained a dictionary, a movie guide, crime novels—some of them in French—and many works on art. *Picasso and His World,* Corot, Boudin, Manet, Mondrian, the Postimpressionists, Rembrandt's portraits, and a surprising number of works on Monet, Pissarro, Seurat, Degas, Sisley—nineteenth-century France dominated. "Did Robert like the Impressionists best?" I asked.

"I guess." She shrugged. "He liked everything best at one time or another. I couldn't keep up with all his enthusiasms."

Her voice held a nasty note, and I turned to the desk. "You're welcome to look through it, as long as you keep things in order. Order—" She rolled her eyes, an afterthought. "Anyway, just keep things together because I'm trying to get all the financial information straight, in case I'm ever audited."

"This is very kind of you." I wanted to be certain I had her permission; I pressed down my distinct thought that looking through a living patient's papers without his own consent was a serious step, even if his ex-wife was encouraging me, bitterly, to do it. Especially if she was encouraging me. But Robert had told me I could talk with anyone I wanted to. "Do you expect there's anything here that would help me?"

"I doubt it," she said. "Maybe that's why I'm feeling so generous. Robert didn't really have personal papers—he didn't write about his emotions or keep a journal or anything like that. I like to write myself, but he said he couldn't really understand the world through words—he had to look at it and get the colors down, paint it. I haven't found much of anything here except his colossal disorganization."

She laughed, or snorted, as if she liked her own description: *colossal.* "I guess it's not quite true that he didn't write things down—he made all these little notes to himself, and lists, and lost them in the mess." She pulled a scrap out of an open box. "'Rope for scenery,' she read aloud. 'Back gate lock, buy alizarin and board, check to Tony, Thursday.' He was always forgetting everything anyway. Or how about this one: 'Think about turning forty.' Can you believe that? Having to *remind* yourself to think about something so basic? When I see all this junk, I'm glad not to have to deal with the rest of it—I mean, not to deal with him anymore. But help yourself." She smiled up at me. "I'm going to make us some lunch so we can eat in peace before I go get the children. There's tomorrow, too, of course." She left the room without waiting for my response.

Chapter 17

Marlow

After a moment I sat down in Robert's desk chair. It was one of those ancient office chairs with cracked leather and rows of brass studs, turning unsteadily on wheels underneath or tipping back a little too far for stability—inherited, I guessed, from a grandfather or even a great-grandfather. Then I got up again and gently closed the door. I felt she wouldn't mind; she'd left me so completely to my own devices there as it was. It seemed to me that Kate Oliver was an all-or-nothing person. Either she was going to conscientiously show and tell me everything, or she was going to keep her privacy intact, and she'd decided on the former course. I liked her; I liked her very much.

I bent over the desk and pulled a wad of paper out of one of the pigeonholes—bank statements, half-crumpled receipts from water and electric bills, some blank notebook paper. It seemed odd to me that Kate had entrusted her scattered husband with the household finances, but perhaps he'd insisted. I shoved the collection back into place. A few of the slots were empty of everything except dust and paper clips; she'd been at work here already. I imagined her pulling all this out, filing it flat and orderly somewhere, eventually wiping the desk clean, polishing it, perhaps. Maybe she'd let me in here because she'd actually already removed anything personal; maybe it was an empty gesture, a false hospitality.

There was nothing of interest in the rest of the pigeonholes except a shriveled object in the far reaches of one that proved to be an ancient joint—I recognized the smell from long ago, as one recognizes a spice from a childhood dessert. I carefully put it back. The top two desk drawers were stuffed with sketches—conventional figure-drawing exercises, none of them anything like the lady with whom he routinely filled his room at Goldengrove—and old catalogs, mostly for art supplies, a few for outdoor gear, as if Robert had also been a hiker or cyclist. Why did I persist in thinking of him in the past tense? He might get well and hike the Appalachian Trail from one end to the other, and it was my job to help him try to do that.

The bottom drawer was harder to open, overflowing with yellow legal pads on which Robert had apparently made notes for teaching ("Previous block sketches, some fruit—still life to end of class, two hours?"). I gathered from these notes that Robert had made only the roughest outlines for his classes, and most of the papers did not have dates on them. His presence alone must have filled the classroom or studio; apparently he hadn't planned for much else. Or had he simply been so gifted a teacher that he kept all his knowledge in his head and could release it in an organized way at will? Or perhaps teaching painting meant to him simply walking around critiquing students' ongoing work? I had had five or six studio courses like that myself, crammed in around the edges of my profession, and I loved them—that feeling of being alone and yet among other painters, left in peace even by the teacher most of the time but also observed, sometimes encouraged, at the odd moment, so that you focused all the harder.

I dug to the bottom of the bottom drawer and was about to turn away from all those legal pads interspersed with old phone bills when a sheet of handwriting caught my eye. It was lined white paper, wrinkled as if it had been wadded up and then partly smoothed out again, a corner torn off. It was the beginning of a letter, or a draft of a letter, written in a strong hand with big upright loops—here and there a word had been crossed out and another choice written in. I knew that handwriting already, from the nest of little notes all around me—it was Robert's, distinctly his. I picked the paper out of the drawer and tried to smooth it on the felt desktop.

You were constantly with me, my muse, and I thought of you with startling vividness, not only your beauty and kind company but also your laugh, your smallest gesture.

The next line was crossed out, scratched out viciously, and the rest of the page was blank. I listened in the direction of the kitchen. Through the closed door, I could hear Robert's former wife moving something—a stool dragged across linoleum, perhaps, a cupboard door being opened and shut. I folded the page into thirds and put it in my inside jacket pocket. Then I bent and dug a last time in the bottom drawer. Nothing—nothing else in his handwriting anyway, although there were tax statements that looked as if they'd hardly been removed from their envelopes.

It seemed silly, but since the door was firmly closed and Kate was still apparently busy in the kitchen, I bent over and began taking Robert's books off the shelves and reaching behind them. Dust streaked my hand. I came up with a rubber ball that might have belonged to one of the children and that had now caught some dust kittens—fluffy masses of human cells, I remembered with something like a shudder. I set four or five books at a time on the floor, so that if Kate opened the door without warning she wouldn't find much out of place and I could always say I'd been looking at the books themselves.

But there were no more papers; there was nothing behind

the books, and apparently nothing—I flipped a couple of them open, rapidly—tucked inside. I saw myself for a moment as if from the doorway, an interior carefully composed of dark shapes with illumination from one bulb on the ceiling, a harsh light, a jarring, suggestive interior in the manner of Bonnard. For the first time, I noticed that there were no pictures on the walls of Robert's office, no postcards taped up, no announcements of exhibitions, no small paintings left unsold from gallery shows. That was strange in an artist's office, but perhaps he had saved them all for his studio.

Then, bending over the bookshelves again, I saw that there actually was something on one wall—not a picture of any sort, but a scrawl of numbers in pencil and a few words next to the shelves, so that the note couldn't have been seen from the door. I thought for a moment it might be the heights and ages of Robert's children, the dates when they had reached a certain stature, but it was down very low for even a small child. I crouched beside the books, still holding *Seurat and the Parisians* in my hand. It was pencil indeed, probably a 5B or 6B, dark and soft for heavy shading. I squinted at it. It said "1879." After that, two words: "Étretat. Joy."

I read it a couple of times. The numbers and letters were untidy on the wall—he must have stretched out on the floor to write them, and it still would have been difficult to make it neat. His long legs would have been cocked behind him like a child's, the office was so small. Or had someone else written that smudge? I thought the looped "É" and "J," the length of the "y," looked like Oliver's hand, the baggy, strong writing on all the self-reminders I'd been reading, the canceled checks. I took the letter draft from my pocket and held it up to compare. The "y" was certainly the same, and the bold, clear lowercase "t." Why would a grown man, a tower of a man, lie down and write something on the wall of his office?

I carefully put the letter back in its hiding place in my pocket—it was already warm from the heat of my body—and began to hunt around for a scrap of paper that wasn't written on. I remembered the yellow pads in the bottom drawer and helped myself to a piece of paper from one of them, recording carefully on it the message from the wall. I thought I knew this word, "Étretat," but I would look it up later anyway.

My search for paper had given me another idea: pulling the wastebasket closer, I went through its contents, glancing at the door every couple of seconds. I wondered whether Kate or Robert himself had stuffed it full—Kate, probably, in the course of her cleanup. It contained more scraps in his handwriting, as well as a set of scribbles that could have been studies for a nude or doodles done in an idle moment, some of them torn in two—evidence at last of the artist. None of Oliver's notes to himself meant anything to me, especially since they tended to be a few words at most and often contained practicalities. I turned over another of them: "Pick up wine, beer for tomorrow night." I didn't dare keep any of them; if I filled my jacket pockets, Kate would hear me rustling, and beyond that very real and humiliating possibility, I would hear myself rustling and feel only ashamed. One shame was enough; I touched the letter through my jacket. "*You were constantly with me, my muse.*" Who was his muse? Kate? The woman in his drawings at Goldengrove? Was that woman "Mary"? It seemed likely, and perhaps Kate would tell me about her if I asked without actually asking.

I went through the rest of the books a few at a time, always listening for the door, finding only some empty slips meant to mark a favorite page, or perhaps a passage or image for Robert's teaching—one such slip lay across a full-color reproduction of Manet's *Olympia*. I'd seen the original in Paris years earlier. She gazed up at me, naked and blankly insouciant, when I removed the paper. Behind the top row of volumes, I found a large white wadded-up sock. No other corner to search, unless I took up the carpet itself. I peered behind the shelves and desk, looked one more time at that date on the wall. A French word, "Étretat," a place. What had been going on in France in 1879, if the name and the date were connected, at least in Robert's mind? I tried to remember, but I'd never known much French history, or I'd unmemorized it soon after my high-school class in Western civilization. Hadn't there been the Paris Commune, or was that earlier? Exactly when had Baron Haussmann designed all those great boulevards in Paris? By 1879, Impressionism was alive and well, if heavily criticized—that much I knew from going to museums and reading the odd book—so perhaps it had been a year of peace and prosperity.

I opened the door to the study, glad Kate hadn't beat me to it from the other side. The kitchen was unnaturally bright after Robert's office; the sun had come out and was making a little water glisten on the trees. It had rained, then, while I was going through Robert's papers. Kate stood at the counter, tossing salad in a bowl; she wore a blue chef's apron over her top and jeans, and her face was flushed. The plates were pale yellow. "I hope you like salmon," she said, as if daring me not to.

"I do," I said honestly. "I like it very much. But I never meant for you to go to such trouble for lunch. Thank you."

"It's no trouble." She was putting pieces of bread into a basket lined with a cloth. "I rarely get to cook for grown-ups these days, and the kids won't eat much except macaroni-and-cheese and spinach. Fortunately for me, they actually like spinach." She turned and smiled at me, and I was struck by this strangeness—here was the former wife of my patient, a woman I'd met only a few hours earlier, a woman I barely knew and half feared, making me a meal. Her smile was friendly, spontaneous, reaching me across the kitchen. I wanted to hang my head.

"Thank you," I said again.

"You can take these plates to the table," she told me, holding them up in her slender hands.

October 30, 1877

Mon cher oncle:

I am writing you this morning to express all our thanks for your presence yesterday evening and for the pleasure you brought. Thank you also for your encouraging words about my drawings, which I wouldn't have wanted to show you had my father-in-law and Yves not insisted. I am working hard in the afternoons at a new painting, but it should be considered only a humble effort. I am pleased to think you liked my jeune fille so much—as I told you, my niece posed and she is a little fairy. I hope to do a painting from that drawing as well—but in the early summer, so that I can use my garden for background; it is magnificent at that time of year, when the roses are overflowing.

Warm regards to you,
Béatrice de Clerval

CHAPTER 18

Marlow

After lunch, which was on the whole silent (but companionably so, I thought), Kate told me she would have to get to work soon, and I took the hint and left, although only after we'd agreed to meet again the next morning. She closed the big front door behind me, but when I turned around on the front walk, she was still gazing out through the glass. She smiled at me, then ducked her head as if regretting the smile, waved once, and vanished before I could even wave in return. Her brick walk was bright with rain, and I picked my way carefully back to the gravel drive. I touched my breast pocket as I got into the car, checking the crinkling sheet there.

I hadn't felt so sad in a long time, somehow. My patients, when they saw me or when I saw them, were surrounded by the uniform setting of my office or the doggedly cheerful rooms at Goldengrove. Now I had talked with a woman who was alone, alone and maybe depressed enough so that she could reasonably have come to my practice herself as a patient, but instead I'd seen her surrounded by her own life, the enormous holly near the front door, the garden beds with her tulips blooming in them, the furniture her grandmother had left her, the smell of salmon and dill in her kitchen, the ruins of her husband's life in evidence behind her. She had still been able to smile in my direction.

I drove back on the springtime roads of her neighborhood,

the woods and glimpses of interesting houses, feeling my way along the route I'd come. I pictured Kate putting on a canvas jacket and getting her car keys off a hook, locking the door behind her. I thought about how she must look bending to kiss her children in their beds at night, her small waist flexible under her blue clothes. The children would both be blond, like her, or one would be pale-haired and the other crowned with Robert's heavy dark locks—but here my mind drew back. She would kiss them every time she saw them again, even after a short absence. That I was sure of. I wondered how Robert could bear to be away from these three exquisite people he had made his own. But what did I know? Maybe he *couldn't* bear it, actually. Or maybe he had forgotten how exquisite they were. I had never had a wife or a child, or two children, or a large old house with a living room full of sunlight. I saw my own hand taking the plates from Kate's—she wore no rings, just a thin gold chain on one wrist. What did I know?

At the Hadleys', I again opened all the windows, then put the scrap of letter from Robert's office on the bureau, lay down on the ugly twin bed, and fell into a doze. At one point, I actually slept for a few minutes. Deep down in my dream was Robert Oliver, telling me about his life with his wife, but I couldn't hear a word and I kept asking him to speak more clearly. There was something else buried in that dream, a memory: Étretat, the name of a coastal town in France—where, exactly?—the scene of Monet's famous cliff paintings, those iconic arches, blue-and-green water, green-and-purple rock.

Finally I got up, unrested, and put on an old shirt. I took my current reading, a biography of Newton, and drove down to the town to hunt for dinner. I found several good restaurants; in one of them, which had tiny white lights in all the windows as if it were Christmas, I had a plate of potato pancakes with various garnishes. The woman sitting at the bar smiled at me and recrossed lovely legs, and the man who joined her a few minutes later looked like a New York businessman. A strange little town, I thought, liking it even more as my Pinot Noir took effect.

Walking around the streets after dinner, I wondered if I might encounter Kate, and if so what I would say to her, how she would react if we ran into each other after this morning's conversation, then remembered that she would surely be at home with her children. I pictured myself driving back into her neighborhood to peer through those huge windows. They would be softly lit, the bushes around them already dark, the roof floating above. Inside, a box of gems: Kate playing with two beautiful children, her hair shining under the lamp. Or I would see her at the kitchen window where she'd made me salmon; she would be washing dishes after the children were in bed, revelling in the silence. I imagined in a rush her hearing me among the bushes, calling the local police, the handcuffs, the fruitless explanations, her anger, my disgrace.

I stopped to compose myself for a moment in front of a boutique window full of baskets and what appeared to be handwoven shawls. As I stood there, I began to long for home. What on earth, after all, was I doing here? It was lonely in this pretty town; at home, I was used to being alone. I kept seeing the words in pencil on Robert's wall. Why had he filled his library with the Impressionists? I made myself walk a little farther, pretending that I hadn't given up on the evening already. Soon I would go home—to the Hadleys', in other words—and lie in bed reading about Newton, who was comfortably from another world, an era without modern psychiatry. Tragically without it, of course. Before Monet, before Picasso, before antibiotics, before my own life. Comfortably dead Newton would keep me better company than these twilit streets, with their restored buildings, café tables, young couples draped in scarves and earrings who went by holding hands in a cloud of musky scent. It was already a long time since I'd been young, and I didn't know how the distance had crept over me, or when.

At the end of the block, the boutiques gave way to a parking lot and then, rather surprisingly, to a festive-looking club that turned out to be a topless bar. Despite the presence of a bouncer at the door, the place had none of the sordid appearance of such operations in Washington. Not that I had been in one in many decades, and then only once, in college, but I had driven past them here and there and noted, at least, their existence. I hesitated for a moment. The man at the door was neatly dressed, gentlemanly, as if even the strip shows in this town had been gentrified. He turned toward me with a friendly, expectant, understanding smile, like a financial consultant at a bank. Was he inviting me in? Did I want to apply for a mortgage?

I stood there wondering if I should indeed go in, because I couldn't think why I shouldn't. I remembered, too, the one really beautiful model from my classes at the Art League School at home—remote, balanced nude before the group, her mind far away and probably going over her college homework or her next dental appointment, her breasts lifted delicately in front of her, her professionalism, the slight quiver that was the only betrayal of her need to move at all during the long, long pose.

"No, thank you," I said to the fellow at the door, but my voice seemed muffled by age and embarrassment. He hadn't invited me in, he hadn't handed me any kind of flyer, so why was I speaking to him? I tucked the biography firmly under my arm and walked on, then turned the next corner so that I wouldn't have to pass him again—him and his festive doorway.

Had he long ago grown used to the sights and sounds within, so that it was no chore to him to have to sit outside in the gathering dark, no hardship to miss it all? Did his mind wander away at last, bored even by what was supposed to excite?

At the Hadleys' quiet house, I lay awake for hours in my twin bed next to the other, empty bed, feeling and hearing the spruces, the hemlocks, the rhododendron scraping at the partly open window, the verdant mountain out there in the night, the burgeoning of nature that did not seem to include me. And when, my restless body asked my teeming brain, had I agreed to be excluded?

Standing on Kate's porch the next morning, I felt not increased embarrassment but a kind of familiarity, an actual ease, as if I'd arrived to see an old friend or as if I were an old friend myself, stepping up to ring the bell. She answered promptly, and again it was like walking onto the set of a play, except that I'd seen the show once now and knew where all the props would be. Today the sun was fully out, streaming through the room. There were only two other changes: one, a great bowl of floating blooms, pink and white, arranged with care on the table by the windows; and Kate herself, who wore a blouse of saffron cotton over her jeans, with the same tourmaline jewelry. Yesterday I had thought her eyes were blue; now they were turquoise, wide and clear. She smiled, but it was a reserved, polite smile, the acknowledgment of a problem, and the problem was me, my renewed presence in her house, my need to ask her more questions about the husband who no longer lived here.

When she'd finished serving our coffee, she sat down on the opposite sofa. "I think we should plan to kind of wrap this up today," she said mildly, as if she'd studied how to say it without hurting my feelings or revealing her own.

"Yes, of course," I said, to show I could take a hint with alacrity. "Of course. You've been very hospitable already. Besides, I should get back to Washington tomorrow night, if possible."

"Then you won't be going out to the college?" She balanced her cup on her neat, small knee, as if to show me how it could be done. Her tone was courteous, conversational. I wondered if I would get less from her today, not more.

"Do you think I should? What would I find there?"

"I don't know," she admitted. "I'm sure there are still plenty of people there who knew him, but I wouldn't feel comfortable putting you in touch with them myself. And I doubt he showed his moods much at school. But his greatest painting is there. It should be in a first-class museum—he should have sold it well. I'm not the only one who considers it his greatest, although I've never really liked it."

"Why not?"

"Go see it for yourself."

I sat considering her elegant, small presence across the room. I felt that I needed to know how Robert's illness had first manifested itself, and we were running out of time. And I needed, or at least wanted, to know who his dark-haired muse was. "Would you like to go on with your story from yesterday?" I asked her as gently as I could. If it didn't lead soon enough to information about the onset of his problems and his subsequent treatment, I could steer her carefully to those more important matters when she was warmed up. I nodded without speaking, although she hadn't said anything more yet. Outside a cardinal landed in the sunlight; a branch swayed.

Chapter 19

Kate

Our lives in New York went on and on, or went by in a flash. We lived three different places in five years—first at my apartment in Brooklyn for a while, and after that in an unbelievably small room on West 72nd near Broadway, a closet with a kitchen counter that folded down out of a smaller closet, and finally on the stifling top floor of a building in the Village. I loved all those places, their Laundromats and grocery stores and even their local homeless people—everything, everything that became familiar about them.

And then one day I woke up and thought, *I want to get married. I want to have a baby.* It was really almost as simple as that—one evening I went to bed young and free, carefree, disdainful of other people's conventional lives, and the next morning by six o'clock, when I got up to take my shower and dress for my editing job of those years, I had become a different person. Or maybe the thought came to me between drying my hair and pulling on my skirt—*I want to get married to Robert and have a ring on my finger and a baby, and the baby will have Robert's curly hair and my small hands and feet, and life will be better than it's ever been before.* It was as if that vision was suddenly so real to me that all I had to do was cover the last bit of ground and make it reality itself and then I would be completely happy. It didn't occur to me just to get pregnant and have a little free-love baby—as my mother might have half humorously said—in Manhattan. I associated babies with marriage, marriage with the long-term, children growing up on tricycles and green lawns—after all, that's what I'd known in my own childhood. I wanted to be like my mother, bending over to put our socks on and tie our little dark-red oxfords. I even wanted to wear the dresses of her youth, which required squatting down with your legs folded neatly together to one side. I wanted a tree with a swing in the backyard.

And just as it wouldn't have occurred to me to produce babies without wearing a wedding ring first, it never occurred to me that I could raise a child in the overwhelming city I had come to love. It's hard to explain these things, because I'd been so sure I wanted nothing but this life of Manhattan and painting and meeting our friends after work at cafés and talking about painting and watching Robert paint in his blue oxford-cloth boxers at a friend's studio late at night while I drew on my lapboard, and then getting up in the morning, yawning before work, waking up as I walked under the stunted trees to the subway. That was my reality, and these curly-haired small people who didn't even exist yet, didn't even have the right to my daydreams, told me to leave it all. And, years later, they are the one thing—our bringing them into existence, despite all the grief, the fear, despite losing Robert, despite the overpopulation of this poor planet and the guilt I feel about having added to it—my children are the one thing I have never regretted.

Robert didn't want to give up any of that life we had in New York. I think it was the persuasion of the body that made him undo it, ostensibly for my sake. Men love to make babies, too, although they will tell you they don't feel the way women do. I think he was drawn in by my passion about the whole thing. He didn't really want the green small town or the job at a little college, but I suppose he knew, too, that sooner or later the postgraduate life we'd pieced together would give way to something else. He'd done well already, had a show with a faculty member from his department, sold a bunch of paintings in the Village. His mother, a widow living in New Jersey who still knitted him sweaters and vests and called him Bob-*bee* in her French accent, had decided he was going to be a great artist after all—she'd actually started sending him some of his inheritance from his father so he could use it to paint.

I think Robert felt invincible, with that much beginner's luck. It was beginner's talent, as well. Everyone who saw his work seemed to recognize the gift, whether or not they liked his traditionalism. He taught an entry-level class at the school he'd graduated from, and day after day he turned out those early paintings that are now in quite a few collections—they *are* wonderful, you know. I still think so.

Just about the time I proposed babies, Robert was working on what he rather seriously called his Degas series—the young girls warming up at the barre at the School of American Ballet, graceful and sexual but not really sexual, stretching their thin legs and arms. He spent hours at the Metropolitan Museum that winter, studying Degas's little ballerinas, because he wanted his to be the same and at the same time different. Each of Robert's canvases contained an anomaly or two—a huge bird trying to get in at the ballet-studio window behind them, or a gingko tree growing up the wall and reflecting in the endless mirrors. A gallery in Soho sold two of them and asked for more. I was painting, too, three times a week after work, rain or shine—I remember the discipline I had then, the feeling that I might not be as good as Robert but that my work was getting stronger every week. Sometimes on Saturday afternoons we took our easels to Central Park and painted together. We were in love—we made love twice a day on the weekends, so why not make babies? He was caught up by the new way I made love to him, too, I'm sure, since that part of our lives was always extremely important to him, and he was intrigued by the feeling of a seed passing between us, the imminent flowering of our connection.

We got married in a chapel on 20th Street. I wanted to go to a justice of the peace, but instead we had a modest Catholic wedding to please Robert's mother. My own mother came from Michigan with my two best friends from high school, and she and Robert's mother liked each other and sat close together during the alien mass, two widows, Robert's mother adding a second child to the "only." My mother-in-law made a sweater for me as a wedding present, which sounds kind of awful, but it was one of my treasures for years—off-white, with a collar like dandelion down. I had loved her from our first meeting. She was a tall, gaunt, cheerful woman who approved of me for no reason I could discern and was convinced that my ten or twelve words of her native language could be transformed into fluency if I worked hard enough. Robert's father, a program officer of the Marshall Plan, had removed her from a postwar Paris she didn't appear sorry to have left. She had never been back, and her entire life revolved around the nursing job for which she'd trained in the United States, and around her prodigy son.

Robert seemed to me unchanged by and during the ceremony, the act of marriage, uncomplicatedly happy to be there with me, oblivious to wearing a suit, the one tie he owned crooked on his shirt front, paint under his nails. He had forgotten to get a haircut, which I'd particularly wanted him to do before we stood up in front of a Catholic priest and my mother, but at least he didn't lose the ring. Watching him as we said the unfamiliar vows, I felt he was as he'd always been—himself, eternally himself, that he could just as well have been standing with me and our friends at our favorite bar, having another beer and debating problems of perspective. And I was disappointed. I had wanted him to stand up next to me changed—transformed, even, by the opening note of this new era of our lives.

After the ceremony, we went to a restaurant in the heart of the Village and met our circle there—they looked unusually cleaned up, and some of the women were wearing high heels. My brother and sister were there, too, from out West. Everyone acted a little formal, and our friends shook hands with our mothers or even kissed them. Once some wine had gone around, Robert's classmates started making bawdy toasts, which worried me. But rather than being shocked, our mothers sat side by side, their cheeks flushed, laughing like teenage girls. I hadn't seen my mother so happy in a long time. I felt a little better then.

Robert did not trouble himself to apply for jobs elsewhere until I'd asked him for several months to do so—now I wanted us to find that cozy town with the houses we might someday be able to afford. In fact, he didn't really apply at all. A job at Greenhill came to him through one of his instructors because he happened to drop by that instructor's office to ask him to go out for an impromptu lunch, and at lunch the instructor happened to think about a job he'd just heard of, for which he could recommend Robert—he, the instructor, had an old friend, a sculptor and ceramist, who taught at Greenhill. It was a great place for an artist, he told Robert at their lunch: North Carolina was full of artists living the real, pure life, just doing their art, and this Greenhill College had ties to the old Black Mountain College because a few of Josef Albers's students had left Black Mountain when the place dissolved and founded an art department at Greenhill—it would be just right, and Robert could paint. Maybe I could, too, come to think of it, and the climate was good, and—well, he would send a letter on Robert's behalf.

In fact, Robert gets most of the good things in his life this way, by luck, and his luck is usually good. The police officer forgives his speeding and reduces the fine to $25 from $120. He's late turning in a grant proposal and he gets the grant, plus an extra grant for equipment. People love to do things for him because he seems so happy even without their help, so oblivious to his own needs and to their wish to help him. I've never understood this. I used to think he was kind of cheating, tricking people without meaning to, but now I sometimes think that life is simply compensating for what's missing in him.

I was pregnant by the time we moved to Greenhill. I pointed out to Robert that all the great loves of my life began with vomiting. In fact, I could hardly think about anything else. I packed everything in our Village apartment and gave away a lot of stuff to the friends who were staying (staying behind, I thought pityingly) in our old life there. Robert had said he would organize a bunch of them to help us load up the truck we'd rented, but he forgot, or they forgot, and in the end we hired a couple of teenagers right off the street to carry everything down from our walk-up. I'd done the packing myself, because he'd had a lot of last-minute something or other to do at school, in his studio. When the apartment was bare and we'd cleaned it so that the landlord wouldn't keep our deposit, Robert drove the truck over to his studio and dragged down boxes of painting supplies and armloads of canvases. He hadn't packed a single piece of his own clothing, a single pot or pan, I realized later—only those essential items from his studio. I went along to sit in the truck and move it if the police or the meter maid showed up.

As I sat there, with the August sun beating down on the steering wheel, I stroked my belly, which was swollen already, not with the peanut-sized baby in the clinic's wall charts but with my eating and throwing up, my new slackness and softness, my not caring to hold it all in. When I slid my hand over the spot, I felt a melting desire for the person growing inside, for the life ahead of us. It was not a feeling I'd ever had before—it was secret even from Robert, mainly because I wouldn't have been able to explain it even to him. When he came down with the last load of shabby boxes, the last easel, I glanced out the truck window at him and saw that he was cheerful and full of energy and selfhood that had nothing to do with me. He wasn't thinking about anything except getting those parts of his old life to fit into a pile with our hopeless furniture in the back. At that moment, more than at any other, I felt the beginning of a mistake, and it was as if my child had been whispering it to me: *Will he take care of us?*

November 5, 1877

Mon cher oncle:

Please do not take amiss my not answering you sooner; your brother, your nephew, and two of the servants have had bad colds—most of the household, in short—and I have been very much occupied as a result. There is nothing serious to worry about, really, or I should have written you much sooner. Everyone is on the mend, and your brother has begun to take his constitutional in the Bois again with his manservant. I am sure Yves will go with him today; he, like you, always has Papa's health at heart. We have long since finished the new book you sent, and I am reading Thackeray to myself and also aloud to Papa. I cannot send much news now, as I am very busy, but I think of you fondly—

Béatrice de Clerval

Chapter 20

Kate

We stopped for lunch a few miles north of DC, pulling off at a rest area and stretching our legs. I was starting to get foot cramps just from thinking about them. The rest area had picnic tables and a grove of oaks—Robert checked the ground for dog piles and then lay down and went to sleep. He'd been out late, packing his studio, and then up late, apparently drawing something and drinking cognac, which I'd smelled on him when he'd tumbled into the not-yet-packed sheets of our bed. I should be driving, I thought, in case he was in danger of falling asleep at the wheel.

I felt actively annoyed—I was pregnant, after all, and had he helped with any of the preparations, even the modest one of getting enough sleep before a long, tough trip? I stretched out next to him in the grass without touching him. I'd be too tired to drive at the end of the day, but if he slept now he might be able to take over again for me when I faded. He wore an old yellow shirt with the button-down collar unbuttoned and curling up unevenly on the right side—probably one of his thrift-store purchases, something that had once been fine fabric and was now worn to a pleasant softness. There was a piece of paper tucked in his shirt pocket, and lying there with nothing else to do, yet not wanting to wake him, I carefully reached over and pulled it out. It would be a drawing, of course, and it was. I unfolded it—skillful, heavy pencil, a sketch of a woman's face.

I knew immediately that I'd never seen her before. I knew the friends he'd used as models in the Village, and the baby ballerinas whose parents had signed forms saying that Robert could draw or paint them, and I knew the improvisations of his brain. This woman was a stranger to me, but Robert understood her well—that thought leapt at me from the page. She glanced up at me as she would have at Robert, under his hand—with recognition, her eyes luminous, her look serious and loving. I could feel his artist's gaze on her. His talent and her face were indistinguishable from each other, and yet she was a real woman, someone with delicately shaped nose and cheeks, the chin a little too square, the hair dark, rumpled and curly like Robert's own, the mouth about to smile but the eyes intense. Those eyes burned from the page—they were large and shining and without any attempt at self-disguise. It was the face of a woman in love. I felt myself falling for her. She was a person as likely to reach out and touch your cheek without warning as to speak.

I had always been certain of Robert's devotion to me, as much because of his obliviousness to his surroundings as because of any sort of innate responsibility on his part. Studying this face, sketched with love, I felt myself jealous, huge with jealousy and yet small, demeaned by my own insistence that Robert was mine. He was my husband, my apartment mate, my soul mate, the father of the little plant in my confused soil, the lover who had made me adore his body without inhibition after my years of relative solitude, the person for whom I'd given up my old self. Who was she, this nobody? Had he met her at school? Was she one of his students, or a young colleague? Or had he simply been copying some other drawing, someone else's work? The face was not youthful, actually—it said instead that age was not a question once the question of beauty had been answered so fully. Was she actually older than Robert, who was older than I was, perhaps a model about whom he'd had some special feeling of kinship but whom he'd never touched, so that if I accused him of doing that I would only be belittling myself? Or had he touched her as well as sketched her and thought I wouldn't understand, because I was less of an artist?

Then I realized with a pang of anger that I hadn't picked up a brush or pencil in the three months since I'd become pregnant and since I'd starting packing and cleaning up our physical, practical lives. I hadn't missed it, which was worse. The last months of my job had been frantic, and my home life filled to exhaustion with planning and doing. Had Robert been out drawing this beauty while I was busy arranging everything? When and where had he met her? I sat in the neatly mown rest-area grass, feeling sticks and ants through my thin dress, the soothing shade from the oaks over my head and shoulders, and I asked myself over and over what I should do.

Finally the answer came to me. I didn't want to do anything. If I thought hard enough, I might be able to convince myself that she was a being from his imagination, since he occasionally drew from that as well. If I asked Robert leading questions, I would make myself less desirable in his eyes. It would make me the pregnant, pestering, paranoid wife, especially if the woman meant nothing, or maybe I would find out something I didn't want to know about, just didn't want to know, didn't want wrecking our new lives.

If she was in New York, we were leaving her already, and if Robert went back there for any reason, I would go with him. I folded the lovely face again and tucked her back into Robert's pocket. He slept so deeply that you could shake him or speak to him for long minutes with no result, so I wasn't afraid of waking him.

*

The drive into North Carolina the next day was spectacular—I was at the wheel and I shouted with happiness, then leaned over and woke Robert. We came in on the north side of Greenhill, over a long pass in the Blue Ridge, and headed east on a smaller highway toward Greenhill College. The college is actually in the town of Shady Creek, in a range called the Craggies. Robert had passed through the region on vacation with his parents long ago but remembered very little, and I had never been this far south. He said he wanted to drive the rest of the way, and we traded places. It was early afternoon, and the countryside seemed asleep in the sun, with its big, old farmhouses and river-valley fields and spreading trees, the haze of ridges in every distance, the sudden roar of a streambed under rhododendron as we climbed onto a back road. The air that came into the sweltering cab was cool, cooled as if from a cave or a refrigerator—it trembled on our faces and caressed our hands.

Robert slowed at a turn, leaned out his window, and pointed to a carved sign: GREENHILL COLLEGE, FOUNDED AS CRAGGY FARM SCHOOL IN 1889. I snapped a picture with the camera my mother had given me before I moved to New York. The sign was framed with gray fieldstones, and it sat in a meadow of grasses and ferns with dark bushes just beyond, a trail leading into woods. It was, I thought, as if we'd been invited into a rustic paradise—I expected to see Daniel Boone or someone like that walk out of the woods with his gun and his dog. It was hard for me to believe that we'd been in New York City the day before, or even that New York existed. I tried to picture our friends walking home from work or waiting in the overheated subway, the constant screech of traffic, the voices in the air. That was all gone. Robert pulled off to the side of the road and stopped the truck, and we got out without speaking. He walked over to the hand-carved sign with its carefully painted letters—made by art students? I took a picture of him leaning against it with his arms crossed in triumph, a hillbilly already. The truck ticked and steamed in the dust. "We can still turn around and go back," I said mischievously, to make him laugh.

He did laugh. "To Manhattan? Are you kidding?"

November 15, 1877

Cher oncle et ami:

Please don't think that because I haven't written I have forgotten you! Your notes are very sweet and bring us all joy, and I treasure the ones you sent to me—yes, I am quite well. Yves will be in Provence for two weeks, which means many preparations in the household. The Ministry is sending him to create a plan for the post office they will give over to him next year. Papa is quite anxious about Yves's departure and says we must find a way to get the government to excuse those with blind fathers from traveling far away. He tells us that Yves is his walking stick and I am his eyes. Perhaps you will assume this is some sort of burden, but please do not think so for an instant—never has any young woman had a kinder father-in-law than I, as I well know. I fear he will languish without Yves, even for this relatively short time, and I do not dare go to see my sister while Yves is gone. Perhaps you will come cheer us some evening—in fact, Papa will insist, I'm sure! In the meantime, thank you also for the brushes you sent me in your package. They are the finest I have seen, and Yves is pleased to think I'll have something new to work with while he's away. My portrait of little Anne is done, and so are two garden scenes showing the approach of winter, but I can't seem to begin anything new. Your brushes will be my inspiration. The modern natural style of landscape pleases me immensely, perhaps more than it does you, and I try to capture it, although of course one can't do much at this season.

In the meantime, warmest greetings from your affectionate

Béatrice de Clerval

CHAPTER 21

Marlow

Kate had set her coffee cup, with its ring of glazed blackberries, on a table at her elbow. She made a little gesture, as if asking me to let her stop talking. I nodded and sat back at once; I wondered if there were tears gathering in her eyes. "Let's take a break," she said, although it seemed to me we were already taking one. I hoped she'd be willing to continue at all. "Would you like to see Robert's studio?"

"Did he work much at home?" I tried not to accept too eagerly.

"Well, at home and at school," she told me. "Mainly at school, of course."

Upstairs, the central hall doubled as a small library, with a faded carpet and windows that looked over that spreading lawn. More novels, collections of short stories, encyclopedias. At one end there was a table equipped with drawing materials, pencils standing in a jar, a large open pad—someone's sketch of windows, apparently. Was this finally a glimpse of Robert? But Kate saw me looking. "My work spot," she said shortly.

"You must be a great reader," I hazarded.

"Yes. Robert always thought I spent too much time reading, in fact. And a lot of these books belonged to my parents."

So they were her books, not his. I noted entrances to various rooms, some with their doors shut, some open to views of carefully made beds. In one of these—at last—I saw the children's toys, scattered joyfully on the floor. Kate opened a closed door and let me in.

The aroma of mineral spirits lingered here still, as well as the smell of oils—I wondered how such a careful housekeeper as she seemed to be (even neater than my mother) could possibly have tolerated that smell in the upstairs of the house. Perhaps, as I did, she actually found it pleasing. We entered without speaking; I had at once a funereal feeling about this room. The artist who had worked here only a short time before was not dead, but now he lay in a bed far away, staring at the ceiling of a psychiatric center. Kate went to the big windows and folded back a series of wooden shutters, and the sunlight for which Robert Oliver must have chosen this room came sweeping in. It fell on the walls, on canvases stacked backward in one corner, a long table, cans full of brushes. And it fell on a handsome adjustable easel with a painting still on it, nearly finished, a painting that electrified my senses.

In addition, the walls were littered with images of paintings—mainly postcards from museums and from every era of Western art. I saw dozens of works I knew and many I didn't. Every inch of space leapt with faces, meadows, dresses, mountains, swans, haystacks, fruit, ships, dogs, hands, breasts, geese, vases, houses, dead pheasants, Madonnas, windows, hats, trees, horses, roads, saints, windmills, soldiers, children. The Impressionists dominated; I could easily pick out masses of Renoir, Degas, Monet, Morisot, Sisley, and Pissarro, although there were other images that were clearly Impressionist but new to me.

The room itself looked as if its occupant had left it on impulse: a heap of paint-hardened brushes—good brushes, wasted—and a stained rag rested on the table. He had not even finished cleaning up, my patient who showered and shaved daily in the heart of an institution. His former wife stood in the middle of the room, the sun touching her sand-dune hair. She glowed with sunlight, with young beauty beginning to ebb, and—I thought—with anger.

Keeping one eye on her, I stepped up to the easel. Robert's familiar subject gazed out of it, the woman with the dark curls, the red lips, and the brilliant eyes. She wore a gown that might have been an old-fashioned nightdress or robe, a garment ruffled and pale blue and barely held in place by her white hand. It was a vivid, romantic portrait, highly sensual—saved from sentimentality, in fact, by a frank eroticism, one curve of the woman's breast pressed roundly under her forearm as she reached up to gather her robe together. To my surprise, the hand that gripped the gown also held a paintbrush, its tip smeared with cobalt as if she herself had been caught in midstroke, working on some canvas of her own. The background seemed to be a sunny window, a window with stone framing and diamond-shaped glass panes, filled in the distance with slate-blue water and ocean clouds. The rest of the background—the room where the woman stood—was unfinished, trailing away into bare canvas in the top right corner.

That face was familiar enough to me, and the wonderfully curling, living dark hair, but two aspects of this portrait were different from the images Robert was constantly painting in his room at Goldengrove. One was the style of the work, the brushwork, the heightened realism; he had abandoned his occasionally rough handling, his modern version of Impressionism, for this painting. It was highly realistic, in places nearly photographic—the texture of her skin, for example, had the smoothness of the late medieval period, the attention to fine surfaces. It reminded me, in fact, of the Pre-Raphaelites and their detailed portraits of women; it had that mythical quality, too, with the loose robe, the woman's broad-shouldered height and splendor. A few fine black curls had escaped to brush her cheek and neck. I wondered if he'd actually painted it from a photograph; but was he a painter who would use photographs at all?

The other thing that startled me—no, shocked me, really—was the subject's expression. In most of the sketches of her at the hospital, Robert's woman was serious, even somber, at least thoughtful—sometimes, as I've mentioned, angry. Here, on a canvas that apparently sat most of the time in shuttered darkness, she was laughing. I had never seen her laugh before. Despite her dishabille, it was not a wanton laugh but a joyful, intelligent mirth, a witty love of life, a natural movement of her lovely mouth, a glimpse of teeth, eyes sparkling. She was utterly, almost terribly, alive on the canvas; she seemed about to move. To see her was to want to reach out and touch her living skin—yes, to long to bring her close and hear her laugh in your ear. The sunlight fell across her in streams. I'll admit it: I desired her. It was a masterpiece, one of the most splendidly conceived and executed contemporary portraits I'd ever seen in the flesh. Unfinished as she was, she had taken—I knew at a glance—weeks or months of work. Months.

When I turned back to Kate, I couldn't help reading her disdain. "You like her, too, I see," she said, and I heard coldness in her tone. She seemed small and worn, even pinched, next to the lady on the canvas. "Do you think my ex-husband is gifted?"

"Without question," I said. I felt myself lowering my voice, as if he might be just behind us, listening—I remembered the contempt I'd so often seen on his face when I spoke to him about his drawings and paintings. This once-married couple might be divided now by their difficult history, but they both knew how to look bitterly disdainful, that was certain. I wondered if they'd sometimes faced each other with that expression. Kate stood staring at the brighter-than-life woman on the easel, who gazed radiantly past us. I had the sudden sense that the portrait was searching for Robert Oliver, her creator, that she, too, saw him standing behind us. I almost turned around to check. It was unnerving, and I wasn't entirely sorry when Kate closed the shutters and the lady was laughing in dusk again. We went out and Kate shut the door. When would I have the courage to ask her the identity of the woman in the portrait? Who had been its model? I had missed the moment; I was afraid that if I asked this, she would stop talking with me altogether.

"You've left his studio as it was," I observed as casually as I could.

"Yes, I have," she admitted. "I keep meaning to do something about it, but I guess I'm never quite sure what to do. I don't want to just put everything in storage or throw it all away. When Robert settles down somewhere, I might pack up these things and send them all to him so he can start a new studio. *If* he ever settles down anywhere." She avoided my gaze. "The children ought to have separate bedrooms soon. Or maybe I'll finally make a studio for myself. I never had one. I always just took my easel outside, but that meant working in good weather, and then we had the kids—" She broke off. "Sometimes Robert offered me a corner of his studio, or said he could work at school and give me this room, but I didn't want a corner. And I certainly didn't want him at school even more of the time."

Something in her tone made me feel I shouldn't ask why not. So I stayed silent, following her down the stairs. Her back in the golden shirt was small and straight, her body firmly controlled, as if she dared me to feel any longing or even curiosity, as if she would turn that ladylike hostility on me in an instant if I let my eyes travel over her. I glanced out the window instead, at a beech tree that threw rosy light into the staircase. She led me to the living room and sat down on her sofa with a purposeful look. I understood that she wanted to get on with our task, and I sat down opposite her and tried to collect myself.

December 14

Mon cher oncle:

We did have a bit of social life last night, and I regretted you could not come to enjoy it with us; in addition to the usual friends, Yves brought home with him Gilbert Thomas, a painter of excellent family who they say is talented—although he was refused at the Salon last year and took it hard. M. Thomas must be about ten years older than I—perhaps in his late thirties. He is charming and intelligent, but there is something angry in him at moments that I do not quite like, especially when he speaks of other painters. He was gracious about asking to see my work, and I believe Yves had the idea that he, like you, might help me. He seemed genuinely struck by my portrait of little Marguerite, the new maid I told you about, who has such white skin and gold hair, and I confess it was flattering to hear it praised. He said he thought I could do great things, given my talent, and complimented my rendering of the figure. I did find him kind then, if a little sure of himself (I won't quite say pompous, so that you will not scold me later for snobbery). He and his brother intend to establish a large new sales gallery, and I daresay he would like to show your work there. He promised Yves to come back one day and bring his brother along, and you must come, too, if that is the case.

There was also a delightful man in the party, a M. Dupré, another artist, one who works for the illustrated papers. He has been in the country of Bulgaria, where they have recently had a revolution. I heard him tell Yves that he knew of your work. He brought us some of his prints, which are very detailed and show all kinds of skirmishes and battles, with cavalry, magnificent uniforms—and sometimes quieter scenes with villagers in their native costumes. He says it is a mountainous country, rather unsafe at the moment for journalists but full of dramatic views. He is doing a series he calls "Les Balkans Illustrés." In fact, he has married a Bulgarian girl with the lovely name of Yanka Georgieva and brought her to Paris to learn French—she was unwell and could not attend this evening, but he wrote down her name for me. I found myself wishing I could go to such places and see them for myself. In fact, we are pretty dull with Yves working so much these days, and I was glad to have a dinner party under my own roof. I do hope you will join us the next time.

I must go now, but I will look forward to whatever lines you can send your devoted

Béatrice de Clerval

CHAPTER 22

Kate

Our new place was a big green cottage provided by the college. After classes started, Robert was gone more than ever, and now he was painting in our attic at night as well. I didn't like to go up there because of the fumes, so I stayed away. I was going through a stage of constantly worrying about the baby, maybe because I'd begun to feel it squirm and kick—"Feeling life," one of the faculty wives told me. Whenever it wasn't moving I was sure it was sick, or more likely dead. I didn't buy bananas at the grocery store anymore when I chugged over there in our new very old car, because I'd read that they had some kind of horrible chemical on them that could cause birth defects. Instead, I went into Greenhill now and then with a big empty basket, filling it with organic fruit and yogurt we couldn't quite afford. How were we going to send a child to college if we couldn't even pay for safe grapes?

It was all a conundrum to me. I had lost hope again that I would be anything but a terrible, awful mother, bored and impatient and popping Valium. I wished we'd never succeeded in conceiving—I wished it nobly, for the sake of the poor baby who was just going to have to make the best of me, and the best of its miserable fate with an artist father—God, maybe his sperm had mutated from all the paint fumes he'd breathed. I hadn't thought of that before. I got into our bed with a book and cried. I needed Robert, and when we had supper together

I told him all my fears and he hugged and kissed me and insisted that there was nothing to worry about, but after dinner he had a meeting at the Art Department because they were about to hire a new specialist in mountain crafts. I never seemed to have enough of him, and he didn't seem to mind that enough either.

In actuality, Robert went up to his attic room more and more when he wasn't in class, which was probably why I didn't know for a long time about the sleeping. One morning I noticed that he hadn't come down to breakfast, and I knew he must have been painting all night, as he sometimes liked to, and then gone to bed as the sun rose—it wasn't unusual for me to wake to find his side of the bed empty on those occasions, because he'd put an old sofa up in his attic soon after we moved in. He appeared sometime around noon on this particular day, his hair standing straight up on the right side. We had lunch together, and he went to his afternoon classes.

I think I remember that day mainly because only a few mornings later I got a call from the Art Department. They were phoning for Robert to know if he was all right, because his students had reported that he'd missed teaching their morning studio twice in a row. I tried to remember his schedule these last days but couldn't—I was in a haze of fatigue myself, my belly so large now that I could hardly bend forward to make our bed. I said that I would ask him when I saw him but that I thought he wasn't home.

The truth was that I'd slept late myself and assumed he'd left before I woke, although now I began to doubt this. I went to the foot of the short flight of stairs that led to Robert's attic and opened the door. The stairs looked like Mount Everest to me, but I hitched my dress up a little and began to climb. It occurred to me that this might bring on labor, but if it did—so what? I was in the safe zone already, or rather the baby was—the nurse-midwife had told me cheerfully the week before that I could have the baby "anytime I wanted to." I was torn between longing to see our son or daughter's face, and the desire to postpone the inevitable day when my baby would look me in the eye and know that I had no idea what I was doing.

There wasn't a door at the top of the stairs, and I could see the whole attic as I clambered up the last step. Two lightbulbs hung from the ceiling, and they'd both been left on. A bleak midday came in through the skylight. Robert slept on the sofa, one of his arms hanging to the floor, the hand twisted inside out, graceful and Baroque. His face was buried in the cushions. I checked my watch—it was 11:35. Well, he'd probably worked until dawn. His easel stood with its back to me, and the smell of paint was still strong. I wanted to gag, as if I'd been flung back into the uneasy stomach of my first trimester, and I turned away instead and lumbered down the stairs. I left him a note on the kitchen counter telling him to call the department, ate some lunch, and went out on a walk with my friend Bridgette. She was pregnant, too, with her second, although not as huge yet as I was, and we'd promised each other we'd walk at least two miles a day.

When I got home, the evidence of Robert's lunch was on the table and the note was gone. He called me to say he'd need to stay late to meet with students and might show up for the college meal. I went down to have dinner in the dining hall, but he never joined me there. I heard the stairs to the attic creak in my dreams, and again the next night and again the next. Sometimes I rolled over in bed and found him a hand-span away from me. Sometimes I woke in the late morning and he was gone. I waited for the baby and for him, although I was more worried about the baby. Eventually I began to worry that

I might go into labor at a time when I wouldn't be able to find Robert. I prayed that he'd be in the attic painting or sleeping whenever the pain began, so that I'd be able to get myself to the foot of the stairs and shriek for him.

One afternoon after I came in from my walk, which had felt like twenty miles, the department called again. They were sorry to ask, but had I seen Robert? I said I would find him. As I counted back, it seemed to me that he hadn't slept in days, at least not in our bed, and that he'd barely been home. I'd sometimes heard the creak of the stairs at night and had assumed he was painting up a storm, perhaps trying to finish extra work before the baby came. I made my way up again, and in the attic I found him stretched out on his back, breathing slowly and deeply, even snoring a little. It was four in the afternoon, and I wasn't sure he had gotten up that day. Didn't he know he had classes to teach, a wife and mammoth belly to support? I felt a flash of anger and hauled myself toward the sofa to shake him awake, then stopped. The easel was turned toward the big skylight, and I'd just gotten a glimpse of it and of the sketches that littered the floor.

I recognized her immediately, as if we were meeting on the street after having fallen out of touch for a while. She was smiling at me, her mouth turned down a little, her eyes shining, an expression I knew from the sketch I'd pulled out of Robert's pocket in the rest area months before. It was a portrait to the waist, clothed. I could see now how lovely her body was, too—slender, strong, full, the shoulders a little broader than you'd expect, the neck sinuous. Up close, I saw there was an indistinctness to the painting, a roughness to the surface, although the forms were real and solid—Impressionism, or something on the verge of it. She wore a ruffled beige dress with crimson stripes curving down the front to emphasize her breasts, an outfit from another era, a studio costume, and her hair was piled up with a red ribbon around it—my favorite alizarin crimson—I knew exactly the tube he'd used for those details. The sketches on the floor were studies for this painting, and I understood on the instant that it was one of Robert's best ever. It was elegant but also full of suppressed action. I'd seldom seen a human expression caught so brilliantly—she was about to move, to laugh softly, to lower her eyes under my gaze.

I turned to the couch in a fury, although whether I was angry about the woman in the painting, or Robert's extreme talent, or his sleeping through calls from the job on which we would depend for future yogurt and diapers, I couldn't have told you at that moment. I shook him. As I did it, I remembered that he'd told me never to shake him awake—it frightened him, he'd said, because he'd once heard a true story about someone who'd lost his mind when startled out of sleep. I didn't care, this time. I shook him roughly, hating his big shoulder, his oblivion, the world in which he slept and dreamed and painted—and admired other women, those with slender waistlines. Why had I married such a slovenly, selfish person? It occurred to me for the first time that this was all my fault, my having such poor judgment.

Robert stirred and mumbled. "What?"

"What do you mean, what?" I said. "It's four in the afternoon. You missed your morning classes. Again."

I was gratified to see him look stricken. "Oh shit," he said, sitting up with apparent effort. "What time did you say it is?"

"Four," I repeated crisply. "Are you planning to keep your job, or shall we raise this baby in abject poverty? Up to you."

"Oh, stop it." He slowly peeled the old blankets off his body, as if they weighed fifty pounds each. "There's no need to be righteous."

"I'm not being righteous," I said. "But the Art Department may be, once you call them back."

He glared at me, rubbing his head and hair, but said nothing, and I felt a lump begin to rise in my throat. I might be alone, as things turned out—or perhaps I was already alone. He got up and put on his shoes and started down the stairs, while I followed cautiously, afraid of slipping, off-balance, miserable. I wanted to stay as close to him as possible, to kiss the back of his curly head, to hold on to his shoulder so I wouldn't sway and fall, to berate him and scratch his back with my fingernails. For a moment I even felt a flash of long-subsumed physical desire, an awareness of the swelling of my own breasts and middle. But he was well ahead of me, and now I could hear him hurrying down to the kitchen. When I arrived, he was on the phone. "Thanks, thanks," he was saying. "Yeah, I guess it's just a little virus. I'm sure I'll be over it by tomorrow. Thanks, I will." He hung up.

"You told them you had the flu?" I had meant to go over to him, put my arms around his neck, apologize for being short-tempered, make him some soup, start over. After all, he worked hard, he painted hard—of course he was tired. Instead, my voice came out flat and nasty.

"It's none of your business what I told them, if you're going to talk to me like that," he said, and opened the refrigerator.

"Did you stay up painting?"

"Of course I stayed up painting." To my further disgust, he pulled out a jar of pickles and a beer. "I'm a painter, remember?"

"What's that supposed to mean?" Now I was folding my arms in spite of myself. I had an entire ledge to rest them on.

"Mean? It means what it means."

"Does it mean painting the same woman all the time?"

I had hoped he would turn to me and scowl, tell me coldly that he had no idea what I was talking about, that he painted whatever he was painting, whatever he felt the need to paint.

To my growing horror, he looked away instead, his face frozen, and began to open his beer without speaking. He seemed to have forgotten the pickles. It was hardly the first time we'd quarreled in our nearly six years together, or even in the past week, but it was the first time he'd ever looked away.

I couldn't imagine anything worse than his expression of guilt, his avoiding my eyes, but a moment later the worse thing happened—he glanced up without seeming to see me, his gaze fixed itself on some point just over my shoulder, and his face softened. I had the awful, creeping feeling that someone had soundlessly appeared in the doorway behind me—the hair actually began to rise on my neck. I struggled not to turn around while he stared, his face blind and gentle. Suddenly I was afraid to know more. If he had fallen in love with someone else, I would find out soon enough. I wanted only to lie down, to hold my baby close and rest myself.

I left the kitchen. If he lost his job through his own irresponsibility, I would go back to Ann Arbor and live with my mother. My baby would be a girl, and we three generations of women would simply hunker down and take care of one another until she could grow up and find a better life. I went to our bedroom and lay down on the bed, which squeaked under my weight, and pulled the comforter over me. Tears of weakness seeped out of my eyes and ran down my cheeks. I wiped them away with my sleeve.

After a few minutes I heard Robert approaching, and I closed my eyes. He sat down on the side of the bed, making it sag further. "I'm sorry," he said. "I didn't mean to be mean. I've just been really wiped out from the term and from working at night."

"Why don't you slow down, then?" I asked. "I never see you anymore. Anyway, it seems as if you're sleeping most of the time, not working." I stole a glance at him. His face seemed normal again. I thought I had been mistaken about the strange look.

"Not at night," he said. "I can't sleep at night. I just get on a roll, a big roll, and I feel as if I need to use every bit of it. I'm thinking about doing a new series, something with a lot of portraits, and I just feel as if I can't sleep until I get some of it done. Then I get really tired and I have to sleep it off. I guess I was up for three nights."

"You could slow down," I repeated. "You'll have to slow down when the baby comes anyway." *Which could be any minute,* I added to myself, although I was too superstitious to say it aloud.

He stroked my hair. "Yes," he said, but it sounded absent-minded and I felt he'd already drifted again. Some of my mother-friends at the sandbox had told me that husbands occasionally "flipped out" before the baby arrived—they laughed about it as if it were nothing serious. "But when they see *that baby*—," they would add, and everyone would nod. Clearly the first glimpse of a baby fixed everything. Perhaps that would fix Robert, too. He would become a morning person, paint at reasonable times, hold down his job automatically, and go to sleep when I did. We would take walks with the stroller and put the baby to bed together in the evenings. I would become a painter again myself, and we could work out some shifts, take turns caring for the baby and painting. Maybe we could keep the baby in our room for a while after all, and use the second bedroom as my studio.

I thought about how to describe this to Robert, how to ask for it, but I was too tired to search for the words. Besides, if he didn't do those things with and for me of his own free will, what kind of a father was he going to be? It worried me already that he never seemed to have any idea how much or little money we had—usually how little—or when the bills needed to be paid. I had always paid them myself, licking the stamps and putting them on straight in the upper corner of the envelope with a sense of satisfaction, even if I knew that when they were deposited at the other end our account would plunge nearly into the red. Robert squeezed my shoulder. "I'm going to finish my painting," he said. "I think I can finish it by tomorrow if I get going again."

"Is she a student?" I made myself ask it, fiercely, afraid I would be unable to ask later.

He didn't seem startled. In fact, he didn't even seem to register the question—there was no guilt. "Who?"

"The woman in the painting upstairs." Again, I made myself form the words, sorry already. I hoped he wouldn't answer.

"Oh, I'm not using a model," he said. "I'm just trying to imagine her." It was strange—I didn't believe him, but I didn't think he was lying either. I knew with a feeling of dread that I would be scanning all the young faces on campus from now on, all the curly dark heads. But this made no sense. He had already been sketching her before we left New York, or at least just as we were leaving. I was certain it was the same face.

"It's the dress that's so hard to get right," he added after a moment. He was frowning, scratching the front of his hair, rubbing his nose—normal, perplexed, absorbed. God, I thought. I am a paranoid fool. This man is an artist, a true artist, with his own vision. He does what he wants, what occurs to him, and the result has been brilliant. It doesn't mean he's sleeping with a student, or with a model in New York. He hasn't even been back there since we moved. It doesn't mean he isn't going to be a good father.

He got up, bent from his height to kiss me, paused at the door. "Oh, I forgot to tell you. The department elected me to do the faculty solo show next year. We take turns, you know, but I didn't think they'd let me go so soon. The museum in town is getting involved. I'll get a raise at the same time."

I sat up. "That's wonderful—you didn't tell me."

"Well, I found out yesterday. Or maybe it was the day before. I want to have this painting done for it, for sure, maybe the whole series." He was gone and I was left smiling, pulling the comforter over me for half an hour. Perhaps, like Robert, I had earned a nap.

But the next time I went to the attic to hunt for him, I found he had scraped the canvas down to its bones, preparatory to cleaning it for a new image—maybe the red-striped dress had not really worked in the end. I almost felt I had imagined that face a second time, that expression full of rueful love for him.

December 18

Mon cher oncle et ami:

How good of you to come yesterday just as the rain was beginning to fall, which always promises a dreary evening. It was lovely to see you and hear your tales. And today it's raining again! I wish I could paint rain—how would one actually do that? M. Monet has managed it, no doubt. And my cousin Mathilde, who loves all things Japanese, has a series of prints in her drawing room that French artists can only dream of emulating—but perhaps rain is more uplifting in Japan than in Paris. How I would love to know that all nature was open to my brush, as it seems to be to Monet's, even if people are unkind about him and his colleagues and their experiments. Mathilde's friend Berthe Morisot exhibits with them, as you may know, and she is already well known (too much exposed, perhaps, in public exhibitions; that must take courage). I wish it would snow again—the beautiful part of winter is all too slow in arriving this year.

Fortunately, there is your note this morning. It was dear of you to write to me as well as to Papa. I don't deserve your kind words about my progress, but my porch studio does help; I while away the hours there when Papa sleeps. We also learned by this morning's post that Yves will be delayed out of town at least two weeks, a blow for us all but especially for Papa. It must be better to have no children, like us, than only one, as my father-in-law has, when that one is so dear and yet constantly called away from home. I feel for Papa, but we sit by the fire and hold hands and read our Villon aloud. His hand is so frail now that it might serve as a study in old age by Leonardo or some ancient Roman sculptor. How wonderful that your big canvas progresses and that your articles will find an even wider sphere—I must insist on my right to be as proud as any blood relative. Please accept the congratulations of your doting niece—

Béatrice

Chapter 23

Kate

Ingrid was born on February 22 at the birth clinic in Greenhill. Nothing ever dims that moment for me, when I realized she was alive and well—exquisite, in fact—or the later moment when I found her hand wrapped in a knot around my finger. And I had not been killed by my ride through flame. Robert stood touching her, the tip of his own finger nearly as big as her nose. I was crying, too, it turned out, and when I looked at Robert I felt a love for him so radiant that I had to avert my eyes from his face, which shone like a gilded ring. I hadn't understood before what it meant to be in love—I couldn't choose which of these two people, the very small or the towering, I loved more. Why had I never noticed Robert's divinity, reproduced now in the tiny head that lay on my skin, the hazel eyes gazing around with such disbelief?

We named her for my long-dead grandmother from Philadelphia. Ingrid was a reasonably good sleeper, and our pattern continued after that first night. Robert and Ingrid slept, and I lay watching them, or reading, or walked around the house, or cleaned the bathroom, or slept with them. Robert seemed too tired to stay up painting—the baby woke us three times every night, which was nothing, I assured him, and he found that exhausting. I offered to let him nurse her, and he laughed sleepily and said that he would if he could, but he thought his milk wouldn't taste good even if he could produce any. "Too many toxins," he said. "All that paint."

I felt a twinge of annoyance that could have been jealousy—did I hear self-congratulation in his tone? There wasn't any paint in *my* bloodstream, only healthy foods and the postnatal vitamins I still felt we couldn't afford but didn't want to deny the baby. That feeling I'd had of love, almost worship, for Robert in the delivery room had slipped away from day to day, fading with the soreness in my stomach and leg muscles, and I'd watched it go, conscious of the loss. It was like the visible end of a teenage crush but far sadder, and it left a gap because now I knew what I'd been capable of feeling, not at fifteen but at past thirty, and it was gone, gone. But I watched Robert holding the baby in the crook of his arm, rather expertly now, and eating with his other hand, and I loved them both—Ingrid was just beginning to turn her head to look up at him, and her eyes were full of the surprise I had always felt myself at the sight of this monumental man with his angular face and heavy, curling hair.

I didn't ask much of Robert at home. He was teaching the early-summer session to bring in some extra money, and I was grateful. After a while, he began to paint late in the attic again, and sometimes he stayed overnight at the school studio. He didn't seem to sleep during the day anymore, at least not that I knew of, despite our night wakefulness with Ingrid. He showed me a small canvas or two, still lifes with sticks and rocks he'd been setting for the students and trying himself, and I smiled and refrained from remarking that to me they seemed dead. *Nature morte*—they reminded me of the French term. A few years before I might have argued with him about them, goaded him a little, debated with him because he liked that kind of attention, told him he lacked only a limp pheasant to complete his canvases. Now, I saw our bread and butter in them rather than just the wood and stones, and I held my tongue. Ingrid needed baby food, preferably organic carrots and spinach, and eventually she might want to go to Barnard, and my only pair of pajamas had worn through the knee the week before.

One morning in June after Robert had left for his class, I decided to go into town to do some unnecessary errands, mainly to break my routine of walks with the stroller around campus. I got Ingrid ready and set her in her crib to play for a few minutes while I collected sweater, car keys, purse. My keys were missing from their hook by the back door, and I knew at once that Robert must have taken them while I was finishing breakfast. Occasionally he drove down to his classes if he was running very late, and he seldom knew where his own keys were. Annoyance rose in me like heat.

As a last resort, I mounted the attic stairs to see if Robert's keys might be in the pile of personal effects on his table, which was often a still life of crumpled paper, pens, cafeteria napkins, phone cards, and even money. I was so intent on my search that I didn't understand at first what I was seeing—I was still looking toward the messy table, the hope of my keys, my outing, as sight registered in the soft gloom. Then I pulled the light string, slowly. It had been a couple of months since I'd been all the way up here, I realized, perhaps even the four months since Ingrid's birth. It was an old house, rustic, as I've mentioned. The underside of the roof was unfinished, the beams and roof slats exposed; the attic ran the short length of the house and was an inferno on hot days, which were fortunately few in the mountains. I glanced hopelessly away, toward the table where the familiar pile of junk lay, then looked around again.

I can't really describe my first impression, except that it had made me give a little scream out loud before I could stop myself, because it was a vision of a woman everywhere, a woman spread across the surfaces of the attic in small parts and versions, repetitions—dissected, cut into pieces, although without blood. Her face I knew already, and I saw it dozens of times around the room, smiling, serious, painted in different sizes and different moods. Sometimes she wore her hair piled up on her head, sometimes with a red ribbon in it, or a dark hat or bonnet, or a low-cut dress, or her hair down and her breasts bare, which gave me a further shock. Sometimes it was a hand by itself with small gold rings on it, or an old-fashioned high-buttoned shoe, or even just a study of a single finger, a bare foot, or, to my horror, a puckering nipple meticulously delineated, a curve of naked back or shoulder or buttock, a deep shadow of hair between spread thighs, and then—even more startling by contrast—a neatly buttoned glove, the somber black bodice of a dress, a hand holding a fan or a bouquet of flowers, a body cloaked and mysterious, and then her face again, in profile, three-quarters, full-face, dark-eyed, sorrowful.

The wood he'd painted on had been sanded smooth—the attic was unfinished but not rough—so that he'd been able to put in fine detail. He had covered the background of this collage with a soft gray-blue and worked in borders of spring flowers, less sharply realistic than all the scattered images of the woman but exquisitely recognizable—roses, apple blossoms, wisteria—flowers we had here on the college grounds, in fact, and which Robert and I both loved. The beams were ornamented with long twisted ribbons of red and blue, a trompe-l'oeil effect that reminded me of wallpaper in Victorian bedrooms.

The two shortest attic walls were given to landscapes, painted freely enough to be called a tribute to Impressionism, with the same lady appearing in each. One showed a beach, with high cliffs rising up on the left side. She stood alone, at a distance, staring out to the sea. She had a parasol over her shoulder and a flower-laden blue hat on her head, and yet she had to shade her eyes—the sun was dazzling on the water. The other landscape was of a meadow, floating with spots of color that must have been summer flowers, and she half lay in the tall grass reading a book, her parasol propped above her and the glow from her pink-patterned dress reflected off her lovely face. This time, to my surprise, there was a child next to her, a little girl perhaps three or four years old, picking at the tops of flowers, and I wondered immediately if this variation had been inspired by Ingrid's presence in our lives. It brought a slight unclenching of my heart.

I sat down in Robert's creaking desk chair. I was sharply aware, especially as I looked at the little girl in the meadow, with her dress and hat and cloud of curly dark hair, that I must not leave Ingrid awake and alone in her crib below much longer. There was one bare corner still, one slanting area of the ceiling that Robert had not yet covered. The rest was filled, bursting, ripe with color and beauty, overflowing with the presence of this woman. The partly finished canvases on Robert's easels also depicted her: in one, she sat shrouded in dark fabric he had only half painted—a cloak, a shawl—her face shadowed, her eyes full of—what? Love? Dread? She gazed at me, and I looked away. The other canvas was even more frightening. It showed her face next to another face, that of a dead woman who lay limp against her shoulder. The dead woman had gray hair, a similar studio costume, a red wound in the center of her forehead—one dark hole, deep, small, somehow more gruesome than any gory gash could have been. That was the first time I saw that image.

I sat there for another long minute. Attic, canvases—I

knew it was the best work from his brush I'd ever encountered. It was transcendent, focused, but the effect was also of a passion filled to bursting, a wild attempt at containment. It had taken days, nights, weeks, probably months. I thought of the purple crescents under Robert's eyes, the way the skin on his cheeks and forehead was beginning to crease with strain. He had told me a couple of times how full of purpose he felt, how he wanted only to paint and paint and didn't seem to need sleep these days, and I had been envious—I felt half asleep all day, after nursing Ingrid at night. We could not sell the attic, with its overwhelming decoration, although perhaps he could show the two paintings. In fact, I prayed no one else would ever see this appalling extravaganza. How could we explain it to the college? No, he would have to paint over the whole thing someday, certainly before we ever left the place. The thought of blotting out all that overflowing, radiant work hurt my stomach. No one else would ever understand it.

Worst of all, whoever she was, she was not me. And she had a child, apparently, with curly dark hair like Ingrid's. Robert's hair—inherited? It was unreasonable, a ridiculous thought. I was more exhausted than I'd realized. After all, the woman herself had curly dark hair, rather like Robert's own. An even worse possibility occurred to me. Perhaps Robert somehow wished he *was* this woman—perhaps this was a portrait of himself as the woman he wanted to be. What did I know about my husband, really? But Robert was and had always been so hugely male that I couldn't believe this hypothesis for more than a second. I didn't know which alarmed me more—the unrelenting work that filled nearly every square inch of all that space closing in on me, or the fact that he had never talked with me voluntarily about the woman who dominated his days.

I got up and made a quick search of the room, my hands trembling as I shook out the blankets on the sofa where Robert apparently no longer slept much. What did I expect to find there? There was no other woman sleeping with him, at least not in my house. No love letter fell out—nothing but Robert's watch, which he'd been looking for. I rummaged through the pile on the table, the papers—sketches, some of them, for the portraits and borders around me. I did come upon his keys on the ring with the brass coins I'd given him a few years before. I put them in my jeans pocket.

By the sofa were several stacks of library books, slipping into an avalanche, mainly large art books. He was always bringing books and photographs into the house, so this, at least, was no surprise. But there were so many of them now, and almost all of them chronicled French Impressionism, something I hadn't known him to find this compelling, apart from his preoccupation with Degas when we were living in New York. There were books on the movement's great artists and their predecessors—Manet, Boudin, Courbet, Corot. Some had been borrowed from distant universities. There were also books about the history of Paris, books about the coast of Normandy, books about Monet's gardens at Giverny, about nineteenth-century women's clothing, about the Paris Commune, about the emperor Louis-Napoléon, the reshaping of Paris by Baron Haussmann, the Paris Opera, French châteaus and hunting, ladies' fans and bouquets in the history of painting. Why had Robert never discussed these interests with me? When had all these books crept into our house? Had he read all of them simply to decorate an attic? Robert was no historian—as far as I knew, he read art catalogs and the occasional crime novel.

I sat holding a biography of Mary Cassatt. This must all be for his show, somehow, some inspiration, some project he had neglected to tell me about. Had I been busy with the baby and neglected to ask? Or was this project so entwined with his feelings about the model he had never mentioned that he couldn't bring himself to talk with me about it? I looked around the attic again, at the tidal wave of images, splintered pieces of a mirror held up to one striking woman. He had dressed her meticulously in the fashions from these books—shoe, glove, ruffled white undergarments. But to him she was clearly a real person, a living part of his life. I heard Ingrid's wail and realized that only a few minutes had elapsed since I'd mounted the stairs to the attic, the brief passage of a nightmare.

Ingrid and I drove to town, and I pushed her stroller around among the retirees and tourists and people on lunch break. At the library, I checked out *Where the Wild Things Are* for her so that I could have the pleasure of reading it aloud—the cover made me feel like a child again every time I saw it. I checked out a biography of Van Gogh that was on display. It was time for me to go on with my education, and I didn't know anything about him except the public legends. I bought a summer dress at one of the boutiques. At least it was on sale, violets on cream-colored cotton, old-fashioned, unlike my usual jeans and solid-colored T-shirts. I thought of asking Robert to paint me in it on our porch, or in the meadow behind the faculty houses, and then had to struggle not to remember the dark-haired child on his attic wall. "Anything else for you today?" the clerk asked me, wrapping up a couple of free sticks of incense to put in the bag.

"No, no, thanks. That's all I need." I straightened Ingrid in her stroller because bending over helped control the prickling behind my eyes.

December 22, 1877

Mon cher oncle et ami:

Thank you for your lovely note, which I hardly deserve but will treasure whenever my small attempts at work need encouragement. A gray day indeed, and I thought I might beguile a little of it by writing you. We expect you, of course, on Christmas, and will look forward to that, whichever day or hour you can come in, and Yves hopes to return for several days then, although his having a reprieve for a longer holiday is far from certain, and he will have to go back to the South to finish his work in the New Year. I think we shall celebrate rather soberly; Papa has a cold again—nothing alarming, I assure you, but he tires easily and his eyes are more painful than usual. I have helped him lie down in his sitting room with warm compresses just now, and when I last glanced in, the fire was cozy and he had fallen asleep. I am a little tired today myself, and can't settle down to anything but letter writing, although my painting went well yesterday because I have found a good model, Esmé, another of my maids; she once told me, shyly, when I asked her whether she knows your own beloved Louve-ciennes, that hers is the very next village, called Grémière. Yves says I shouldn't torment the servants by making them sit for me, but where else could I find such a patient model? Today, however, she is out on errands and I must listen for Papa while I sit to write you.

You, who have seen my studio, know that it contains not only easel and worktable but also this desk, which I have had since childhood; it belonged to my mother, who painted its panels herself. I always do my correspondence here, looking out the window. You can picture, I'm sure, how sodden the garden is this morning—I can hardly believe it the same little paradise where I painted several scenes last summer. But it is beautiful even now, if stark. Imagine this garden, my winter consolation, mon ami*—imagine it for me, if you will.*

With affection,
Béatrice de Clerval

Chapter 24

Kate

When Robert came home, I didn't mention the attic to him. He was tired from a day of teaching, and we sat in silence over the lentil soup I'd cooked, with Ingrid bubbling applesauce and carrots cheerfully down her front. I fed her and wiped her mouth over and over with a damp washcloth and tried to get up the courage to ask Robert something about his work, but I couldn't. He sat with his head propped on one hand, deep rings under his eyes, and I sensed that something had changed for him, although I didn't know what it was or how it was different from anything else. Every now and then he glanced past me to the kitchen doorway, his eyes flickering hopelessly, as if he expected someone who never arrived there, and I felt again that shiver of confusion, apprehension, and willed myself not to follow his gaze.

After dinner he went to bed and slept for fourteen hours. I cleaned up the kitchen, got Ingrid to sleep, got up with her in the night, got up with her in the morning. I thought about inviting Robert for a walk, but when I came back from my stroll to the campus post office, he was gone, the bed unmade, a half-eaten bowl of cereal on the table. I went up to the blossoming attic to be sure and caught a glimpse again of the kaleidoscope woman, but no Robert.

The third day I couldn't bear it any longer, and I saw to it that Ingrid was down for her nap when Robert came home from his afternoon classes. It would make her sleep too late and stay up too long in the evening, but that was a small price to pay for the chance to set the world back on its feet again. When Robert came in, I had some tea waiting for him and he sat at the table. His face was weary, gray, one side of it drooping a little as if he might be about to sleep, or cry, or have a mild stroke. I knew he must be tired and I wondered at my own selfishness in putting him through a big discussion. Of course, it was partly for his own good—something was really wrong, and I had to help him.

I put our cups on the table and sat down as calmly as I could. "Robert," I began, "I know you're tired, but could we talk for a few minutes?"

He glanced at me across the tea, his hair partly on end, his face sullen. I realized now that he hadn't been bathing—he looked greasy as well as tired. I would have to remonstrate with him about overwork, whether it was teaching or painting attic walls. He was simply overtiring himself. He set his cup down. "What have I done now?"

"Nothing," I said, but the lump in my throat was already growing. "Nothing at all. I'm just worried about you."

"Don't worry about me," he said. "Why should you worry about me?"

"You're exhausted," I said, keeping the lump in place. "You're working so hard that you seem exhausted, and we hardly see you."

"That's what you wanted, wasn't it?" he growled. "You wanted me to work a good job and support you."

My eyes began to fill despite my best efforts at composure. "I want you to be happy, and I see how tired you are. You sleep all day and you paint all night."

"When am I supposed to paint except at night? Anyway, I'm usually asleep then, too." He ran his hand angrily through the front of his hair. "Do you think I get any real work done?"

Suddenly the sight of that unkempt, greasy hair made me angry, too. After all, I was working just as hard. I never slept more than a few hours at a time, I did all the dull work of keeping the household going, I had no chance to paint unless I skipped even more sleep, and I couldn't do that, so I didn't paint. I made it possible for him to do whatever work he did get done. He never had to do the dishes or clean a toilet or make a meal—I had freed him. And I managed to wash my hair now and then anyway, thinking that might make some difference to him. "There's another thing," I said, more curtly than I'd planned to. "I went up in the attic. What is that all about?"

He leaned back and fixed his eyes on me, then sat very still, straightening his powerful shoulders. For the first time in our years together, I felt afraid of him—not afraid of his brilliance or his talent or his ability to hurt my feelings, but simply afraid, in a subtle, animal way. "The attic?" he said.

"You've been painting a lot up there," I tried more cautiously. "But not on your canvases."

He was silent for a moment, and then he spread one of his hands on the table. "So?"

I had wanted above all to ask him about the woman herself, but instead I said, "I just thought you were getting ready for your show."

"I am."

"But you've done only a canvas and a half," I pointed out. This was not what I'd wanted to discuss. My voice was beginning to tremble again.

"So now you have to keep track of my work as well? Do you want to tell me what to paint while you're at it?" He was suddenly sitting bolt upright in the small kitchen chair, his presence filling the room.

"No, no," I said, and the cruelty of his words, and the cruelty of my own self-betrayal, made tears spill down my cheeks. "I don't want to tell you what to paint. I know you have to paint whatever you need to. I'm just worried about you. I miss you. I'm scared to see you look so exhausted."

"Well, save your worry," he said. "And stay out of my space. I don't need someone spying on me, on top of everything else." He took a sip of his tea, then put it down as if the taste disgusted him, and left the kitchen.

Somehow his refusal to stay and talk shattered me as nothing else had. The sense of a bad dream broke over me in one bitter wave. I thrashed my way through it and found myself jumping up after him. "Robert—stop! Don't just walk out!" I caught him in the hall and grabbed his arm.

He shook me off. "Get away from me."

My self-control gave way completely. "Who is she?" I wailed.

"Who is who?" he asked, and then his brow darkened and he pulled away and went into our bedroom. I stood in the doorway, watching, my face running with tears, my nose dripping, my sobs humiliatingly audible, while he lay down on the bed I had made that morning and covered himself with a quilt. He shut his eyes. "Leave me alone," he said without opening them again. "Leave me alone." To my horror, he fell asleep as I stood there. I stayed in the doorway, muting my weeping and watching as his breath slowed and then became soft and even. He slept like a baby, and upstairs Ingrid woke with a cry.

CHAPTER 25

Marlow

I imagined Béatrice's garden. It would have been small and rectangular—the book I found of paintings of Paris in the late nineteenth century didn't include any by Clerval, but there was an intimate scene by Berthe Morisot showing her husband and daughter on a shady bench. The text explained that Morisot and her family lived in Passy, a grand new suburb. I pictured Béatrice's garden at the end of autumn, the leaves already brown and yellow, some plastered onto the slate walk by a heavy rain, the ivy on the back wall the color of burgundy—*vigne vierge,* one caption noted beside a painting of a similar wall: the original Virginia creeper. There would be a few roses—now stark brown stems, scarlet rose hips—around a sundial. I considered all this, mentally discarding the sundial. Instead I concentrated on the soggy flower beds, the corpses of chrysanthemums or some other heavy flower darkened by rain, and in the center a small formal arrangement of bushes and a bench.

The woman sitting at her desk looking out at all this would be twenty-six years old, a mature age for the era, married for five years but childless—that lack, a secret anguish, judging from her love for her nieces. I saw her at the desk painted by her mother, the full, pale-gray skirts of her dress—didn't ladies wear different dresses for morning and afternoon?—billowing against the chair, lace at her neck and wrists, a silver ribbon around the knot of her heavy hair. She herself would be anything but gray, her face strong-featured and clear even in the dull light, her hair dark but also bright, her lips red, her eyes bent wistfully to the page that was already her favorite company, this wet morning.

Chapter 26

Kate

All that summer Robert slept off and on, taught, painted at odd hours, and held me at arm's length. After a while I stopped crying in secret and began to get used to it. I hardened myself a little, in the midst of my love for him, and waited.

In September the rhythm of the school year resumed. When I took Ingrid for tea and conversation with faculty-wife friends, I listened to them chat about their husbands and contributed innocuous tidbits myself, to show how normal things were at home. Robert was teaching three studio classes this term. Robert liked chili. I should get that recipe.

I secretly gathered information, too, for comparison. Their husbands apparently got up in the morning when they did—or earlier, to go out running. One of them had a husband who cooked on Wednesday nights, since he had fewer classes to teach that day. When I heard that, I wondered if Robert had ever noticed which night was Wednesday and which was any other day of the week. He had certainly never cooked a meal, unless you counted opening cans. One of my friends swapped off child care with her husband two evenings a week, so that she could have a little time to herself. I had seen him swooping in at just the right hour to pick up their two-year-old. How did he know what time it was, where he was supposed to be? I kept myself to myself and smiled with the rest of them about their husbands' little foibles. *He doesn't pick up his clothes?* I wanted to say. *That's nothing.* And for the first time I wondered how the women who were actually on the faculty managed their lives—I knew one who was also a single mother, and I felt unexpectedly sad and guilty that the rest of us met in this pleasant group while she was teaching her classes. We had never made an effort to include her. Our own lives were so free—we counted pennies but didn't work for them. But my life did not seem quite as free as my friends', and I wondered how that had happened.

One day that fall, Robert came home almost exhilarated and kissed the top of my head before telling me he'd accepted an invitation to teach up north for a semester—soon, in January. It was a good position, good money, at Barnett College, in striking distance of New York. Barnett had a famous art museum and a guest lectureship for painters—he named some of the great ones who'd preceded him there. He would have to teach only one class, and the rest was essentially a painting retreat. He would be able to paint full-time, more than full-time.

For a minute, I couldn't understand what he meant, although I got the part about being happy for him. I put down the dish towel I was holding. "What about us? It's not going to be easy moving a toddler to a new space for just a few months."

He stared at me as if this hadn't occurred to him. "I guess I thought—," he said slowly.

"What did you think?" Why was I so angry at him for even a look, a crumpling of his eyebrows?

"Well, they didn't say anything about bringing a family. I thought I would go by myself and get some work done."

"You could at least have asked them if they'd mind your bringing along the people you happen to live with." My hands had begun to shake, and I put them behind my back.

"There's no need to be hostile. You don't *know* what it's like not to be able to paint," he said. As far as I knew he'd been painting for weeks.

"Well, then don't sleep all the time," I suggested. In fact, he hadn't been sleeping during the day. I was actually getting worried again about his staying up at night, staying out at the studio, his seeming to sleep so little, although my picture of him now, indelibly, was of a body sprawled horizontal.

"You have no idea how to be supportive." Robert's nose and cheeks were white and pinched. At least he was truly paying attention. "Of course I would miss you and Ingrid a lot. You could come up with her in the middle, for a visit. And we'd be in touch all the time."

"Supportive?" I turned away. I fixed my gaze on the woodwork and asked myself what sort of husband would elect to leave for a semester for the sake of his own work without even consulting me or asking me if I wanted to be alone with a small child. What sort. What sort. The kitchen cupboards were all neatly shut. I wondered if looking at them long enough would keep me from exploding. I wondered if it was possible to live with someone crazy without becoming crazy oneself. Maybe I could become a genius, too, although I wasn't sure I wanted to be one if this was what they were like up close. The truth was that I would have let him go without a murmur if he'd asked me, if he'd checked with me. I pushed down an image of the dark-haired muse—why did she have to be so vivid? Why did he want to be in striking distance of New York? He might well go away and focus and feel accomplishment and finish his big series, and be healed by that.

"You could have asked me," I said, and I heard my own voice as a growl, the nasty nipping to the bone, one member of the pack finally turning on another. "As it is, do whatever you want. Help yourself. I'll see you in May."

"The hell with you," Robert said slowly, and I thought I'd never seen him so enraged, or at least so quietly enraged. "I will." Then he did a strange thing. He got up and turned around slowly two or three times, as if he wanted to leave the room but had lost track of the direction of the kitchen door. It was somehow more frightening to me than anything that had happened yet. Suddenly he found his way out, and I didn't see him again for two days. Whenever I picked up Ingrid, I started to cry and had to hide my tears from her. On his return, he never mentioned our conversation, and I didn't ask where he'd been.

Then one morning Robert appeared at breakfast while I was making it—making it for me and for Ingrid, that is. His hair was wet and clean and smelled of shampoo. He put some forks on the table. The next day he got up in time for breakfast again. The third day he kissed me good morning, and when I went into the bedroom for something I found he had made our bed—crookedly, but he had made it. It was October, my favorite month, the trees golden, leaves streaming off them in the wind. He seemed to have come back to us—how or why I didn't know, but I gradually became too happy to ask. That week he came to bed on time—or, rather, when I did—for the first time in longer than I could remember, and we made love. It was astonishing to me that his body had not changed from having a child. It was as handsome as ever: big, warm, sculpted, his hair wild on the pillow. I felt ashamed of my own compromised, baby-gnawed flesh and whispered that to him, and he silenced my doubts with his ardor.

In the weeks that followed this, Robert began to paint after class instead of working at night, and to come down to eat when I called. Sometimes he worked in his studio on campus, especially on larger canvases, and Ingrid and I wandered down with the stroller to pick him up for dinner. That was a blissful moment, when he put away his brushes and walked home with us. I was happy when we passed friends and they saw us together, the three of us, organized and complete and on our way home for the meal I had already left warm under second-hand china covers. After dinner he painted in the attic, but not very late, and sometimes he came to bed and read while I dozed with my head tucked under his chin.

At the studio and in his attic (I checked now and then when he wasn't there), Robert was working on a series of still lifes, beautifully rendered and often with some comical element in them, something out of place. The strange brooding portrait and the big painting of the dark-haired woman holding her dead friend stood turned against the attic wall, and I was careful not to ask him about them. The attic ceiling was still festive with her clothes and body parts. The books next to his sofa were again exhibition catalogs, or an occasional biography, but nothing about the Impressionists or Paris. I thought sometimes I had dreamed his chaotic obsession, invented it myself, whatever it meant. Only the too-colorful attic reminded me of its reality. I avoided going up there whenever I felt new doubts.

One morning when Ingrid was already crawling, Robert did not get up until noon, and that night I heard him upstairs pacing around, painting. He painted for two nights without sleeping, and then he took the car and disappeared for a day and a night, returning just after breakfast. While he was gone I did not sleep much either, and I wondered several times with tears in my eyes whether to call the police, but the note he'd left prevented me from doing that. "Dear Kate," it said. "Don't worry about me. I just need to sleep in the fields. It's not too cold. I'm taking my easel. I think I'll go crazy otherwise."

It was true that we'd been having mild weather, one of those occasional gifts of warmth in the late Blue Ridge autumn. He came home with a new landscape, a subtle one showing fields just under the fringe of the mountains, the sunset. Walking in the brown grasses was a figure, a woman in a long white dress. I knew her form so well that I could have felt it under my own hands, the line of her waist, the drape of her skirt, the swell of her breasts below lovely wide shoulders. She was just turning around, so that her face showed, but she was too far away for any expression other than a hint of dark eyes. Robert slept until twilight, missing his morning studio class and an afternoon faculty meeting, and the next day I called the doctor at the campus health center.

Chapter 27

Marlow

I imagined her life.

She is not permitted to go out unchaperoned. Her husband is away all day, but she can't speak with him by telephone—that strange invention won't be installed in most Parisian homes for at least another twenty-five years. From early morning, when her husband leaves home in his black suit and tall hat and overcoat to take a horse-drawn omnibus along Baron Haussmann's wide boulevards to his job directing postal operations at a big building in the center of the city, until the time he arrives home, tired and sometimes smelling faintly of spirits, she does not see him and she hears nothing of him.

If he tells her he has worked late, she cannot know where he's been. Her mind sometimes wanders over possibilities that range from hushed meeting rooms, where men in suits, white shirtfronts, and soft black ties like his gather around a long table, to what she pictures as the pointedly tasteful decorations of a certain kind of club, where a woman dressed only in a silk camisole and stays, ruffled petticoats and high-heeled slippers (but otherwise respectable-looking, with nicely coiffed hair), lets him trail his hand over the top half of her white breasts—scenes she knows only vaguely from whispers, a hint in a novel or two, hardly part of her upbringing.

She has no proof that her husband visits such establishments, and perhaps he never does. It isn't clear to her why this recurrent picture inspires little jealousy in her. Instead it gives her a sense of relief, as if she is sharing a burden. She knows that the genteel alternatives to these extremes are restaurants where men—mainly men—eat their midday dinner, or even their evening meal, and talk together. Occasionally he comes home needing no supper and reports pleasantly that he's had an excellent *poulet rôti* or *canard à l'orange*. There are also *cafés chantants* where both men and women can sit with propriety, and other cafés where he can sit alone with *Le Figaro* and a late-evening cup of coffee. Or perhaps he simply does work late.

At home he is attentive: he bathes and dresses for their evening meal if they dine together; he puts on his dressing gown and smokes by the fire if she's already eaten and he has dined out, or he reads aloud to her from the newspaper; sometimes he kisses her on the back of the neck with exquisite tenderness when she sits bent over her work, crocheting lace or embroidering dresses for her sister's new baby. He takes her to the opera in the glittering new Palais Garnier and occasionally to the nicer places to hear an orchestra or drink champagne, or to a ball in the heart of the city, for which she dons a new dress in turquoise silk or rose-colored satin. He makes it clear that he is proud to have her on his arm.

Above all, he encourages her to paint, nodding with approval at even her most unusual experiments with color, light, rough brushwork in the style she has seen with him at the more radical new exhibitions. He would never call her a radical, of course; he has always told her she is simply a painter and must do as she sees fit. She explains to him that she believes painting should reflect nature and life, that the light-filled new landscapes move her. He nods, although he adds cautiously that he wouldn't want her to know *too* much about life—nature is a fine subject, but life is grimmer than she can understand. He thinks it good for her to have something satisfying to do at home; he loves art himself; he sees her gift and wants her to be happy. He knows the charming Morisots. He has met the Manets, and always remarks that they are a good family, despite Édouard's reputation and his immoral experiments (he paints loose women), which make him perhaps too modern—a shame, given his obvious talent.

In fact, Yves takes her to many galleries. They attend the Salon every year, with nearly a million other people, and listen to the gossip about favorite canvases and those the critics disdain. Occasionally they stroll in the museums in the Louvre, where she sees art students copying paintings and sculpture, even an unchaperoned woman here and there (surely Americans). She can't quite bring herself to admire nudes in his presence, certainly not the heroic males; she knows she will never paint from a nude model herself. Her own formal training was in the private studios of an academician, copying from plaster casts with her mother present, before she married. At least she has worked hard.

She wonders sometimes if Yves would understand if she elected to submit a painting to the Salon. He has never said anything slighting about those few paintings at the Salon that are by women, and he applauds whatever she herself puts on canvas. In like fashion, he never complains about the household, which she runs so well, except to say politely once a year that he would like something cooked a little rarer or that he wishes she would put another arrangement on the table in the hall. In the dark now and then, they know each other in a completely different way, with a warmth, even a fierceness, that she cherishes but doesn't dare think about during the day, except to hope that one morning she will wake up realizing she hasn't recently needed to get out those neatly folded clean napkins for her underclothing, the hot-water bottles, the glass of sherry that takes the edge off her monthly cramps.

But it has not yet happened. Perhaps she thinks about it too often, or too seldom, or in the wrong way—she tries to stop thinking about it at all. She will wait instead for a letter, and that letter will be her main diversion for the morning. The post comes twice daily; it is delivered by a young man in a short blue coat. She can hear his ring through the rain, and Esmé answering the door. She will not seem eager; she is not, in fact, eager. The letter will appear on a silver tray in her boudoir while she is dressing for her afternoon calls. She will open it before Esmé goes out and then tuck it into her desk, to reread later. She hasn't yet taken to putting the letters inside the bodice of her dress, carrying them on her person.

In the meantime, there are other letters to write and to answer, meals to order, the dressmaker to see, the warm coverlet to finish for her father-in-law's Christmas present. And there is her father-in-law himself, the patient old man: he likes to have his drinks and books brought by her in person after he naps, and she actually looks forward to the moment when he strokes her hand with his transparently veined one and gazes at her with almost empty eyes, thanking her for her care. There are the flowering plants she waters herself instead of leaving them to the servants, and most important of all there is the room next to hers, originally a sunporch, that contains her easel and paints.

The maid sitting for her these days—not Esmé but the younger Marguerite, whose gentle face and yellow hair she likes—is hardly more than a girl. Béatrice has begun a painting of her sitting by the window with a pile of sewing; since the maid likes to busy her hands while she poses, Béatrice is happy to let her mend collars and petticoats, as long as the girl keeps her drooping golden head sufficiently still.

It is very light in there; even when rain streams down the many panes, they can get a little work done together, Marguerite's hands moving on the delicate white goods, the cotton and lace, and Béatrice's measuring shape or color, reproducing the roundness of the young shoulders bent over the needle, the folds of dress and apron. Neither speaks, but they are united by the peace of women at their tasks. In those moments, Béatrice feels that her work is a part of the household, an extension of the lunch simmering in the kitchen and the flowers she arranges for the dining table. She daydreams about painting the daughter she does not have, instead of this silent girl she likes but hardly knows; she imagines that her daughter reads poetry aloud to her as she paints, or chatters about her friends.

In fact, when Béatrice is actually working, she ceases to worry about the significance of her paintings, whether they are good, whether she could ever raise with Yves the notion of submitting one to the Salon—they are not good enough yet for that anyway, and probably never will be. Nor does she worry about whether her life has a wider meaning. She finds it enough for now to contemplate the blue of the girl's dress, perfectly matched at last by a smear on the palette, the curling stroke that gives color to the young cheek, the white that she will add the next morning (it needs more white, and a little gray, to convey that rainy autumn light, but she has run out of time before lunch).

If painting fills her mornings, then the afternoons when she does not feel like painting more, and doesn't make calls or receive them, can be a little empty. The characters in the novel she is reading seem with a certainty dead, so she writes instead a letter she's been gathering in her mind, an answer to the one now sitting in a pigeonhole of her painted desk. She crosses her feet at the ankles and tucks them under her chair. Yes, her desk sits in the window; she moved it there last spring, to take advantage of the view of the garden.

As she writes, she sees that this is one of those strange days that sometimes come to Paris in autumn, the driving rain turning to sleet, then snow. *Effet de neige, effet d'hiver*—she saw that phrase at an exhibition last year, where some of the new painters were showing not only sunlight and green fields but snow as well, accomplishing revolutionary things out in the cold. She stood, humbled, in front of those canvases the newspapers reviled. Snow, when it sits on the ground, contains flecks of gray. It contains blue, depending on the light, the time of day, the sky; it contains ocher and even brown or lavender. She has already stopped seeing snow as white herself a year ago; she almost remembers the moment when she recognized that, examining her garden.

Now, the first snow of a new winter materializes in an instant before her eyes; the rain has transformed itself without warning. She stops writing and cleans her pen on the flannel pen-wipe at her elbow, keeping the ink away from her sleeve. The wilted garden is already covered with subtle color—indeed, it isn't white. Beige, today? Silver? Colorless, if there is such a thing? She adjusts her paper, dips her pen, and begins to write again. She tells her correspondent about the way the new snow settles on each branch, the way the bushes, some of them green all year, huddle together under their weightless veil of nonwhite, about the bench, bare in the rain one moment and collecting a fine soft cushion the next. She feels him listening, unfolding the letter in his graceful, aging hands. She sees his eyes, with their restrained warmth, absorbing her words.

When the post comes later, there is another letter from him, one that is lost to posterity but that tells her something of himself, or of his own garden not yet covered by snow—he would have written it earlier in the day or the evening before; he lives in the heart of the city. Perhaps he deplores—with humorous charm—the emptiness of his own life: he has been a widower for years, and he is childless. Childless, she remembers sometimes, like her. She herself is young enough to be his daughter, even his granddaughter. She refolds his note with a smile, then unfolds it and reads it again.

Chapter 28

Kate

Robert consented, stonily, to see the campus doctor, but he would not let me go with him. The health center was in walking distance of our house, like everything else, and in spite of myself I stood on the porch, watching him go. He walked with his shoulders bowed, putting one foot in front of the other as if every movement pained him. I prayed to whatever I could think of that he would be communicative enough or desperate enough to tell the doctor all his symptoms. They might have to do tests. He might be exhausted from some blood disease: mononucleosis or—God forbid—leukemia. But that wouldn't explain the dark woman. If Robert didn't report much from this visit, I would have to meet with the doctor myself and explain things, and I might have to do it in secret, so as not to anger Robert.

He had apparently gone on to his classes after the appointment, or to paint at the campus studio, because I didn't see him until dinnertime. He didn't tell me anything until after I'd put Ingrid down to sleep, and even then I had to ask him what the doctor had said. He was sitting in the living room—not sitting, actually, but sprawled on the sofa with an unopened book. He raised his head when I spoke to him. "What?" He seemed to be looking at me across a great distance, and one side of his face drooped a little, as I'd noticed before. "Oh. I didn't go."

Rage and grief rose in me, but I took a deep breath. "Why not?"

"Lay off me, will you?" he said in a thin voice. "I didn't feel like it. I had work to do, and I haven't had time to paint in three days."

"Did you go paint instead?" That, at least, would be a sign of life.

"Are you checking up on me?" His eyes narrowed. He put the book in front of him like a breastplate. I wondered if he might even decide to throw it at me. It was a photographic essay on wolves he'd bought on impulse earlier in the year. That was a change, too, his frequently buying new books he later didn't read. He'd always been too thrifty to buy anything that wasn't secondhand, or much of anything at all, apart from the big well-made shoes he loved.

"I'm not checking up on you," I said carefully. "I'm just concerned about your health, and I'd like you to go to the doctor and look into it. I think just doing that will help you feel better."

"Do you?" he said almost nastily. "You *think* it will help me feel better. Do you have any idea how I feel? Do you know what it's like not to be able to paint, for example?"

"Certainly," I said, trying not to fire up. "There are very few days when I get to do that myself. Almost none, in fact. I know that feeling."

"And do you know what it's like to think about something over and over until you wonder . . . never mind," he finished.

"Until you wonder what?" I tried to speak very calmly, to show only that I was a good listener.

"Until you can't think about or see anything else?" His voice was low and his eyes flickered to the doorway. "So many terrible things have happened in history, including to artists, even artists like me, who tried to have normal lives. Can you imagine what it would be like to think about that all the time?"

"I think about terrible things sometimes, too," I said staunchly, although this sounded to me like a rather strange digression. "We all have those thoughts. History is full of awful things. People's lives are full of awful things. Every thinking person reflects on them—especially when you have children. But that doesn't mean you have to make yourself ill over them."

"Or what if you started thinking about one person? All the time?"

My skin began to crawl, whether from fear or from anticipated jealousy or both, I couldn't have said. Here was the moment when he would wreck our lives. "What do you mean?" I got the words out with some difficulty.

"Someone you could have cared about," he said, and his eyes traveled the room again. "But she didn't exist."

"What?" I felt a long blankness in my own mind—I couldn't find the end of it.

"I'll go to the doctor tomorrow," he said angrily, like a little boy resigned to punishment. I knew he'd agreed so that I wouldn't ask him anything more.

The next day he went out and came back, slept, and then got up to eat some lunch. I stood silently beside the table. I didn't have to ask. "He can't find anything wrong physically—well, he took a blood test for anemia and some other things, but he wants me to get a psychiatric evaluation." He put the words deliberately out into the room, so that something in them rang just short of contempt, but I knew that his telling me at all meant he was afraid, and willing to go. I went to him and put my arms around him and caressed his head, the heavy curls, the massive forehead, feeling that surprising mind inside, the vast gifts I had always admired and wondered about. I touched his face. I loved that head, his crisp uncontrollable hair.

"I'm sure everything will be all right," I said.

"I'll go for you." His voice was so quiet I could hardly hear it, and then he put his arms tightly around my waist and leaned over to bury his face against me.

CHAPTER 29

1878

The snow has deepened overnight. In the morning she gives orders for dinner, sends a note to her dressmaker, and leaves the house for the garden. She would like to know how the hedge looks, the bench. When she shuts the back door of the house behind her and steps into the first drift, she forgets everything else, even the letter tucked inside her dress. The tree planted ten years ago by the house's original occupants is festooned with snow; a tiny bird sits on a wall, ruffled up to twice its size. Her laced boots let in a rim of snow at the tops as she makes her way among the dormant flower beds, the shriveled arbor. Everything is transformed. She remembers her brothers as children, lying in the drifts while she watched from an upstairs window, waving their arms, flailing their legs, pummeling one another, floundering, their woolen coats and long knitted stockings engulfed in white. Or was it white?

She scoops a generous helping—a dessert, *Mont Blanc*—with her gloved hand and puts it into her mouth, swallows a little of the tasteless cold. The flower beds will be yellow in the spring, this one pink and cream, and under the tree will bloom the small blue flowers she has loved all her life, brought here most recently from her mother's grave. If she had a daughter, she would take her out in the garden on the day they bloomed and tell her where they came from. No—she would take her daughter out every single day, twice a day, into the sunshine and the bower, or the snow, sit with her on the bench, have a swing built for her. Or for him, her little son. She holds back the sting of tears and turns angrily to the sweep of snow along the back wall, tracing a long shape in it with her hand. Beyond the wall are trees, then the brownish haze of the Bois de Boulogne. If she finishes the maid's dress in her painting with more white, in the quick flecking she favors these days, it will lighten the whole picture.

The letter inside her clothes touches her, a sharply folded edge. She brushes the snow off her gloves and opens her cloak, her collar, draws it out, conscious of the back of the house behind her, the eyes of the servants. But they will be especially busy at this hour, in the kitchen or airing her father-in-law's parlor and bedroom while he sits at his dressing-room window, too blind to see even her dark figure in the white garden.

The letter does not use her name but an endearment. The writer tells her about his day, his new painting, the books by his fireplace, but beneath these lines she hears him saying something quite different. She keeps her wet, gloved fingers away from the ink. She has memorized every word of it already, but she wants to see the curving black proof again, his handwriting with its consistent carelessness, his economy of line. It is the same casual directness she has seen in his sketches, a confidence different from her own intensity—riveting, even puzzling. His words are also confident, except that their meaning is more than it seems to be. The *accent aigu,* a mere brush with the pen's tip, a caress, the *accent grave* strong, leaning away, a warning. He writes of himself, assured yet apologetic: *Je,* the "j" in capital form at the beginning of his precious sentences a muscular deep breath, the "e" quick and restrained. He writes of her and the renewal of life she has given to him—accidentally? he asks—and as in his last few letters, with her permission, he calls her *tu,* the "t" respectful at the beginnings of sentences, the "u" tender, a hand cupped around a tiny flame.

Holding the edges of the page, she ignores the sound of each line for a moment, for the pleasure of understanding it afresh a moment later. He intends no disruption of her life; he knows that at his age he can offer her few attractions; he wants only to be allowed to breathe in her presence and encourage her noblest thoughts. He dares to hope that, although they may never even speak of it, she sees him at the very least as her devoted friend. He apologizes for disturbing her with unworthy feelings. It frightens her that underneath the long flourish of his *pardonne-moi* and its delicate hyphen, he guesses that she is already his.

Her feet grow cold; the snow is beginning to soak through her boots. She folds the letter, tucks it away in a secret place, and puts her face against the bark of the tree. She can't afford to stand there long, in case anyone with sufficient sight should come to the windows behind her, but she needs a sustaining pause. The trembling at her core comes not from his words, with their graceful half retreat, but from his certainty. She has decided already not to reply to this one. But she has not decided never to reread it.

Chapter 30

Kate

Robert insisted on visiting the psychiatrist alone, and when he returned he told me matter-of-factly that he had some medication to try and the name and number of a therapist. He didn't say whether or not he would call the therapist, or whether he would take the medication. I couldn't figure out where he'd even put it, and I decided not to pry for a week or two. I would just wait to see what he did and encourage him in any way I could. Eventually, the bottle appeared in our medicine cabinet in the bathroom—lithium. I heard it rattle morning and night when he took a dose.

Within a week, Robert seemed calmer and began to paint again, although he slept at least twelve hours out of every twenty-four and ate in a daze. I was thankful that he was holding his studio classes without further interruptions and that I hadn't perceived any unease on the part of the college, although how such unease would have reached me I wasn't sure. One day Robert told me that the psychiatrist wanted to see me and that he, Robert, thought it was a good idea. He had an appointment that afternoon—I wondered why he hadn't mentioned it sooner—and when the time came, I packed Ingrid into her car seat because it was short notice to find a babysitter. The mountains flowed by, and I realized as I watched them pass that I hadn't even been to town in a while. My life revolved around the house, the sandbox and swings when it was warm enough outside, the supermarket up the road. I watched Robert's grave profile as he drove and finally asked him why he thought the psychiatrist wanted to see me. "He likes to get a family member's perspective," he said, and added, "He thinks I'm doing well so far. On lithium." It was the first time he'd mentioned the drug by name.

"Do you think so, too?" I put my hand on his thigh, feeling the muscles shift when he braked.

"I feel pretty good," he said. "I doubt I'll need it for long. I wish I weren't so tired, though—I need the energy to paint."

To paint, I thought, *but to be with us, too?* He fell asleep after dinner without playing with Ingrid, and was often still asleep when I left on my walks with her in the morning. I said nothing more.

The clinic was a long, low building made of expensive-looking wood and planted around with raw little trees in paper tubes. Robert went in matter-of-factly, holding the door for me as I passed through with Ingrid in my arms. The waiting room inside, which seemed to serve a number of doctors, was spacious, with a large patch of sunlight at one end. Eventually a man came out, smiled and nodded at Robert, and called me by name. He didn't wear a white coat or carry a chart—he was dressed in a jacket and tie, ironed khaki trousers.

I glanced at Robert, who shook his head. "This is for you," he said. "He wants to talk with you. He'll call me in, too, if he needs me."

So I left Ingrid with Robert and followed Dr.—well, what does his name matter? He was kind and middle-aged and doing his job. His office was lined with framed diplomas and certificates, his desk very neat, a large bronze paperweight sitting on the only loose piece of paper. I sat down facing the desk, my arms empty without Ingrid. I wished now I'd brought her in, and it worried me that Robert might put his face back in his hands instead of watching her cruise past electrical outlets and floral arrangements. But when I studied Dr. Q a little, I found I liked him. His face was gentle and reminded me of my Michigan grandfather's. When he spoke, his voice was deep, a little guttural, as if he had come from somewhere else as a teenager and whatever his accent was had become untraceable, just a slight rasping on the consonants.

"Thank you for coming to see me today, Mrs. Oliver," he said. "It's helpful to me to talk with a close family member, especially with any new patient."

"I'm glad to," I answered honestly. "I've been really worried about Robert."

"Of course you have." He rearranged the paperweight, leaned back in his seat, looked at me. "I know this must have been hard for you. Please be sure that I am paying very close attention to Robert and I'm satisfied that our first trial of medication is having a good effect."

"He certainly seems calmer," I admitted.

"Can you tell me a little about what you first noticed in his behavior that seemed different or that concerned you? Robert has told me that you were the one who got him to see a doctor originally."

I folded my hands and recited our problems, Robert's problems, the dizzying ups and downs of the last year.

Dr. Q listened silently, without changing expression, and his expression was kind. "And he seems to you more stable on the lithium?"

"Yes," I said. "He sleeps a lot still, and he complains about that, but he does seem able to get up and go to teach almost all the time. He complains about not being able to paint."

"It takes time to adjust to new medication, and it takes time to find out what medication works and what dosage works." Dr. Q arranged the paperweight thoughtfully again, this time in the top left corner of the one paper. "I do think in your husband's case it's important for him to take lithium for a while, and he will probably need it permanently, or some other medication if this one doesn't turn out to be just what we want. The process will require quite a bit of patience on his part—and on yours."

I began to feel new alarm. "Do you mean you think he will always have these problems? Won't he be able to stop the medicine when he's better?"

The doctor recentered the bronze lump on the document. It reminded me suddenly of that childhood game—rock, paper, scissors—where one element could win out over the other, but something else could always win out over the winner, a fascinating cycle. "It takes some time to develop any accurate diagnosis. But I believe Robert is probably experiencing—"

And then he told me the name of an illness, one I knew only vaguely and associated with nameless things, things that had nothing to do with me, things that people were given electric shock therapy for, or that caused them to kill themselves. I sat there for a few seconds, trying to fit these words to Robert, my husband. My whole body was bathed in cold. "Are you telling me that my husband is mentally ill?"

"We don't really know what part of any condition is mental illness and what is environmental or a function of personality," Dr. Q demurred, and I hated him for the first time—he was hedging. "Robert may stabilize on this medication, or we may have to try some other things. I think given his intelligence and his dedication to his art and his family, you can be hopeful that he'll achieve quite a bit."

But it was too late. Robert was no longer only Robert for me. He was someone with a diagnosis. I knew already that nothing would be the same, ever, no matter how much I tried to feel about Robert as I had before. My heart ached for him, but it ached even more for myself. Dr. Q had taken away the dearest thing I had, and he clearly didn't know what that felt like. He had nothing to give me in return, just the view of his hand arranging his empty desk. I wished he'd had the grace to apologize.

Chapter 31

Kate

Robert was sleepy on lithium. One day he ran into another car on his way to the museum in town—at low speed, fortunately. After that, Dr. Q put him on a different drug, combining it with something for anxiety. Robert explained these things to me when I asked for details, which I did as often as I could without irritating him.

By mid-December the new drug seemed to work well enough to allow him to paint and to get to his classes on time, and he seemed more like the old energetic Robert. He worked in the campus studio during that period, staying there late at night several times a week. When I visited once with Ingrid, I found him deep in a portrait—the lady of my nightmares. She sat in an armchair, her hands crossed in her lap. It was one of the brilliant paintings that later got him his big show in Chicago—a reasonably cheerful image this time—she was dressed in yellow, smiling as if to herself, as if remembering something pleasant and private, her eyes soft, a spray of flowers on the table beside her. I was so relieved to see him working, and in happy colors, that I almost stopped wondering who she was.

That made the shock greater when I went by a couple of days later to bring Robert some cookies that Ingrid and I had managed to make together, and found him working on the same picture but from a live model. She looked like a student, and she sat in a folding chair, not in the midst of overstuffed damask. For a moment my heart froze. She was young and pretty, and Robert was chatting with her, as if to keep her still while he repainted the angle of the head and shoulder. But she was nothing like the lady of his attic. She had short blond hair and light eyes and wore a college soccer jersey. Only her beautiful body and the square cut of her jaw provided her any sisterhood with the curly-headed woman I'd first seen in a sketch from his pocket. Furthermore, Robert seemed unabashed by my appearance, greeting Ingrid and me with kisses and introducing the girl as one of the regular studio models, a student job. The girl herself seemed a good deal more entranced with Ingrid and the fact that exams were almost over than with Robert. He was clearly just using her for the pose, and I knew as little as before.

I remember only a couple of moments from Robert's departure for New York State in early January. He held Ingrid for a long time, and I realized that she was so tall now that she could wrap her legs partway around his waist—the child with Robert's own long body, his crisp dark hair. The other moment I remember is going back in the house after his car disappeared down the drive into the woods—it must have been after, unless I refused to stand on the porch in the cold air for even a second longer to watch him go. I remember going inside to finish cleaning up our breakfast and asking myself in crisp, clear words, although silently, *Is this a separation?* But there was no answer in my own head or in the warm kitchen, with its smells of applesauce and toast. Everything seemed normal, if bleak. There was even a breath of relief in the house. I had managed before, and I would keep managing.

Robert's notes were usually scrawled on a postcard and addressed to Ingrid as much as to me, and his phone calls, too, came in an uneven rhythm, although frequently enough. The winter in upstate New York was fierce, but the snow was wonderful, Impressionist. He painted outside once and almost got frostbite. The college president had welcomed him. His room was in faculty guest quarters and had a good view of woods and the quad. His students were mostly ungifted, if interesting. The studio space was too small, but he was painting. He'd gone to bed at four that morning.

Then a little space, a short silence, and the notes would begin again. I liked his postcards better than his calls, which were full of unspoken tension between us, a chasm even harder to cross when we couldn't see each other's face. I tried not to call him any more often than he called me. Once, he sent a sketch for Ingrid, as if he knew she could understand this language best. I taped it to the wall of the nursery. It showed Gothic buildings and heaps of snow, bare trees. If Ingrid cried in the night, I brought her into bed with me, and we woke the next morning in a tangled pile. In late February, Robert flew home for his winter break and Ingrid's birthday. He slept a great deal, and we made love but didn't talk about anything difficult. He would have a break in early April as well, he said, but he'd decided to spend it painting up north. I didn't protest. If he returned in the summer with more work done, he might be easier to live with.

When Robert was gone again, my mother came for a stretch and sent me to the campus pool to swim every day. I'd lost much of my baby weight that year, and the rest came off as I plowed through the water, remembering how it had felt, such a short time ago, to be young and optimistic. On that visit, I first saw the trembling of my mother's hands and the little burst capillaries in her cheeks, the slight swelling of her ankles. She hadn't slowed in her helping me—when she was there, the dishes were always clean and drying in the rack, Ingrid's endless cotton suits washed and folded, and Ingrid read to as much as she could wish for.

But something had begun to slip in Mom's physical confidence, and after she went back to Michigan she started telling me she was afraid to walk on the ice. She would step out the front door to go to the grocery store, or to the dentist, or to volunteer at the library, and she would see the ice—and then she would go back inside and eventually call me. One day she told me she hadn't been out of the house in nearly a week. I didn't want to wait, alone, with the question that woke me in the early mornings now, and when I asked Robert, he said yes, without hesitation, that Mom should come to live with us.

I shouldn't have been surprised, but I was. I think I had forgotten his quick generosity, his use of yes instead of no, his habit of giving jackets to friends or even strangers. It made love quicken in me as I stood there waiting for him, far away from that cold New York State campus. I thanked him from my heart, told him about the azaleas beginning to bloom, the green leaves everywhere. He said he'd be home quickly, and we both seemed to be smiling over the phone.

When I called Mom, she didn't protest as I'd thought she would—instead she said she would think about it, but that if she came, she would want to help us buy a bigger house. I had never known she had that much money, but she did, and someone had offered to buy her house in Ann Arbor the year before, as well. She would think about it. Maybe it wasn't such a bad idea. How was Ingrid's cold?

CHAPTER 32

1878

In May, Yves insists that his uncle accompany them to Normandy, first to Trouville and then to a village near Étretat, a quiet place they have visited several times in the past and loved. It is Papa's idea to return with his brother, but Yves puts his own force behind it. Béatrice demurs; why should it not be just the three of them, as before? She can look after Papa by herself, and the house Yves always rents has only one small room for guests, with no parlor for Uncle Olivier if Papa stays in his usual quarters. If they move Papa, he will not be able to find anything, or might fall down the stairs in the night. It is hard enough for Papa to travel at all, although he is patience itself and relishes the feeling of the Channel sun and breeze on his face. She begs Yves to reconsider.

But Yves is firm. He may be called away on business in the midst of the vacation, so she will at least have Olivier to assist her. Strange—Olivier is even older than Papa, but he seems fifteen years Papa's junior in health and agility. Olivier's hair was not white before the death of his wife, Yves told her once, but that occurred a couple of years before she met the family. Olivier is strong, vibrant for his age; he can be helpful. Insisting that Olivier accompany them is the closest Yves ever comes to complaining about having the care of Papa on their shoulders.

She protests again—feebly this time—and three weeks later they are on a train moving slowly out of the Gare Saint-Lazare,

Yves tucking a lap robe over Papa's legs and Olivier reading aloud the art news in the paper. He seems to avoid Béatrice's eye. She is grateful, since his presence fills the small space until she wishes she could sit in another car. He appears to have grown younger in the months since their correspondence began; his face looks tanned even before they reach the coast. His beard is thick silver, neatly trimmed. He tells them he has been painting in the Forêt de Fontainebleau, and she wonders if he thought about her as he walked along those paths with his easel or stood in glades she will probably never see. For a moment she envies the trees that gathered around him, the grass that probably lay under his long frame when he rested, and she turns her mind at once to other thoughts. Is she merely jealous of his ability to travel and paint at will, his constant freedom?

Outside the train window, cinders blow by between her and the newly green fields, the glimpses of winding water. Yves keeps the window shut against the coal smoke and the dust, although the compartment grows too warm. She watches cows under a grove of trees, the dusting of red poppies, white and yellow daisies across a field. She has removed her gloves, her hat, and its matching jacket, since they are alone, all family, and the curtains are drawn between them and the corridor. When she leans back and closes her eyes, she senses Olivier's gaze and hopes her husband will not notice. But what is there to notice? Nothing, nothing, nothing, and that is the way she will keep it—nothing between her and this white-haired man Yves has known since birth, now her own relative.

The steam whistle blows far ahead, at the front of the train, a sound as hollow as she feels. Life is going to be long, for her at least. Is that not a good thing? Hasn't she always felt time stretching ahead of her in a lovely expanse? What if—she opens her eyes and keeps them resolutely on a distant village, a pale smudge, a church tower far away in the fields—what if that expanse contains neither children nor Olivier? What if it contains no more of Olivier's letters, his hand on her hair—she looks directly at him now, while Yves opens a second newspaper, and is gratified to see she has startled him. He turns his handsome head toward the window, picks up his book. There is so little time. He will die decades before she does. What if that in itself were enough to compromise her resistance?

CHAPTER 33

Kate

It actually took Mom several years to decide what to do, then to sell her house and go through all those books. Robert and I stayed in the cottage on campus during that time. Once, I went up to Michigan to help her give away most of my father's possessions, and we both wept. I left Ingrid with Robert, and he seemed to take good care of her, although I worried that he would forget where she was or let her wander around alone outside.

In the fall, Robert went to France for ten days, his turn to get away. He wanted to see the great museums again, he said—he hadn't been there since college. He came back so refreshed and excited that I felt it had been worth the money. He also had a rather grand show in Chicago the following January, an invitation of one of his former instructors—we all flew up there at horrifying cost, and I saw in the course of a day or two that he was becoming something bordering on famous.

In April the flowers Robert and I liked came out on campus again. I went into the woods to find the wild ones, and we walked around the college gardens so Ingrid could see the blooming beds. At the end of the month, I bought a little kit in the supermarket and watched a pink line soak across a white oval. I dreaded telling Robert, although we'd agreed to try for another child. He was so often tired or discouraged, but he seemed pleased with my news, and I felt that Ingrid's life would be complete. What was the point of having only one child? This time we found out it was a boy, and I got a boy doll for Ingrid to hold and to diaper. In December we drove to the birth center again. I had the baby with a kind of fierce, efficient concentration, and we brought him home—Oscar. He was fair-haired and looked like my mother, although Robert insisted he looked more like his own mother. Both mothers came to help for a few weeks—mine was still in Michigan—staying in our neighbors' spare rooms, and they enjoyed debating the question. Now I was pushing the stroller again, and my arms and lap were constantly full.

I have an indelible picture of Robert from the time when our children were small and we were living at the college. I'm not sure why I remember him so well from that period, except that that time was a kind of perfect peak of our lives, although it was also the time when Robert began to really go to pieces inside, I think. Even someone you've inhabited rooms with, and seen naked every day, seen sitting on the toilet through a half-opened door, can fade out after a while and become an outline.

But Robert, from that whole time when the children were toddlers and before Mom came to live with us, is all filled in for me, color and texture. He had a thick brown sweater that he wore almost daily in cool weather, and I can remember the strands of black and chestnut, seen up close, and the other things that got caught in it—lint and sawdust, sticks, all kinds of little bits of roughness that came from his studio at school, from his walks and painting excursions. I bought that sweater for him secondhand soon after we met—it was in great condition, from Ireland, knitted by someone's actual strong hands, and it lasted for years and years—outlasted us, in fact. The sweater filled my arms when he came home. I stroked its sleeves when I stroked his elbows. Under it, he wore an old long-sleeved T-shirt or a stretched cotton turtleneck, always in a color that vibrated with the sweater—frayed scarlet or deep green, not necessarily matching but compelling somehow. His hair got long or short—it curled over the collar of the sweater or it was shorn in soft bristles across the back of his neck, but the sweater was always the same.

My life was mostly touch in those days—I suppose his was color and line, so that we couldn't see each other's worlds very well, or he couldn't quite feel my presence. All day long I touched the clean plates and bowls as I put them away, and the children's heads slimy under shampoo in the tub, and the softness of their faces, and the scrape of poop off their goose-pimpling backsides, the hot noodles, the heavy wet laundry as I threw it into the dryer, and the brick front steps as I sat reading to myself for eight minutes while they played just beyond the page in the prickling new grass, and then when one of them fell down I touched the grass and the mud and the scraped knee, and the sticky Band-Aids, and the wet cheek, and my jeans, and the dangling shoelace.

When Robert came home from teaching, I touched his brown sweater and his curling, separating locks of hair, his stubbly chin, his back pockets, his calloused hands. I watched him lift up the children and felt just by seeing it how his rough face brushed their delicate ones and how that pleased them. He seemed completely there with us at those moments, and his touch was the proof of this. If I wasn't exhausted from the day, he touched me to keep me awake a little longer, and then I reached for his smooth, hairless flanks and the soft, crisp hair between his legs, his flat, perfect nipples. He seemed to stop looking at me then and to finally enter my world of touch, in that moving space between us, until we closed the gap with a fiery familiarity, a routine of release. In those days I always felt covered with secretions, the dripping milk, the spray on my neck when I changed Oscar a few minutes too early, the foam on my thighs, the saliva on my cheek.

Maybe this was why I was converted to touch and left the world of vision, why I stopped drawing and painting after all those years of doing it nearly every day. My family, the way they licked and chewed me, kissed me and pulled at me, spilled things on me—juice, urine, semen, muddy water. I washed myself again and again, I washed the mountains of laundry, I changed the beds and the breast pads, I scrubbed and wiped the bodies. I wanted to get clean again, to clean all of them, but in the moment before I had the energy to wash everything, there was always another kind of goodness, an immersion.

Then we were shopping for real estate, like grown-ups, and sending my mother photos of front porches, and finally we moved into our house the summer Ingrid was five and Oscar was one and a half. It was what I had wanted in the first place—two lovely children, a yard with a swing that Robert finally put up after I'd asked him for a couple of months to please do it, a small town whose very name was green, and at least one of us employed at a good job. Should we ever get what we think we want? And I had my mother. In the first years with us, she gardened and vacuumed and read for an hour or two a day in the shade on the terrace, where an elm tree threw the shadows of small leaves over her silvery head and the white pages of her book. From there she could even watch Ingrid and Oscar hunting for caterpillars.

In fact, I think those years were good ones for us *because* my mother was here. I had company, and Robert was at his best in her presence. Occasionally he stayed up for a couple of nights or slept at school and seemed tired afterward, and now and then he went through a period of irritability and then slept late for a few days. On the whole, things were peaceful. Robert had voluntarily painted over the chaos of his studio attic before we'd left the campus. I didn't know how much of that was due to the orange plastic bottles in our medicine cabinet. Once in a while he mentioned that he'd been to see Dr. Q, and that was enough for me—Dr. Q couldn't help me, of course, but he was apparently helping my husband.

During our second year in the new house, Robert taught at a painting retreat in Maine. He didn't talk about it much, but I thought it had done him good. We laughed together about the children, and sometimes at night, if I was not too tired, Robert reached for me, and things were the way they had always been. I used some of his shirts, torn into thirds, to dust the furniture—I could have pulled one of them out of any pile of rags and known it was his, known it was him, his lingering smell, his fabric. He seemed happy in his work, and I had started some part-time editing, mostly from home, to help with our part of the mortgage while my mother watched the children.

One morning after she had taken them to the park and I had done the breakfast dishes, I went upstairs to make beds and start work at the desk in the hall, and I saw the door to Robert's studio open. He had left with his coffee mug in one hand as I was getting up—he was in a phase of waking very early and going to school to paint. This morning I noticed he'd dropped something on the floor, a scrap of paper, which lay near the open door. I picked it up without thinking about anything in particular. Robert often scattered paper—notes, reminders, bits of drawings, crumpled napkins.

What I found on the floor was about a quarter of a sheet of writing paper, torn off, as if the writer had gotten frustrated. The writer was Robert—it was his handwriting, but neater than usual. I still have those lines hidden in my desk, not because I kept the original piece of paper—in fact, I eventually wadded it up and threw it at his head, and he caught it and put it in his pocket, and I never saw it again. I have those lines still because some instinct made me sit down at my desk and copy them over for myself and hide them before I confronted Robert. I suppose I was thinking vaguely that I might need them in court someday, or at the very least want to have them for myself later and might begin to forget some of the details. "My dearest one," the note said, but it was not a letter to me, nor had I ever seen any of those words before, lined up in this particular order and flowing from Robert's black pen.

My dearest one:

I am in receipt this very moment of your letter and am moved by it to write you at once. Yes, as you compassionately hint, I have been lonely these years. And strange as this may seem, I wish you had known my wife, although if that had been possible, then you and I would have come to know each other under proper circumstances and not in this otherworldly love, if you will permit me to call it that.

I hadn't known that Robert could be so flowery in a letter, or anywhere else—his notes to me had always been short and brisk. For a moment I felt more sickened by this surprise than by the fact that it was a love letter. The courtly, almost old-fashioned tone of it was a Robert I could hardly recognize, a gallant Robert who had never wasted his gallantry on his wife, whom he wished the addressee of the letter knew, or had known at some point.

I stood holding his words in the sunny library and wondered what I was reading. He had been lonely. He had fallen in otherworldly love. Of course it had to be "otherworldly," since he was married and had two children and was also possibly crazy. And what about me? Had I not been lonely? But I didn't have anything otherworldly, only all the reality of the world to cope with: the children, the dishes, the bills, Robert's psychiatrist. Did he think I liked the real world any more than he did?

I went slowly into his studio and looked at the easel. The woman was there. I thought I'd gotten used to her, to her presence in our lives. It was a canvas he'd been working on for weeks—she was alone in it, and her face was not yet fully painted, but I could have filled in that rough pale oval myself with the right features. He had placed her at a window, standing, and she was wearing a revealing, loose robe, pale blue. She held a paintbrush in one hand. Within another day or two she would be smiling at him, or gazing seriously, steadily, her dark eyes full of love. I had come to believe that she was imaginary, a fiction, part of the vision that drove his gifts. That had been trusting, too trusting, because it turned out my first instincts had been correct. She was real, and he wrote to her.

I had a sudden desire to wreck the room, tear up his drawing pads, knock the lady-in-progress to the floor, smear her and stamp on her, rip the posters and chaotic postcards from the wall. The cliché of it stopped me, the humiliation of being like a jealous wife in a movie. And a kind of sneakiness, too, a stealth that crept over my brain like a drug—I could learn more if Robert didn't know I knew. I put the scrap of paper on my desk, already planning to copy the words for myself and put it back on the floor at the open door of his studio in case he missed it. I pictured him stooping for it, thinking, *I dropped this? That was a close call.* And putting it in his pocket or in the drawer of his table.

Which was my next move—I went delicately through the drawers of his studio table, replacing with the care of an archivist anything I moved: big graphite pencils, gray erasers, receipts for oil paints, a half-eaten chocolate bar. Letters in the back of one drawer, letters in a handwriting I didn't recognize, replies to letters like his. *Dear Robert. Darling Robert. My dear Robert. I thought of you today while I worked on my new still life. Do you think still lifes are worth doing? Why paint something that is more dead than alive? I wondered how to put life into something with just your hand, this mysterious force that jumps like electricity between the sight and your eye, and then your eye and your hand, and then your hand and the brush, and so on. And back to your eye; it all comes down to what you can see, doesn't it, because no matter what your hand can do, it can't fix dimness of vision. I have to run to class now, but I think of you constantly. I love you, you know. Mary.*

My hands shook. I felt nauseated, felt the room trembling around me. I knew her name, then—and knew she must be a student, or possibly a faculty member, although in that case I would probably have recognized the name. She had to run to class. The campus was full of students I hadn't met and hadn't even seen—I wouldn't have seen all of them even in the time we lived there. Then I remembered the sketch I'd found in his pocket during our move to Greenhill several years earlier. This had been going on a long time; he had surely met her in New York. He had traveled north often since then, including his long semester away—had he gone so he could see her? Had that been the reason for his sudden leave of absence, his reluctance to take us with him? Of course she was another painter, an art student, a working painter, a real painter. He was painting her himself with her brush in hand. Of course she was a painter, as I had once been.

And yet—Mary—such an ordinary name, the name of the person with the little lamb, the name of the mother of Jesus. Or Queen of Scots, or Bloody Mary, quite contrary, or Mary Magdalene. No, it didn't always guarantee blue-and-white innocence. Her handwriting was large and girlish but not crude, the spelling correct, the turns of phrase intelligent and sometimes even striking, often humorous, sometimes a little cynical. Sometimes she thanked him for a drawing or added a skillful sketch of her own—one took up a whole page and showed people sitting around in a café with mugs and teapots on the tables. One of the notes was dated from a few months earlier, but most had no dates and none had envelopes. He had somehow thought to throw those out, or perhaps he'd opened the letters elsewhere and not cared about the envelopes, or carried them around without envelopes—a few of them were frayed, as if they'd been in a pocket. She didn't mention any meetings or plans to see him, but she wrote once about a time they had kissed each other. There was nothing else really sexual in those letters, in fact, although she said often that she missed him, loved him, daydreamed about him. In one she referred to him as "unattainable," which made me think that maybe nothing more had ever happened between them.

And yet everything had happened, if they loved each other. I put the notes back in the drawer. It was Robert's letter that upset me most—but there were no others from him, only from her. And I found nothing else in the studio, nothing in his office, nothing in his extra jacket, nothing in his car when I searched that, too, that evening, on the pretext of looking for a flashlight in the glove compartment—not that he would have followed me or noticed much. He played with the children, smiled at dinner—he was energetic, but his eyes were distant. That was the difference, the proof.

CHAPTER 34

Kate

I confronted him the next day, asking him to stay home for a few minutes after my mother had gone out with the children—I knew it was a day when he didn't have class until afternoon. I had hidden the letters in the dining-room sideboard, with the exception of the one in Robert's handwriting, which I put in my pocket, and I sat him down at the table to talk. He was impatient to be off to school, but his body stilled when I asked him if he realized that I knew what was going on. He frowned. Now I was the one trembling—with rage or fear, I wasn't yet certain. "What do you mean?" His frown seemed genuine. He was wearing something dark, and his remarkable handsomeness leapt out at me, as it sometimes did, without warning—the regal body, the strong features.

"First question—do you see her at school? Do you see her every day? Did she come here from New York, maybe?"

He leaned back. "See who at school?"

"The woman." I said. "The woman in all your paintings. Does she model for you at school or in New York?"

He began to glower. "What? I thought we'd been through this before."

"Do you see her every day? Or does she send you letters from a distance?"

"Send me letters?" He looked flabbergasted at this, pale. Guilt, surely.

"Don't bother to answer. I know she does."

"You know she does? What do you know?" There was anger in his eyes but also bewilderment.

"I know because I found her letters to you."

Now he was staring at me as if he had no words, as if he actually didn't know what to say. I had seldom seen him so disoriented, at least not in response to something from outside himself. He put both hands on the table, where they rested against the sheen of the grain, Mom's polishing. "You found letters from her to me?" The strange thing was that he didn't sound ashamed. If I'd had to characterize his voice and face at that moment, I would have said he seemed somehow eager, alarmed, hopeful. It enraged me—the note in his voice made me realize that he loved her uncontrollably, loved even the mention of her.

"Yes!" I shouted, jumping to my feet and pulling the pile of notes from under the place mats in the sideboard. "Yes, I even know her name, you stupid fool! I know it's Mary. Why did you leave them in this house if you didn't want me to find out?" I dropped them in front of him on the table, and he picked one up.

"Yes, Mary," he said, and then he glanced up and began almost to smile, but sadly. "That's nothing. Well, not nothing, but not so important."

I began to cry in spite of myself, and I felt it was not because of what he'd done so much as what he'd seen me do, that dramatic pulling out of letters and tossing them down in front of him. It was as humiliating as I ever could have dreamed. "You think it's nothing that you love another woman? What about this?" I pulled his own scrap of letter from my pocket, the one indisputably in his handwriting, crumpled it up, and hurled it at him.

He caught it and smoothed it out on the table. I thought I

read disbelief in his face. Then he seemed to rally. "Kate, what the hell do you care? She's dead. She's dead!" He was white around the nose and lips, his face rigid. "She died. Do you think I wouldn't give anything to have saved her, to have let her go on painting?"

Now I was sobbing in confusion as much as anything else. "She's dead?" The one dated letter from Mary meant she must have been alive even a couple of months before. I had the weird social impulse to say, *Oh, I'm so sorry.* Had she been in a car accident? Why had he not acted traumatized these last months or weeks? Nothing had seemed different. Perhaps whatever the relationship had been, he'd cared so little, actually, that he hadn't grieved for her. But this struck me as terrible in itself—could a person be that coldhearted?

"Yes. She is *dead.*" He gave the word a bitterness I wouldn't have thought him capable of. "And I still love her. You're damn right about that, if that satisfies you. I don't know why you should care. I love her. And if you don't understand the kind of love I mean, I'm not going to explain." He stood up.

"It doesn't satisfy me." Now that I had started weeping, I couldn't stop. "It makes it all worse. I don't know what you've been up to or what you mean. You have no *idea* how hard I've tried to understand you. But we're done, Robert, and that satisfies me—that does satisfy me." I picked up our Chinese vase from the sideboard, where it had always sat well out of child-reach, and threw it across the room. It smashed to heartrending bits on the hearth, under the portraits of my father's parents, stalwart people from Cincinnati. I regretted its destruction already. I regretted everything, except my children.

Chapter 35

1878

The village where they stay is quieter than nearby Étretat, but Yves says he likes it better for that very reason; their day in Trouville he found even more unsettling—in summer there must be as many people on the promenade there as on the Champs-Élysées, he tells Béatrice. They can always take a horse-drawn cab to Étretat for some quiet elegance, if they like, but this hamlet of houses in walking distance of the broad beach pleases all of them, and most days they stay there in serenity, walking the pebbles and the sands.

Every evening Béatrice reads Montaigne aloud to Papa in the rented parlor with its cheap damask chairs and shelves full of seashells. The other two men listen or talk in low voices near them. She has started a new piece of embroidery as well, to be sewn into a cushion for Yves's dressing room, a birthday present. She applies herself to this task day after day, straining her senses over the fine, small flowers in gold and purple. She likes to work on it while she sits on the veranda. When she raises her head, there is the sea, the gray-brown, green-topped cliffs off to the left and far right, the peeling fishermen's shacks and the boats pulled up on the beach, the clouds above a blustery horizon. Every few hours it rains, and then the sun breaks through again. Every day is a little warmer until a stormy morning suddenly keeps them inside; the next day is brighter still.

Her pastimes all help her avoid Olivier, but one afternoon he comes to sit beside her on the veranda. She knows his habits, and this is a change. In the mornings and again in the late afternoons, when the weather is fine, he paints on the beach. He has invited her to accompany him, but her hurried excuses—she doesn't have a canvas prepared—always put a stop to that, and he goes by himself, cheerfully, whistling, touching his hat as he passes her in her chair on the porch.

She wonders if he walks more briskly because she is watching; she again has that strange sense that he is shedding years under her gaze. Or is it merely that she has learned to look through his years, now more transparent to her—that she sees through them to the person they have made him? Whenever he takes leave of her, she watches his straight back, his favorite old painting suit retreating down the beach. She is trying to unlearn what she knows about him, to view him again as her husband's elderly relation who happens to be on holiday with them, but she knows too much about his thoughts, his turns of phrase, his dedication to his work, his regard for hers. Of course, he doesn't send her letters here in this house, but words linger between them—his slanting handwriting, the sudden leap of his mind on paper, his caressing "*tu*" on the page.

Today there is a book instead of an easel under his arm. He settles down next to her in a big chair as if determined not to be rebuffed. She is glad in spite of herself that she has put on her pale-green dress with the yellow ruching at the neck, which a few days before he said made her look like a narcissus; she wishes he were even nearer so that his gray-jacketed shoulder could brush hers, wishes he would go away, wishes he would get on a train back to Paris. Her throat tightens. He smells of something pleasant from his toilette, some unknown soap or eau de cologne; she wonders if he has worn this scent for many years, whether it has changed with time. The book in his lap stays closed, and she is certain that he doesn't intend to read it, a suspicion borne out when she sees the title, *La loi des Latins*; she recognizes it from the dull shelf just inside. He obviously snatched it up before coming to sit with her, a ploy that makes her smile down at her needlework. "Bonjour," she says with what she hopes is a housewife's neutrality.

"Bonjour," he answers. They sit in silence for a moment or two, and that, she thinks, is the proof, even the problem. If they were genuine strangers or ordinary family members, they would already be chatting about nothing in particular. "May I ask you a question, my dear?"

"Of course." She finds her tiny scissors with their stork's beak and embossed legs; she cuts her thread.

"Do you intend to avoid me for a full month?"

"It's been only six days," she says.

"And a half. Or six days and seven hours," he corrects her. The effect is so droll that she glances up and smiles. His eyes are blue, not elderly enough to put her off as they should. "That's much better," he says. "I had hoped the punishment would not last four weeks."

"Punishment?" she asks as mildly as she can. She tries in vain to rethread her needle.

"Yes, punishment. And for what? For admiring a young painter from a distance? After all my good manners, you could surely afford to give me a little cordiality."

"You understand, I think," she begins, but the needle is giving her unusual trouble.

"Allow me." He takes the needle and threads it carefully with the fine gold silk, then hands it back. "Old eyes, you know. They get keen with use."

She can't stop herself from laughing. It is this spark of humor between them, his ability to mock himself, more than anything else, that undoes her. "Very well. With your keen eyes, then, you will understand that it is impossible for me to—"

"To pay me as much attention as you would pay a stone in your pretty shoe? Actually, you'd pay much more to the stone, so perhaps I will simply have to become more annoying."

"No, please—" She has begun to laugh again. She hates the joy that sparkles between them at such moments, the pleasure that might become visible to anyone else. Doesn't this man understand that he is part of her family? And elderly? She feels again the elusiveness of age. What he has already taught her is that a person doesn't feel old inside, at least until the body claims its dismal due; that is why Papa seems old although he is younger, while this white-haired, silver-bearded artist seems not to know how he should behave.

"Stop it, *ma chère*. I'm too ancient to do any harm, and your husband thoroughly approves of our friendship."

"And why shouldn't he?" She tries to sound offended, but the strange pleasure of his closeness is too great, and she finds herself smiling at him again.

"All right, then. You have argued yourself into a corner. If there's no reason for objections anyway, you can come out and paint with me tomorrow morning. My fisherman friend down on the beach says it will be fine, so fine that the fish will be leaping into his boat. For my part, I thought they leapt higher on rainy days." He is imitating the dialect of the coast, and she laughs. He gestures toward the water. "I don't like your languishing here with all this sewing. A great artist in the making should be out with her easel."

Now she feels herself flushing from the neck up. "Don't tease me."

He turns serious at once and takes her hand as if without thinking, not as a gesture of courtship. "No, no—I am in earnest. If I had your gifts, I would not be wasting a minute."

"Wasting?" She is half angry, half ready to cry.

"Oh, my dear. I *am* clumsy." He kisses her hand in apology and lets it go before she can protest. "You must know what faith I have in your work. Don't be indignant. Just come out and paint with me tomorrow, and you'll remember how you love it and forget all about me and my clumsiness. I'll merely escort you to the right view. Agreed?"

Again, that vulnerable boy gazing out of his eyes. She passes a hand over her forehead. She cannot imagine loving anyone more than she loves him in this moment—not his letters, not his politeness, but the man himself and all the years that have polished him and made him both confident and fragile. She swallows, puts the needle neatly through her embroidery. "Yes. Thank you. I will come."

When they return to Paris three weeks later, she takes with her five small canvases of the water and the boats, the sky.

CHAPTER 36

Kate

Robert didn't move out right away, and neither did I—in fact, I had no intention of uprooting my mother and children or leaving the house I'd dreamed about and come to love and that my mother had helped us buy. After I broke that vase, Robert collected his pile of letters, put them in one of his pockets, and went out without getting so much as a toothbrush or a change of clothes. I might have felt better about him even then if he'd gone upstairs and prudently packed a suitcase.

I didn't see Robert for several days, and I didn't know where he was. I told my mother only that we'd had a bad quarrel and needed some time off, and she was concerned but also neutral—I saw that she thought it would blow over. I tried to convince myself that he was staying with Mary, wherever she lived, but I couldn't shake the feeling I'd had that he'd been telling the truth when he'd said so bitterly, "She's *dead.*" He didn't seem capable of real mourning. That was almost the worst of it. The fact that the affair had ended with her death didn't ease my hurt. In fact, it added a sense of haunting to my days, of eeriness, that I couldn't shake.

One afternoon that week when I was reading—not very attentively—on the front steps and my mother was doing our mending in the chair on the terrace and we were both watching the children overwater the garden, Robert drove up without any fanfare and got out of his car. I could see that he had some things stowed in the back of it—easels and portfolios and boxes. My heart knotted in my throat. He came up the front walk and made a detour to kiss my mother and ask how she was. I knew she was telling him that she felt fine, although I'd had to take her to the doctor for another dizzy spell the day before. And although she now knew he'd all but moved out.

Then Robert came slowly up the walk toward me, and for a moment I saw the sum total of his presence, his big body that was not lean and not heavy, the broad movements of muscle under his shirt and pants. His clothes seemed grubbier than ever, and he had been more than usually careless with paint, so that his rolled sleeves bore flecks of red and his khakis were smudged with white and gray. I could see the skin of his face and neck beginning to age, the lines under his eyes, the deep brown-green of his gaze, his thick hair, the angelic curls threaded with silver, his largeness, his distance, his self-sufficiency, his loneliness. I wanted to jump up and throw myself at him, but that was what he should have been doing for me. Instead, I sat where I was, feeling smaller than ever, framed, in a frame—a little, straight-haired, too-clean person he had forgotten to look after in his big quest for art, an essential nobody. He had forgotten even to tell me what his quest was for.

He paused at the steps. "I'm just going to get a few things."

"Fine," I said.

"Do you want me to come back? I miss you and I miss the kids."

"If you came back," I said in a low voice that I tried to keep from trembling, "would you really come back, or would you still be living with a ghost?"

I thought Robert would get angry again, but after a moment he said simply, "Leave it alone, Kate. You can't understand."

And I knew that if I shouted something like "I can't understand? *I* can't understand?" I would never stop shouting at him, even in front of the children and my mother. Instead I closed my fingers in my book so that they hurt, and I let him go on up the steps and come back down after a while with the proverbial suitcase, actually an old duffel bag from one of our closets.

"I'll be gone a few weeks. I'll call you," he said. He went and kissed the kids and threw Oscar up in the air, letting their wet clothes dampen his shirt. He lingered. I hated him even for his pain. Finally he got into the car and drove away. Only then did I wonder how he could leave his job for weeks at a time. It hadn't occurred to me yet that he might stop teaching, too.

As it turned out, that was one of the last days my mother felt like herself. Her doctor called us into his office to tell us she had leukemia, far gone. She could have chemo, but that would probably cause her more discomfort than anything else. She opted instead to accept a brochure for hospice care, and pressed my arm as we left, to save me from my own grief.

CHAPTER 37

Kate

I will pass over some of this part. I will pass over it, but I do want to describe how Robert came back. I called him that night, and he came back for the six weeks it took my mother to weaken to almost nothing. It turned out he hadn't gone farther than the college, although he never told me where he slept while he was there—maybe at the studios or in one of the empty cottages. I wondered if our old house there was empty. Maybe he was sleeping among our own ghosts, in a pile of blankets on the floor, the rooms to which we'd brought Ingrid and Oscar home as newborns.

When he returned for that brief period to help me with my mother, he camped out in his studio room, but he was calm and kind and he sometimes drove off with the children on excursions so I could sit with my mother while she took painkillers and long naps, longer and longer. I didn't ask him about his work at the college. I thought Robert and I would wait together for the time when the hospice nurses would come in; everything was arranged, and my mother had even helped me arrange it—she would tell me, give me a sign, and I would call the number by the phone in the kitchen.

But in the end only Robert and I were there, and that was the real finish of our marriage, unless you count the previous endings, or the dwindling calls later, or his disappearance to Washington, or my filing for divorce and leaving his office untouched for more than a year, or my beginning to clean out his office at last, or my putting away most of his paintings of Mistress Melancholy, whatever you want to call her. Or even the moment when I heard he'd attacked a painting and been arrested for it, or when I heard later he had consented to enter a mental institution. Or when I realized that I wanted to help his mother at least a little with his bills, still wanted him to get better, if that was possible, so that someday he could come to the children's graduations and weddings.

People whose marriages haven't collapsed, or whose spouses die instead of leaving, don't know that marriages that end seldom have a single ending. Marriages are like certain books, a story where you turn the last page and you think it's over, and then there's an epilogue, and after that you're inclined to go on wondering about the characters or imagining that their lives continue without you, dear reader. Until you forget most of that book, you're stuck puzzling over what happened to them after you closed it.

But if there was a single ending for Robert and me, it happened the day my mother died, because she died more suddenly than we had expected. She was resting on the sofa in the living room, in the sunlight. She'd even been willing to let me fix her a little tea, but then her heart failed. That's not the technical term, but that's how I think of it, because mine failed me, too, and I reached her as it happened, dropping the tray on the living-room carpet in my rush to her. I knelt holding her by the arms while our hearts failed us, and it was terrible, and terrible to watch, but very fast, and it would have been much more terrible if I hadn't been there to watch and hold her after all the years she had taken care of me.

When it was over and she was no longer herself, I put my arms around her and held her more tightly, and my voice finally came back. I called for Robert, screamed for him, although I was still afraid it would disturb her. He must have heard the tone from his office behind the kitchen, because he came running in. My mother had lost most of her weight already, and I held her up easily in my arms, my cheek pressed to hers, partly so that I wouldn't have to look at her directly again right away. I stared up at Robert instead. What I saw in his face finished our marriage just as my mother's life vanished. His eyes were blank. He was not seeing us, me holding her lifeless body in my arms. He was not thinking how he could comfort me in those first moments, or how he could honor her death, or how he mourned her himself. I saw clearly that he was watching someone else, something that set his face alight with horror, something I could not see or possibly understand because it was even worse than this, this worst moment of my life. He was not there.

November 1878
Paris

Très chère Béatrice:

Thank you for your touching note. I don't like to think I missed another evening with you, even for the best of Molière; forgive my absence. I wonder, rather jealously, if the stylish Thomas pair was there again; perhaps it is knowing they are closer to your age than I am that makes me a little protective. In fact, I don't care, these days, for the way they hang over you—or, for that matter, ogle your work, which ought to be seen only by discerning eyes (not theirs). Excuse my unbecoming grumpiness. If I could prevent myself from writing, I certainly would, but the beauty of the morning is too much for me, and I must share it with you. You will be at your window, perhaps with your embroidery or some book, possibly the one I left last time, resting in your hand. You told me, when I committed the indiscretion of admiring them, that your hands are too large; but they are lovely—capable—and in proportion to your graceful height. Moreover, they are not capable only in appearance but in your handling of brush and pencil, and, no doubt, everything else you do. If I could hold each of them in mine (mine being, after all, still larger but less capable), I would kiss each in turn, respectfully.

Forgive me; I am already forgetting my purpose of sharing the morning's beauty with you. I've walked as far as the Jeu de Paume this morning, shaking off my late night at the theater and feeling, my dear, that I am after all not up to many late nights, since I always wake early;

I would rather have been at your side yesterday evening, and perhaps tomorrow night I shall again be reading to you by your cheerful fire or saying nothing at all so that I can watch your thoughts. Do sit that way sometimes, when I cannot sit there with you.

Again, I wander. Walking to the Jeu de Paume, I saw a family of sparrows fed by an old gentleman who might have witnessed Napoléon's last charge and once looked very fine in a cocked hat. You will laugh at my innocent fantasies. Walking through the park, too, was a young priest (who in some other realm might have blessed us), kicking his gown impatiently ahead of him; he was in a hurry, that's certain. And I, who was not, sat down on a bench to dream for ten minutes, even in the cold, and you can perhaps guess some of my reflections. Please do not laugh at their wistfulness.

Now that I've come home, warmed up, and breakfasted, I must ready myself for a day of meetings and work, during which I will think of you incessantly and you will forget me entirely. But I'll have news for you by tomorrow, I hope, news that will please you, and at least one of my meetings concerns this news. It concerns also the new painting, my probable submission to this year's Salon. You will excuse my attempt at mystery! But I would like to talk with you about it, and it is of sufficient importance that I must beg you to come to the studio sometime tomorrow morning between ten and twelve, if you are free, on a matter of business—one of the utmost propriety, since Yves has urged me to seek your approval of the work. I have enclosed the address and a little map; you will find the street picturesque but not unpleasant.

Until then, I do kiss your slender hand with respect, and await a welcome scolding—and acceptance of my invitation—aimed at your devoted friend.

O. V.

CHAPTER 38

Marlow

I left Kate with heartfelt thanks, and with my notes on our sessions in my briefcase. She shook my hand warmly but also seemed relieved to watch me go. At the edge of downtown, I stopped at a coffee shop, but stayed in my car and got out my cell phone. It took only a little searching. The switchboard operator at Greenhill College sounded friendly, casual; there was some kind of rustling in the background, as if she might be eating lunch on the job. I asked for the Art Department and found an equally receptive secretary there. "I'm sorry to call out of the blue," I said. "I'm Dr. Andrew Marlow. I'm writing an article on one of your former faculty, Robert Oliver, for *Art in America*. That's right. Yes, I realize he's not there anymore—I've actually interviewed him in Washington, DC, already."

I could feel some sweat at my hairline, although until that moment I'd been completely calm; I wished I hadn't named a particular journal. The question was, did they know at the college that Robert had been arrested and institutionalized? I hoped that the incident in the National Gallery had been publicized mainly in the Washington papers. I thought of Robert stretched out like a fallen colossus on his bed, arms behind his head, legs crossed at the ankle; he was staring at the ceiling. *You can talk to anybody you want.*

"I'm passing through Greenhill today," I pressed on cheerfully, "and I know it's short notice, but I wonder if any of his colleagues might be able to sit down with me for a few minutes this afternoon or—or tomorrow morning—and comment on his work a bit. Yes. Thank you."

The secretary went away for a moment and came back with surprising rapidity—I pictured a big warehouse studio, loft-style, where she could stop anyone at an easel and ask a question. But that couldn't be correct. "Professor Liddle? Thank you very much. Please tell him that I'm sorry about the short notice and that I won't take too much of his time." I clicked the phone off, went in and got an iced coffee, and wiped my forehead with the paper napkin. I wondered if the young man at the counter knew from looking at me that I was a liar. *I haven't been one in the past,* I wanted to tell him. *It crept up on me.* No, that wasn't quite accurate. *It happened recently, by accident.* An accident named Robert Oliver.

The drive to the college was short, perhaps twenty minutes, but my suspense made it feel endless: a big arching sky above the mountains, highways planted with vast triangles of wildflowers, something pink and white that I didn't recognize, smooth asphalt. "You can even talk with Mary," Robert had said to me. It was easy to remember what he'd said because he'd said so little in front of me.

There were only three possibilities, I thought. The first was that his condition had deteriorated to the point of delusions since the time of his break with Kate, and he now thought a dead woman was still alive. I hadn't seen real evidence of this, however. Surely if he were plagued by delusions he wouldn't be able to maintain his silence in such a studied way. Another possibility was that he had been lying to Kate, elaborately, and Mary was not dead. Or—but the third possibility wouldn't quite take shape in my mind, and I gave up on it around the time I had to start watching for the exit to the college.

The area wasn't my picture of backwoods Appalachia; perhaps you had to go farther off the interstate for that. Greenhill College was responsible for the stretch of neat country road I turned onto, a sign informed me, and—as if to prove it—there was a group of young people in orange vests picking up negligible amounts of trash in the ditch off the shoulder. The road wound into mountains and past a sign that I realized must have been the one Kate had described, weathered carving framed with gray fieldstones, and then I entered the drive to the college.

This wasn't the backwoods either, although some of the buildings near the entrance were mellowed old cabins, half hidden in stands of hemlock and rhododendron. A big official hall turned out to be the dining center; wooden dormitories and brick classroom buildings climbed the slope behind it, and beyond that in every direction were woods—I had never seen a campus so nestled in woodland. The trees on the grounds were even bigger than those at Goldengrove—patrician, wild—oaks scraping the blustery sky, a great sycamore, skyscraper spruces. Three students played Frisbee on the lawn in a neatly balanced triangle, and a golden-bearded professor was holding class on the piazza, all the students balancing their notebooks on their cross-legged laps. It was idyllic; I wanted to go back to school myself, start over. And Robert Oliver had lived for several years in this little paradise, ill and frequently depressed.

The Art Department proved to be a concrete box at one end of campus; I parked in front and sat looking at the gallery building next door to it, a long narrow cabin with a colorfully painted door. A board outside announced a student art show. I hadn't expected to be so nervous. What was I afraid of? I was there on an errand of mercy, essentially. If I wasn't being open about my profession or its relation to former painting instructor Robert Oliver, that was because I knew I'd get no information otherwise. Or less information, at least—perhaps far less.

The secretary turned out to be a student, or young enough to be one, wide-hipped in jeans and white T-shirt. I told her I was there for a meeting with Arnold Liddle, and she showed me along hallways to an office with a door; I got a glimpse of someone with his legs on his desk. They were scrawny legs in faded gray trousers, ending in sock feet. When we came in, the legs went down and the person on the phone hung up abruptly—it was a normal phone, the old kind, not wireless, and it took him a second or two to uncurl the spiral cord from his arm. Then he stood up and shook my hand. "Professor Liddle?" I asked.

"Just Arnold, please," he corrected me. The secretary was already gone. Arnold had a lively thin face and hair that receded to a ginger haze around the back of his shirt collar. His eyes were blue—large, pleasant—and his nose long and red. He smiled and motioned me to a seat in the corner, facing him, and put his feet back up. I had the urge to slip off my shoes, too, but didn't. The office was cluttered: there were postcards of gallery shows on a bulletin board, a big poster of a Jasper Johns over the desk, snapshots of a couple of skinny children balanced on their bicycles. Arnold settled more deeply into his chair as if he loved it there. "How can I help you?"

I folded my hands and tried to appear at ease. "Your receptionist may have told you that I'm doing some interviews about the work of Robert Oliver—she thought you might be able to help me." I watched Arnold carefully.

He seemed to consider this, falling silent, but not with any special awareness. Perhaps he hadn't heard or read about the incident at the National Gallery after all. I felt a small surge of relief.

"Certainly," he said at last. "Robert was—has been—a colleague of mine for about seven years or so, and I know his work pretty well, I think. I wouldn't say we were friends, exactly—private kind of guy, you know—but I've always respected him." He didn't seem to know quite where to go after this, and it surprised me that he didn't ask for my credentials or why I wanted to know about Robert Oliver. I wondered what the secretary had told him—whatever it was, he seemed satisfied by it. Had she repeated the *Art in America* claim? What if the editor had been his art-school roommate?

"Robert did a lot of good work here, didn't he?" I hazarded.

"Well, yes," Arnold admitted. "He was prolific, kind of a superman, always painting. I have to say that I find his paintings a little derivative, but he's quite a draftsman—a great one, actually. He told me once he'd done abstract for a while in school and didn't like it—that didn't last long for him, I guess. While he was here he was working mainly on two or three different series. Let's see—one of them was about windows and doors, kind of a Bonnard interior, but more realistic, you know. He showed a couple of those in the entry of our center here. One of them was still lifes, brilliant, if you like still lifes—fruit, flowers, goblets, kind of like Manet but always with something odd in them like an electrical outlet or a bottle of aspirin—I don't know what. Anomalies. Very nicely done. He had a big show of them here, and the Greenhill Art Museum picked up at least one. So did some other museums." Arnold was rummaging through a can on his desk; he pulled out a stub of pencil and began to twiddle it between two fingers. "He was working on a new series for a couple of years before he left, and toward the end he had a solo show of them here. That batch was, I'll be frank, bizarre.

I saw him working on them in the studio. Mostly he worked at home, I guess."

I tried not to look too interested; by now I'd managed to get my notepad out and arrange myself in journalistic calm. "Was that series also traditionalist?"

"Oh yes, but weird. All the paintings showed basically the same scene—pretty gruesome scene—a young woman holding an older woman in her arms. The young woman is staring down at her in shock, and the older woman is—well, shot through the head, shot dead, you can tell. Kind of Victorian melodrama. Clothes and hair and incredible detail, with some soft brushwork and some realism, a mix. I don't know who he got to pose for those—maybe students, although I never saw anyone working with him on it. There's still one painting from that series at the gallery here—he gave it for the lobby when they renovated. I've got a piece there, too—all the current faculty were represented, which means they had to build a lot of pottery cases and all. Do you know Robert Oliver well?" he asked suddenly.

"I've interviewed him a couple of times in Washington," I said, alarmed. "I wouldn't say I know him that well, but I find him interesting."

"How is he?" Arnold was looking at me with more keenness than I'd previously noted; how had I missed the intelligence in his pale eyes? He was a disarming person, sort of loose and comfortable, with his skinny legs and arms splayed around the desk; you couldn't help liking him, and I feared him now, too.

"Well, I understand he's working on some new drawings these days."

"He won't be coming back, I suppose? I've never heard anything about his coming back."

"He didn't mention any plans to return to Greenhill," I

admitted. "At least, we didn't discuss that, so maybe he's planning to—I don't know. Do you think he liked teaching? How was he with his students?"

"Well, he ran off with a student, you know."

This time I was completely off my guard. "What?"

He seemed amused. "Didn't he tell you that? Well, she wasn't a student here. Apparently he met her when he was teaching at another college for a term, but we heard after he took a leave of absence all of a sudden that he had gone to live with her in Washington. I don't think he even mailed in an official resignation. I don't know what happened. He just didn't come back. Very bad for his teaching career. I've always wondered how he could afford to do that. He didn't seem like someone who had a lot of extra money stashed away, but I guess you never know. Maybe his paintings were selling well enough—that's a real possibility. Anyway, it was a shame. My wife knew his wife a little, and she said his wife never said a word about it. They had been living in town for a while already, not on campus. She's a lovely woman, his wife. I can't imagine what old Bob was thinking, but—you know. People go crazy."

I found it hard to follow this speech with any coherent comment, but Arnold didn't seem to notice. "Well, I wish Robert all the best anyway. He was a good guy at heart, or I always thought so. He's big-league, I guess, and probably this place couldn't hold him. That's my theory." He mentioned this without bitterness, as if the place that hadn't been able to hold Robert was as comfortable for him—Arnold—as the chair he was settled in. He ruminated on his pencil stub and then began to draw something on a notepad. "What are you focusing on in your article?"

I collected myself. Should I ask Arnold that former student's name? I didn't dare. I thought again that she must have been his muse, the woman in the painting Kate so disliked. *Mary?* "Well, I'm concentrating on Oliver's paintings of women," I said.

Arnold would have snorted if he'd been that kind of person. "He did plenty of those, I guess. His show in Chicago was mainly women, or all the same woman, kind of curly, black-haired. I saw him painting some of those, too. The catalog's around here somewhere, if his wife didn't haul it away. I asked him once if that was someone he knew and he didn't answer, so I don't know who posed for those either. The same student, maybe, although she didn't live here, as I said. Or—I don't know. Odd bird, Robert—he had a way of answering you and you realized only afterward that you hadn't gotten any info out of him."

"Did he seem—did you notice anything out of the ordinary with him before he left the college?"

Arnold let his sketch fall to the desk. "Out of the ordinary? No, I wouldn't say so, except for that last weird bunch of paintings—I shouldn't say that about a colleague's work, but I'm known for speaking my mind, and I'll be honest—they freaked me out a little. Robert has a great ability to paint in nineteenth-century styles—even if you don't like imitation, you have to admire his skill. Those still lifes were amazing, and I saw a kind of Impressionist landscape he did once, too. You would have thought it was the real thing. He told me once that only nature mattered, that he hated conceptual art—I don't do conceptual either, but I don't *hate* it—and I thought, *Then why on earth paint all that heavy Victorian stuff?* I don't know what that is, if not conceptual, these days—you're making a statement just by doing it. But I'm sure he told you all about it."

I saw that I wasn't going to get much more out of Arnold. He was an observer of paintings, not of people; he seemed to shimmer and fade in front of me, as smart and insubstantial and good-natured as Robert Oliver was deep and substantial and troubled. I would take sullen, subtle Oliver in a minute, I thought, if it were a matter of choosing friends.

"If you need some more notes, I can walk you over to see Bob's painting," Arnold was telling me. "That's about all of him you'll find here these days, I'm afraid. His wife came out one day and cleaned out his office and took all the paintings he'd left in the faculty studio. I wasn't here when she did it, but someone told me about it. Maybe he just didn't want to do it himself and those paintings would have stayed here forever—who knows? I don't think he was that close to anyone here. Come on—I need a walk anyway."

He unbent his legs, storklike, and we ambled out together. The sunlight beyond the front door was gorgeously bright, urgent; I wondered how any artist could stand that little concrete office, but perhaps it wasn't up to Arnold, and he seemed to have made the best of it.

CHAPTER 39

Marlow

I followed him into the log-cabin gallery next door, which turned out to be large and sophisticated inside, with a hidden back wing of glass and whitewashed frames, an addition some architect had nurtured toward a local prize. The skylighted entryway was lined with canvases and softly bright glass cases filled with ceramics.

Arnold indicated a big painting opposite the door, and I saw at once what he meant—it was bizarre, terribly alive and yet overdramatic, stilted like a Victorian stage piece. It showed a woman in billowing skirts and fitted bodice, her slender body bent over. She was kneeling on a roughly cobbled street; as Arnold had promised, she cradled in her arms an older woman, sickeningly dead. The older woman's face was ashen, her eyes closed, her mouth slack, and through her forehead was a bullet hole, a distinct horrible tunnel drilled there, so that a gush of blood was already drying down one side of her loosened hair and shawl.

The younger woman had been elegantly dressed, but her pale-green gown was dirty and torn, stained with blood on the front where she clasped the murdered woman's head against her. Her own lustrous, curly hair had come undone, her hat fell by its ribbons onto her shoulder, her face was bent over the dead woman's so that I couldn't see the luminous eyes I was already so used to meeting. The background was hazier, but it seemed to be a wall, a narrow city street, one storefront overhung with words whose letters blurred in the paint, unreadable, figures in red and blue crouching nearby but indistinguishable. There were piles of something at one end—brown, beige—chopped wood? Sandbags? A lumberyard?

The whole thing was riveting but also purposely overdone, it seemed to me, appalling as well as moving. It smelled of fear and hopelessness. The pose, the grief in it, made me remember my first glimpse of the Michelangelo Pietà—a work too famous for anyone to look at it clearly anymore, except perhaps when one is young enough. I'd seen it on my trip to Italy after college; at that time it was not yet behind glass, so I was separated from the figures by only a rope and a distance of five feet or so. The daylight coming down on Mary and Jesus touched them with different tones, and it was as if both bodies were alive, the blood pulsing in their veins—not only the grieving mother but also the freshly dead son. The incredibly touching thing was that he wasn't dead. For me, without faith, it was not a prediction of resurrection but a portrayal of Mary's shock, and of the lingering aliveness one sees in the hospital when a young person is wrested out of life by some terrible injury. I learned, in that moment, the difference between genius and everything else.

What struck me most about Robert's painting, apart from the horror of the scene, was that it was narrative, whereas all the images I'd seen of his lady before this were portraits. But what was the story? Possibly Robert hadn't been using any models at all; I remembered what Kate had said about how he sometimes drew and painted from his imagination. Or perhaps he'd been using models but had invented the story—the nineteenth-century dress would support this idea. Had he dreamed up his lady character holding her murdered mother? Perhaps he'd even been painting his own bright and dark sides, the two parts of his psyche divided by illness. I hadn't expected Robert Oliver to come up with actual stories.

"You don't like it either?" Arnold looked pleased.

"It's very skillful," I said. "Which one of these is yours?"

"Oh, on this wall," Arnold said, gesturing toward a large canvas behind us, next to the door. He folded his arms in front of it. It was abstract, large soft squares of pale blue melting into one another, a silver sheen over it all, as if you could drop a square pebble in water and it would make concentric squares. It was rather appealing, actually. I turned to Arnold and smiled. "I do like this."

"Thanks," he said cheerfully. "I'm doing yellow now." We stood gazing at the blue, Arnold's child of a couple of years earlier, Arnold with his head fondly to one side; I could see he hadn't really looked at it in a while. "Well," he said.

"Yes, I should let you get back to office hours," I told him gratefully. "You've been very kind."

"If you talk with Robert again, tell him I said hello," he prompted. "Tell him he's not forgotten here, no matter what."

"I'll certainly tell him," I—lied?

"Send me a copy of that article if you think of it," he added, waving me out the door.

I nodded and then shook my head and covered my error with some return waving before I got into my car, but he was gone. I sat behind the steering wheel for a moment, trying not to actually put my head in my hands. Then I got out again, slowly, feeling the eyes of the building on me, and went back into the gallery. I walked deliberately past the paintings in the entryway, the platforms of glowing bowls and vases, the linen and wool tapestries. I went into the main hall and viewed one by one the student paintings hung on show there, reading the placards without remembering them, staring at the glaze of red, green, gold—trees, fruit, mountains, flowers, cubes, motorcycles, words, a jumble of work, some of it excellent, some of it surprisingly clumsy. I looked at every item until the colors whirled, and then, slowly, I went back to Robert's painting.

She was still there, of course, bending over her terrible burden, pressing the loosened floppy head with its bullet hole against the green curve of her breast, her own face concentrated with grief rather than slack, her jaw set against tears, her dark eyebrows drawn together in a fine, furious, unbelieving misery, her anger showing also in the line of her shoulder, her skirts still trembling from her swift movement: she had knelt on the dirty street and seized the precious body. She knew and loved the dead woman; this was no abstract mercy. It was an incredible painting. With all my training, I couldn't begin to figure out how Robert had conveyed such emotion, such motion, in paint; I could see some of the strokes he'd used, the blends of color, but the life with which he'd imbued the living woman and the lifelessness with which he portrayed the dead one were beyond my understanding. If it was a work of the imagination, that made it all the more horrifying. How could the college bear to have this image hanging in front of its students day after day?

I stood gazing at her until she seemed about to start up with a cry of anguish or a call for help, or run, or brace her lovely back and waist to try to raise and carry the heavy body. At any moment something might happen; that was the remarkable thing. He had caught the instant of shock, of total change, of disbelief. I put my hand to my throat and felt my own warmth there. I waited for her to lift her head. Would I—this was the question—would I be able to help her if she looked up? She was inches away from me, breathing and real, in the second of unreal calm before complete distress, and I knew myself powerless. I realized then, for the first time, what Robert had accomplished.

CHAPTER 40

Marlow

It took me hours, that afternoon, to make up my mind. By the time I reached Kate's door again, it was dark; I'd lost another day and would have to drive to DC starting early in the morning, drive hard to make an evening appointment. Instead of leaving Greenhill, I'd taken a restless walk and eaten dinner in town, then turned my wheels away from the Hadleys' mountain road, at the last moment, and back toward the other side of the valley. The trees loomed around me in Kate's neighborhood, and there were lights in the windows of the Tudor houses; a dog barked. I pulled slowly up her drive. It wasn't late, but it wasn't courteously early either. Why the hell hadn't I called ahead? What was I thinking? By then, however, I couldn't stop myself.

When I reached her porch, the light went on automatically, and I almost expected an alarm to sound. One lamp was lit in the living room. There was no other sign of life, although I could see a glow in the back rooms as well. I raised my hand to ring the bell, then changed my mind with my last bit of sense and knocked firmly instead. A shadow came out of the far interior doorway and approached—Kate, her delicate body passing into and again out of the lamplight, her hair glinting, her movements wary. She peered through the glass with a tense face and then, apparently recognizing me but all the more cautious because of that, came to the door and opened it slowly.

"I'm so sorry," I said. "I'm sorry to disturb you this late, and I haven't lost my mind—" Although I wasn't completely sure about that, and it sounded worse than if I hadn't said it, once it was out. "I'm leaving in the morning, you know, and—please show me the other paintings."

She let her hand drop from the door handle and turned her head to look fully at me. It was an expression of sorrow, of disdain, a last-straw look but full of an infinite patience as well. I stood my ground, losing hope every second. In a moment she would deny me, tell me I had indeed lost my mind, remark that she didn't know what I was talking about, that I had no real business here, that she wished I would leave. Instead, she moved aside to let me in.

The house was deeply peaceful, and I felt like the worst kind of intruder, clumsy and heavy-footed. At what cost had she created this peace? There was comfort around me, lamplight, perfect order, a gentle breathing of wood and flowers that could have been the breathing of the children themselves; presumably they were asleep upstairs, and their unseen vulnerability made me feel all the guiltier. I dreaded going up those stairs and hearing their actual soft sighs, but to my surprise Kate opened a door in the dining room instead and led me down steps: the basement. It smelled of dust, dry dirt, old dry wood. We went slowly down the stairway; despite one lightbulb overhead, I had the feeling that we were descending into darkness. The smell reminded me of something from my childhood—oddly pleasant, someplace I'd visited or played. Kate's slender shape moved ahead of me; I looked down on the top of her gold-brown head in that bare yet inadequate lighting, and she seemed to slip away from me into a dream. There was a woodpile in one corner, an ancient spinning wheel in another, plastic buckets, empty ceramic flowerpots.

Kate led me without words to a wooden cabinet at the other

end of the one room. I opened the door, still as if in a dream, and saw that it had been specially built to hold canvases neatly and separately, like a drying rack in a studio, and that it was full of paintings. She held the door ajar for me, her hand white against the wood. I reached in and carefully took out a painting in the thrumming dimness and set it against the wall nearby, then another, then the next, and another, until the cabinet was empty and eight big framed canvases stood against the walls. Some of these must have been from Robert's shows; I wondered if he'd sold many others there and to what homes and museums they'd gone.

The light was bad, as I mentioned, but that only made them more real. Seven of the paintings showed some version of the scene I'd encountered that afternoon at the Greenhill College gallery—my lady bent over a beloved corpse, sometimes a close-up of the two faces near each other, huge on the canvas, the still-young, strong-featured face hovering over the older ashen one. Sometimes it was a similar scene, but she had buried her sobs in the dead woman's neck as if drinking her blood or mixing it with her tears—melodramatic, yes, but also wrenchingly moving. In another she stood upright with a handkerchief pressed over her lips, the body at her feet, looking wildly around for help—was this the moment before or after the one depicted in the painting at Greenhill College? Over and over, the curly-haired woman was taken by surprise, horrified, grieving. The story never moved forward or backward; she was caught forever in that one event.

The eighth painting was the largest, and quite different, and Kate had already moved to stand in front of it. It was a full-length view of three women and a man, in a weirdly formal arrangement, breathtaking realism, with none of Robert's usual stamp of the nineteenth century—no, this one was unmistakably contemporary, like the sensuous painting I'd seen in Robert's home studio two floors above us. The man stood in the foreground, two of the women behind him to his right and one to his left, all four figures gravely facing the viewer and dressed in modern clothing. The three women wore jeans and pale silky shirts, the man a ripped sweater and khaki pants. I recognized all but one of them. The smallest of the women was Kate, her old-gold hair longer than she now wore it, her blue eyes wide and sober, every freckle in its place, her body upright. Beside her stood a woman I didn't know, also young, and much taller, long-legged, with straight reddish hair and a sharp face, her hands jammed in the front pockets of her jeans. Or had I seen her somewhere? Who could she be? To the man's left was a familiar figure, womanly under unfamiliar modern gray silk and faded denim, her feet bare, her strong face as I saw it in my dreams, her curly dark hair falling past her shoulders. Seeing her in the clothes of my own era made my heart contract with the possibility of actually finding her.

The man in the painting was Robert Oliver, of course. It was almost like having him present: his rumpled hair and worn clothes, his greenish eyes huge. He seemed only half aware of the women around him; he was his own main subject, the foreground, gazing out with flat resistance, refusing to relinquish anything of himself even to the viewer. Alone, in fact, despite the three Graces around him. It was an embarrassing painting, I thought—blatant, egocentric, puzzling. Kate stood staring at it almost the way she stood looking out of it, her eyes wide, her little body straight as a dancer's. I moved hesitantly over to her and stood against her shoulder, then put my arm around her. I meant only to comfort. She turned to me with something cynical in her expression, almost a smile.

"You didn't destroy them," I said.

She looked steadily up at me, not resisting my arm. She had the shoulders of a bird, hollow little bones. "Robert is a great artist. He was a pretty good father and a pretty bad husband, but I know he is great. It's not my place to destroy these."

There was nothing noble in her voice; it was a matter-of-fact, bald statement. Then she drew back, disengaging herself gracefully from my arm: closed door. She didn't smile. She smoothed her hair, staring at the largest painting.

"What will you do with them?" I said finally.

She understood. "Keep them until I know what to do."

This made so much sense that I didn't ask her further questions. It seemed to me that these disturbing images might one day put her children through college, if she handled them well. She helped me set the paintings back in their tracks, and we shut the door together. Finally I was following her again, up the wooden stairs, across the living room, and onto the porch. There we paused. "I don't mind what you do," she said. "Whatever you think is right." I knew this meant that I had her permission to eventually tell Robert that I had seen his wife, that I had not seen his children except in picture frames, that I had seen the gracious clean house in which he'd once lived, the paintings she was saving for a future she could not look far into.

Neither of us spoke for a moment, and then she stood a little taller—although not the stretch it must have been to Robert Oliver's cheek—and kissed me sedately. "Have a safe trip back," she said. "Drive carefully." She did not send any message.

I nodded, unable to speak, and went down the stairs, hearing her door close behind me for the last time. Once I was out on the road, I turned up my car radio, then switched it off and sang loudly into the silence, more loudly, thwacked my hand against the steering wheel. I could see Robert's paintings shining under the bare bulb, and I knew I might never view them again. But I had broken open my life, or perhaps she had done it for me.

Chapter 41

1878

The outside of his studio building in the rue Lamartine is unprepossessing. She sits looking at it from her carriage. She has told herself since yesterday that she will bring her maid up with her. But at the last minute, before leaving her house, she realizes she wants no witness at all. Her unnecessary note to the housekeeper explains that she will be calling on a friend and orders a tray to be taken up to her father-in-law at midday.

The facade of the building is thoroughly real, and she swallows hard under the bow of her bonnet; she has tied it too tightly. Late morning—the streets are full of the bustle of carriages, the heavy clopping of paired horses, the delivery wagons. Waiters push the chairs outside their cafés into straight lines, and an old woman sweeps up rubbish at the curb. Béatrice watches as the woman, who wears tattered gloves and a patched skirt, accepts a few coins from a man in a long apron and moves on down the street with broom and pail.

The note in Béatrice's little bag contains a street number and a sketch of the building. His invitation is to see a new large canvas, which he would like to send to the Salon jury next week, so that she must view it now or wait until then—and who knows if it will be accepted? It is a flimsy pretext; she will see the painting later with Yves, she knows, whether or not it is hung in the Salon. But Olivier has mentioned the submission several times, an unwieldy canvas, his uncertainty. The thought of the painting, his struggles with it, have become their mutual concern, almost a shared project. It is the portrait of a young woman, he has most recently told her. Béatrice dares not ask who she is—a model, no doubt. He has also thought about sending an earlier landscape instead. She knows all this and feels the pride of involvement, of being consulted—that is her thin justification for appearing alone there in a new bonnet. Besides, it is not as if she is going to see him at his home; he has only lured her to his studio, and perhaps there will be others there as well, taking refreshments and studying the paintings.

She excuses the carriage for an hour and lifts her skirts to descend. She has dressed herself in a walking suit the color of plums, and over it a cloak of blue wool trimmed with gray fur. Her bonnet goes with the cloak; it has the new shape for hats, in blue velvet lined with silver and heavy with blue silk forget-me-nots, chicory, lupine—marvelously real, like a hat decorated in a field. The mirror at home has told her that her cheeks are already flushed, her eyes bright with something like guilt.

She watches her own foot in black leather leave the carriage first, step onto the paving stones, avoiding some slimy water. This is a part of town where some of the troubles occurred, she realizes, and tries to imagine it eight years before, piled with barricades and perhaps even bodies, but her imagination will not quite be diverted; she is thinking only about the man waiting for her somewhere above. Can he see her? She is careful not to glance up again. With skirts gathered in one gloved hand, she makes her way to the entrance, knocks, then realizes that she must simply walk in—there is no servant to answer. Inside, a worn staircase leads her to the third floor, to his studio. None of the closed doors on the other floors open as she passes them. She stands looking at his name and catching her breath—her stays are tight—before knocking.

Olivier answers at once, as if he has been just behind the door, listening for her, and they regard each other without speaking. They have not been face-to-face in more than a week, and during that time something has deepened between them. Their eyes meet, inevitably, across this knowledge, and she sees that he is aware of the change. For her part, she feels the shock of his age, because she hasn't seen him recently and she knows him more and more as a man, objectively; he is handsome, only a little past middle age, but there are deep vertical lines from the corners of his nose to the corners of his mouth and beneath his eyes, and his hair is pale silver.

Under his face she sees the younger man he must once have been, and this young man gazes back at her as if through a mask he never wanted to wear, vulnerable and expressive, revealing eyes still bright—but not as they must once have been; they droop redly in the lower rims and their blue is compromised, diluted. He has combed his hair away from a pink parting, which she can see when he bows over her hand. His beard still has some brown in it, a warmth at the roots, and his lips are also warm as they touch the back of her hand. In their brief contact, she feels his essence—neither the boy in love looking out of his eyes nor the aging man. She feels instead the artist himself, ageless and in the midst of a long accumulated life. His presence goes through her like the unexpected sound of a bell, so that she cannot catch her breath after all.

"Please, come in," he says. "*Entrez, je vous en prie.* My studio." He does not call her "*tu.*" He holds the door for her, and she realizes now that he is wearing an old suit, shabbier than what she has seen him in before, with an open linen smock over the jacket. The sleeves of the smock are rolled back, as if they are too long even for him. His white shirt has a few spatters of paint on the breast, and his four-in-hand tie is black silk, also threadbare. He has not dressed up for her visit; he is allowing her to know him as he actually works. She passes into the room, noting that no one else is there, feeling his proximity at the door. He shuts it behind her gently, as if not wishing to draw attention to the point they both understand, the possible compromise to their two reputations. The door is shut. It is done. She wishes she felt more regret, more shame; she reminds herself that the outside world can still consider him merely a relative, a dignified elder who might well invite his nephew's wife to see a painting.

But it is as if instead of shutting a door he has opened one, making a long space of daylight and air between them. After a moment, he moves, saying, "May I take your cloak?"

She remembers the ordinary gestures, unties her bonnet and lifts it straight up and off so as not to disarrange the coils of her hair. She unfastens her cloak at the throat and folds it once, vertically, inside out, to protect the delicate fur. She hands him both, and he carries them away through another door. Standing alone in the studio, she feels the increased intimacy of a room without its occupant. It is full of light from long windows, clean inside and badly streaked on the outside, and there is an ornate skylight above her. She can hear the sounds of the street below—muffled thumps; rattling, screeching iron; horses' hooves—all so faint that there is no need for her to believe in its existence anymore, nor to think about her coachman taking a hot drink at a stable up the street, where perhaps he knows other coachmen and will not think of her for an hour. Olivier returns and gestures toward his paintings; she has deliberately not looked at them. "I have censored nothing," he says. "You are a fellow artist." He says it without ostentation, almost shyly, and she smiles and glances away.

"Thank you. You have done me an honor by leaving your studio as it is." But she needs some courage to view the paintings.

He points. "Here is the one that hung in the Salon last year. Perhaps you remember it, if I am not flattering myself." She remembers well; it is a landscape three or four hand-lengths across, a subtle piece, a floating field with a layer of white and yellow flowers on the surface, a cow grazing at the far edge, brown trees mixed with green. It is a little bit old-fashioned, rather in the style of Corot, she thinks, and chides herself—he paints the way he has always painted, and he is good. But it is another reminder of the years that separate them. "You like it, but you think it passé," he says.

"No, no," she protests, but he puts up a hand to stop her.

"Between friends," he says, "there can be only honesty." His eyes are very blue; why has she thought them old? Now they radiate a vigor that is better than mere youth.

"Very well," she says. "Then I like the bravery of this one more." She has turned to a large canvas standing on the floor. "Is that the one you will submit?"

"No, alas." He is laughing now—the reality of his body next to hers. As long as she doesn't actually look at him, she feels again the presence of the young man inside that body. "This one is a little too brave, as you say—they might not take it." The painting shows a tree in the foreground, a fellow in an elegant suit and hat seated beneath it on the grass, his legs crossed negligently and his long hands hanging down over his knee. It is done in a skillful perspective that makes her want to walk around behind the tree to see what is on the other side. The brushwork is more modern than that in the cow painting—here she can see an influence.

"This one shows an admiration of the work of Monsieur Manet?"

"A grudging admiration, my dear, yes. You have a sharp eye. At the Salon, they might say that it is offensive because it has no purpose."

"Who is the boy?"

"The son I never had." He speaks lightly, but she studies his face, feeling puzzled, afraid of revelations. "Oh, I simply think of him that way—my godson from Normandy, who lives in Paris now—I see him several times a year, and we go for a long walk or two. A dear boy, son of some young friends. He will make a good doctor in a few years—he studies incessantly. I am the only one who can get him out to the country for exercise, and I believe he thinks it does *me* good, his poor old godfather—that's why he goes, pretending to take my orders for his health. Thus each of us attempts to fool the other."

"It's very fine," she says in earnest.

"Ah, well." He touches her plum-colored sleeve. "Come, I'll show you the rest, and then we'll have some tea."

The other paintings are harder for her to look at, but she does it unflinchingly; models half-dressed, the back of a nude woman, graceful, unfinished—does that mean the woman will return to the studio one of these days and take off her clothes for him again? Has she ever been his lover? Isn't that the way of artists? She tries not to think of it except as a fellow painter, not to mind. Models are often women of loose conduct, as everyone knows, but she herself has come alone to a man's private rooms, his studio—is she any better? She hardens herself against her own fear and turns to examine his still lifes, fruit and flowers, which he explains are youthful works. To her they appear a little dull, but skillful, delicate; she sees the Old Masters. "I had been to Holland just before I painted these," he says. "I took them out the other day to see how they had held up. They are antiques, aren't they?"

She is careful not to answer. "And your submission for this year? Have I seen it?"

"Not yet." He crosses the long room, beyond the two shabby armchairs and little round table where, she assumes, he will serve tea. Leaning against the wall is a canvas draped in cloth, a large one; he has to lift it with both hands. He leans it against a chair. "You are sure you want to?"

For the first time she is frightened, almost afraid of the man himself, this familiar figure whom she understands now in a wholly new way because of his letters, his forthrightness, the revelation of himself, the strange response of her own heart as she stands at his shoulder. She turns to him questioningly but can't think of the question. Why is he hesitant to show her his painting? Perhaps it is a genuinely shocking nude or some other subject she can't imagine. She has a sense of her husband's presence, disapproving, his arms folded to indicate that she has gone too far. But Olivier has told her in his letter that Yves wants her to see this painting. She doesn't know what to think or say.

When Olivier lifts the sheet, she catches her breath, the sound audible to them both. It is her painting, her golden-haired maid seated at work, her own rose-colored sofa, the brushwork she tried to make loose and free and yet seeing, all-seeing. "You understand why I have chosen this one to submit to the Salon this year," he says. "It is by a better artist than I."

She puts her hands to her face, and her vision is smeared, embarrassingly, with tears. "What do you mean?" Her own voice sounds weak in her ears. "Are you playing with me?"

He turns to her, swift in his concern. "No, no—I didn't mean to offend you. I took it home with me last week, after you had said good night to us. You must let me submit it for you. Yves approves completely and asks only that you protect your privacy a little by using another name. But it is remarkable—you have merged in it something old and something very new. When you showed it to me, I understood that the jury must see this painting, even if it turns out to be too modern for them. I wanted only to persuade you."

"And Yves knows that you took it?" She somehow does not want to say her husband's name here, in this other man's rooms.

"Yes, of course. I asked him first, but not you—I knew he would say yes and you would say no."

"I do say no," she tells him, and the tears brim over and run down her face. She is humiliated, she who seldom cries, even in front of her husband. She can't explain how it feels to see this private painting in strange surroundings, or—above all—to hear it praised. She wipes her face, searches for a handkerchief in the velvet bag at her wrist. He has moved closer, pulling something from inside his jacket. Now he is carefully wiping her face—patting, drying, arranging with hands that have spent years holding brush and pencil and palette knife. He takes her elbows deliberately in his cupped palms, as if weighing them, and then he draws her toward him.

For the first time she puts her head against his neck, his cheek, feeling that it is permissible to both of them because he is comforting her. He strokes her hair and the back of her neck, and at his touch a network of cool strands runs down it. His fingertips move over the mass of braids at the back of her head, touching them without disturbing their meticulous arrangement, and his arm goes around her shoulders. He pulls her against his chest, so that she has to put one hand on his back to steady herself. He strokes her cheek, her ear; he has already come very close, so that his mouth finds her mouth before his hand does. His lips are warm and dry but rather thick, like softened leather, and his breath tastes of coffee and bread. She has been kissed many times, but only by Yves, so it is the alien nature of these new lips she understands first; only after that does she realize that these lips are more skilled than her husband's, more insistent.

The impossibility of his kissing her and of her wanting him

to kiss her puts a wave of heat into her face and down her neck, a fist clenching inside her, desire that she hasn't known before to associate with desire. He holds her by the upper arms now, as if afraid she will pull away. His grip is strong, and again she feels the years when she hasn't known him, when he built up that strength simply by living and working.

"I can't let you," she tries to say, but the words disappear under his lips, and she doesn't know whether she means that she can't let him send her painting to the Salon or that she can't let him kiss her. He is the one who gently puts her away from him. He is quivering, as nervous as she is.

"Forgive me." His words come out choked. His eyes hold hers but blindly. Now that she can look at him again, she sees he is indeed old. And brave, she realizes. "I didn't mean to offend you further. I have forgotten myself."

She believes him; he forgot himself, remembering only her. "You have not offended me," she says in a voice she can hardly hear herself, straightening her sleeves, her bag, her gloves. His handkerchief is at their feet. She can't stoop for it in her stays; she is afraid of losing her balance. He bends to pick it up, but instead of giving it to her again he tucks it slowly inside his jacket. "The fault is mine," he tells her. She finds herself staring at his shoes, brown leather, the tips a little worn, the edge of one spattered with yellow paint. She is seeing the shoes he works in, his real life.

"No," she murmurs. "I should not have come."

"Béatrice," he says. He picks up her hand seriously, formally. She remembers with sharp misery the moment when Yves asked her to marry him years ago, the same formality. They are, after all, uncle and nephew, so why would they not share gestures, family characteristics?

"I must leave," she says, trying to withdraw her hand, but he retains it.

"Before you go, please understand that I respect and love you. I am dazzled by you, by who you are. I will never ask anything of you except to kiss your feet. Allow me to tell you everything, just once." The intensity of his voice moves her, the contrast of it with his familiar face.

"You honor me," she says helplessly, looking around for her cloak and hat. She remembers that they are in the other room.

"I also love your painting, your instinct for art, and I love them apart from my love for you. You have a splendid gift." He speaks more calmly this time. She realizes that, in spite of the nature of the moment, he is sincere. He is sad, earnest—a man time has already left behind, and who has little time left. He stands before her a moment longer and then disappears into the next room for her things. She ties the bonnet on with shaking fingers; he holds the cloak carefully around her while she buttons it at her throat.

When she turns back, there is such loss in his face that she goes to him without allowing herself to think. She kisses his cheek, pauses, then his mouth, swiftly. To her regret, it already feels and tastes familiar. "I really must go," she says. Neither of them mentions tea or her painting. He holds the door open for her, bowing in silence. She clutches the balustrade all the way down the stairs to the street. She listens for the sound of his door closing but does not hear it; perhaps he is still standing in the open doorway at the top of the building. Her carriage will not return for at least another half hour, so she must either walk up to the stables at the end of the block or find a hansom to take her home. She leans against the front of his building for a moment, feeling the facade through her glove, trying to steady her mind. Succeeding.

But later, when she sits alone on her sunporch, trying to make everything simple, the kiss returns, fills the air around her. It floods the high windows, the carpet, the folds of her dress, the pages of her book. "Please understand that I respect and love you." She cannot make the kiss disappear. By the next morning she no longer wants it to. She means no harm—she will do no harm—but she wants to keep that moment with her as long as she can.

CHAPTER 42

Marlow

Before dawn, I loaded the car and daydreamed my way up into Virginia, along highways whose embankments had gotten even greener since my trip down. It was a softly chill day, rain falling for a few minutes and then ceasing, falling and ceasing, and I began to long for home. I went straight to my one late appointment at Dupont Circle. The patient talked; out of long habit, I asked the right questions, I listened, I adjusted a prescription, I let him go, confident in my decisions.

When I reached my apartment in the dark, I unpacked quickly, heated a can of soup. After the Hadleys' dreary cottage—I could admit it now; I would have torn the place down in a minute and put up something with twice as many windows—my rooms were pristine, welcoming, the lamps perfectly adjusted on each painting, the linen curtains smooth from last month's dry cleaning. The place smelled of mineral spirits and oil paint, something I don't usually notice unless I've been away for a few days, and of the narcissus blooming in the kitchen; it had burst out while I was gone, and I watered it gratefully—careful, however, not to overwater. I went to my father's old set of encyclopedias and put my hand on one spine, then stopped myself. There would be time; I took a hot shower instead, turned out the lights, and went to bed.

*

The next day was busy: my staff at Goldengrove needed me more than ever because I'd been away; some of my patients had not done as well as I'd hoped and the nurses seemed cranky; my desk was covered with paperwork. I managed in the first few hours to stop by Robert Oliver's room. Robert was sitting in a folding chair at the edge of the counter that served as a desk and supply shelf, sketching. His letters lay next to him, arranged in two piles; I wondered how he'd divided them. He closed his sketchbook when I came in and turned to look at me. I took this as a good sign; sometimes he ignored my presence altogether whether he was working or not, and he could keep this up for disconcertingly long periods. His expression was weary and raw, and his eyes shifted from his recognition of my face to a contemplation of my clothes.

I wondered, for perhaps the hundredth time, if his silence was allowing me to underestimate the degree to which his illness currently affected him; possibly it was much more serious than I could judge by observing him, however closely. I also wondered if he could possibly have guessed where I'd been, and I considered settling down in the big chair and asking him to clean his brush and sit on the bed opposite me, to listen while I gave him news of his ex-wife. I could say, *I know that when you first kissed her, you lifted her off the floor.* I could say, *There are still cardinals at your bird feeder, and the mountain laurel is beginning to bloom.* I could tell him, *I know even better now that you are a genius.* Or I could ask, *What does "Étretat" mean to you?*

"How are you, Robert?" I stayed in the doorway.

He turned back to his drawing.

"Fine. Well, I'm off to see some other folks." Why had I used that word? I'd never liked it. I made a quick scan of the room. Nothing seemed different, dangerous, or disturbed. I wished him good sketching, pointing out that the day promised to be sunny, and left him with as genuine a smile as I could manage, although he wasn't looking.

I fought my way through rounds until the end of the day and stayed late to catch up at my desk. When the day staff was gone and dinner had already been served to the patients and was being cleared away, I shut my office door and locked it, then sat down at the computer.

And saw what I'd begun to remember. It was a coastal town in Normandy, in an area much painted during the nineteenth century, particularly by Eugène Boudin and his restless young protégé, Claude Monet. I found the familiar images—Monet's tremendous rough cliffs, the famous arch of rock on the beach. But Étretat had apparently attracted other painters—lots of them, including Olivier Vignot and even Gilbert Thomas of the self-portrait with coins in the National Gallery; they had both painted that coastline. Almost every painter who could afford to get on one of the new northern railway lines had gone out and had a crack at Étretat, it seemed—the masters and the minor ones, the weekend painters and the society watercolorists. Monet's cliffs rose above all the others in the history of paintings of Étretat, but he'd been part of a tradition.

I found a recent photograph of the town; the great arch looked as it had in the Impressionists' day. There were still wide beaches with boats pulled up and overturned on them, cliffs green on top with grass, little streets lined with elegant old hotels and houses, many of which might have been there when Monet was painting a few yards away. None of this seemed in any way related to the scrawl on Robert Oliver's wall, except perhaps through his personal library of works on France, where he would surely have come across the name of the town and some depictions of its dramatic setting. Had he been there himself, to experience "joy"? Perhaps on the trip to France that Kate had mentioned? I wondered again if he might be mildly delusional. Étretat was a dead end, a beautiful one, the cliff on my screen arching down toward the Channel, disappearing into the water. Monet had painted an astonishing number of views of it, and Robert, unless I'd missed something, had painted none.

The next day was Saturday, and I took a run in the morning, just to the National Zoo and back, thinking about my glimpse of those mountains around Greenhill. Leaning against the gates, stretching my tight hamstrings, I thought for the first time that I might never be able to make Robert well. And how would I know when to stop trying?

CHAPTER 43

Marlow

The Wednesday morning after my run to the zoo, there was a letter with a Greenhill return address in the upper corner of the envelope waiting for me at Goldengrove. The handwriting was neat, feminine, organized—Kate. I went into my office without stopping to see Robert or any other patients first, shut the door, and took out my letter opener, which had been a gift from my mother on my graduation from college; it often occurred to me that I shouldn't keep such a treasure in my rather public office, but I liked to have it near me. The letter was one page and, unlike the address on the envelope, typed.

Dear Dr. Marlow:

I hope this finds you well. Thank you for your visit to Greenhill. If I was of any assistance to you or (indirectly) to Robert, I'm glad. I don't feel I can continue our communication much, and I'm sure you'll understand. I valued our meeting and am still thinking about it, and I believe that if anyone can help Robert, it will be someone like you.

There was one thing I did not give you while you were here, partly for personal reasons, and partly because I didn't know if it would be ethical, but I've decided I do want you to have it. It's the last name of the woman who wrote Robert the letters I told you about. I didn't tell you then that one of them was written on a piece of stationery, and it had her full name at the top. She was a painter, too, as I mentioned to you, and her name was Mary R. Bertison. This is still a very painful topic for me, and I wasn't sure I wanted to share this detail with you, or if it might even be wrong for me to do so. But if you are going to seriously try to help him, I feel I have to give you her name. Perhaps you will be able to find out something about who she was, although I'm not sure exactly how that could be useful.

I wish you all the best in your work, and especially in your efforts to help Robert.

Yours truly,
Kate Oliver

It was a generous, upright, irritable, awkward, kind letter; I could hear in every line Kate's determination, her decision to do what she thought was right. She would have been sitting at her table in the upstairs library, maybe in the early morning, typing her way stubbornly through her pain, sealing the letter before she could change her mind, making tea in the kitchen afterward, affixing the stamp. She would have been grieved by her own exertions on Robert's behalf, and yet satisfied with herself—I could see her in neat-fitting top and jeans, sparkling jewels in her ears, setting the letter on a tray by the front door, going to wake the children, saving her smile for them. I felt a sudden pang of loss.

But the letter was the same—the closed door I'd observed before, even if it opened another one, and I had to respect her wishes. I typed a brief response, grateful and professional, and sealed it in an envelope for my staff to mail. Kate had offered me no e-mail address, nor had she used the one on the card I'd handed her in Greenhill; apparently she wanted only this official, slower communication between us, an actual missive crossing the country on an anonymous tide of correspondence. All of it sealed. It was what we might have done in the nineteenth century, I thought, this polite, secret exchange on paper, conversation at a remove. I put Kate's letter away in my personal files rather than in Robert's chart.

The rest was surprisingly easy, not a detective story at all. Mary R. Bertison lived in the DC limits, and her full name was listed, bold and clear, in the phone book, which said she resided on 3rd Street, Northeast. In other words, as I'd suspected, she was quite possibly alive. It was strange to me to see this artifact of silent Robert Oliver's life lying out in the open. There could, I supposed, be more than one woman with this name in the city, but I doubted it. After lunch I phoned the number from my desk, my door shut once more against other eyes and ears. Mary Bertison might, I thought, be at home, since she was a painter; on the other hand, if she was a painter she probably had a day job, as I did—in my case, the little matter of my being a licensed doctor of medicine fifty-five hours a week. Her line rang five or six times. My hope diminished with each ring—I wanted to catch her by surprise—and an answering machine clicked on. "You have reached Mary Bertison at—," a female voice said firmly. The voice was a pleasant one, made a little harsh, perhaps, by the necessity of recording a phone message, but firm on the ear, an educated alto.

It occurred to me now that she might actually respond better to a courteous message than to a startling live call, and it would give her time to think over my request. "Hello, Ms. Bertison. This is Dr. Andrew Marlow—I'm an attending psychiatrist at Goldengrove Residential Center in Rockville. I'm currently working with a patient who I understand is a friend of yours, a painter, and I wondered if you might be willing to give us a little assistance."

That careful "us"—it made me flinch in spite of myself. This was hardly a team project. And the message itself was enough to worry her, if she still considered him a close friend, at the least. But if he'd lived with her, or come to Washington to be with her, as Kate suspected, why on earth hadn't she turned up at Goldengrove herself by now? On the other hand, the papers hadn't reported his being placed in psychiatric care. "You can call me here at the center most weekdays, and I will get back to you as soon as possible. The number is—" I gave it clearly, added my pager information, and hung up.

Then I went to see Robert, feeling in spite of myself as if I had visible blood on my hands. Kate hadn't told me not to mention Mary Bertison to him, but when I reached his room I was still thinking about whether or not to do this. I had called someone who might not otherwise ever have learned that Robert was in psychiatric care. *You can even talk with Mary,* he had told me contemptuously on his first day at Goldengrove. He had said nothing more, however, and there must be twenty million Marys in the United States. He might remember exactly what he'd said. But would I have to explain where I'd gotten her last name?

I knocked and called in to him, although his door was slightly open. Robert was painting, standing calmly at the easel with his brush raised and his great shoulders relaxed and natural; I wondered for a moment if he'd experienced some recovery over the last few days. Did he really need to be here just because he wouldn't speak? Then he looked up with a frown, and I saw the red in his eyes, the stark misery that came over his face at the sight of me.

I sat down in the armchair and spoke before I could lose my nerve. "Robert, why don't you simply tell me about it?"

It came out sounding more like frustration than I'd intended. He seemed startled, to my sneaking pleasure—at least I'd gotten a response. But I was less pleased to see a faint smile of what I took to be triumph, conquest, touch his lips, as if my question proved he'd flushed me out again.

In fact, that made me mad as hell after a moment, and perhaps precipitated my decision. "You could tell me, for example, about Mary Bertison. Have you thought about getting in touch with her? Or, a better question—why hasn't she been here to see you?"

He started forward, raising his hand with the brush in it before controlling himself again. His eyes were huge, full of that choked intelligence I'd seen in them the day we'd met, before he'd learned to veil it in my presence. But he could not respond without losing at his own game, and he managed to say nothing. I felt a twinge of pity; he'd painted himself into this corner, and now he had to sit there. If he spoke even of his rage at me, or at the world, or possibly at Mary Bertison—or asked me how I knew about her—he would give up the only piece of privacy and power he'd kept for himself: the right to remain silent in the face of his torment. "All right," I said—gently, I hoped. Yes, I was sorry for him, but I knew he would take an extra advantage now as well; he would have ample time in which to ponder and guess at my activities, the possible sources of my knowledge of Mary Bertison's last name. I considered assuring him that I would let him know myself, if and when I found his particular Mary, and what, if anything, she communicated to me.

But I had already given away so much that I decided to keep my own counsel again; if he could, so could I. I sat with him in silence another five minutes, while he fiddled with the brush in his big hand and stared at the canvas. Finally, I got up. I turned at the door for a second, almost repenting; his rumpled head was bent, his eyes on the floor, and his misery went through me in a wave. It followed me, in fact, down the hall and to the rooms of my other, more ordinary (I confess that was my feeling, although it's not a word I like to apply to any case) patients with their more ordinary derangements.

*

I had patients to see all afternoon, but most of them were reasonably stable, and I drove home with a feeling of satisfaction, almost contentment. The haze over Rock Creek Parkway was golden, and the water glinted in its bed as I took each curve. It seemed to me that a painting I'd been working at all week ought to be set aside for a while; it was a portrait from a photograph of my father, and the nose and mouth simply weren't right, but perhaps if I worked on something else for a few days I could come back to it with more success. I had some tomatoes—not much good for eating at this season, but sufficiently luminous—that wouldn't spoil for a week. If I set them in the window of my studio, they might constitute a kind of updated Bonnard, or—if I wanted to be less self-denigrating about it—a new Marlow. The light was the problem, but I could catch a little evening sunshine after work now that the days were longer, and if I could muster the energy I might get up even earlier and start a morning canvas as well.

I was already thinking about colors and the placement of the tomatoes, so that I hardly remembered swinging my car into the garage, a dank space under my apartment building whose rent costs nearly half the apartment's. Every now and then I wished for another job, one I didn't have to drive to regularly alongside all of bad-tempered suburban DC, so that I could give up my car. But how could I leave Goldengrove? And the idea of sitting in the office at Dupont Circle full-time with patients well enough to walk in there for counsel did not appeal to me.

My mind was full of these things—my still life, the sunset glancing off the trickle of Rock Creek, the tempers of my fellow drivers—and my hands were occupied fishing out my keys; I took, as always, the stairs, for extra exercise. I didn't see her until I was nearly at my own door. She stood leaning against the wall as if she'd been there awhile, relaxed and yet impatient, her arms folded, her boots braced. As I remembered, she wore jeans and a long white shirt, this time with a dark blazer over them, her hair mahogany in the bad lighting of the hall. I was so astonished that I stopped "in my tracks"; I knew then, and would know ever after, what that phrase really meant.

"You," I said, but it did not begin to undo my confusion. She was without a doubt the girl from the museum, the one who had smiled conspiratorially at me in front of the Manet still life at the National Gallery, the one who had studied the Gilbert Thomas *Leda* with attention and smiled at me again on the sidewalk. I had thought of her perhaps once, perhaps twice, and then forgotten about her. Where had she come from? It was as if she lived in a different realm, like a fairy or an angel, and had reappeared without any passage of time, without human explanations.

She stood straight and put out her hand. "Dr. Marlow?"

Chapter 44

Marlow

"Yes," I said, balanced there with my keys hanging limp in my fingers, my other hand uncertain in hers. I was struck by the muted ferocity in her manner, and again, inevitably, by her looks. She was as tall as I was, somewhere in her thirties, lovely and yet not in any conventional way; she was a presence. The light shone on her hair, her bangs cut too straight and too short across her white forehead, the long, smooth purple-red wave of the rest of it falling far past her shoulders. Her grip on my hand was strong, and I instinctively tightened mine to meet it.

She smiled a little, as if seeing things from my point of view. "I'm sorry I startled you. I'm Mary Bertison."

I couldn't stop staring at her. "But you were at the museum. The National Gallery." And then a moment of disappointment washing over even my confusion: she was not the curly-haired muse of Robert's dream life. Another wash of wonder: I had also seen her recently in a painting, dressed in her blue jeans and a loose silk shirt.

Now she frowned, clearly confused in turn, and dropped my hand.

"I mean," I repeated, "we've met once already, more or less. In front of *Leda,* and that Manet still life, you know, with the glasses and the fruit." I felt foolish. Why had I thought she would remember me? "I see—you—yes, you must have gone to see Robert's painting. That is, Gilbert Thomas's painting."

"I do remember you now," she said slowly, and it was clear that she wasn't a woman to lie about this, to flatter. She stood straight, unabashed at having invaded my very home, gazing at me. "You smiled, and then outside—"

"Did you go there to see Robert's painting?" I repeated.

"Yes, the one he tried to stab." She nodded. "I had just found out about it, because someone gave me the article a few weeks late—a friend happened on it. I don't usually read the papers." Then she laughed, not bitterly but with a kind of amusement at the strangeness of the situation, as if she found it fitting. "How funny. If you'd known or I'd known—who the other was—we could have talked right there instead."

I collected myself and unlocked the door. It was without question unorthodox for me to have a discussion about a patient in my own apartment—in fact, I knew it wasn't a good idea, letting in this attractive stranger—but hospitality and curiosity were getting the better of me already. I had called her, after all, and she had appeared almost at once, as if magically summoned. "How did you find my apartment?" Unlike her, I wasn't listed in the phone directory.

"The internet—it wasn't difficult, once I had your name and number."

I ushered her in ahead of me. "Please. Now that you're here, we might as well talk."

"Yes, otherwise we'd be throwing away a second opportunity." Her teeth were creamy and bright. I remembered now that jaunty poise, her balance in boots and jeans, the delicate blouse under her jacket, as if she were part cowboy and part fine lady.

"Please sit down and give me a minute to organize myself. Can I get you some tea? Juice?" I decided to ameliorate my having invited her in by at least not pouring her any alcohol, although I was beginning to long uncharacteristically for a drink myself.

"Thank you," she said with great politeness, and sat as gracefully as a guest in a Victorian drawing room, arranging herself with a single neat motion in one of my linen chairs, her boots crossed, feet tucked to one side, hands thin and elegant in her lap. She was a puzzle. I noticed the educated sound of her speech, as I had noticed it in her answering machine message, her deliberate, refined way of speaking. Her voice was soft but also firm and carrying. A teacher, I thought again. She followed me with her eyes. "Yes, some juice, please, if it's no trouble."

I went into the kitchen and poured two glasses of orange juice, all I had on hand, and put a few crackers on a plate. As I returned with the tray balanced before me, I remembered Kate serving me in her living room in Greenhill, letting me carry the salmon in to the lunch table. And later giving me this strange, graceful girl's last name, the key to finding her.

"I wasn't a hundred percent certain I had the right Mary Bertison," I said, handing her a glass. "But if you hang around in front of paintings Robert Oliver has tried to slash, that can't be coincidence."

"Of course not." She sipped her juice, set down the glass, faced me with pleading in her eyes for the first time, the bravado gone. "I'm sorry I'm intruding on you like this. I haven't had firsthand news of Robert in almost three months, and I was worried—" She did not add "brokenhearted," but I wondered, from the sudden control she seemed to be exercising over her mobile face, if this might be a better adjective. "I certainly wasn't going to get in touch with him myself. We'd had a big fight, you see. I thought he'd just shut himself away somewhere to work, to ignore me, and that I'd hear from him eventually. I was worried for weeks and then very surprised when I got your message, and since it was already the end of the workday I realized I wouldn't catch you at Goldengrove and wouldn't sleep all night if I couldn't get some news from you."

"Why didn't you try my pager?" I asked. "Not that I'm sorry to have this chance to speak with you—I'm very glad you showed up."

"Are you?" I saw that she forgave me, in turn, for being glib. Robert Oliver certainly chose interesting women. She smiled. "I did try your pager number, but if you check it, you'll discover it's turned off."

I checked; she was right. "I'm sorry," I said. "I try never to let that happen."

"This is better anyway, that we can talk in person." The quiver was gone, the self-confidence back, the smile breaking forth. "Please tell me Robert's all right. I'm not asking to see him—in fact, I really don't want to. I just want to know he's safe."

"He's safely under our care, and I think he's all right," I reported cautiously. "For now, and as long as he's with us. But he's also been depressed and sometimes agitated. What concerns me most is his lack of cooperation. He won't speak."

She appeared to take this in, biting the inside of her cheek for a few seconds and staring at me. "Not at all?"

"Never. Well, the first day, a little. In fact, one of the few things he said to me that day was 'You can even talk with Mary if you want.' That's why I felt at liberty to call you."

"That's all he's ever said about me?"

"It's more than he's said about almost anyone else. It's almost all he's ever said in my presence. He mentioned his ex-wife as well."

She nodded. "And that's how you found me, because he mentioned me."

"Not exactly." I took the plunge, on instinct. "Kate told me your last name."

It did startle her, and to my astonishment her eyes filled with tears. "That was good of her," she said brokenly. I got up and fetched her a tissue. "Thank you."

"Do you know Kate?"

"In a way. I've seen her only once, briefly. She didn't know who I was, but I knew who she was. You know, Robert told me once that some of Kate's family were Quakers from Philadelphia, like mine. Our grandparents could have known each other, or our great-grandparents. Isn't that strange? I liked her," she added, patting her lashes dry.

"I did, too." I hadn't expected to say this.

"You've met her? Is she here?" She looked around, as if expecting Robert's ex-wife to join us.

"No, not in Washington. In fact, she hasn't come to see Robert at all. No one has been to visit him."

"I always knew he would end up alone." This time her voice was matter-of-fact, a little hard, and she tucked the tissue into the pocket of her jeans, straightening her leg to make room for it. "He can't really love anyone, you know, and in the end such people are always alone, no matter how much other people once loved them."

"You loved him? Or love him?" I asked, matter-of-fact myself, but in as kind a voice as I could manage.

"Oh yes. Of course. He's remarkable." She said this as if it were an identifying characteristic, like brown hair or big ears. "Don't you think so?"

I finished my juice. "I've seldom met anyone so gifted. That's one reason I want to see him make progress, get better. But I'm confused about something—several things. Why didn't you know sooner he'd vanished, or where he'd gone? Didn't he live with you?"

She nodded. "Yes, when he came to Washington. It was wonderful at first, being with him all the time, and then he began to have regrets, to be silent for long periods, to be angry with me about small things. I think he was sorry—in some terrible way he couldn't express—that he'd left his family, and I guess he knew he couldn't go back even if his wife would take him. He wasn't happy with her, you know," she added simply, and I wondered if this were wishful thinking on her part. "We broke up months ago. Now and then he called me, or we tried to have dinner or go to a gallery show or a movie, but it never worked—deep down I just wanted him to come back, and he always figured that out and vanished again. I finally gave up, because that was better for me—it brought me some peace of mind, at least a little. It helped that we had a huge fight just before the last time he left—we fought partly about art, although it was really about us."

She raised one hand, a gesture of resignation. "I believed that if I left him alone, he might eventually call me himself, but he didn't. The problem with someone like Robert is that he's an impossible act to follow. You can't imagine ever wanting anyone else, because everyone begins to seem kind of pale by contrast, kind of dull. I told Robert that once, that he was an unfollowable act, with all his faults, and he laughed. But then it turned out to be true."

She drew a heavy breath. Her sadness, when it surfaced, made her look ten years younger, girlish, not older or more tired—an odd trick. She was young enough, surely, to be my daughter, at least if I'd married and had a daughter at twenty, like some of my high-school classmates. "So you hadn't seen him in—how long, before he was arrested?"

"About three months. I didn't even know where he was living by then—I still don't. Sometimes he borrowed friends' apartments or slept on their sofas, I think, and probably sometimes he stayed in fleabags downtown. He didn't have a cell phone—he hates them—and I never knew how to reach him. Did he stay in touch with Kate, do you know?"

"I'm not sure," I admitted. "He seems to have called her a few times to talk with the children, but that was all. I think he was having a gradual breakdown, isolating himself, which probably culminated in this idea of attacking a painting. The police contacted her when he was arrested." I noted as if from a distance that I no longer felt I was breaking patient confidentiality when I talked with Robert's women.

"Is he really ill?" She said "ill," I noticed, rather than "sick" or "crazy."

"Yes, he's ill," I said, "but I'm optimistic about his getting quite a bit better if he'll only talk and participate more fully in his own treatment. A patient has to want to get well, at some important level, in order for that to happen."

"That's true of everything," she said pensively, which made her seem younger than ever.

"Were you aware while you were living with him that he was suffering from psychological problems?" I handed her the plate of crackers, and she accepted one but held it in both hands instead of eating.

"No. Vaguely. I mean, I didn't think of them as psychological. I knew he took medication from time to time if he got upset or anxious about things, but a lot of people do, and he said that it helped him sleep. He never told me he had any serious problems. He certainly never mentioned having any breakdowns in the past—I don't think he'd had a real one, ever, or he would have said something about it, because we were very close." She made this last assertion a little belligerently, as if I might choose to contradict her statement. "I suppose I just saw certain problems emerge without knowing what they were."

"What did you see?" I took a cracker myself. It had been a long day, with this confusing denoucment outside my apartment door. And it wasn't over yet. "Did you notice anything that worried you?"

She mused and brushed a strand of hair back with one hand. "He was unpredictable, most of all. Sometimes he would say he'd be home for dinner and then stay out all night, and sometimes he would say he was going to go to a play or an opening with a friend and then never move from the sofa—he'd just sit there reading a magazine and fall asleep, and I didn't dare ask him what the friend waiting for him would think. I got to the point where I was afraid to ask him any of his plans, because he was always irritable about such questions, and I was also afraid to make plans with him because he might change his mind at the last minute. I thought in the beginning that it was just that we were both used to having a lot of freedom, but I didn't like being left in the lurch. I disliked it even more if we had planned something with other people and he left them in the lurch as well. You see what I mean."

She fell silent, and I nodded encouragement until she went on. "For example, once we made a date for him to meet my sister and her husband, who were in town for a conference, and Robert simply never showed up at the restaurant. I had an entire dinner with them, and every bite of it was worse than the last. My sister is very organized and practical, and I think she was astonished. She didn't act very surprised later when Robert left me and she had to mop me up over the phone. After that dinner, I came home and found Robert asleep on our bed with his clothes on, and I shook him awake, but he didn't remember anything about the dinner plan. He refused to talk about it even the next day, or to admit he'd done anything wrong. He refused to talk about his feelings in general. Or to admit mistakes."

I refrained from repeating her insistence that they'd been

very close. She drooped over her cracker and finally ate it, as if the memory made her hungry, then wiped her fingers delicately on the napkin I'd given her. "How could he have been so rude? I invited him to meet my sister and brother-in-law because I thought we were serious—he and I. He'd told me he'd left his wife, that she no longer wanted him to stay anyway, and that he felt we would be together a long time. Later he told me she'd filed for a divorce and he'd complied. It's not that we talked about marriage. I've never wanted to actually get married to anyone—I'm not sure I see the point, since I don't think I want children—but Robert was my soul mate, for want of a better word."

I thought her eyes might fill with tears again; instead she shook her glossy head, defiant, disillusioned, angry. "Why am I telling you all this? I came here to get information about Robert, not give you my private life." Then she was smiling again, but sadly, at her hands. "Dr. Marlow, you could get a stone to talk."

I started; it was my friend John Garcia's line for me, the compliment I most valued, one of the cornerstones of our long friendship. I had never heard it on anyone else's lips. "Thank you. And I wasn't trying to draw out of you anything you don't want to tell me. But what you've shared with me already is very useful."

"Let's see." She gave a real smile, jaunty again, amused in spite of herself. "You now know that Robert was taking some sort of medication before he reached you, if you didn't know that already, and you feel a little better because you know that Robert refused to talk about his feelings even to the woman he lived with, so you haven't really failed."

"Madame, you are frightening," I said. "And correct." I didn't see any reason to mention to her that I'd learned these things from Kate as well.

She laughed aloud. "So tell me now about your Robert, since I've told you about mine."

I told her then, honestly and thoroughly, and with a more tangible sense of breaking patient confidentiality, which I certainly was. I did not tell her, of course, anything Kate had told me, but I described much of Robert's behavior since he'd come to me. The means—telling her all this—would have to justify the ends; I had a great deal more to ask her and ask of her, and with a person so acute, so intense, I would have to pay up front for the privilege. I finished by assuring her that we watched Robert carefully at Goldengrove and that I felt he was safe at the moment, and that he didn't seem inclined to hurt himself or anyone else, even if he had gotten there by trying to stab a painting.

She listened with attention and without interrupting to ask questions. Her eyes were large and clear, candid, a strange color like water, as I remembered from the museum, with a darker rim around them that might be skillful makeup. She could have gotten a stone to talk, too, and I told her so.

"Thank you—that's an honor," she said. "I thought for a while of becoming a therapist, to tell you the truth, but it was a long time ago."

"Instead you're an artist and a teacher," I hazarded. She sat looking at me. "Oh, that wasn't so difficult to figure out. I saw you studying the surface of *Leda* at an oblique angle, very close—normally only a painter does that, or possibly an art historian. I don't picture you in the purely academic role—that would bore you—so you must teach painting itself, or do something else visual to support yourself, and you have the confidence of the born teacher. Am I being impertinent yet?"

"Yes," she said, clasping her hands on her jean-clad knee. "And you are an artist, too—you grew up in Connecticut, and that painting over your mantel there is by you, with the church from your small town. It's a good painting, you're serious, and you have talent, as you know perfectly well. Your father was a minister, but a rather progressive one who would have been proud of you even if you hadn't gone to medical school. You have a special interest in the psychology of creativity and the disorders that plague many creative or even brilliant people such as Robert, which is why you've thought about making him the subject of your next article. You're an unusual mix of the scientist and the artist yourself, so you understand such people, although you hang on to your own sanity very efficiently. Exercise helps—you run or work out, and have for years, which is why you look ten years younger than you are. You like order and logic, and they sustain you, so it doesn't matter as much that you live alone and work such long hours."

"Stop!" I said, putting my hands over my ears. "How do you know all that?"

"The internet, of course. Your apartment, and observing you. And your painting is initialed in the lower right corner, you know. Put the information from those sources together, and that's what you get. Besides, Sir Arthur Conan Doyle was my favorite writer when I was a little girl."

"One of mine, too." I thought about holding her hand, with its long ringless fingers.

She hadn't stopped smiling. "Do you remember how Sherlock Holmes once read someone's whole character and profession—his history—from a walking stick the man left in his rooms? And I have an entire apartment to work with, here. Holmes didn't have the internet either."

"I think you can help me help Robert more than anyone," I said slowly. "Would you be willing to tell me all of your experiences with him?"

"All?" She was not quite looking at me.

"I'm sorry. I meant everything you think would be helpful to someone trying to understand him." I didn't give her time to refuse yet, or accept. "Do you know about the painting he stabbed?"

"*Leda*? Yes. Well, a little. Some of it is just a guess, but I did look it up."

"What are you doing for dinner, Ms. Bertison?"

She put her head to one side and touched her mouth with her fingertips as if surprised to find a bit of smile still there. When she turned her face, the smudges under her crystalline eyes deepened, gray-blue, shadows on snow, an *effet de neige*. Her skin was very pale. She sat upright in her blazer, her beautiful hips and legs in faded jeans against my sofa, her slim shoulders raised against a blow. This young woman had grieved for weeks, months even, and she didn't have two children to comfort her. Again, I felt that ugly anger toward Robert Oliver, the sudden extinction of my physician's objective caring.

But she was not angry. "For dinner? Nothing, as usual." She folded her hands. "It's fine as long as we split the bill. But don't ask me to talk about Robert any more for now. I'd rather write some of it down, if that's all right with you, so that I don't end up crying in front of a complete stranger."

"I'm only a stranger," I said, "not a *complete* stranger—don't forget that we went to the museum together."

She sat facing me across the twilight of my living room—she was right, it was all very orderly, logical, and in a moment I would stand up to turn on another lamp, would ask her if I could get her anything more before we left, would excuse myself to use the bathroom, would wash my hands and find a light coat. At dinner we would surely talk about Robert at least a little, but also about painting and painters, our childhoods with Conan Doyle, our ways of making a living. And we would, I hoped, talk about Robert Oliver anyway, this time and in the future. Her eyes were expressive—not happy but faintly interested in what they saw across the room, and I had at least two hours at the finest table in walking distance to make her smile.

1878

Ma chère:

Forgive, please, my inexcusable behavior. It came out of no premeditation, no lack of respect, believe me, but rather from a longing that only you have had the power to awaken, in recent years. You may one day understand how a man who faces the end of life can forget himself completely for a moment, can think only of the sudden increase of what he must lose. I have meant no dishonor to you, and you must know already that my motives for inviting you to see the painting were pure. It is an extraordinary work; I know you will do many more, but please do permit me, by way of atonement and apology, to allow the jury to see this first great one. I do not think they will fail to recognize its delicacy, subtlety, and grace, and if they are foolish enough not to accept it, it will still have had a chance to be seen, if only by the jurors. I shall do whatever you command me in the way of using your name or changing it. Indulge me in this so that I may feel I have done your gift—and you—some small service.

For my part, I've decided to submit the painting of my young friend, since you admired it, but that, of course, will be under my own name and has an even greater chance of rejection. We must brace ourselves.

Your humble servant,

O.V.

Chapter 45

Mary

There are some things about my time with Robert Oliver that I have never been able to set straight even for myself, and that I would still like to set straight if such an act is possible. Robert said during one of our final arguments that our relationship had been twisted from the beginning because I had taken him away from another woman. This was terribly, patently untrue, but it was certainly true that he was already married when I fell in love with him the first time, and still married when I fell in love with him the second.

This morning I told my sister, Martha, that a doctor had asked me to tell him everything I could think of about Robert, and she said, "Well, Mary, here's your chance to talk about him for twenty-five hours without annoying anybody." I said, "You of all people won't have to read it." I don't blame her for this caustic, loving remark—at the worst point, her shoulder caught most of my tears over Robert Oliver. She's an excellent sister, a long-suffering one. Maybe Robert would have done me more harm than he did if she hadn't helped me get away from him. On the other hand, if I'd followed her advice, I might not have experienced a lot of things that I can't quite bring myself to regret now. Although my sister is a practical woman, she occasionally regrets things; I usually don't. Robert Oliver almost qualifies as an exception.

*

I'd like to be thorough about this story, so I'll begin with myself. I was born in Philadelphia, and so was Martha. Our parents divorced when I was five and Martha was four, and my father was a receding figure after that: in fact, he left our neighborhood in Chestnut Hill and receded into Center City, into his suits and his handsome, bare apartment, where we visited once every week, then once every two weeks, and mostly watched cartoons while he read stacks of paper he called "briefs." He called his underwear by this name, too, and once I found a pair of his briefs tangled under his bed with another pair of underwear. The other pair was made of beige lace. We weren't sure what to do with either pair, and it didn't seem right to leave them there, so when Daddy went to the corner for the Sunday *Inquirer* and our bagels, which usually took him three or four hours, we carried the two pairs of underwear into the back garden of his brownstone apartment building in a soup pot and buried them together between the wrought-iron railing and an ivy-covered tree trunk.

When I was nine, Daddy left Philadelphia for San Francisco, where we visited him once a year. San Francisco was more fun; Daddy's apartment there sat high above a fog-blanketed ocean, and we could feed seagulls right on the balcony. Muzzy, our mother, sent us there on the plane alone as soon as she thought we were old enough. Then our San Francisco visits faded to once every two years, or every three years, then now and then when we felt like it and Muzzy was willing to pay, and finally Daddy faded away into a job in Tokyo and sent us a photo of himself with his arm around a Japanese woman.

I think Muzzy was pleased when Daddy disappeared to San Francisco. It left her completely free to attend to Martha and me, and she did this with so much vigor and energy that neither of us has ever wanted children. Martha says she knows she would feel obliged to do everything our mother did for us and more, and it would bore her, but I think we both secretly know we couldn't measure up. Using her parents' excellent old Quaker bank account—we were never sure whether it was filled with oil, oats, railroad stock, or actual money—Muzzy put us through twelve years of a fine Friends' school, a place where soft-voiced teachers with perfectly cut gray hair got down on their knees to see if you were all right when someone hit you with a block. We studied the writings of George Fox and attended meeting and planted sunflowers in a bad neighborhood in North Philly.

My first experience of love occurred while I was in middle school among the Friends. One of the school's buildings was a house that had been a stop on the Underground Railroad; there was a trapdoor blended with the floor of an old cupboard in the attic. That building held the seventh- and eighth-grade classrooms, and when I moved up to those years, I liked to stay inside for a few minutes after everyone left for lunch recess, to listen for the spirits of men and women escaping to freedom. In February 1980 (I was thirteen), Edward Roan-Tillinger stayed in at lunchtime, too, and kissed me in the seventh-grade reading niche. I had been hoping for this for a couple of years, and as a first kiss it was not bad, although the edge of his tongue felt like a tough cut of meat, and I could see George Fox staring down at us from his portrait at the other end of the room. By the next week, Edward had turned his attention to Paige Hennessy, who had smooth red hair and lived out in the country. It took me a few weeks, not more, to stop hating her.

It's a shame for a woman's history to be all about men—first boys, then other boys, then men, men, men. It reminds me of the way our school history textbooks were all about wars and elections, one war after another, with the dull periods of peace skimmed over whenever they occurred. (Our teachers deplored this and added extra units about social history and protest movements, but that was still the message of the books.) I don't know why women so often tell stories that way, but I guess I've just started to do the same thing myself, maybe because you've asked me both to tell who I am and to describe my contact with Robert Oliver.

My high-school years, to continue being thorough, were certainly not only about boys; they were also about Emily Brontë and about the Civil War, about botany in the sloping Philadelphia parks, about tombstone rubbings, *Paradise Lost,* knitting, ice cream, and my wild friend Jenny (whom I drove to the abortion clinic before I took even my shirt off in front of a boy). In those years I learned to fence—I loved the white clothes and the spongy, damp smell of our undersized Quaker gymnasium, and the moment when the tip of the foil whipped your opponent's vest—and I learned to carry a bedpan without spilling it, in my volunteer job at Chestnut Hill Hospital, and to pour tea for Muzzy's endless charity meetings and to smile, so that her charitable friends said, "What a lovely girl you have, Dorothy. Now, was your own mother blond, too?" Which was what I wanted to hear. I learned to brush on eye shadow and put in a tampon so I couldn't feel it there (from a friend; Muzzy would never have discussed such a thing), and to hit the ball squarely with my field-hockey stick, and to make colored popcorn balls, and to speak French and Spanish not at all like a native, and to feel privately sorry for another girl as I gave her the cold shoulder, if that was necessary, and to reupholster little chairs in needlepoint. At the margins of all this, I first found out about the feel of paint under my brush, but I'll save that for a little later.

I thought I learned many of these things on my own, or from my teachers, but I understand now that they were always part of Muzzy's comprehensive plan. Just as she scrubbed between our toes and fingers every night in the bathtub when we were toddlers, getting the tender webbed places with a firmly washclothed finger, she also made sure her girls knew to tighten their bra straps before each wearing, to hand wash silk blouses in cold water only, to order salad when we ate out. (To be fair, she also wanted us to know the names and centuries of the most important English kings and queens and the geography of Pennsylvania and the way the stock market worked.) She went to our parent-teacher conferences with a little notebook in her hand, she took us shopping for a new party dress every Christmas, she mended our jeans herself but had our hair cut at a special salon in Center City.

Today, Martha is glamorous and I am passable, although I went through a long stage of wearing only dilapidated old clothes. Muzzy has had a tracheostomy, but when we go to see her—she still lives at home, with a maid on the second floor and a kindergarten teacher renting the top-floor apartment—she gasps, "Oh, you girls have turned out beautifully. I'm so grateful for that." Martha and I know that her gratitude is mainly to herself, but even so we feel larger-than-life in the little antique-filled living room, we feel large and graceful and accomplished, undefeatable, like Amazons.

But what was all this dressing, polishing, finishing, strap-adjusting for? Which brings me back to men. Muzzy did not discuss men or sex, we had no father at home to threaten our boyfriends or even ask about them, and Muzzy's attempts to protect us from boys were too polite to amount to much. "Boys will want something from you if they pay for a whole date," she would say.

"Muzzy"—Martha would begin her customary eye-rolling—"this is the nineteen eighties. It is not nineteen fifty-five anymore. Hello."

"Hello, yourself. I know what year it is," Muzzy would say mildly, and go to the phone to order pumpkin pies for Thanksgiving dinner, or call her sick aunt in Bryn Mawr, or stroll down to the lamp place to see if they also repaired antique candlesticks. She always said that she would gladly have gone out to get a job, but that as long as she could pay for our education herself ("herself" meant the oil or oats in the bank), she felt she was most useful being home for us.

For my part, I thought she stayed home mainly to keep track of us, too; but since she never asked about boys, we didn't tell her much, unless the boy was a prom date, in which case he came into the house exactly once, in his tux, to shake hands and call her "Mrs. Bertison." ("What a nice boy, Mary," she would say later. "Have you known him long? Doesn't his mother do the organic-vegetable drive at school, or am I thinking of someone else?") This little ritual somehow made me feel less guilty, somehow actually sanctioned—as the prom years went by—when the boy later slipped a hand down the low back of my dress, for example. As I grew up, I told Muzzy less and less, and by the time Robert Oliver entered my life, I had already spent my adolescence in a world I shared with myself, the occasional friend or boyfriend, and my journals. Robert told me while we were living together that he had also felt alone since childhood, and I think that was one of the things that most endeared him to me.

Chapter 46

Mary

I took two years off to work at a downtown bookstore before starting college, to Muzzy's endless consternation, but then I went dutifully enough, and with cash of my own in my pocket. Barnett College was good to me. I ought to be able to say I was filled with angst in college, that I struggled with the question of my future, the meaning of my life—spoiled sheltered rich girl collides with great books and is devastated by her own banality. Or maybe spoiled sheltered rich girl realizes that Barnett is more of the same, sells possessions, and flees into world to see real life, sleeps on street with dog for ten years.

Maybe I hadn't been quite spoiled enough—Muzzy made it clear that Quaker Oats wouldn't buy us ski trips and fancy Italian shoes, and she put us on a strict clothing allowance. And maybe I hadn't been quite sheltered enough—the Friends' service projects, the North Philly housing, the shelter for battered women, the bloody vomit at Chestnut Hill Hospital, had all brought me news of a suffering world. Barnett's curriculum didn't hold great revelations for me, and I worked at the library to help Muzzy buy my textbooks and train tickets home. In fact, I didn't experience much more than the usual undergraduate crises about boys and term papers. However, I discovered one thing there that no one will ever take away from me, and in a way that was a crisis in itself, a crisis of joy.

I had always liked art class at the Friends' school—I liked

our feisty little high-school art teacher and her stained purple smocks, and she liked my painted clay people, direct descendants of the fourth-grade hippopotamuses in Muzzy's treasure cabinet. I had never been one of the school's art stars, the group of loners who won state prizes and applied to RISD or Savannah College of Art and Design while the rest of us wondered if we could get into the Ivy League. But at Barnett I learned about the art inside myself.

Strangely, it began with a disappointment, almost a mistake. I had planned to be an English major, but I had to take some kind of distributional requirement in the arts. I can't remember what the distribution was—Creative Expression, maybe—and at the beginning of my second semester I signed up for a class in writing poetry, because the junior I thought I might soon be dating was a poet and I didn't want to feel completely ignorant with him.

As it turned out, this class was already full, and I was tracked over into a subdistribution called Visual Understanding. I found out much later that Robert Oliver, a pampered visiting painter whose punishment it was to teach the course that term, privately called it "Visual Misunderstanding." The college prided itself on giving non–art majors access to an established artist, and Visual Understanding was the only burden of his Barnett visit, an all-purpose painting and art-history class that drew unwilling students from across the curriculum. One January morning, I found myself among them at a long table in the painting studio.

Professor Oliver was late, and I sat there trying not to make eye contact with my classmates, none of whom I knew. I always felt shy at the beginning of any course; to avoid meeting anyone's eyes, I looked out the high grimy windows. Through them I could see white fields, the drift of snow on the window ledge. The sunlight fell in on a long clutter of easels and stools, the battered table, the nicked and paint-stained floor; on the still life of hats, puckering apples, and African statuettes arranged on a platform at the front; on the color wheels and museum posters. I recognized Van Gogh's yellow chair and a faded Degas, but not some squares within squares, vibrating with color, that Robert would later tell us were reproductions of the work of Josef Albers. My classmates talked to one another, popping their gum, scribbling in notebooks, scratching their midriffs. The girl next to me had purple hair; I'd noticed her in the dining hall that morning.

Then the studio door opened, and Robert came in. He was only thirty-four, although I didn't have any idea of that. I thought in the way undergraduates do that he and all my other instructors must be over fifty—ancient, in other words. He was a tall man, and he gave an impression of height and energy even greater than his actual size. He had rangy hands and a rather gaunt face without being gaunt in body; he was solid, strong (if probably elderly) under his clothes. He was dressed in heavy, smudged corduroy pants of a deep golden-brown, with rubbed spots on the knees and thighs. Over these he wore a yellow shirt, sleeves rolled to the elbows, and a threadbare olive sweater-vest that appeared to be hand-knitted. It was—his mother had knitted it for his father during his father's last years.

In fact, I knew so much about Robert later that it's hard for me to differentiate my first glimpse of him from all the rest of it. He was frowning deeply, his brow furrowed. He would have been interesting-looking if he hadn't been grouchy and disheveled, I thought in that first moment. His mouth was wide, loose, thick-lipped, his skin slightly olive, his nose fiercely long, his hair dark but also reddish and curly, poorly cut—it was partly this outdated bushiness that made me think he was older than he actually was.

Then he seemed to see us sitting around the table, and he

stopped moving for a second and smiled. When he smiled I saw that I must have been wrong to think he was untidy and bad-tempered. He was so obviously pleased to see us. He was a warm person, a warm-skinned, warm-eyed person dressed in soft-colored old clothes. You could forgive him his out-of-date, rumpled look when you saw him smile.

Robert had two books under his arm; he closed the door behind him, went to the head of the table, and set the books down. We all stared expectantly at him. I noticed that his hands were a little gnarled, as if they were even older than he was; they were unusual hands, very large and heavy yet graceful. He wore a wide wedding ring of dulled gold.

"Good morning," he said. His voice was both sonorous and raspy. "This is painting for nonmajors, also known as Visual Understanding. I trust that you're all glad to be here, as I am"—an ironic lie, but he was convincing in the moment—"and that this is the class you're supposed to be in." He unfolded a sheet of paper and read off our names, slowly and carefully, stopping to check the way he should pronounce them and nodding at each of us when we confirmed. He scratched his forearms; he was still standing in front of us. He had dark hair on the backs of his hands, and paint clotted around his nails as if they never quite washed clean. "That's all the names I have. Any stowaways?"

One girl raised her hand; like me, she hadn't been able to get into another class, but unlike me she wasn't on his list and wanted to know if she could stay. He appeared to think this over. He scratched his hairline through the dark locks of hair that sprouted there. He had nine students, he said, which was fewer than he'd been promised. Yes, she was welcome to stay. She should get a note from the chair of the department. That wouldn't be a problem. No other questions? No worries? Good. How many of us had ever painted before?

A few hands went up, but hesitantly. Mine stayed firmly on the table. Only later did I know how those first days of teaching any beginning course made his heart sink. He was as shy, in his way, as I was in mine, although he hid it well enough in class. "As you know, there is no requirement of previous experience for this course. It's also important to remember that every painter is a beginner, in a real sense, every day of his life." This line was a mistake, as I could have told him; undergraduates particularly hate to be patronized, and the feminist elements in the class were sure to resent that "his" as a stand-in for all artists—I included myself among those elements, although I wasn't given to hissing aloud at lectures like some of the young women I knew. He was likely to let himself in for a rough time in this class. I watched him with increased interest.

But he seemed to be taking a different tack now. He tapped the books in front of him and sat down. He folded his paint-stained hands together as if about to pray. He sighed. "It's always hard to know where to begin with painting. Painting is almost as old as human beings, if the caves of Europe are any indication. We live in a world of form and color, and of course we want to reproduce it—although the colors of our modern world have become a lot brighter since synthetic color was invented. Your T-shirt, for example"—he nodded at a boy across the table from me. "Or—if you'll excuse my using this example—your hair." He smiled at the girl with the violet tufts, gesturing loosely toward her with his big, ringed hand. Everyone laughed, and the girl grinned proudly.

I suddenly liked it there, liked the beginning-of-semester feeling, the smell of paint, the winter sunlight flooding the studio, the rows of easels waiting to receive our inept paintings, and this untidy but somehow debonair man offering to initiate us into all the mysteries of color, light, and form. Sitting in his classroom returned to me for a moment the pleasures of my high-school art studio, out of context among my other studies here but an important memory now that I'd gotten back to it.

I don't remember the rest of that day's class—I suppose we must have listened to Robert talk about the history of painting or some technical fundamentals of the medium. Maybe he passed around the books he'd brought with him, or gestured to the Van Gogh poster. We must have moved to the easels eventually, either in that class meeting or the next. At some point—maybe not until the next time—Robert must have shown us something about how to squeeze paint out of a tube, how to scrape a palette, how to sketch a figure onto canvas.

I do remember that he said once that he didn't know whether it was ridiculous or sublime for us to attempt oil painting when most of us hadn't taken courses in drawing or perspective or anatomy, but that we would at least understand something of what a difficult medium this was, and we would remember the smell of the paint on our hands. Even we could see that it had been an experiment, a departmental decision, not his, to expose a few non-majors to paint before anything else. He tried to convince us that he didn't really mind.

But I was more struck by his noting the smell of the paint on our hands, because this was one of my favorite parts of taking the Visual Understanding class, as it had been in high-school art; I loved sniffing my hands after I washed them for dinner, to prove to myself over and over that the smell of the paint was ineradicable. It really was. You couldn't wash it off with any kind of soap. I sniffed my hands during other classes and looked at the paint that clung to my fingernails if I didn't keep them safely clean, as Robert instructed us. I smelled my hands on my pillow when I went to sleep, or when they were clasped around the soft hair of the junior poet, whom I was now dating. No scent could mask or even overtake that pungent, oily odor, which was mixed every day on my skin with the equally sharp smell of the turpentine that didn't quite get the paint off.

This pleasure of smell was second for me only to the pleasure of applying the paint to the canvas. The forms I drew in Robert's class were certainly clumsy, despite my high-school teacher's previous efforts—I sketched the rough shapes of bowls and driftwood in the studio, the African statuettes, the tower of fruit Robert brought in one day, piling it up carefully in his almost-gnarled hands with their wedding band. Watching him, I wanted to tell him that I already loved the smell of paint on my hands and already knew I would never forget it, even if I didn't paint anymore after the class was over; I wanted him to know that we weren't all as insensitive to his lessons as he probably thought. I didn't feel I could tell him something like that in class; it would have invited the mockery of the girl with the purple hair and the track star who used his running shoes when we had to create our own still lifes. On the other hand, I couldn't go to Professor Oliver's office hours and sit down to tell him that I valued the smell of my hands—that would have been equally ridiculous.

Instead, I watched and waited for some real question to ask, something I might genuinely inquire of him. I hadn't had any questions until then. I knew only that I was clumsier with pencil and brush than my old teacher had ever pointed out to me, and that Professor Oliver hadn't really liked my blue bowl with the oranges in it; the proportions of the bowl were off, he'd told me one day, although the colors of the oranges were well mixed—and he'd gone on immediately to someone else's canvas, where there were even worse problems. I wished I had drawn the bowl better, spent more time on it, instead of being so eager to get to the oranges.

But there was no intelligent question I could ask about this.

I had to learn to draw, and somewhat to my own surprise I began to apply myself to this enterprise, checking books out of the art library and taking them to my dorm room, where I could sit copying apples and boxes, cubes, the rumps of horses, an impossible drawing of a satyr's head by Michelangelo. I was fascinatingly bad at this, and I drew them over and over until some of the lines seemed to come more easily out of my hand. I began to indulge in dreams of art school, to Muzzy's concern; she approved my moving along the table that served up the liberal arts smorgasbord, trying something new every semester (music history, political science), but she hoped all of that sampling would lead to law or medicine in the end.

Since art school was clearly still far off, I began to draw actual objects in my room: the vase my uncle had brought me from Istanbul years before, the lattice of the window, neatly framed in for the dormitory around 1930. I drew sprays of forsythia my naturalist roommate brought home from her walks, and my poet's fine hand as he lay asleep in my bed while my roommate was at her four-hour Great Books seminar. I bought sketchbooks in different sizes so that I could keep them on my desk or carry them in my book bag. I went to the university art museum, a surprisingly fine collection for a college, and tried to copy what I saw there—a Matisse print, a drawing by Berthe Morisot. Each task I set myself had a special flavor, a flavor that got stronger whenever I made a new effort to learn to draw; I was doing it partly for myself and partly so that I would have a good question to take to Professor Oliver.

1878

My dearest one:

I am in receipt this very moment of your letter and am moved by it to write you at once. Yes, as you compassionately hint, I have been lonely these years. And strange as this may seem, I wish you had known my wife, although if that had been possible, then you and I would have come to know each other under proper circumstances and not in this otherworldly love, if you will permit me to call it that. It is the fate of every widower to be pitied, and yet I felt no pity emanating from your letter, but only a generous regret for my sake that does you honor as a friend.

You are correct: I mourn her and always will, although it is the manner of her death that has caused me the greatest anguish, not the mere fact of her not being still alive—and that, I cannot speak about, even to you, at least not yet. One day I will, I promise.

I also will not try to tell you that you have filled this void, because no one fills the absence left by another; you have simply filled my heart again, and for that I am more indebted to you than your years and experience will permit me to explain. At the risk of sounding lofty, or even patronizing—you will find a way to forgive me—I assure you that you will one day understand the comfort that loving you has brought me. I'm quite certain that you think that your loving me is what comforts me, but when you have lived as long as I, you will know that it is your allowing me to love you, my dearest, that has eased the bleakness I carry inside me.

Finally, I am grateful that you accept my offer, and I only hope I have not been too insistent. And of course we will use the name you suggest—

Marie Rivière will be my honored colleague henceforth, and this painting will go out to the jury from my own hand and with complete discretion. I shall take it myself tomorrow, since the time is short.

With gratitude, ton
O.V.

A postscript: Yves's friend Gilbert Thomas came by the studio with his rather silent brother—you know Armand as well, I believe—to buy one of my landscapes from Fontainebleau, which I agreed some time ago to sell through their gallery. He might be of assistance to you, don't you think? He admired your golden-haired girl exceedingly, although naturally I said nothing about her real creator; in fact he remarked once or twice that the style reminded him of something familiar, but he couldn't think what. I fear he is unscrupulous in raising the prices on the paintings in his gallery, but perhaps I am too particular. And his admiration of your brush speaks well for him, even if he doesn't know who holds it—you might one day sell him some work, if you wanted to.

Chapter 47

Mary

Finally, I realized that I didn't have a question for Professor Oliver: I had a portfolio of sorts. I had my sketchbook, a largish one filled with the satyrs and boxes, the still lifes. I had individual sheets on which I'd drawn one of Matisse's women, made up of just six lines, dancing with abandon on the page (I couldn't make her actually dance, no matter how many times I copied those lines), and five versions of the vase with a shadow on the table next to it. Was the shadow in the right place? Was that my question? I bought a heavy cardboard sleeve at the art shop and put everything in it, and at our next class I watched for an opportunity to schedule a meeting with Professor Oliver.

He was setting a new lesson for us—we were going to paint a doll this week and a live model the next. The doll had to be finished outside of class time and brought in for critique. I didn't like the idea of painting a doll, but when he got her out and set her in a wooden doll chair, I felt a little better. She was an antique, slender and stiff, apparently made of painted wood, with matted old-gold hair and staring blue eyes, but there was something canny and observant in her face that I liked. He put her stiff hands in her lap, and she faced us, wary and half alive. She wore a blue dress with a ragged red silk flower pinned to the collar. Professor Oliver turned toward the class. "She belonged to my grandmother," he said. "Her name is Irene."

Then he got a sketch pad and silently demonstrated how we should articulate her form as related limbs—the oval head, the jointed arms and legs under the dress, the upright torso. We should look carefully at the foreshortening of the knees, he said, since we would see her head-on. Her skirt would hide her knees, but they were still there—we should find a way to show the front of the knees under her dress. This got into the area of drapery, he said, which we wouldn't study that semester—it was simply too involved. But the exercise would give us a feel for limbs under fabric, for the solidity of a body in its clothes. Not a bad thing for a painter to think about a little, Robert assured us.

He set to work on a demonstration, and I watched him; I watched his faded shirtsleeve rolled up on his sketching arm, his green brown eyes flicking back and forth to the doll while the rest of his body was still and focused on its quarry. The back of his curly hair was flattened as if he'd slept on it and then forgotten to brush it, and a lock at the front stuck up, growing like a plant. I could see that he was unaware of us and of his hair, unaware of anything but the doll with her knees rounding the front of her fragile dress. Suddenly, I wanted that unawareness for myself. I was never unaware. I was always watching other people; I was always wondering if they were watching me. How could I become an artist like Professor Oliver unless I could lose myself in front of a whole group of people, lose myself like that to everything but the problem at hand, the sound of my pencil on the page and the flow of line emerging from it? I felt a wave of despair. I focused so hard on his long-nosed profile that I started to see a halo of daylight around his whole head. I couldn't possibly ask him my nonquestion, bring him my pretend portfolio to look at. It would be more mortifying to me if he saw the rest of my work than if he never saw it at all. I hadn't even taken my first art-major drawing class yet—I was an example of art-for-nonmajors, a dilettante who knew how to upholster little chairs and play Beethoven sonatinas on the piano. For people like me, he provided this sampler of the difficulties of real painting—there's anatomy, there's drapery, there are shadows, there is light, there is color. At least you will all know how difficult this really is.

I turned to my canvas and got ready to pretend to sketch the jointed doll and put some color over her. Everyone set to work, even the flippant students taking it seriously out of relief at being somewhere quiet, in a class where you didn't have to speak, a little space away from talking, away from dorm life. I worked, too, but blindly, moving my pencil and then squeezing oil onto my carefully scraped palette only because I didn't want anyone to see me standing still. Inside I was standing still. I felt tears come to my eyes.

I might have quit painting forever that day, before I really got started, but suddenly Robert, who had been moving from easel to easel, stopped just behind me. I hoped I wouldn't start trembling; I wanted to ask him please not to look at what I was doing, and then he leaned over and pointed one of his strangely large fingers at the head I had sketched in. "Very nice," he said. "You've come an impressively long way with this." I couldn't speak. His yellow cotton shirt was so close that it filled my vision when I turned my head to try to acknowledge those words. His arm and pointing hand were tanned. He was amazingly real, ugly, vivid, confident. I felt that who I was, everything I had been brought up with, was all puny, boring, but his presence made it important for a moment.

"Thank you," I said bravely. "I've been working hard—in fact, I was wondering if I could come to your office and ask

ask you some questions, show you some other things I've been doing to get ready for my drawing class in the fall."

As I spoke, I turned farther and looked at him. His angular face was softer than I'd noticed before, a little fleshy around nose and chin, the skin just beginning to slip—a face that would age quickly because its owner was unaware of it. I felt how firm my own smooth face was, my curve of chin and neck, the gloss of my hair, carefully brushed and cut with a shining straight edge. He was frightening, but he was old and battered. I was new and ready for the world. Perhaps I had the advantage. He smiled, a kind smile, although not a personal one—a warm smile, the smile of a man who didn't actually dislike people, even if he could forget all about them while he sketched a doll. "Certainly," he said. "You're welcome to stop by. I have office hours Monday and Wednesday from ten to twelve. Do you know where my office is?"

"Yes," I lied. I would find it.

About a week after Robert Oliver had invited me to stop by his office, I got up enough courage to bring him my portfolio. The door, when I arrived clutching my big cardboard folder, was ajar, and I could see his large figure moving around inside a tiny room. I pushed timidly past the bulletin board on his door—postcards, cartoons, and, oddly, a single glove tacked up with a nail—and entered without knocking. I realized I should have knocked, and I turned back, then gave up because Robert had already seen me. "Oh, hello," he said.

He was putting some papers into a file cabinet, and I noticed that he shoved them into the drawer in flat piles because there were no standing files inside, as if he just wanted to hide them or get them off his desk and didn't care about finding them ever again. His office was a jumble of notebooks, drawings, painting supplies, odds and ends from still lifes (some of which I recognized from our class), boxes of charcoal and pastels, electric cords, empty water bottles, sandwich wrappers, sketches, coffee mugs, university paperwork—papers everywhere.

The walls were almost as littered: postcards of places and paintings taped above his desk, memos, quotations (I couldn't get close enough to read any), the few big art posters half obscured by them. I remember one of the posters was from the National Gallery for the exhibition *Matisse in Nice,* which I'd seen myself on a trip with Muzzy. Robert had slapped Post-it notes covered with handwriting all over Matisse's lady in her open striped robe.

I also remember that, for some reason (that was how I thought of it), there was a book of poetry lying on top of the mess on his desk—it was Czesław Miłosz's *Collected Poems* in translation, new—and I was surprised to think that a painter read poetry, my poet boyfriend having convinced me temporarily that only poets were allowed to do so. That was the first time I had ever heard of Miłosz's poetry, which Robert loved and later read to me; I still own that very volume, the one I saw lying on his desk that day. It's one of the only gifts from him I've kept; he gave possessions away as casually as he helped himself to other people's, a characteristic that looked at first glance like generosity, until you realized he never remembered anyone's birthday and never paid off small debts.

"Please come in." Robert was clearing a chair in one corner, which he did by shuffling the papers from it into the drawer of the file cabinet. He shut the drawer again. "Sit down."

I sat obediently, between an aloe plant in a tall pot and some kind of native drum that he'd used once in our studio still life. I knew the beads and shells around it by heart. "Thank you for letting me drop by," I said as easily as I could. His physical presence in the crowded little room was even more intimidating than it was in the classroom; the walls seemed to curve in around him, as if his head brushed the ceiling, dislodged it. He certainly could have reached out and touched opposite walls at the same time, with his great wingspan. I was reminded of our childhood book of Greek myths, in which the gods were described as being a lot like human beings but larger. He twitched his khaki pants at the thighs and sat down in the desk chair, swiveling around to look at me. His face was kind and teacherly, interested, although I sensed his distraction; he already wasn't really listening.

"Absolutely. My pleasure. How is the class going and what can I do for you?"

I fiddled with the edges of my portfolio, then tried to sit still. I had thought many times of what he would say to me, especially when he saw the hard work I'd put into my drawings, but I had forgotten to rehearse what I was going to say to him—strange, when I'd dressed so carefully and brushed my hair one more time before walking into the building.

"Well," I said. "I really like the class—in fact, I love it. I've never thought before about being an artist, but I'm working on—I mean, I'm starting to see things differently. Everywhere I look." This wasn't what I'd meant to say, but with his narrow eyes fixed on me, I felt that I was discovering something and it tumbled out. His eyes were remarkable, especially up close, not large unless he opened them wide, but beautifully shaped, green-brown, the color of green olives; they put to shame his unkempt hair and what seemed to me then his aging skin—or was it that the contrast between those perfect eyes and his rumpled self was so astonishing? I never figured that out, even much later when I'd been allowed to scrutinize them and him with every cell of my being. "I mean, I'm starting to look at things instead of just seeing them. I walk out of my dorm in the morning and I notice the tree branches for the first time. I make a note to myself and then I go back later and sketch them."

He was listening now. His gaze was intent, not on that inward voice he often seemed to hear in the midst of class; he was no longer handsomely uncaring, no longer casual. His huge hands lay on his knees, and he looked at me. He wasn't being charming; he wasn't concerned with himself; he was not even concerned with me and my perfectly brushed hair. He was caught by my words, as if I'd offered him a secret handshake or uttered a phrase from the language he'd known in childhood and hadn't heard in years. His tangled dark eyebrows went up, surprised. "Is that your work?" He pointed to the cardboard folder.

"Yes." I handed it to him, fumbling the edges. My heart was pounding. He opened it across his lap and studied the first drawing: my uncle's vase, standing next to a bowl of fruit stolen from the dining hall. I saw it upside down on his knee; it was terrible, a travesty. He sometimes turned our work upside down in class, so that we would think about arranging forms, working on a composition rather than a lamp or a doll—he did that to show us pure shape, to flush out our inaccuracies. I wondered why I had shown that sketch to anyone at all, let alone Robert Oliver. I should have hidden from him, hidden everything. "I know I have to work for at least ten more years."

He said nothing in response, holding my sketch a little closer to his eyes, then moving it slowly away. I realized that ten years might actually sound too optimistic. At last he spoke. "This is not very good, you know," he said.

My chair seemed to heel like a boat in rough water. I didn't have time to think.

"However," he said, "it is alive, and that's something that can't be taught. That's a gift." He turned through a few more sketches. I knew he must be studying my tree branches now, and the junior poet with his shirt off—I had ordered the big sheets carefully. Now my copy of some Cézanne apples, and then my roommate's hand, held obligingly still on a table for me. I had tried a little of everything, and for each of the sketches I'd included, I'd discarded ten others; I'd had that much sense, at least. Robert Oliver looked quickly up again, not seeing me but seeing into me. "Did you take art in high school? Have you been drawing a long time?"

"Yes and no," I said, feeling that here were some questions I could actually answer. "We had an art class every year, but it was pretty lax. We didn't really learn to draw. Apart from that, I've had just this class—yours—and I started drawing on my own a few weeks ago because I couldn't paint things right, just like you said. You said we couldn't really paint until we learned to draw."

"That's right," he muttered. He turned slowly back through my sketches. "So you just started this?" He had this way of fixing his eyes on you suddenly, as if he'd just found you—it was unnerving and thrilling. "You are really rather talented." He turned a page around again, as if puzzled, then closed the portfolio. "Do you love doing this?" he asked gravely.

"I love it more than anything I've ever found," I said, realizing as I said it that it was true and not merely the right answer.

"Then draw everything. Do a hundred drawings a day," he said fiercely. "And remember that it's a hellish life."

How could the heaven yawning above me be hellish? I didn't like being commanded to do anything—that always got something stirring in my stomach—but he had made me happy. "Thank you."

"You won't thank me," he said, not grimly but sadly. *Has he forgotten about joy?* I wondered. *How terrible it must be to get older*. I felt very sorry for him, very glad for myself, for all my youth and optimism and my sudden knowledge that my life was going to be magnificent. He shook his head, smiled—an ordinary, tired smile. "Just work hard. Why don't you apply to the summer painting workshop here? I can put in a word for you."

Muzzy will love *that,* I thought, but I said, "Thank you—I was considering applying." I hadn't even been planning to stay on campus for the summer; all my friends were going to New York to get jobs, and I had almost decided to do the same. "Are you teaching the workshop?"

"No, no," he said. He seemed absentminded again, as if he had things he needed to get back to—more papers to stuff into drawers, maybe. "I'm here just this semester. Visiting. I have to get back to my life." I had forgotten that. I wondered what his life could be, apart from the paintings and drawings he could do anywhere and of course his all-important students, like me. There was the wedding ring on his left hand, but probably his wife was here with him, although I'd never seen her. "Do you usually teach somewhere else?" I realized too late that I probably should already know this about him, but he didn't seem to notice my ignorance.

"Yes—I'm at Greenhill College in North Carolina. Nice little place with good studios. I've got to get home." He smiled. "My daughter misses me."

This was rather shocking. I'd thought artists didn't have children, certainly that they shouldn't. It gave him a mundane existence I didn't think I liked very much. "How old is she?" I asked, to be polite.

"One and two months. A budding sculptor." His smile deepened; he was far away, some domestic place where he felt he belonged.

"Why didn't they come with you?" I asked this to punish him a little for having them at all.

"Oh, they're so settled there—good nursery co-op at the college, and my wife just started working part-time. I'll be back down there soon."

He looked wistful; he loved his baby, I saw, in that mysterious realm, and perhaps he loved the diligent wife as well. It was disappointing, the way older people always turned out to have these ordinary lives. I thought I shouldn't overstay my welcome or court any further disillusionment. "Well, I'd better let you get back to your work. Thank you very much for looking at my sketches and for—and for your encouragement. I really appreciate it."

"Any time," he said. "I hope it goes well for you. Feel free to bring me some more, and remember to sign up for that workshop. James Ladd is teaching it, and he's terrific."

But he's not you, I thought. "Thanks." I put out my hand, wanting to close this meeting with some ritual. He stood up, very tall once more, and accepted my grasp. I shook his hand firmly, to show I was serious, grateful, maybe even a future colleague. It was wonderful, that hand; I'd never touched it before. It engulfed mine. The knuckles were thick and dry, his grip strong in return, if automatic—it felt like an embrace. I swallowed hard to make myself let go. "Thanks," I said, turning incoherently toward the door with my portfolio under my arm.

"See you soon." I felt rather than watched him return to some sort of work at his desk. But I had seen, also, in that last second, something in him that I couldn't name—possibly he had been moved by my touch, too, or—no, perhaps he'd just noticed that I'd been moved by his. I was covered with shame at the thought; it took half the walk back to my dorm, under the windy, bright sky and past throngs of students going to lunch, to cool my face. Then I remembered: *Do a hundred drawings a day*.

Robert, I remembered it for nearly ten years. I remember it still.

Mon cher ami,

I do not know where to begin writing you, except to say that your letter moved me very much. If it would bring you relief to tell me about your beloved wife, you may be certain you will find me ready. Papa told me once, but ever so briefly, that you had lost her unexpectedly, and had grieved almost to the point of illness before your departure from the country. I can only assume that your years abroad were solitary because of this and that you left Paris partly to mourn her. If it eases you to talk with me, I will listen as well as I can, although I know little of such loss myself, thank heaven. That is the least I can do for you after what you have done for me, your encouragement and faith in my work. I find myself going eagerly to my studio-porch every morning now, knowing that these paintings have at least one kind admirer. In other words, although I shall wait with as much eagerness as you do for the jury's verdict, your words mean more to me than good news or bad from that source ever will. Perhaps you think this the bravado of the young artist, and perhaps you will be right, in part. But I am also sincere.

With deepest affection,
Béatrice

Chapter 48

Mary

That was not the last time I was alone with Robert Oliver before he left Barnett; we had one more encounter, but first I have to tell you about a few other things. Our class was finished; we had painted, mostly badly, three still lifes, one doll, and one model—discreetly robed, not nude, a muscular male chemistry student. I couldn't help wishing Robert would paint and draw more along with us, so that we could watch how it was really done. Some of his work was included in the faculty spring show, and I went to see it. He had contributed four new canvases, all painted—where? at home? at night?—during the term he'd been with us. I tried to see in them the lessons he taught in class: form, composition, color choices, mixing the paint. Had he turned them upside down while he was working on them? I tried to find triangles in them, verticals, horizontals. But they were so strong in their subject matter, their living, breathing brushwork, that it was hard to look behind the scenes.

One of Robert's paintings in the show was a self-portrait (I saw this again years later, before he destroyed it) full of detached intensity, and two others were almost Impressionist and showed mountain meadows and trees, with two men in modern clothes walking off the edge of the canvas. I liked the contrast between the nineteenth-century brushwork and the contemporary figures. I was learning that Robert did not care whether or not people thought he had a style; he considered his work one long experiment and rarely used a single look or technique for more than a few months.

Then there was the fourth painting. I stood in front of that one for a long time because I couldn't help it—you see, I encountered her long before Robert and I were lovers ourselves; she was already there, always there. It was the portrait of a woman in a low-cut, old-fashioned dress, a sort of ball gown, holding a closed fan in one hand and a closed book in the other, as if she couldn't decide whether to go out to a party or stay home and read. Her hair was thick and dark, piled in soft curls and ornamented with flowers. I thought her expression was musing and deeply intelligent, a little wary. She'd been pondering something and then had suddenly become aware that she was being watched. I remember wondering how he could have caught such a fleeting expression.

She must be his wife, I thought, posing in costume—the portrait had that kind of intimacy. I didn't like meeting her that way, for some reason, especially since I'd already imagined her as dull and hardworking, with her toddler, her practical job. I found it a vaguely unpleasant surprise to think she might be this vital and lovely to Robert. She was young, but not too young to belong to Robert, and so full of subtle suspended movement that you felt in another moment she would smile—but only once she'd recognized you. It was eerie.

The other thing that was remarkable about the painting was the setting. The lady sat on a great black sofa, leaning back a little, with a mirror on the wall behind and above her. The mirror was so skillfully rendered that I expected to catch myself reflected there. Instead, at a distance, I saw Robert Oliver with his easel, in his rumpled modern clothes, painting himself painting her, and at the center of the mirror was the back of her softly coiffed hair and slender neck. His face was serious and preoccupied as he glanced up at her—she was model as well as wife.

So he was the one at whom she would smile in a moment. I felt a stab of actual jealousy, although I couldn't have said whether it was because I'd expected her to smile at me instead or didn't want Robert to smile back at her. The mirror showed him and his easel further framed by a window that was the source of light behind him as he painted, a latticed window bordered by stonework. Barnett had some Gothic Revival buildings from the 1920s and '30s; he might have gone to a dining hall or one of the old classroom buildings to find those details. Through the window reflected in the mirror, you could see what looked like a beach, cliffs off to one side, blue sky coming down to the horizon of water.

Portrait and self-portrait, subject and viewer, mirror and window, landscape and architecture: it was an extraordinary painting, one that messed with your mind, to use the lingo of our dorms and dining halls. I wanted to stand in front of it forever, trying to decipher the story. He had called it *Oil on Canvas,* although the other three canvases had real titles. I wished Robert would stroll into the gallery so that I could ask him what it meant, tell him how chokingly lovely and puzzling it was. I felt a kind of anguish at walking out and leaving it—I checked the catalog in my hand, but the college gallery had chosen to reproduce one of his other paintings and discuss it in detail, while this work was simply listed and dated. Once I left, I might never see it again, might never see this woman whose gaze met mine with such longing—that was probably why I went back to it a couple of times before the show was taken down.

Chapter 49

Mary

And then one day I saw Robert again, alone, just at the end of the semester. Our class had concluded with a little party in the studio, and he had graciously seen us all out the door at the end, bestowing special notice on no one and a smile of pride on everyone; we'd done better, all of us, he confessed, than he'd ever thought we could. I was walking to the library a few days later, during exam week, and I turned up a petal-strewn walk and almost bumped against him.

"Fancy running into you here," he said, stopping abruptly and holding out his long arm as if to catch me, or to prevent me from actually colliding with him. His hand closed over my upper arm. It sounded more intimate than he'd probably meant, but then I had almost barreled into his rib cage.

"Literally," I added, and was gratified when he laughed heartily, something I hadn't seen before. He threw back his head a little; he was lost in the pleasure of it, unself-conscious. It was a happy sound—I laughed, too, when I heard it. We stood there contentedly under the spring trees, an older person and a younger person whose work together was done. Because of that, there was nothing to say, and yet we stood there, smiling, because it was a warm day and the long upstate winter hadn't scuttled our differing dreams, and because the semester was about to end and release everyone—a transition, a relief. "I'm going to take that painting workshop in the summer term," I said to fill up the pleasant silence. "Thanks again for your recommendation." And then I remembered: "Oh, I went to see the gallery show. I loved your paintings." I didn't mention that I'd gone three times.

"Well, thank you." He said nothing more; I had just learned something else about him, which was that he didn't like to comment on people's comments on his work.

"I actually had a lot of questions for you about one of them," I hazarded. "I mean, I was very curious about some things you did in it and I wished you'd been there to ask on the spot."

A strangeness crossed his face then; it was slight—a thin, fine cloud across the spring day, and I never knew whether he'd guessed which painting I was going to name or whether it was my "I wished you'd been there" that sent through him—what? A premonitory shiver? Doesn't every love express itself this way, with the seeds of both its flowering and its ruin in the very first words, the first breath, the first thought? He frowned and looked attentively at me. I wondered whether the attention was for me or for something just outside the frame. "You can ask me," he said a little shortly. Then he smiled. "Would you like to sit down for a moment?" He glanced around and so did I—the chairs and tables at the back of the student café were in plain view on the other side of the quad. "How about there?" he asked. "I was thinking of taking a break and having some lemonade."

We ate lunch instead, sitting outside among the students and their backpacks, some of them studying for exams, some talking in the sunshine, stirring coffee. Robert had an enormous tuna sandwich with pickles and an overflow of potato chips on the side, and I had a salad. He insisted on paying for the meal, and I insisted on buying us two big paper cups of lemonade—out of a roiling tank, but still it was good. We ate in silence at first. I'd turned in my final painting, we'd said good-bye at the last class, and although I was waiting now for the moment to ask him about *Oil on Canvas,* it felt to me as if we might already be something like friends, since we were no longer instructor and student. I dismissed this thought as presumptuous the minute it occurred to me; he was a great master and I was a nobody with a little talent. I hadn't fully noticed the birds before then—that they had returned after the snowbound winter—or the brightness of the trees and buildings, the latticed windows of the dining hall thrown open to let in spring.

Robert lit a cigarette, apologizing first. "I don't usually smoke," he said. "I just got a pack this week, to celebrate. I'm not planning to buy any more. It's once a year." He went back into the café to get an ashtray, and when he came out he settled himself in his chair and said, "All right, go ahead, but you know I don't usually answer questions about my paintings." I hadn't known; I wanted to say that I didn't know a thing about him. He looked amused, however, or prepared to be amused, and his eyes seemed to register my hair when I pushed it over my shoulders—it still reached my waist, then, and it was still blond, my natural color.

But he said nothing else, so I had to speak. "Does that mean I shouldn't ask you?"

"You can ask me, but I might not answer, that's all. I don't think painters have the answers about their own paintings. No one knows anything about a painting except the painting itself. Anyway, a painting has to have some kind of mystery to it to make it work."

I drank the last of my lemonade, gathering courage. "I liked all your paintings a lot. The landscapes are really wonderful."

I was too young, then, to know how this might sound to a genius, but at least I knew better than to say anything about the self-portrait. "What I wanted to ask you about is that big one, with the woman sitting on the sofa. I assume she's your wife, but she's wearing this incredible, old-fashioned kind of dress. What's the story behind that?"

He looked at me again, but this time he was absent, guarded. "The story?"

"Yes. I mean, it's so detailed—the window and the mirror—it's so complicated and she seems completely alive. Did she sit for you, or did you maybe use a photograph?"

He was looking through me, apparently all the way through to the stone wall behind me, the wall of the student union. "She's not my wife, and I don't use photographs." His voice was mild, if distant, and he drew on his cigarette. He examined his other hand on the table, flexing the fingers, massaging the joints: a painter's long slide toward arthritis, I understood later. When he glanced up again, his eyes were narrowed, but this time on me, not on some vague horizon. "If I tell you who she is, will you keep it a secret?"

Something prickled in me at this, the sort of horror you feel as a child when an adult proposes to tell you something adult—to report some private sorrow, for example, or a financial problem that you've already guessed but should be allowed to ignore for a few years more of childhood, or something, God forbid, frightening, sexual. Was he going to tell me about a hidden, sordid love life? Middle-aged people had such things sometimes, although they were too old for them and ought to know better. How much sweeter it was to be young and free and allowed to flaunt one's affections and mistakes and body. It was my habit to pity everyone over thirty, and I cruelly made no exception for weather-beaten Robert Oliver with his single springtime cigarette.

"Sure," I said, although my heart beat fast. "I can keep a secret."

"Well—" He tapped his ash into the borrowed tray. "The truth is that I don't know who she is." He blinked rapidly. "Oh God," he said, his voice full of despair. "If I just knew who she was!"

This was so surprising, so unanswerable, so chilling and weird, that I said nothing for a few moments; I almost pretended he hadn't uttered that last line. I simply couldn't figure it out, didn't know how to respond. How could he paint someone and not know who she was? I'd assumed he worked from friends or from his wife or hired models whenever he wanted to, that people sat for him. Could he have pulled some gorgeous woman off the street, like Picasso? I didn't want to ask him outright, to expose my confusion and ignorance. Then a possibility occurred to me. "Do you mean you imagined her?"

He looked grim this time, and I wondered if I liked him after all. Maybe he was mean, in fact. Or crazy. "Oh, she's real, in a way." Then he smiled, to my ineffable relief, although I felt vaguely offended, too. He knocked a second cigarette out of his package. "Would you like another lemonade?"

"No, thank you," I said. My pride was hurt; he'd posed an agonized mystery without giving me even a clue, and he seemed to feel no sense of having excluded me, his student, his lunch guest, the girl with the beautiful hair. There was something scary about it, too. I had the idea that if he could explain to me what he'd meant by these strange statements, I would instantly be enlightened about the nature of painting, the miracle of art, but obviously he'd assumed I couldn't understand. Part of me didn't want to know his weird secrets, but at the same time it stung. I put my cup and the white plastic fork neatly on my plate, as if I were at one of Muzzy's friends' little dinner parties. "I'm sorry—I have to get back to the library. Exams." I stood up, defiant in my jeans and boots—taller, for once, than my instructor, since he was still seated. "Thank you so much for the lunch. That was very nice of you." I gathered up my garbage without looking at him.

He stood, too, and stopped me with a large gentle hand on my arm, so that I put down the plate again. "You're angry," he said, with a kind of wonder in his voice. "What have I done to upset you? Was it that I didn't answer your question?"

"I can't blame you for thinking I wouldn't understand your answer," I said stiffly, "but why did you play with me? Either you know the woman or you don't, right?" His hand was miraculously warm through the sleeve of my blouse; I didn't want him to remove it, ever, but a second later he did.

"I'm sorry," he said. "I was telling you the truth—I don't understand who the woman really is, in my painting." He sat down again, and he didn't need to gesture: I sat down with him, slowly. He shook his head, staring at the table with its smear of what appeared to be bird droppings at one edge. "I can't explain this even to my wife—I think she wouldn't want to hear about it. I encountered this woman years ago, at the Metropolitan Museum of Art, in a crowded room. I was working on a show that was all paintings of young ballet dancers, some of them really just children, in New York—they were so perfect, like little birds. And I started going to the Met to see a lot of Degas, as a reference, because obviously he was one of the master painters of dance, probably the greatest ever."

I nodded proudly; this time I knew.

"I saw her one of the last times I went to the museum, before we moved to Greenhill, and I just could never shake the image of her from my mind. Never. I couldn't forget her."

"She must have been beautiful," I hazarded.

"Very," he said. "And not only beautiful." He seemed lost, back at the museum, staring at a woman in a crowd who vanished a second later; I could sense the romance of the moment, and I felt a continued envy of the stranger who'd lingered in his mind so long. It didn't occur to me until later that even Robert Oliver couldn't have memorized a face that quickly.

"Didn't you go back to try to find her?" I hoped he hadn't.

"Oh, of course. I saw her a couple more times, and then I never saw her again."

An unrealized romance. "Then you started imagining her," I prompted.

This time he smiled at me, and warmth spread down the back of my neck. "Well, I guess you were correct to begin with. I guess I did." He stood again, reassured and reassuring, and we walked companionably back to the front of the student union. He paused in the sunshine and put out his hand. "Have a good summer, Mary. Best of luck with your studies in the fall. I'm sure you're going to do fine work if you keep at it."

"And you, too," I replied miserably, smiling. "I mean, good luck with your teaching—your work. You're going back to North Carolina right away?"

"Yes, yes, next week." He bent and kissed my cheek, as if saying good-bye to the whole campus and every one of his students there, and to the wintry north, all in the convenient form of me. The impersonality of it winded me. His lips were warm and pleasantly dry.

"Well, bye," I said, and I wheeled around, made myself walk off. The only surprising thing was that I didn't hear him turn and walk the other way; I felt him there for a long time, and I was too proud to look back. I thought he was probably standing there, staring down at his feet or the sidewalk, lost in his vision of the woman he'd glimpsed a few times in New York, or perhaps daydreaming of his wife and children at home. He was surely excited about leaving all this and going back to his family and his real life. But he had also told me, *I can't explain this even to my wife*. I'd received his random attempt to say something about his vision; I had been privileged. It stayed with me, as the face of a stranger had stayed with him.

Chapter 50

Mary

After Robert and I broke up, months ago, I started sketching in the mornings at a café I still frequent sometimes. I've always loved that phrase, to "frequent" a café. I needed a place to be away from the university studios where I now teach. Not many cafés in that area are private enough for faculty to sit around in them. You're too likely to run into your former (or, worse, current) students and get into conversation. Instead I found a café between where I live and where I work, at a metro stop with a chic address.

It's not that I don't like my students; on the contrary, they are my lifeblood now, the only children I will ever have, my future. I love them, with all their crises and their excuses and their selfishness. I love seeing them lifted into a sudden revelation about painting, or a sudden predilection for watercolors, a love affair with charcoal—or an obsession with azure, which starts to appear in all their paintings so that they have to explain to the rest of the class what's going on. "I'm just . . . into it." Usually they can't explain why; each new love simply takes them over. If it's not painting, it's unfortunately sometimes alcohol or coke (although they don't actually tell me about that), or a young woman or man in their history class, or rehearsals for a play; they have heavy smudges under their eyes, they slouch in class, they light up when I pull out a Gauguin they loved in high school. "That's mine!" they shout.

They make me end-of-term presents out of painted egg cartons. I love them.

But you do have to get away from students, too, to do your own work, so for a while I was in the habit of sketching from life in my favorite café, just after breakfast, if I could spare time before my classes began. I sketched the rows of teapots on a shelf, the fake Ming vase, the tables and chairs, the exit sign, the too-familiar Mucha poster next to a newspaper rack, the bottles of Italian syrup with their different but almost matching labels, and finally the people. I got bold again about drawing strangers, the way I used to be when I was a student myself—three middle-aged Asian women talking fast over scones and paper cups, or a young man with a long ponytail, half asleep on his table, or a fortysomething woman with her laptop.

It made me see people again, and that made the hurt of Robert lessen a little, this feeling that I was one among many and that those other people—with their different jackets and glasses and variously shaped and colored eyes—all had had their Roberts, their incredible disasters, their pleasures and regrets. I tried to put pleasure and regret into my sketches of them. Some of them liked being sketched and smiled sideways at me. Those mornings made it easier, in a small way, for me to accept that I was alone and didn't want to look at other men, although perhaps that would wear off eventually. After about a hundred years.

1879

Mon cher ami,

I cannot understand why you have not written or visited these weeks. Have I done something to offend you? I thought you were away still, but Yves says you are in town. Perhaps I have been wrong in assuming your affection as strong as I have, in which case please excuse the error of your friend

Béatrice de Clerval

Chapter 51

Marlow

Traffic was heavy the morning after my dinner with Mary Bertison, possibly because I'd gotten a late start. I like to be ahead of the crowds, to arrive before the receptionists, to have the roads and then the parking lot and corridors of Goldengrove to myself, to catch up on paperwork for twenty minutes alone. That morning I'd lingered, watching the sun across my solitary breakfast table, cooking a second egg. I'd put Mary in a taxi after our genial dinner—she'd refused my politely couched offer of a ride to her door—but in the morning the apartment to which she hadn't returned, my apartment, had seemed full of her. I saw her sitting on my sofa, restless, hostile, confiding, by quick turns.

I'd poured a second cup of coffee I knew I'd regret later; I stared out my window at the trees on the street, which were now thoroughly green, leafed out for summer. I remembered her long hand waving aside some point I'd made and making one of her own. At dinner we had talked about books and painting; she'd made it clear that she'd had enough conversation about Robert Oliver for one evening. But this morning I could still remember the quiver in her voice when she told me she'd rather write about him than talk.

Halfway to Goldengrove I switched off my current favorite recording, which I'd usually have turned up louder at this point—András Schiff playing some of J. S. Bach's French

Suites, a glorious torrent, then a ripple of light, then the rush of water again. I told myself I was turning off the music because I couldn't focus on such heavy traffic and listen appreciatively at the same time; people were cutting one another off at the entry ramps, leaning on their horns, stopping without warning.

But I wasn't sure, either, that there was space in my car for both the Bach and Mary's presence, the sight of her eagerness over dinner when she forgot Robert Oliver for a few minutes and talked about her recent paintings, a series of women in white. I'd asked respectfully if I might see them sometime—after all, she'd gotten a glimpse of my small-town landscape, and I didn't even consider that one of my best. She'd hesitated, agreed vaguely, keeping a line between us. No, there was not room in my car for the French Suites, the deepening green of the roadsides, and Mary Bertison's alert, pure face. Or perhaps there was not room for me. My car had never seemed so small, so much in need of a roof to roll down.

After my morning rounds were done, I found Robert's room empty. I'd saved him for last, and he was gone. The nurse in the hall said he was walking outside with one of the staff, but when I strolled through the back doors and across the veranda, he wasn't immediately in sight. I don't think I've mentioned that Goldengrove, like my office in Dupont Circle, is a relic of grander days, a mansion that saw great parties in the era of Gatsby and MGM; I often wonder whether the shuffling patients in its halls aren't uplifted and perhaps even a little healed by the Deco elegance around them, the sunny walls and faux-Egyptian friezes. The building was restored inside and out a few years before I arrived. I particularly like the veranda, which has a serpentine adobe wall and tall flowerpots, kept filled (partly at my insistence) with white geraniums. From there you can see across the property to the smudge of trees along the Little Sheridan, a halfhearted tributary of the Potomac. Some of the original gardens have been rejuvenated, although to bring them all to life would take more than we can give. There are flower beds and a large sundial, not original to the house. In the dip beyond the gardens spreads a small shallow lake (too shallow to drown oneself in) with a summerhouse on the other side (too low for a damaging jump from the roof, the rafters inside covered with a dropped ceiling to prevent hangings).

This all impresses the families who usher their loved ones into the relative silence of the place; I see family members drying tears out here on the veranda sometimes, assuring one another—*Look how pretty it is, and it's only for a while.* And usually it is only for a while. Most of these families will never see the public city hospitals where people with no money at all are sent to wrestle with their demons, the places with no gardens, no new paint, and sometimes not enough toilet paper. I saw some of them as an intern, and it's hard for me to forget those sights, although here I am, employed in a private hospital and likely to remain. We don't know exactly when we get stuck, or lose the energy to work for change, but we do. Perhaps I should have tried harder. But I feel useful, in my own way.

Coming out on the other side of the veranda, I saw Robert some distance down the lawn. He was not walking; instead he was painting, the easel I'd given him set up so that he could face the long vista to the river at the edge of it. A staff member wasn't far off, strolling with a patient who'd apparently insisted on staying in his bathrobe—how many of us would get dressed, ultimately, given the choice? I was pleased to see that the staff was following my orders to keep a close but respectful watch on Robert Oliver. He might not like being watched at all, but he'd certainly appreciate this bit of privacy allowed him in the process.

I stood observing his figure while he studied the landscape; he would be choosing that taller, rather misshapen tree to the right, I predicted, and ignoring the farm silo that showed over the trees to the far left, across the Sheridan. His shoulders (in the faded shirt he wore almost every day, ignoring the fact that I'd obtained a few others for him) were straight, his head bowed a little toward the canvas, although I estimated that he'd extended the legs on their screws as tall as they'd go. His own legs in graceless khakis were graceful; he shifted balance, considering.

Watching him paint was extraordinary—I'd done it before, but always indoors, where he was aware of my presence. Now I could watch him without his knowing, although I couldn't see the canvas. I wondered what Mary Bertison would give to have this vantage for a few minutes; but, no—she had told me she didn't want to see Robert again. If I helped him get well and he returned to the world, if he became again teacher, painter, exhibitor of work, ex-husband, father with some loving custody, a man who bought vegetables and went to the gym and paid rent on a little apartment in DC or downtown Greenhill, or Santa Fe, would he still choose to stay away from Mary? And, more important, would her anger at him hold? Was it rotten of me to hope it would?

I strolled up to him, hands behind my back, and I didn't speak until I was a few feet away. He turned quickly, gave me a baleful look—the caged lion, the bars you shouldn't bang on. I bowed my head to indicate that my interruption was well-meant. "Good morning, Robert."

He went back to his work; that, at least, showed a certain trust, or perhaps he was too absorbed to let even a psychiatrist interrupt. I stood next to him and gazed frankly at the canvas, hoping that might goad him to some reaction, but he went on with his looking and checking and dabbing. Now he held the brush up against the distant horizon, now he dropped his gaze to the canvas, bent his frame to focus on a rock at the edge of his painted lake. He'd been working on the canvas for at least a couple of hours before this, I saw, unless he was unimaginably fast; it was beginning to round up to fully realized forms. I admired the light on the surface of the water—the surface of his canvas—and the soft liveliness of the distant trees.

But I said nothing aloud about my admiration, dreading his silence, which would smother even the warmest words I might be able to come up with. It was heartening to see Robert painting something other than the dark-eyed lady and her grieving smile, especially something from life. He had two brushes in his painting hand, and I watched silently as he switched between them—the habit, the dexterity, of half a lifetime. Should I tell him that I'd met Mary Bertison? That, over a good wine and fish in parchment, she'd begun to tell me her story and part of his? That she still loved him enough to want to help me heal him; that she never wanted to see him again; that her hair shone in whatever light glanced off it, illuminating its auburn, its gold and purple lights; that she couldn't speak his name without either a tremor or defiance in her voice; that I knew how she held her fork, how she stood balanced against a wall, how she folded her arms against the world; that, like his ex-wife, she was not, after all, the model for the portrait he brought forth over and over from his angry brush; that she, Mary, somehow contained the secret of that model's identity without knowing it; that I was going to find the woman he loved above all people and learn why she had stolen not only his heart but his mind?

That, I thought, watching him pick up a little white, some cadmium yellow for his treetops, was the very nature of mental illness, if you deserted clinical definitions and considered only human life. It was not illness to let another person—or a belief, or a place—take over your heart. But if you gave away your mind to one of those things, relinquished your ability to make decisions, it would, in the end, render you sick—that is, if your doing that wasn't already a sign of your condition. I looked from Robert to his landscape, the gray-washed spaces in the sky where he probably intended to flesh out clouds, the ragged spot on his lake that would surely become their reflections. It had been a long time since I'd had any new thought about the maladies I was trying to treat, day in and day out. Or about love itself.

"Thank you, Robert," I said out loud, and left him. He did not turn to see me go, or if he did, I'd already presented my own back.

Mary called that evening. It surprised me considerably—I'd decided to call her myself but to wait a few days first—and for a moment I couldn't quite understand who was on the line. That alto voice I'd come to like even more over dinner was hesitant as it told me she'd been thinking about her promise to write down for me her memories of Robert. She would do it in installments. It would be good for her, too; she would mail them to me. I could make a complete narrative of them if I wanted, or use them as a doorstop, or recycle the whole pile. She had already begun writing. She laughed rather nervously.

I was disappointed for a moment, because this arrangement meant that I wouldn't see her in person. Although what business did I have, wanting to see her again? She was a free, single woman, but she was also my patient's former girlfriend. Then I heard her say she'd like to have dinner again sometime—it was her turn to invite me, as I'd insisted on paying the bill for our first meal, over her protests—and perhaps it would be better for her to wait until she'd sent me her memories. She didn't know how long that might take, but she'd look forward to another meal; it had been fun to talk with me. That simple word, "fun," touched me to the quick, for some reason. I said I'd like that, that I understood, that I would wait for her missives. And hung up smiling in spite of myself.

CHAPTER 52

Mary

Being in love with someone unattainable is like a painting I saw once. I saw this painting before I got into my habit—now of many years—of writing down basic information about any picture that strikes me in a museum or gallery, in a book or somebody's home. In my home studio, in addition to all my postcards of paintings, I keep a box of index cards, and on each of them is my own handwriting: the title of the painting, the artist's name, the date, the place I encountered it, a synopsis of any little story about the painting that I've discovered on the plaque or in the book, sometimes even a rough sketch of the work—the church steeple is to the left, the road in the foreground.

When I'm frustrated and coming up short on my own canvas, I flip through my cards and find an idea; I add the church steeple, drape the model in red, or break the waves into five sharp separate peaks. Once in a while I find myself flipping through my card file, in actuality or just mentally, searching for that important painting for which I have no card. I saw it when I was in my twenties (I can't even remember what year), probably in a museum, because after college I went to every museum I could, everywhere I went.

This particular work was Impressionist; I'm certain only of that. It showed a man sitting on a bench in a garden, that wild, luxuriant garden the French Impressionists favored and even planted when they needed one, an all-out rebellion against the formality of French gardens and French painting. The tall man was sitting there on the bench, in a kind of bower of green and lavender, dressed like a gentleman—I guess he *was* a gentleman—in formal coat and vest, gray trousers, pale hat. He looked content, complacent but also slightly alert, as if listening for something. If you backed away from the painting, you saw his expression more sharply. (This is another reason I think I saw the painting in life, not in a book; I remember backing away from it.)

Near him in a garden chair—on another bench? perched on a swing?—sat a lady whose costume matched his in elegance, black stripes on a white ground, a little hat tipped forward on her high hair, a striped parasol next to her. If you stepped back farther, you could see another female figure walking among flowering shrubs in the background, the soft colors of her dress almost merging with the garden. Her hair was light, not dark like theirs, and she didn't wear a hat, which I guess made her young or somehow lacking in respectability. The whole had a gold frame, glorious, ornate, rather grimy.

I don't remember connecting this painting with myself at the time I saw it; it simply stayed in me like a dream, and I've gone back to it again and again in my mind. In fact, for years I've checked in surveys of Impressionism without finding it. To begin with, I don't have any proof that it was French, only that it looked like French Impressionism. The gentleman and his two women could have been in a late-nineteenth-century garden in San Francisco, or Connecticut, or Sussex, or even Tuscany. Occasionally I find I've thumbed that image in my mind so many times that I think I've invented it, or that I dreamed it at some point and remembered it the next morning.

And yet those people in the garden are vivid to me. I would never want to unbalance their composition by taking the fine, formal, striped woman from the left side of the painting, but there is tension in the image: Why doesn't the younger woman in the thickets of blossom seem to have a place? Is she the man's daughter? No, something tells you—me—no. She is forever wandering off the canvas toward the right, reluctant to leave. Why doesn't the elegantly dressed gentleman start up and catch her sleeve, detain her for a few minutes, tell her before she wanders away that he loves her, too, that he has always loved her?

Then I picture just those two figures moving, while the sun shines permanently down on the tumbling, rough-stroked flowers and bushes, and the well-dressed lady stays imperturbably in her chair, holding her parasol, certain of her place at the man's side. The gentleman does rise; he leaves the bower with a fierce step, as if on impulse, and takes the girl in the soft dress by her sleeve, her arm. She is firm, too, in her way. There are only flowers between them, brushing her skirt and streaking his tailored trousers with pollen. His hand is olive-skinned, a little thick, a little gnarled, even, at the joints. He stops her with his grip. They have never spoken like this before—no, they aren't speaking now. They are instantly in each other's arms, their faces warm together in the heavy sun. I don't think they are even kissing in the first moment; she is sobbing with relief because his bearded cheek feels the way she imagined it would against her forehead, and maybe he is sobbing, too?

1879

My beloved,

Forgive my weakness in not writing to you, and in staying away in such an unseemly manner. At first it was, yes, a normal absence—as I told you, I went to the south for a week or so and rested a little after a minor indisposition. That was also an excuse, however; I removed myself there not only to recover from my cold, and with the idea of painting a landscape I had not seen in years, but also to recover from a more profound ailment, about which I hinted to you some time ago. I made no progress, as you can see from the salutation of this letter. You were constantly with me, my muse, and I thought of you with startling vividness, not only your beauty and kind company but also your laugh, your smallest gesture, every word you have spoken to me since I first came to care for you more than I should, the affection I feel in your presence and out of it.

So I returned to Paris no less ailing than when I went away, and on my arrival I resolved to try even here to throw myself into work and leave you in peace. I will not hide from you the pleasure your note brought me—the thought that perhaps in some little way you had wished me not to leave you alone—that you had missed me, too. No, no—there is no offense taken, except what I have perhaps in my own foolishness given you. I can only resolve to live in proximity to you with all the composure I can summon.

How foolish for an old man to be so stirred, you will think, even if you are too kind to tell me so. You will of course be right. But in that case you will also underestimate your own power, my dearest, the power of your presence, your receptivity to life and the way that moves me. I shall leave you in peace as much as possible, yet not separate myself completely any longer, since you do not seem to wish it any more than I. For which all those imperious, crumbling gods I saw in Italy be praised.

This is only a part of my story, however. Here I must draw a deep breath and put down for a moment or two the task of writing you, to reach for the extra strength I shall need. I felt all the time I was away that I could not, even if you should wish it, return to you either in person or on paper without fulfilling the hardest promise I have made you.

As you will recall, I said I would one day tell you about my wife. I have hourly regretted that declaration. I am selfish enough to feel that you cannot know me without knowing about her, and even that I might—as you surmised—gain some small relief by doing so. And I would not intentionally break any promise to you as long as I live. If I could give you all of my past, and abscond with all of your future, I would do that, as you must guess; and it is perennial grief to me that I cannot. You see how abundant is my selfishness—to think as I do that you might be happy with me when you already have every reason to be happy.

At the same time, I have felt deeply my mistake in making this promise, because my wife's story is not one I would willingly put into your mind, with its lovely innocence, its hopes for the world. (This will, I know, annoy you, and you will see the sad truth in my assessment only too late.) In any case, I beseech you to save the following pages for an hour when you feel able to hear something terrible, yet all too real—and I ask you to realize that I shall regret every word. When you have read this, you will know a little more than my brother does, and a great deal more than my nephew. And more, certainly, than all the rest of the world. You will know, also, that this is a political matter, and as a consequence some of my safety will rest in your hands. And why should I do such a thing—tell you something that can only dismay you? Well, that is the nature of love: it is brutal in its demands. The day you recognize its brutal nature for yourself, you will look back and know me even better, and forgive me. Probably I will be long gone, but wherever I am I will bless you for your understanding.

I met my wife rather late in life; I was already forty-three and she was forty. Her name, as you may know from my brother, was Hélène. She was a woman of good family, from Rouen. She had never married, not because of any ineligibility on her part but because of her care of her widowed mother, who died only two years before we met. After her mother's death, she came to live with her older sister's family in Paris, and she made herself as indispensable to them as she had been to her mother. She was a person of dignity and sweetness, serious but not humorless, and from our first meeting I was attracted by her bearing and by her consideration of others. She was interested in painting, although she had had little in the way of education in art and was more inclined to books; she read German and some Latin as well, her father having believed in learning for his daughters. And she was devout in a sense that put my own lighthearted doubts to shame. I admired her steadfastness in everything she did.

Her brother-in-law, an old friend, was my advocate in the courtship (although he knew too much about me, perhaps, for the good of my reputation), and he settled a generous dowry on her. We were married in the church of Saint-Germain l'Auxerrois, with a few friends and relations in attendance, and went on to a house in Saint-Germain. We lived quietly. I pursued my painting and exhibitions, and she kept an excellent household in which my friends felt welcome. I came to love her very much, with a love that had perhaps more esteem than passion in it. We were too old to expect children, but we were content with each other, and I felt in her influence a deepening of my own nature and a taming of some of what she doubtless considered my wayward earlier life. Thanks to her steady belief in me, my absorption in painting also deepened and my skill increased.

We might have lived happily forever in this way if our emperor had not considered it his right to plunge France into that most hopeless of wars, invading Prussia—you were, my dear, a girl, but news of the Battle of Sedan must be shocking in your memory, too. Then came the terrible retribution of their armies—and the siege that ravaged our poor city.

Now I must tell you, and frankly, that I was among those whom all of this angered beyond endurance. True, I was not part of the barbaric rabble but was one of those moderates who believed that Paris and France had suffered more than enough at the hands of unthinking, luxurious despotism and who rose against it.

You know that I spent many of these last years in Italy, but what I have not told you is that I was an exile, removing myself from what would undoubtedly have been peril, until I could be certain of resuming a quiet life in my native city—removing myself in grief and cynicism as well. I was in fact a friend of the Commune, and in my heart I have no shame about that, although I grieve for my comrades who were not forgiven by the state for their convictions. Why, indeed, should any citizen of Paris have endured without revolutionary response—or the strongest complaint, at least—what we had not sanctioned in the first place? I have never abandoned that belief, but the price I paid for it was so dear that I might not have committed myself to action had I known what that cost would be.

The Commune established itself on March 26, and there was little real trouble for my unit until the beginning of April, when fighting began in the streets where we were stationed. You would have been living in the suburbs already, and safe, as I know from questions I have put to Yves since my return; he tells me that he did not know your family until later, but that you went through the calamity unscathed, apart from deprivations none could escape. Perhaps you will tell me you heard shooting in distant streets, perhaps not even that. Where there was gunfire, I involved myself with taking messages from one brigade to another, making sketches of the historic scene wherever I could do so without risking lives other than my own.

Hélène did not share my sympathies. Her faith allied her strongly with the rights of the recently fallen regime, but she was tender toward all I believed; she asked me not to share with her anything that might compromise me, were either of us to be caught. In honor of this wish, I did not tell her where the brigade with which I was most deeply involved was bivouacked, and I will not tell you now. It was an old street, and a narrow one; we blockaded it during the night of May 25, knowing that this rampart would be of great importance in the defense of the area if, as we expected, the false government sent in militia to try to break us the next day.

I promised Hélène that I would not be late, but during the night the need arose to relay a round of messages to our comrades in Montmartre, and I volunteered to take those messages, as I was not yet suspected by the police. I traveled without detection, in fact, to that area, and would have returned in the same manner had I not been caught and detained. It was my first encounter with the militia. My questioning was prolonged and threatened several times to become violent, and I was not released until noon the next day. I thought for many hours that I might well be executed on the spot. Again, I will not tell you the details of my interrogation, as I don't wish you to be privy to them, even eight years afterward. It was a terrifying experience.

But I will and must tell you what is infinitely worse: Hélène, missing me during the night and taking alarm, began to search for me at first light, asking among our neighbors until her apprehension finally persuaded one of them to take her to our barricade. I was still imprisoned. She arrived before the barricade to inquire after me at the very moment troops from the center appeared. They opened fire on everyone present, Communards and bystanders alike. The government, of course, has denied all such incidents. She fell, shot through the forehead. One of my companions recognized her, pulled her from the skirmish, and protected her body behind the rubble.

When I arrived, having run first to our home and found it empty, she was already growing cold. She lay in my arms with the gush of blood from her wound drying on her hair and clothing. Her face showed only surprise, although her eyes had closed by themselves. I shook her, called to her, tried to rouse her. My only, and pitiful, consolation lay in her having died instantly—that and the belief that if she had known what was about to happen, it would have been in her nature to commend herself in that moment to her God.

I buried her, more hastily than I wanted to, in the cemetery of Montparnasse. Within days my grief was increased by the swift defeat of our cause and the execution of thousands of comrades, and especially our organizers. During this final extinction, I slipped out of France with the help of a friend who lived near one of the city gates. I traveled alone toward Menton and the border, feeling that I could do nothing more for a country that had refused its only hope of justice, and unwilling to live in fear of future arrest.

My brother remained faithful to me throughout this ordeal, tending Hélène's memory and grave in silence and writing to me from time to time during my absence to advise me whether or not I might return. I was a small player in that drama and not, in the end, of interest to a government with much rebuilding to accomplish. I returned, indeed, not out of any desire to contribute to France's well-being but out of gratitude to my brother and the wish to be of service to him in his afflictions. I discovered, not from him but from Yves, that he was losing his sight. Whatever assistance I could give him, and the dogged habit of pursuing my painting, were the only pleasures left to me until I met you. I was a wretch without wife, children, or country. I lived without the dream of society's improvement that must be the motivation of every thinking man, and my nights were a horror because of the death that had filled my arms with useless, cruel sacrifice.

The radiance of your presence, your natural gifts, the delicacy of your affection and friendship, have meant more to me than I can say. Now I think I will need less than ever to explain that to you. I will not demean you by insisting on secrecy—most of my happiness already rests in your hands. And, lest I find myself unable or unwilling to fulfill my promise and send you these truths about myself, I will close quickly by signing myself, heart and soul,

Your
O. V.

Chapter 53

Marlow

I'd paid particularly close attention to Mary's report that Robert Oliver had first met the woman of his obsession in a crowd at the Metropolitan Museum of Art, and now I considered whether I could ask Robert about the incident directly. Whatever had happened there, whatever he had seen in her, had absorbed much of his attention—and probably shaped his illness—since then. If he had imagined the woman in that crowd at the Met—in other words, if she had been his hallucination, this would imply a rethinking of my diagnosis of Robert, and a serious shift in his treatment. Did he now paint from memory, whether he'd originally seen a real woman or not? Or was he still hallucinating? The fact that he was apparently painting a modern woman, glimpsed once, in nineteenth-century clothing, implied in itself some act of imagination, perhaps involuntary. Did he have other hallucinations? If he did, he wasn't painting them, at least not at the moment.

Whatever the case, by the time of his move to Greenhill with Kate, he'd been imagining the woman's face at least occasionally; after all, Kate had found a sketch of her in Robert's shirt pocket during their drive south. But if I asked Robert about his first sighting of the woman and included any information about the museum, he would know at once that I'd been talking with someone he was close to, and the pool of possibilities would be very small, then—perhaps a pool of one, since he already knew I had Mary's last name. He appeared to have confided in Mary but not Kate and was unlikely to have talked with anyone else at all, unless he'd had friends in New York to whom he might have mentioned his unforgettable first sight of the woman. He'd implied to Mary that he'd seen the stranger only a few times, but I found that difficult to believe, especially after viewing those powerful paintings at Kate's. Surely he'd known her intimately and absorbed her face and presence over time. Robert claimed he didn't work from photographs, but might he have been able to persuade a stranger to model live for him until he had enough material to work from for future portraits?

But I couldn't risk asking Robert any of this; if I revealed the extent of my knowledge to him, I'd never win his trust. My telling him I knew Mary's name had probably been an error. I did go so far as to inquire, during one of my morning visits to the big armchair in his room, where he'd first gotten to know the woman who inspired most of his work. He looked briefly at me, then went back to the novel he was reading. After a while I could only excuse myself and wish him a good day. He'd taken to borrowing crime thrillers from the shelves of well-thumbed paperbacks in the patients' sitting room, reading them with a kind of bored dedication when he wasn't painting; he chewed up about one a week, and they were always the crudest kind of potboiler about the Mafia, or the CIA, or murder mysteries set in Las Vegas.

I had to wonder whether Robert felt some kind of sympathy for the criminals in these books, since he'd been arrested himself with a knife in his hand. Kate had said he sometimes read thrillers, and I'd seen them on his office shelves, but she'd also said he read exhibition catalogs and works of history. There were much better books than those detective novels in the patients' sitting room, including some biographies of artists and writers (I confess I tucked a few of those into the shelves myself, to see if he'd pick them up), but he never touched them. I could only hope that he wasn't acquiring any further taste for violence, from tales of murder, although I saw no signs of it. He was as unlikely to tell me where and how he'd encountered his favorite model as to explain why he limited his reading to the very dregs of the sitting-room shelf.

Mary's story about his first glimpse of his lady had given me another thought, however, and perhaps it was also her reminding me laughingly of the genius of Sherlock Holmes that made me hold that little tale up to the light again and again. I even called Mary one day and asked her to repeat the story as Robert had told it to her at Barnett College, and she did, in very nearly the same words. Why was I asking? She had promised to explain more later, and she would. I thanked her politely, acknowledging the installments she was sending and careful not to press her for a meeting of any sort.

I couldn't shake my feeling about that moment, however, and a Holmesian idea about it took hold of me—a particular suspicion, but also a sense that, on principle, one should go see the scene of the event for oneself. It was just the Met, and I'd been there many times over the years, but I wanted to find the spot of Robert's first hallucination, or inspiration, or—had it been falling in love? Even if there was no gun at the scene, no bit of rope hanging from the ceiling, nothing one could pull out a magnifying glass to examine—well, it was silly, but I would go, partly because I could combine it with a more important mission, a visit to my father. I hadn't been up to Connecticut in nearly a year, which was six months too long, and although he sounded cheerful on the phone and in the little notes he sent on his parish stationery (it needed using up, he said, and he disdained e-mail), I worried that if anything was wrong he'd never tell me by any of those media. And what might be wrong, if something really was, would likely be a drooping of his spirits, which he certainly wouldn't report.

With all this in mind, I chose an upcoming weekend and bought two train tickets, one a round-trip to Penn Station from Washington, and the other a loop up to my hometown and back to New York. I splurged on a reservation for a night in a dingy but pleasant old hotel near Washington Square, a place I'd once spent a weekend with a young woman I'd half expected to marry; surprising, now, how long ago that had been and how much I'd forgotten about her, a woman I'd once embraced in a hotel bed and with whom I'd sat on the benches in Washington Square Park while she pointed out all the species of trees that grew there. I didn't know where she was now; probably she'd married someone else and become a grandmother.

I thought fleetingly of inviting Mary to go with me to New York but couldn't puzzle out what that might entail or how she'd take it, how I could solve or even bring up the matter of hotel rooms. It might have been appropriate to go to the museum with her, since Robert Oliver's past consumed her even more deeply than it did me. But it was too much of a conundrum. In the end I didn't tell her about my plans; she hadn't called in a couple of weeks anyway, and I assumed she'd get more of her account of Robert to me when she was ready. I'd call her on my return, I decided. I told my staff that I would miss one day of work to see my father, and then I gave the usual orders for Robert and my other worrisome patients to be watched with special care.

I went straight from Penn Station to Grand Central to catch the Metro-North New Haven Line; I'd have a long overnight with my father before my visit to the city. It's not a bad ride, and I've always liked the train, which I use for both reading and daydreaming. This time I read some of the book I'd brought, a translation of *The Red and the Black,* but also watched the early-summer scenery go by, the miserably damaged heart of the Northeast Corridor, brick warehouses, the backyards of railroad neighborhoods in small towns and city suburbs, a woman hanging up laundry in slow motion, kids on an asphalt school playground, a towering landfill with gulls circling above it like vultures, the glitter of metal sticking out of the ground here and there.

I must have drowsed, because the sun was lighting up salt water by the time we reached the Connecticut coast. I've always loved that first glimpse of Long Island Sound, the Thimble Islands, the old pilings, the marinas full of shiny new boats. I grew up on this coast, more or less; our town is ten miles inland, but a Saturday in my childhood meant a picnic at the public beach in nearby Grantford, or a stroll on the grounds of Lyme Manor, or a walk along marsh roads that ended in some little platform from which you could view red-winged blackbirds through Mother's binoculars. I've never lived far from the smell of salt water, or its tributaries.

Our town, in fact, was built on a bank of the Connecticut River that the British would have taken by fire in 1812 had not the town's leading citizens hurried down to negotiate with the British captain, at which point the captain discovered that the mayor was his father's cousin and there was some quiet bowing and exchanging of home news. The mayor asserted his general willingness to acknowledge the king, the captain overlooked the obvious halfheartedness of his cousin's declaration, and everyone parted friends. That evening the town gathered in the church—not my father's but a very old one that stands right on the water—to offer thanks. The towns all around them fell to the British torch, and the mayor took in and sheltered their citizens with what must have been generosity but also guilt. Our town is the pride of the local historic preservationists: our churches and inn and oldest houses are original—virgin timber, spared by the ties of family. My father loves to tell that story; I wearied of it as a child but never fail to remember and feel moved by it when I see the water of the river again and the cluster of colonial structures, many of them now shops full of expensive candles and handbags, in the old center.

The railroad came in only thirty years after the gentlemanly captain left, but it arrived at the other end of town. The earliest station is long gone, and there's a fine building from about 1895 in its place; the waiting room—brass, marble, dark wood—has exactly the smell of furniture wax it had when my parents and I waited for the train that would take us to New York to see the Christmas show at Radio City Music Hall in 1957. Today, a couple of passengers were reading the *Boston Globe* on the wooden benches I had loved before my feet could even reach the floor.

My father was waiting there for me, his tweed hat in one papery, transparent hand, his blue eyes bright and pleased when they found my face. He gave me a hug, a squeeze on the shoulders, and held me back for viewing, as if I might still be growing and he needed to check my progress. I smiled, wondering if he saw me with all my hair still brown and on my head, or with the flannel pants and bulky sweater I wore home from college, instead of seeing a man in his fifties, reasonably trim, in plain slacks and a polo shirt, a weekend jacket. And I felt that familiar pleasure of being someone's grown child. It shocked me that I hadn't seen him in so long; in previous years I'd come up more often than this, and I resolved on the spot to visit again much sooner. This man of nearly ninety was my proof of the continuity of life, the buffer between me and mortality—immortality, he would have said with a chiding smile, the clergyman in him tolerating the scientist in me. I had little doubt he'd go to heaven when he left me, although I hadn't believed in heaven since I was ten. Where else could such a person end up?

It occurred to me as I felt his arms around me that I already knew all the trauma that accompanies a parent's death, and knew also that the trauma of losing my father when the time came would be deepened by the earlier loss of my mother, of our shared memories of her, and by the fact that he was my last caretaker, the second to go. I'd helped patients through such passages, in fact, and their grief was often lingering and complex; after I'd lost my mother I'd come to understand that even the quietest slipping away of parental presence could be a devastation. If there were more serious symptoms in a patient, some ongoing struggle with mental illness, a parent's death could tip delicate balances, break down carefully maintained coping patterns.

But none of my professional understanding could console me ahead of time for the eventual loss of this mild, white-haired man in his lightweight summer coat, with his mingled optimism and cynicism about human nature, his calm ability to pass his vision test year after year despite the doubtful glances of the DMV clerks. When I saw him standing in front of me now, eighty-nine this fall and yet so much himself, I was seeing both his presence and his looming absence. When I saw him waiting for me in his good clothes, the bulge of car keys and wallet in his pants pockets, his shoes polished, I felt as always both his reality and the thin air that would one day replace him. In a strange way, I sometimes believed that he would not be complete for me until he was gone, perhaps because of the suspense of loving someone at the far edge of life.

While he was still here, I hugged him back solidly—hard,

even—surprising him so that he had to steady himself on his feet. He'd shrunk; I was now a head taller than he. "Hello, my boy," he said, grinning and taking my upper arm in a firm grasp. "Shall we get out of here?"

"Sure, Dad." I slung my overnight bag on my shoulder, refusing the hand he stretched out for it. In the parking lot, I asked if he wanted me to drive, then regretted my request; he looked at me severely, humorously, and got his glasses out of the inside pocket of his sport jacket, wiping them with his handkerchief before putting them on. "When did you start driving with those?" I asked, to cover my gaffe.

"Oh, I was supposed to years ago, but I didn't really need them. Now it's a little easier with them on my nose, I'll admit." He started the engine, and we pulled magisterially out of the lot. I noticed that he drove more slowly than I remembered and that he sat peering forward; they were probably old glasses. It seemed to me that his stubbornness was one of the main characteristics he'd passed to his only child. It had preserved and strengthened us both, but had it also made loners of us?

CHAPTER 54

Marlow

Our house is only a few miles from the station, set back in the historic part of town and a short walk from the water. This time, for some reason, I felt a pang when I saw the front door at the end of its short but melancholy row of arborvitae. It had been decades since I'd last watched my mother open that door; I don't know why that hit me harder than usual this time.

I covered for myself—nothing would have pained my father more than for me to mention such a twinge aloud—by noting how good the yard looked and letting my father point out the hedges he'd trimmed the week before, the grass he kept neatly cut with his push mower. There was the familiar smell of boxwood, pots of impatiens around the small front door. It wasn't a large yard, in front at least, because the seventeenth-century merchant who'd built the house had wanted it close to the street. The backyard stretched farther, into the ragged remains of an orchard, as well as into a kitchen garden that my mother had somehow maintained in her spare hours. My father still put in tomatoes every summer, and a few gnarled parsley roots burgeoned out among them, but he wasn't the gardener she'd been.

My father unlocked the house and ushered me in, and as always I was assailed by objects and scents with which I'd grown up, the threadbare Turkish rug in the front hall, the corner shelf that housed a ceramic cat I'd made in art class once and glazed to look like those in my mother's book on ancient Egyptian art—she'd been so proud of my initiative, my eye. I suppose every child makes a few lumpy things of this sort, but not every mother keeps them forever. The radiator clanged and slurped in the front hall; it was distinctly not eighteenth century, but it kept the downstairs warm and gave off a smell I'd always loved, like scorched cloth. "I turned it on just this morning," my father apologized. "It's been darn cold for summer."

"Good idea." I set my bag beside it and went into the kitchen bathroom to wash my hands. The house was neat, clean, pleasant, and the floors glowed—my father had succumbed in the last year to my insistence on a housekeeper, a Polish lady from Deep River who came every other week. My father said she scrubbed even the pipes under the kitchen sink. That would have pleased Mother, I pointed out, and he had to agree.

When we'd both washed up, he reported that he had some soup to give me for a late lunch and began to pour it into a pan on the stove. His hands shook a little, I noticed, and this time I prevailed on him to let me fix our meal, heating the soup and putting out the pickles and pumpernickel bread and English tea he loved, warming the milk so that it wouldn't cool his tea. He sat in the wicker chair my mother had bought for the corner of the kitchen, telling me about his parishioners without mentioning their names, although I knew who most of them were anyway because they or their grown children had lingered with him for years: one had lost her husband in a car accident, another had retired after teaching at the high school for forty years and celebrated by having a very private but despairing crisis of faith. "I told him that we couldn't be sure of anything except the power of love," he said, "and that he was under no requirement to believe in a particular source of that love, as long as he could keep giving and receiving some in his own life."

"Did he go back to believing in God?" I asked, squeezing out the tea bags.

"Oh, no." My father sat with his hands tucked serenely between his knees, his watery eyes fixed on me. "I didn't expect him to. In fact, he probably hadn't believed in years, and his teaching just kept him too busy to worry about the matter. Now he comes to see me once a week and we play chess. I make sure I beat him."

And you make sure he's loved, I added in silent admiration. My father had never shown the slightest disrespect for my natural atheism, even when I'd wanted to argue with him in high school and again in college, wanted to provoke him. "Faith is simply whatever is real to us," he always told me in response, and then he'd quote Saint Augustine or a Sufi mystic and slice a pear for me, or set up the chessboard.

As we made our way through the lunch and later some pieces of dark chocolate, my father's thrifty pleasure, he asked me how my work was going. I'd intended not to mention Robert Oliver to him—I felt vaguely that my concern for the man might sound unbalanced, unjust to my other patients, among other things, or, worse, that I might not be able to justify to him the actions I'd taken on Robert's behalf. But in the deep quiet of the dining room, I found myself telling him nearly the whole story. Like my father, I didn't mention the name of my parishioner. My father listened with what I could tell was genuine interest, buttering his pumpernickel; like me, he loved nothing better than a human portrait. I told him about my conversations with Kate; I left out the fact that I'd gone back in the evening to Kate's house and had invited Mary to dinner. Perhaps he would have forgiven even those things, assuming as he naturally would that I had Robert's best interests at heart.

When I described how Robert wore the same clothes over and over, changing them only long enough to have them washed; his dogged reading of books below his intellect; and his endless silence, my father nodded. He finished the last of his soup, set down the spoon. It slipped from his hand, clattering on the dish, and he put it straight. "Penance," he said.

"What do you mean?" I took a last square of chocolate.

"This man is doing penance. That's what you're describing, I think. He punishes his flesh and suppresses the longing of his soul to speak about its misery. He mortifies body and mind to atone for something."

"To atone? But for what?"

My father poured another cup of tea, carefully, and I refrained from helping him. "Well, you are more likely to know that than I, aren't you?'

"He left his wife and children," I mused. "Possibly for another woman. But I think it wasn't that simple. His ex-wife doesn't seem to feel he was really ever hers, somehow, and neither does the woman to whom he went. He left the second woman, too, after a short time. And since he won't talk with me, I have no way of guessing how guilty he feels toward either of them."

"It seems to me," said my father, dabbing his lips with a blue paper napkin, "that all those paintings are a part of his penance. Perhaps he is apologizing to her?"

"You mean the lady he paints? She may be a figment of his imagination, remember," I pointed out. "If he based her on a real person, as his wife believed, it was a person he didn't really know. And the woman he most recently left also seems to think he couldn't have known the mysterious lady well, even if she was real, although I'm not sure I agree."

"Isn't it in her interest to think so?" My father was leaning back in his chair, contemplating our empty lunch dishes with the same attention he usually gave to my queen's pawn. "Surely it would be horrifying for her to discover that he'd been painting over and over a live woman he knew intimately, especially given the nature of the portraits you described, the passion in them."

"True," I said. "But whether his model is real or a hallucination, why would he need to do penance for her sake? Could she be someone real he somehow injured? If he's apologizing to a hallucination, he's in worse shape than I've thought up to now."

Oddly, my father said again what he'd always told me in high school, an echo of the line I'd been thinking of just a little while earlier. "Faith is what is real to us."

"Yes," I said. I felt sudden resentment—I couldn't return even to my family home, my shrine, without being pursued by Robert Oliver. "He has his goddess, that's certain."

"Maybe she has him," observed my father. "Here, I'll get these dishes, and probably you'd like a nap after your trip."

I couldn't deny that the house was lulling me, as it always did. The clocks in each room, some of them nearly as old as the mantel-pieces they sat on, gave off a sound that seemed to say, "Sleep, sleep, sleep." It was so rare for me, in the outside world, to get quite enough rest from week to week, and I never liked to waste my weekends napping. I helped my father clear up and left him with a soapy sponge in his hand, then climbed the stairs.

My room was reserved for me forever, and in it hung a portrait of my mother that I'd painted (from a photograph; I was not a purist like Robert) a year or so before her death. It struck me that if I'd known what was soon to happen to her I would have painted it from life, no matter how inconvenient that might have been for either of us, arranging sittings—I would have done it not because it could have improved the portrait (I hadn't been much good in those days anyway) but because it might have given us another eight or ten hours together. I could have memorized her face from life, then, measured its small irregularities with a brush held up horizontally or vertically, smiled into her eyes whenever I glanced up from my work. As it was, the portrait showed a neat, nearly pretty, dignified woman with a deep thoughtfulness on her face but none of the life and strength I'd known in my mother in real life, none of that flash of matter-of-fact humor. She wore her black cardigan and her dog collar, a formal smile; the photograph must have been taken for a parish newsletter or office wall.

I wished now, as I often had, that I'd painted her in the deep-red dress my father had bought for her at Christmas with my approval when I was twelve, the only clothing I ever knew him to purchase for her. She had put it on for us, put her hair up, and clasped around her neck the string of pearls she'd worn for their wedding. It was a modest dress of soft wool, fitting for a pastor's wife and for the pastor she'd recently become. When she came down the stairs for Christmas dinner, we had both sat speechless, and my father had taken a photograph of my mother and me, black and white: my mother in her rich dress and me in my first sport jacket, which was already getting short in the sleeves—where had that picture gone? I must remember to ask him if he knew.

My room was wallpapered in a pattern of faded brown-and-green stripes; the small rug looked freshly washed, I thought, a little too fluffy, and the wood floor polished—the Polish housekeeper. I lay down on the narrow bed I still thought of as mine and drifted off, coming to in the silence and realizing that I'd slept only twenty minutes, then plunging into a deeper sleep for another hour.

Chapter 55

Marlow

When I woke, my father was standing in the doorway with a smile, and I realized that the creaking of the stairs as he made his slow way up them had been my alarm clock. "I know you don't like to nap too long," he said apologetically.

"Oh, I don't." I struggled to one elbow. The clock on my wall said it was already five thirty. "Would you like to go for a walk?" I liked to get my father out walking whenever I visited, and he brightened.

"Certainly," he said. "Shall we go walk out Duck Lane?"

I knew this meant to my mother's grave, and my heart was not in it today, but for his sake I agreed at once, sat up, and began to put on my shoes. I heard my father make his way back downstairs, holding the railing, no doubt, and bringing both feet to each step before moving on; I was thankful for his caution, although I couldn't help remembering the quick thud of his feet coming down to breakfast or clattering back up for a forgotten book before he went to the church office. We walked slowly along the road, too, his hand on my arm and his hat on his head, and I could see on each side the beginning of summer, cool and shifting by the moment, bulrushes in the marsh, a crow rising out of them, some late-afternoon sun breaking over the neighbors' houses with the dates above their front doors—1792, 1814 (that one had just missed the British invasion, I realized, and the mayor's civil refusal to have his town burned).

As I'd known he would, my father paused in front of the gates to the cemetery, which stood open until dark, and gave my arm the gentlest pressure; we went in together past lichen-stained markers that bore the names of forgotten founders, a few with that winged Puritan skull at the top to warn us of the end to which we all come whether we've sinned or no, and then back to the more recent graves. My mother's sat next to a family named Penrose, whom we'd never known, and the plot was big enough to accommodate my father's presence once he joined her. I thought for the first time that I ought to decide whether or not to purchase a plot here; unlike them, I'd already opted to donate my body to science, then be cremated, but perhaps there was room to stick an urn between my parents; I imagined the three of us sleeping together forever in this king-size bed, my reduced self between their protective bodies.

The image wasn't real enough to me to give me any further regrets; what lowered my spirits was the sight of my mother's name and her dates, chiseled in simple letters on the granite, her too-fleeting years—what was the line from Shakespeare, the sonnet? Something, something— "and summer's lease hath all too short a date."

I quoted it aloud to my father, who had bent to remove a branch from the plot, and he smiled and shook his head. "There's a better sonnet for this occasion." He threw the branch slowly but with sure aim into the bushes near the fence. "'But if the while I think on thee, dear friend, / All losses are restor'd, and sorrows end.'"

I felt he meant me, his remaining friend, as well as my mother, and was grateful. I had tried in recent years to think of her at peace, not as I'd seen her in those last minutes, struggling against her departure from us. I wondered, as I often did, which was worse, the fact that she'd had to die at fifty-four or the way she'd gone. They went together, those two sad realities, but I never tired of trying to tease them apart, to extricate one misery from the other. I couldn't bring myself to take my father's arm as we stood there, or put mine around him, and I was very touched when he did just that for me, his skinny old hand gripping my back. "I grieve for her, too, Andrew," he said matter-of-factly, "but you learn that a person is not so far away, especially when you're my age."

I refrained from pointing out the usual difference in our perspectives: I believed the extent of my reunion with my mother would be the mingling, over millions of years, of the atoms that had composed our bodies. "Yes, I feel her nearby sometimes, when I'm doing my best." I couldn't say more around the fist in my throat, so I didn't try, and for some reason I remembered Mary, sitting on my sofa in her white blouse and blue jeans, telling me that she didn't want to see Robert Oliver ever again. There are different ways of taking grief in different circumstances; my mother had never abandoned me, except unwillingly, in those minutes that had constituted her good-bye.

We walked a bit farther up Duck Lane, and then my father indicated with a little pause and a shuffling turn that he'd had enough, and we ambled back to the house even more slowly. I commented that the neighborhood had remained tranquil despite the new expansion of the town to the west, and he said he was grateful for the presence of the river, which had prevented the interstate from coming any closer. The very quiet of the street worried me; how much company could my father have here, when we hadn't seen a single neighbor outside since setting out on our excursion? My father nodded, as if the silence around him was all to the good. At our own front walk, I paused to say something else I'd thought in the cemetery but had been unable to utter—not my longing for Mother but the other ghost who had haunted me there. "Dad? I'm not sure I've been doing the right thing. This patient I told you about."

He understood at once. "You mean, by questioning the people close to him?"

I put a hand on one of the trunks of our arborvitae. It had the hairy, peeling texture I remembered from my childhood, the hardness of the wood itself just underneath. "Yes. He gave me verbal consent, but—"

"Do you mean because he doesn't know you're doing it, or because you aren't sure of your own motives?"

As always, when I approached him about something important, I was left a little speechless at his shrewdness. I hadn't actually told him either of those things. "Both, I guess."

"Look at your motives first, then, I think, and the rest will fall into place."

"I will. Thanks."

Over dinner, which I insisted on making for us, and our subsequent game at the chess table in the living room—he laid and lit a fire by sitting on a low chair near the fireplace and poking sticks into the grate—he told me about his writing projects and about a woman ten years younger than he was who drove over from Essex once or twice a month to read aloud to him, although he could still read to himself. This was the first he'd said about her, and I asked how he'd met her, a little surprised. "She used to live here and come to the church before I retired, and then she and her husband moved away, but not far, so later they would come to hear my annual emeritus sermon. He died and I didn't hear from her for a long time, but she finally sent a note and now we have these nice meetings. At my age, it can't be much, of course," he added, "or at hers, but it means a little companionship." I knew he was saying, too, that he could never love anyone but my mother and me enough to rearrange his short future. He reached for his queen and then changed his mind. "What sort of company do you keep these days?" he asked me.

This was a rare question from him, and I welcomed it. "You know I'm a worse old bachelor than you are, Dad. But I almost think I've met someone."

"The young woman, you mean," he said mildly. "Right? The one your patient abandoned most recently."

"I can't put anything over on you." I watched him move a bishop out of harm's way. "Yes. But she really is too young for me, and I think she's still wrapped up in what this other man did to her." I didn't add that my relationship with her was complicated by my having used her for professional research, or that even if she was now single, she had been my patient's lover and was therefore an ethical puzzle; all that would be equally obvious to my father. "Recently abandoned women can be complicated."

"And she's not only complicated but independent, unusual, beautiful," my father said.

"Of course." I pretended to be alarmed for my king's safety, to amuse him.

He wasn't fooled. "And you are worried, first of all, because she recently belonged to your patient."

"Well, it's hardly a matter to overlook."

"But she's single now, and done with him, in practical terms?" He gave me a sharp glance.

I was glad to be able to nod. "Yes, I very much think so."

"How old is she, exactly?"

"Early thirties. She teaches painting at a local university and paints a good deal on her own as well. I haven't seen her work, but I have the sense she's probably quite good. She's done all kinds of odd jobs in order to pursue her painting seriously. She has guts."

"Your mother was in her twenties when I married her. And I was quite a few years older than she was."

"I know, Dad. But that was a much smaller gap. And not everyone is meant for marriage the way you and Mother were."

"Everyone is meant for it," he observed with a flash of pleasure; in the gentle light from lamp and fire, he was calling my bluff. He knew I'd never risk my king, even to let him win. "The problem is simply finding the right person. Ask Plato. Just make sure she finishes your thoughts and you finish hers. That's all you need."

"I know, I know."

"And then you must say to her, 'Madame, I observe that your heart is broken. Allow me to repair it for you.'"

"I wouldn't have thought you had that in you, Dad."

He laughed. "Oh, I could never have said it to any woman myself."

"But then you didn't need to, did you?"

He shook his head, his eyes bluer than usual. "I didn't need to. Besides, if I'd ever said such a thing to your mother, she'd have told me to pull myself together and take out the garbage for her."

And kissed you on the forehead as she said it. "Dad, why don't you come to New York with me tomorrow? I'm going to the museum, and there's an extra bed in my hotel room. It's been a long time since you got down there."

He sighed. "That's an unimaginably big trip for me now. I couldn't walk around properly with you. Even the grocery store is an odyssey these days."

"I understand." But I couldn't help persisting; I didn't want this to be the end, already, of his seeing the world. "Well, then, wouldn't you like to come visit me in Washington this summer? I'll come up and drive you down. Or maybe in the fall, when it cools off?"

"Thank you, Andrew." He put me in check. "I'll think about it." I knew he wouldn't.

"How about at least getting your glasses replaced, Cyril?" It was an old joke, that I could use his first name when I had a special request to make of him.

"Don't be a common scold, my boy." He was grinning at the board now, and I decided to let him win, which he almost had anyway; certainly he was having no problem seeing the pieces.

CHAPTER 56

1879

She wakes with a scream. Yves, in his nightcap, is shaking her shoulder, bringing her a little cognac from his dressing room. It is only a dream, she tells him, gasping. He says that of course it is only a dream. What did she dream about? Nothing, she says—just a strange working of her imagination. Once he has comforted her, he is sleepy again; he has worked like a dray horse these last weeks, she knows; she lets him think she is calm so that he can burrow back into his own dreams. He breathes gently, in and out, while she lights a candle and sits in her rose-trimmed dressing gown on the edge of the bed until light begins to seep through the curtains.

Eventually she needs the chamber pot; she takes it carefully out from under the bed and uses it, her gown tucked up out of the way. When she wipes herself there is a streak like red cadmium, and she has to fumble in the bureau of her dressing room for the cloth pads Esmé has left folded in the top drawer. Another month without hope. The blood itself is horrifying after her dream; she sees it bubbling over a white face, seeping onto the paving stones, a woman's blood mingling in the dirt with the blood of men who have died for their convictions.

She blows out the candle, afraid Yves will wake again; tears sting her eyes. She thinks of Olivier. She cannot tell him her dream—she would not give him such pain. But now she wishes he were here, sitting in the damask chair by the window, holding her. She finds a warmer robe and sits there alone, her hair loose and tears trickling down her neck. If he were here, he would sit down in her chair first, his long, rather spare body filling the space; then she would curl up in his lap like a child. He would hold her, dry her face, draw the robe across her shoulders and knees. He is the most loving person she has ever known, this man who once dodged bullets with a sketchbook in his hand. But then, she wonders, why should he comfort her? Surely his own need is greater. This brings the dream back again, and she makes herself smaller in the chair, crushing her breasts in her arms, waiting for his past to subside in her.

Chapter 57

Marlow

The ride into New York from that direction was, as always, kind of splendid, the tip of the skyline appearing before the city did, like a row of advancing lances: World Trade Center, Empire State, Chrysler, and a lot of towering nonentities whose names and functions I don't know and never will—banks, I suppose, and megalithic office buildings. It's hard to picture the city without that skyline, as it must have looked even forty years ago, and now it's increasingly hard to imagine the Twin Towers back into it. But on the train that morning, I felt the buoyancy that comes with plenty of sound sleep and the anticipation of the city's vitality. It was a feeling of being on vacation, too, or at least away from work—twice already in the space of a couple of months. I checked my cell phone for the hundredth time; there were no pages from Goldengrove or from any of my private patients, so I was truly at liberty. It occurred to me that Mary might have called, but she hadn't, and why should she? I would have to wait at least a few weeks longer before I could call her again myself—I wished once more that she'd allowed me to interview her, as Kate had, but there was a particular pleasure in seeing her words on the page, and her story was possibly more candid than it would have been if she'd had to tell me face-to-face.

I didn't realize until I'd left my bags at the Washington

Hotel and walked out into the Village why I'd chosen this area, if unconsciously. These were Robert's streets, and Kate's; he'd walked from here to school every day, sat in bars with the friends with whom he swapped opinions and sweatshirts, exhibited his work in little galleries not far away. I wished Kate had told me their address, although I couldn't quite see myself actually looking for the building, craning up at it: *Robert Oliver slept here*. But, strangely, I did feel his presence; it was easy to imagine him at twenty-nine or so, just as he was now but with no silver in his snaky hair. Kate was more of a puzzle; she'd surely been different then, but I couldn't picture how.

I searched the streets for them, as a game: that young woman with the blond crew cut and long skirts, the student with a portfolio slung by its strap over one shoulder—no, Robert was taller and more powerful-looking than anyone on this crowded sidewalk. He would have loomed here, as he did at Goldengrove, although New York would have better absorbed his vividness. I wondered for the first time if some of his depression had come from simple displacement: a person larger than life, larger than most, needed a setting to match his energy. Had he gradually wilted, away from Manhattan? It had been Kate who wanted the move to a quieter place, a haven for children. Or had his exile from this pulsating city simply increased his determination to pursue his calling—was that the ferocity Kate had observed when he painted in the attic and slept through his classes at Greenhill? Had he been trying to get himself actually fired from the college so he could justify a return to New York? Why, when he finally fled, had he gone to Washington instead of New York? His having chosen a different city argued for the strength of his bond with Mary, or perhaps it was proof that his dark mistress wasn't in New York anymore, if she ever had been.

I walked past the spot where Dylan Thomas had more or less died in the gutter, or at least been fished out of it for his last ride to the hospital, and the row of houses where Henry James had set *Washington Square*—my father had reminded me of that one this morning, pulling a copy down from his study shelves and eyeing me over his inadequate glasses—"You do still find time to read, don't you, Andrew?" The heroine of that book had lived in one of the prim rows facing the square, and when she'd finally rejected her money-grubbing suitor, she'd sat down to her embroidery "'for life, as it were,'" my father read aloud.

The late nineteenth century again; I thought of Robert and his mysterious lady, with her full skirts and tiny buttons, her dark eyes more alive than paint was supposed to be. This morning Washington Square was tranquil with summer sun, people talking on the benches, as generations had before them, as I once had with a woman I'd thought I might marry, all this time slipping past everyone and disappearing, all of us disappearing with it. There was a comfort in the way the city went on and on without us.

I had a sandwich at a sidewalk café, then took the subway from Christopher Street up to West 79th and changed to a crosstown bus. Central Park was overflowing with green, with people rollerblading and bicycling, joggers narrowly avoiding death by those on wheels—a sublime Saturday, New York exactly as it should be, as I hadn't seen it in years. More than ever, I remembered my world here, its spokes radiating south from Columbia, from my undergraduate classrooms and dormitories. New York meant youth to me, as it had to Robert and Kate. I alighted from the bus and went up a couple of blocks to the Met. The museum steps were covered with visitors, settled there like birds, taking photographs of one another, noisy, fluttering down to buy hot dogs or Cokes from the food carts nearby, waiting for their rides, or their friends, or resting their feet. I threaded a path among them and up to the doors.

I hadn't walked in there in almost a decade, I realized now; how could I have let such acres of time stretch between me and this miraculous entrance, the soaring lobby with its urns of fresh flowers, the hubbub of people flowing through it, the entrance to ancient Egypt yawning at one side? Some years later, my wife went up for a visit to the museum by herself and told me that a new area had been opened just under the main staircase; she had turned in there, tired from wandering, and found an exhibition on Byzantine Egypt. Only two or three people at a time could fit in the space; she'd come around a corner into it and found herself alone with just a few ancient objects, perfectly lit. And she told me afterward that her eyes had filled with tears because the sight had made her feel her connection to other human beings. (*But you were by yourself there,* I said. She said, *Yes, alone with those objects someone had made.*)

I knew I'd want to stay all afternoon, even if my visit on Robert's behalf took only five minutes. I was remembering now treasures half forgotten: colonial furniture, Spanish balconies, Baroque cartoons, a big languid Gauguin I'd particularly liked. I shouldn't have come here on a Saturday, when the crowds swelled to their peak; would I be able to see a thing up close? On the other hand, Robert had glimpsed his lady through a crowd, so perhaps it was appropriate that I was here as part of one. With a colored metal museum button folded over the top of my shirt pocket and my jacket over my arm, I went up the great staircase.

I had forgotten to ask if the Degas collection was all in one place, and whether it had been moved since Robert's obsession with it in the '80s. It didn't matter much; I could always go back to the information desk, and perhaps I wasn't looking for information anyway. I found the Impressionist rooms where I'd remembered them, more or less, and was transfixed by their verdant expanse—the crowds were thick here, but I had sudden visions of orchards, garden paths, tranquil water, ships, Monet's regal arched cliffs. A shame that these images had become iconic, a tune we were all tired of humming. But every time I stepped closer to one of those canvases, the old tune was silenced by a swell of something enormous, color that really was almost melody, thick paint on surfaces that actually conveyed the smells of pasture and ocean. I remembered the stack of books Kate had found next to Robert's attic sofa, books that had inspired his vigorous painting of walls and ceiling. These works had not been dead for him, a contemporary artist, but somehow fresh and refreshing, even in glossy color reproductions from the library. He was a traditionalist himself, of course, but he'd seen through the endless exhibits and posters to something still revolutionary.

The Degas collection was mostly housed in four rooms, with a few other examples of his work—mainly large portraits I didn't remember—spilling into the halls of the nineteenth-century collection. I'd forgotten, too, that the Met's collection of his work must be one of the largest in any museum anywhere, perhaps the largest in the world; I made a mental note to check that. The first room contained a bronze cast of Degas's most famous sculpture, *The Little Fourteen-Year-Old Dancer,* with her skirt of real faded netting and the satin ribbon slipping off the braid down her back. She stood in the path of anyone who entered, her face turned up, blind and submissive but perhaps touched by a dream no non-dancer could understand, her hands clasped behind her, her lower back delicately arched, her right foot forward and impossibly turned out in the beautiful deformity for which she'd been trained.

The walls around her were dominated by Degas, with a few other painters here and there: his portraits of rather ordinary women smelling flowers in their homes, and canvases of dancers. The dancers filled the next two rooms almost completely, young ballerinas with feet on barre or chair, tying their shoes, their skirts upended as they leaned over, like the feathers of swans fishing underwater, the sensuality that made you scan the lines of their bodies just as you might have scanned them at the ballet itself, the heightened intimacy of seeing them in training, offstage, behind the scenes, ordinary, tired, shy, mutilated, ambitious, underage or overripe, exquisite. I made my way from one to another and then stopped in front of a third to look around.

Beyond the dancers was a little room of Degas nudes, women stepping from baths and swathing themselves in huge white towels. The nudes were heavily fleshed, as if the ballerinas had aged and gained weight, or turned out to be curvaceous after all under the discipline of their tight bodices and fluffy skirts. Nothing spoke to me of Robert's presence or the lady he'd once seen in these galleries; although perhaps she'd been here as a Degas fan herself. He'd had permission to sketch in the museum, he'd set up his easel or held his drawing pad before him on some busy morning in the late '80s, he'd seen a woman in the crowd and then lost her. If he'd wanted to sketch, why had he been there in a crowd? I didn't even know if these rooms had been arranged the same way then, and checking it would make me appear fanatical, if only to myself. This was a ridiculous pilgrimage to have made; I was already weary from the jostling of the crowd, all these people out gathering impressions of impressions of Impressionists, collecting firsthand images they already knew thirdhand.

I sent a thought out to Robert and resolved to go downstairs to some quiet room full of furniture or Chinese vases that fewer people cared about. Perhaps it had been like this for him; he'd been tired that day, turned and glanced through the crowd—I tried it myself, and my eyes lit on a gray-haired woman in a red dress holding a little girl by the hand, the child tired already, too, staring vacantly around her at people rather than paintings. But that day Robert had looked straight through the mass to a woman he could never forget, a woman possibly dressed up in nineteenth-century clothing for a rehearsal or a photograph or a prank—these possibilities hadn't occurred to me before. Maybe he had gone up to her and talked with her, even in a crowd.

"Are there any more paintings by Degas?" I asked the guard in the doorway.

"Degas?" he said, frowning. "Yes, two more in that room." I thanked him and made my way there, to be thorough; perhaps Robert had had his epiphany, or his hallucination, here. There were fewer people in the next room, possibly because there were fewer Monets. I examined a pastel on brown, drawn in pink and white, a dancer stretching long arms down her long leg, and another of three or four ballerinas with their backs to the painter and their arms around one another's waists or their hands adjusting hair ribbons.

I was done. I turned away, searched for an exit at the other end of the gallery, in the opposite direction from the crowds I'd left. Then she was there, across from me, a portrait in oils about two feet square, painted loosely but with absolute precision, the face I knew, the elusive smile, the bonnet tied under her chin. Her eyes were so alive that you couldn't turn around without meeting them. I went numbly across the room, which seemed huge; it took hours for me to reach her. It was indisputably the same woman, depicted from her blue-clad shoulders up. As I drew close, she seemed to smile a little more; her face was wonderfully alive. If I'd had to guess the painter,

I would have said Manet, although the portrait didn't have his genius. It must be the same period, however: the careful strokes that made up the shoulders of her dress, the lace at her throat, the dark luxury of her hair, were not quite the domain of Impressionism; her face had some of the realism of earlier work. I scanned the plaque—"*Portrait of Béatrice de Clerval,* 1879. Olivier Vignot." Béatrice de Clerval! And painted by Olivier! She was a real woman, all right. But not a living one.

The fellow at the information desk on the first floor helped as much as he could. No, they didn't have any other work by Olivier Vignot, nor any other titles involving Béatrice de Clerval. The piece had been in the collection since 1966, bought from a private collection in Paris. During Robert's tenure in New York City, it had been loaned for a year to a traveling exhibition, one on French portraiture during the rise of Impressionism. He smiled and nodded; that was all he had—did it serve my purposes?

I thanked him, my lips dry. Robert had seen it once or twice before it had been removed to travel with an exhibition. He had not hallucinated, only been struck by a marvelous image. Had he really not asked someone what had happened to the painting? Perhaps he had or perhaps he hadn't; what suited his myth about her was that she had disappeared. And if he had returned to the museum in the years since then, it had not mattered to him whether the painting was actually there or not; by then he'd been producing his own version of her. Even if he'd seen this painting only a few times, he had surely made a sketch of it, a very good one, for his later paintings to resemble her so accurately.

Or had he found the painting again in a book? Obviously, neither artist nor subject was well known, but the quality of Vignot's work had attracted the Met enough to make them purchase the portrait. I tried the gift shop as well, but there was no postcard of it, no book with a reproduction. I climbed the staircase again, went back into the gallery. She was waiting there, glowing, smiling, about to speak. I took out my sketch pad and drew her, the pose of the head—if only I could do it better. Then I stood looking into her eyes. I could hardly bear to leave without taking her with me.

Chapter 58

Mary

After art school I did any job I could find until I finally got some teaching in DC. Now and then I showed a piece of work, or received a small fellowship, or even got into a good workshop. The workshop I want to tell you about is one I went to a few years ago, late August. It was held at an old estate in Maine, on the coast, an area I had always wanted to see and maybe paint. I drove up there from Washington in my little pickup truck, my blue Chevy, which I've junked since then. I loved that truck. I had my easels in the back, my big wooden box of gear, my sleeping bag and pillow, the duffel bag from my father's military service in Korea stuffed full of jeans and white T-shirts, old bathing suits, old towels, old everything.

Packing that bag, I realized I had come a long way from Muzzy and her education; Muzzy would never have tolerated my packing job or what I'd packed, that nest of fraying clothes and gray tennis shoes and boxes of art supplies. She would have hated my Barnett sweatshirt with the cracked lettering across the front and my khakis with the torn pocket flap on the back. I was no grunge, however; I kept my hair long and shining, my skin supple, the ancient clothes very clean. I wore a gold chain with a garnet pendant around my neck, I bought new lace bras and underwear with which to adorn myself under the ratty surface. I loved myself like this, slim swelling roundness dressed up in secret, out of sight—not for any man (I was tired of them all, postcollege)—but for the moment at night when I took off my paint-stained white blouse and the jeans that my knees showed through. It was all for me; I was my own treasure.

I started very early and followed back roads toward Maine, spending the night in Rhode Island at a half-empty roadside motel from the '50s, little white cottages with a sign in fancy black script, the whole place uncomfortably reminiscent for me of the motel in *Psycho*. There were no killers in the place, though; I slept peacefully until almost eight, and had fried eggs in the smoke-filled diner next door. I sketched a little in my notebook as I sat there, recording the fly-specked sheer curtains tied back on either side of window boxes full of artificial flowers, the people drinking coffee.

At the Maine border there was a sign for moose crossing, and the roadsides became crowded with evergreens, which pressed in on either side like armies of giants—no houses, no exits, just miles and miles of tall firs. And then the very edge of the road showed a drift of pale sand, and I realized that I was getting close to the ocean. It gave me a stabbing excitement, like what I used to feel when Muzzy drove us to Cape May in New Jersey for our annual vacation. I imagined myself painting the beach, the landscape, or sitting on rocks by water in the moonlight, all alone. In those days, I still thoroughly enjoyed the romance I called "by myself"; I didn't know yet how it gets lonely, picks up a sharp edge later on that ruins a day now and then—ruins more than that, if you're not careful.

It took me some study to find the right road through that town and out to the retreat; the workshop flyers had a little map on them ending at an inlet away from civilization. The last couple of roads I took were dirt, pushed through dense pinewoods like logging cuts, but mellowed, too, pine seedlings springing up on the shoulder in the shadow of the forest. After a few miles of this, I came to a gingerbread house—it looked like one, anyway—a wooden gatehouse with a sign on it that said ROCKY BEACH RETREAT CENTER, with no one around, and a little farther on I found myself rounding a bend toward a stretch of green lawn. I could see a big wooden mansion with the same gingerbread trim under the eaves, woods, and a glimpse of ocean just beyond. The house was enormous, painted a dull pink, and the lawn was not only a lawn but gardens, trellises, paths, a pink summerhouse, old trees, a flat area where someone had set up croquet, a hammock. I glanced at my watch; I was in plenty of time for registration.

The dining hall, where everyone met that night for the first meal, was in a carriage house with its dividing walls knocked out. It had high, rough rafters and windows edged with squares of stained glass. Eight or ten long tables were arranged on a peeling wood floor, and young men and women—college students; they already looked younger to me than myself—were moving around setting out water pitchers. There was a buffet at one end of the hall with a few bottles of wine on it, glasses, a bowl of flowers, and next to it open coolers full of beers. I had a queasy feeling; it was like the first day in a new school (although as a child I'd gone to the same school for twelve years), or like my college orientation, where you realize that you know no one at all and therefore no one there cares about you, and you're going to have to do something about it. I could see some people talking in little groups near the drinks. I made myself stride over toward those beers (I was proud of my stride in those days) and pluck one from its bed of ice without looking around. When I straightened up to search for a bottle opener, my shoulder and elbow hit Robert Oliver.

It was certainly Robert. He stood there in three-quarter profile, talking with someone, moving out of my way, sidestepping the interruption that was me without even glancing around. He was talking to another man—a man with a thin head and a graying thin beard. It was absolutely, positively Robert Oliver. His curly hair was a little longer in the back than I remembered, with some new silver making it glint, and one of his elbows showed brownly through the hole in his blue cotton shirt. There had been no mention of him in the workshop catalog; why was he here? He had paint or grease on the back of his light-colored cotton pants, as if he'd wiped his hand on his buttocks like a little kid. He was wearing heavy slip-on sandals despite the cool of the New England summer evening already reaching in through the door. He had a beer in one hand and was gesticulating with the other to the man with the narrow head. He was as tall as I remembered, imposing.

I stood frozen, staring at his ear, at the heavy curl of hair around that ear, at his still-familiar shoulder, at the blade of his long hand raised in argument. He half turned, as if he felt my gaze, and then went back to the conversation. I remembered that solid, graceful balance from his perambulations around the studio. Then he glanced around again, with a frown, but it was no double take from the movies; it was more as if he had misplaced something, or was trying to remember what he'd come into a room to look for. He recognized me without recognizing me. I edged away, averting my face. I found it an alarming idea that if I wanted to, I could walk over and tap his shoulder through the blue shirt, interrupt his conversation more firmly. I dreaded his perplexity, the vague *Oh, I'm sorry—where do I know you from?*, the *Good to see you again, whoever you are.* I thought of the hundreds (thousands?) of students he had probably taught since then. Better not to speak to him than to find myself one more blur in the crowd.

I turned quickly to the first person whose eye I could catch, who happened to be a wiry young man with his shirt unbuttoned to his breastbone. It was an impressive breastbone, tanned and prominent; it sported a big chain with a peace sign lying on it. His tanned, flat breasts curved away from it like two lean cuts of chicken. I raised my eyes, guessing he would have long retro locks to match the pendant, but his hair was shorn to a pale stubble. His face was as stark as the breastbone, his nose a beak, his eyes light brown, small, flickering uncertainly at me. "Cool party," he said.

"No, not particularly cool." I was filled with dislike, which I knew was unfairly left over from that moment of seeing Robert Oliver's shoulder turn toward me and then away.

"I don't like it either." The young man shrugged and laughed; his bare chest caved in for a moment. He was younger than I'd thought, younger than I. His smile was friendly and it brightened his eyes. Perversely, I disliked him again; of course he would be too cool to like any gathering of human beings, or at least to admit that he did if someone else disagreed. "How do you do—I'm Frank." He put out his hand, renouncing all the retro cool in a moment, a mama's boy, a gentleman. The timing was impeccable, disarming. There was deference in it that recognized my—oh, six years—seniority; there was a spark, too, that said I was a sexy older woman. I had to admire the skill of his admiration. He seemed to know I was almost thirty, elderly, and to tell me in the dry warmth of his hand that he liked thirty, he liked it very much. I wanted to laugh, but I didn't.

"Mary Bertison," I said. Robert had moved, at the edge of my vision; he was making his way toward the dining-hall doors to talk with someone else. I kept my back turned. My hair made a partial curtain, a cloak, which protected me.

"So, what made you come here?"

"Confronting past lives," I said. At least he hadn't asked if I was one of the faculty.

Frank frowned.

"Just kidding," I said. "I'm here to take the landscape workshop."

"Very cool." Frank beamed. "Me, too. I mean, I'm taking it, too."

"Where did you go to school?" I asked, trying to replace the distraction of Robert Oliver's profile with a sip of my beer.

"SCAD," he said casually. "MFA." The Savannah College of Art and Design was becoming quite a good school, and he seemed pretty young to have finished his degree already; I felt a flicker of respect in spite of myself.

"When did you graduate?"

"Three months ago," he admitted. That explained the college-party manners, the recently practiced smile. "I got a fellowship to do the landscape course here, because I'm teaching in the fall and I need to kind of add that in to the picture."

The picture, I thought, *the picture of me, Frank the gifted artist, and my wonderful future*. Well, a few years out of art school would cure him nicely of his picture; on the other hand—he already had a teaching job? Robert Oliver was entirely out of my range of vision now, even when I tilted my head and my perspective shifted. He had gone somewhere else in the room without recognizing me at all, without even sensing in the room all of my longing to be recognized. Instead, I was completely stuck with "Frank."

"Where are you teaching?" I asked, to cover my internal meanness.

"SCAD," Frank said again, which gave me pause. He had been hired straight into the faculty of his own program, as a graduating MFA student? That was quite unusual; maybe he was right to dream about his future. I said nothing for a few seconds, wondering when dinner would start and how I could sit either as far away from or as close to Robert Oliver as possible. Far away would be better, I decided. Frank was scrutinizing me with interest. "You have great hair," he said finally.

"Thanks," I said. "I grew it out in third grade so I could be the princess in my class play."

He frowned again. "So you're doing landscape? It should be great. I'm almost glad Judy Durbin broke her leg."

"She broke her leg?"

"Yeah. I know she's really good, and I don't really enjoy that she broke her leg, but how cool is that, to get Robert Oliver?"

"What?" I glanced around in Robert's direction in spite of my best efforts not to. He was standing in the midst of a group of students now, head and shoulders above nearly everyone, his back to me—distant, distant across the room. "We get Robert Oliver?"

"I heard when I got in this afternoon. I don't know if he's here yet. Durbin broke her leg on a hiking trip—the secretary told me Durbin said she could actually hear the bone crack. Bad break, big surgery and everything, so the director called his buddy Robert Oliver. Can you believe that? I mean, lucky. Not for Durbin."

A sort of film reel went snapping and spinning around me—Robert Oliver walking in the fields with us, pointing out angles of light and fixing the perspective on those low blue hills inland, the ones I'd driven past. Could we see them from the shore? I would have to say to him the first day, *Oh, hello, I guess you don't remember me, but . . .* And then I'd have to paint all week with him right there, walking around among our easels. I sighed aloud.

Frank was looking puzzled. "Don't you like his work? I

mean, he's a traditionalist and everything, but, God, can he paint."

I was saved from this by the heavy clamor of a bell apparently rung outside to announce the meal, a sound I would hear twice a day for five days, a sound that still goes straight through my stomach when I think about it. Everyone began collecting around the tables. I hung back next to Frank until I saw that Robert had sat down at the table closest to his little group, as if to continue the conversation. Then I edged Frank into a seat as far away as possible from Robert and his illustrious colleagues. We sat together and critiqued the dinner, which was the very definition of wholesome, followed up by strawberry pie and cups of coffee. It was served by students Frank said were work-study artists who were in art school or college; there was no waiting in line, just these beautiful young people putting down our full plates in front of us. Someone even poured my water for me.

While we ate, Frank talked steadily about his classes, his student show, his talented friends who were scattering from Savannah to big cities all over the country. "Jason's going to Chicago—I might join him for a while next summer. Chicago's the next big place, that's pretty obvious." And so on. It was deadly, but it kept my confusion at bay, and by the time the strawberry pie came I felt safe for a whole night from being either recognized by or unrecognized by Robert Oliver. I could sense Frank's muscular shoulder next to mine, his mouth coming closer to my ear, his unspoken *Maybe this is the beginning of something / My room is down at the far end of the men's dorm.* During dessert the director of the program stood up behind a microphone at one end of the carriage house—he turned out to be the bullet-headed man with the thin gray hair—and told us how glad he was to have such a fine incoming group, how talented we were, how hard it had been to turn away all those other fine applications. ("And all those other workshop fees, too," Frank muttered to me.)

After the speech everybody got up and milled around for a few minutes while the work-study artists darted in to collect plates. A woman in a purple dress and huge earrings told Frank and me that there would be a bonfire behind the stables and we should come hang out there. "It's a tradition the first night," she explained, as if she'd been to these workshops many times. We walked out into the dark—I could smell ocean again, and the stars were showing overhead—and when we came around the edge of the buildings, there was a tremendous shower of sparks already raining upside down, toward the sky, and lighting up people's faces. I couldn't see beyond the trees at the edge of the yard, but I thought I could hear the pounding of waves. The application brochure had said the camp was a short stroll from the beach; tomorrow I would explore. There were a few paper lanterns hung in the trees, as if we'd come to attend a festival.

I felt an unexpected wave of hope—this would be magical, would erase the recent long tedium of my low-level teaching jobs, one at a city college and one at a community center, would close the gap between my work life and my secret life at home with my paintings and drawings, would end my hunger for the company of fellow artists, a longing that had grown unchecked since I'd finished my degree. Here, in just a few days, I would become a better painter than I'd ever dreamed I could be. Even Frank's cheerfully disdainful comments couldn't derail my sudden wild hope. "A mob scene," he said, and used that as an excuse to enclose my arm in confident fingers and steer us both away from the smoky side of the fire.

Robert Oliver stood among the older people—faculty,

regulars (I recognized the woman in the purple dress)—also out of range of the smoke, a bottle of beer in his hand. The bottle had picked up the light of the fire, which made it glow from the inside, like a topaz. He was listening now to the director. I remembered that trick he had, which possibly wasn't a trick, of listening more than he talked. He had to bend his head a little to listen to almost anyone, and that gave him an intent, attentive appearance, and then he looked up or away with just his eyes as he listened, as if what the speaker was saying was printed on the sky. He had put on a sweater with part of the neck frayed away; it occurred to me that we shared an affinity for old clothes.

I considered stepping closer to the fire, out in its light, and trying to catch Robert's eye, and then dismissed the thought. Tomorrow's embarrassment would come soon enough. *Oh yes, I (don't) remember you.* The interesting thing would be seeing whether he lied about it. Frank was handing me a beer—"Unless you want something stronger." I didn't. He was pressing up against my shoulder now, my old sweatshirt, and after I'd had a little of the beer that sensation of his hard arm against mine was not unpleasant. I could see Robert Oliver's head in the starlight, his bright eyes fixed for a moment on the flames before us, his rough hair devilishly upright, his face gentle and composed. It was a more deeply lined face than I remembered, but he must have been at least forty by now; there were heavy grooves at the corners of his mouth, which vanished when he smiled.

I turned to Frank, who was pressing more distinctly against my sweatshirt. "I think I'll head to bed," I said with what I hoped was insouciant uncaring. "Have a good night. Big day tomorrow." I regretted the last statement; it wouldn't be as big a day for Frank the Great Artist as it would be for me, the talented nobody, but he didn't need to know that.

Frank gazed at me over his beer, regretful and too young to hide it. "Hey, yeah. Sleep well, okay?"

No one was in bed yet in the long dormitory, another converted barn, which held the women students in its little closed-in stalls. No privacy here, certainly, in spite of the attempt to put solid walls among the guests. It still had a faintly horsey smell, which I remembered, with a stab of nostalgia, from Muzzy's three years of enforced riding lessons for me and Martha. "You *sit* so well on a horse," she would tell me approvingly after every session, as if that were justification enough for all the time and expense. I used the cold-seated toilet down the hall—down the aisle, rather—and then shut myself into my cubicle to unpack. There was a desk big enough to draw on, a hard chair, a tiny bureau with a framed mirror above it, a narrow bed made up with narrow white sheets, a bulletin board with nothing on it but thumbtack holes, and a window with brown curtains.

After standing there disoriented for a moment or two, I pulled the curtains shut and unzipped my sleeping bag to spread on the bed for extra warmth. I put my ratty clothes in the drawers and my sketch pads and journal on top of the desk. I hung my sweatshirt up on the back of the door. I laid out my pajamas and my book. Through the closed window I could hear the sounds of merriment, voices, distant laughter. *Why am I excluding myself from all that?* I wondered, but with as much pleasure as melancholy. My truck was parked in the lot near the camp and I was bone-weary from my long drive, ready for bed, or nearly. Standing in front of the mirror, I performed my nightly undressing ritual, pulling my T-shirt off over my head. Underneath was my delicate, expensive bra. I stood very straight, looking at myself. Self-portrait, night after night. Then I took off the bra and set it aside and stood looking again: myself, and all for me. Self-portrait, nude. When I had finished that long gaze, I put on my graying pajamas and dove into the bed; the sheets were cold, my book one I thought I should be reading, a biography of Isaac Newton. My hand found the light switch, and my head found the pillow.

1879

My darling friend,

Your letter touched me greatly and filled me with the pain of having caused you pain, which I see when I read between your brave and selfless lines. Since I sent my letter to you, I have regretted it every moment, fearing that it would not only put hideous images in your head—the ones I must live with myself—but also appear a pitiable bid for sympathy. I am human, and I love you, but I swear neither of these has been my intention. This shame makes me glad that you told me your nightmare, my dear, despite your reservations about doing so; this way I can suffer with you in turn, sorry as I am to have caused your sleepless night.

If my wife had indeed died in such loving arms as yours, she would have felt herself in the embrace of an angel, or of the daughter she never had. Your letter has already brought a strange alteration in my thoughts about that day, which occupy and torment me frequently—until this morning my keenest wish was always that she might have died in my arms, if she had to die. And now I think that if she could have died in the gentle embrace of a daughter, of a person with your instinctive tenderness and courage, that might have been more comforting still, both to her and to me. Thank you, my angel, for lifting some of this weight and for making me feel the generosity that is your nature. I have destroyed your letter, although reluctantly, so that you can never be implicated in any knowledge of a dangerous past. I hope you will destroy mine as well, both this one and the last.

I must go out for a while; I cannot collect or calm myself indoors this morning. I will walk a little and will make certain this is delivered in perfect safety to you, wrapped in the grateful heart of your

O. V.

CHAPTER 59

Mary

The next morning I woke early, as if someone had whispered to me—fully awake, knowing exactly where I was—and my first thought was of the ocean. It took me only a few minutes to put on clean khakis and a sweatshirt and to brush my hair and teeth in the chilly dorm bathroom with spiders on the ceiling. Then I crept out of the barn, wetting my tennis shoes in the dew; I would regret that later, I knew, since I didn't have another pair with me. The morning was gray with mist, clearing in uneven patches overhead to show pellucid sky, the evergreens full of crows and cobwebs, the birches already turning over a few yellow leaves.

A track led out of the camp just beyond the ash-heaped fire ring, as I'd hoped. I was going in the right direction, toward the ocean, and after a few minutes of listening to my shoes tap the path and to the sounds of the woods, I came out onto a stony beach, the slop of water and sea wrack, the bubbling tide among gray fingers of land. Fog hung right over the water, struggling to clear, so that I got glimpses of pale sky above but could see just a yard or two of waves. There was no view out to sea, only that fog and the edges of the continent lined with dark upright firs, a few cottages breaking their ranks. I took off my shoes and rolled my khakis to the knee. The water was cool, then cold, then very cold, penetrating the bones of my feet and making my calves pimple with chill. The seaweed reached over my ankles.

I felt suddenly afraid, alone with the woods, the smell of pine, the invisible Atlantic. Everything was still, apart from the surge of water. I couldn't bring myself to wade in deeper than my ankles—I had that sudden childhood fear of sharks and entangling weeds, the sense I might be pulled under and lost at sea. There was nothing to gaze out at; the fog returned my stare like a kind of blindness. I wondered about how to paint fog and tried to remember if I'd ever seen a painting that was mostly fog. Maybe something by Turner, or a Japanese print. Snow, yes, and rain, and clouds hovering on mountains, but I couldn't think of any paintings of this kind of fog. At last I backed out of the tide and found a rock to sit on, a high enough, dry enough, smooth enough rock to save the backside of my khakis, with a higher rock to lean against. There was an equally childish pleasure in that, finding one's own throne, and I fell into a dream. I was still sitting there when Robert Oliver came out of the woods.

He was alone and he seemed lost in thought, as I'd just been; he walked slowly, gazing down at his feet on the path and occasionally around him at the trees or out to the foggy water. He was barefoot, in old corduroy pants, and he wore a crumpled yellow cotton shirt hanging open over a T-shirt with some letters on it that didn't quite form words, from where I sat. Now I would have to introduce myself whether I wanted to or not. I thought of standing up and greeting him and immediately missed the moment—I started to get up and then realized I was still out of his line of vision. I sat down again behind my boulders in an agony of embarrassment. If things went well, he would put his feet in the ocean for a moment, check the temperature, and turn around to go back to the camp; I would wait twenty minutes, let my face cool off, and sneak back alone. I huddled against the cold rock. I couldn't take my eyes off him; for one thing, if he saw me, I wanted to see him recognize me. Which he probably wouldn't.

Then he did what I'd most feared and longed for, without knowing it: he took off his clothes. He didn't turn away toward the ocean or hide in the edge of the forest; he simply reached down and unbuttoned his trousers, pulled them off—he wasn't wearing underwear—and then pulled off his shirts, dropping everything in a pile above the tide line and walking toward the water. I was paralyzed. He stood only a few yards away from me, his long, muscled back and legs bare, rubbing his head as if to subdue his hair or rouse his mind from sleep, then rested his hands loosely on his hips. He could have been a studio model, stretching stiff limbs while the class took a break. He stood looking out to sea, relaxed, completely alone (as far as he knew). He turned his head a little, away from where I sat. He twisted his body, gently, warming up, so that in spite of myself I got a glimpse of wiry dark hair, of dangling cock. Then he waded swiftly out into the water and—while I sat shivering, watching, wondering what to do—dove in, a long, shallow dive away from the last rocks, and swam a few strokes. I knew already how cold the water covering him must be, but he didn't turn back until he'd swum out twenty yards.

Finally he wheeled around in the water, came back more swiftly, and found his feet, stumbling a little, wading in. He dripped and gasped; he wiped his face. Drops glittered from the hair on his body and the heavy wet curls on his head. At the shore he finally saw me. You can't look away at such a moment, even if you want to, and pretense is impossible: how could you miss Poseidon stalking out of the ocean; how could you pretend to be checking your nails or scraping snails from the rock? I just sat there, mute, miserable but also transfixed. I even thought at that moment that I wished I could paint the scene—a cliché kind of thought, something I rarely consider in the midst of experience. He stopped and studied me for a moment, a little startled, but didn't make any move to cover himself. "Hello," he said, attentive, wary, possibly amused.

"Hello," I answered as firmly as I could. "I'm sorry."

"Oh, no—no worries." He reached for his clothes on the pebbly beach and, using the T-shirt, dried himself modestly but without hurry, then dressed himself in his pants and yellow oxford. He came a little closer. "Sorry if I was the one who startled you," he said. He stood there studying me, and I saw the dreaded expression of half recognition come into his eyes; saw, miserably, that he couldn't quite place me.

"To make it worse, we used to know each other." It came out sounding flatter, harsher, than I'd intended.

He put his head to one side, as if the ground could tell him my name and what he should remember about me. "I'm sorry," he said at last. "I'm terrible about this, but remind me."

"Oh, it's no big deal." I punished him by staring him down anyway. "I'm sure you teach a million students. I was in one of your classes at Barnett a long time ago, just for a term. Visual Understanding. But you really started me toward art, so I've always wanted to thank you for that."

He was looking hard at me now, not bothering to hide his search for my younger presence, as a more polite person might have done. "Wait." I waited. "We had lunch one time, didn't we? I remember something about that. But your hair—"

"Fair enough. It was a different color, blond. I dyed it because I was tired of having people see only that."

"Yes, I'm sorry. I do remember now. Your name—"

"Mary Bertison," I said, and now that he was dressed I put out my hand.

"Good to see you again. Robert Oliver."

I was no longer his student, or wouldn't be again until ten

o'clock this morning. "I *know* you're Robert Oliver," I said as sardonically as I could.

He laughed. "What are you doing here?"

"Taking your landscape class," I said, "except that I didn't know it was going to be you."

"Yes, it was an emergency." He was rubbing his hair now with both hands, as if he wished he had a towel. "But what a nice coincidence. Now I can see how you're coming along."

"Except that you won't remember what I was doing before," I pointed out, and he laughed again, that lovely release of all troubles, with nothing wry or knowing in it—Robert laughed like a child. I remembered now those gestures of hand and arm, and the curling edges of his mouth, the oddly sculpted face, the charm that was charming because there was no awareness behind it, as if he were simply renting his body and it had turned out to be a good one, although he treated it with a renter's lack of caring. We walked slowly back together, and where the path allowed only single file, he went ahead, not a gentleman, and I was relieved because I didn't have to feel his eyes on my back and wonder what their expression might be. When we reached the edge of the lawns, with the mansion in full view and dew glittering across the grass, I could see people hurrying in to breakfast and realized that we had to join them. "I don't know anyone here except you," I confessed on impulse, and we both paused at the edge of the woods.

"I don't either," he said, turning his uncomplicated smile on me. "Except the director, and he's an incredible bore."

I needed to flee, to be alone for a few minutes, not to have to walk into a public meal beside a man I'd just seen coming out of the ocean naked—he seemed already to have forgotten this incident, as if it had happened as long ago as our Visual Understanding class. "I've got to grab some things from my room," I told him.

"See you in class." He seemed about to pat me on the shoulder or to slap me on the back, man-to-man, then apparently thought better of it and let me go. I walked slowly to the stables and shut myself in my whitewashed stall for a few minutes. I sat still, feeling the blessing of the locked door. Huddled there, I remembered how, on a hard-earned trip to Florence three years before, my first and only time in Italy, I'd gone to the monastery of San Francesco and seen the Fra Angelico murals in the former cells of the monks, now empty. There were tourists in the halls, and modern monks on guard here and there, but I had waited until no one was looking, gone into a small white cell, and illegally closed the door. I'd stood there, finally alone, guilty but determined. The tiny room was bare except for a Fra Angelico angel, radiant gold and pink and green on one wall, its wings folded behind it, and sunlight coming in through the grated window. I had understood even then that the monk who had once lived alone in that space, which was otherwise like a prison, had wanted nothing else, nothing but to be there—nothing, not even his God.

Chapter 60

Marlow

Outside the Metropolitan Museum, I walked up a block and into the edge of Central Park. It was glorious there, green and full of blooming flower beds, as I'd hoped it would be. I found a clean bench and took out my cell phone, dialed the number I hadn't called for a couple of weeks. It was Saturday afternoon; where would she be on a Saturday? I actually knew nothing about her current life, except that I was trespassing on it.

She answered after the second ring, and I could hear sounds in the background, a restaurant, some public place. "Hello?" she said, and I remembered the firmness of her voice, the spare look of her long hands.

"Mary," I said. "It's Andrew Marlow."

It took Mary about five hours to reach me in Washington Square; she arrived in time for dinner, which we ate together in the restaurant at my hotel. She was famished after her unplanned bus ride—she had taken the bus rather than the train because it was cheaper, I was sure, although she didn't say that. As she ate, she told me about her comic struggles to obtain the last ticket for that departure. I'd been surprised by her insistence on coming up at all. Her face was flushed with the excitement of having done something spontaneous, her long hair caught back at the sides with little clips; she wore a thin turquoise sweater and heavy ropes of black beads around her throat.

I tried not to mind that the exquisite color in her face was for Robert Oliver, for the relief or possibly even the pleasure of uncovering something about his life that would explain his defection and justify her previous devotion to him. Her eyes were blue this time—I thought of Kate—because of the sweater. Apparently they changed like the ocean; they depended on the sky, the weather. She ate like a polite wolf, using her knife and fork with grace and putting away an enormous plate of chicken and couscous. At her bidding, I described in greater detail Béatrice de Clerval's portrait and the loan that must have removed it just after Robert had seen it.

"Odd that he should have remembered it well enough from one or two viewings to paint her for years afterward, though," I added. My elbows were already on the table, and I'd ordered coffee and dessert for both of us, over her protestations.

"Oh, he didn't." She laid her knife and fork to rest together on the plate.

"Didn't remember? But he painted her so accurately that I recognized her on sight."

"No—he didn't have to remember. He had her portrait in a book."

I put my hands in my lap. "You knew about this."

She didn't flinch. "Yes. I'm sorry. I was planning to tell you, when I got to that part of the story. I've actually written it down for you already. But I didn't know about the painting at the museum. The book didn't say where the painting was; in fact, I assumed it must be in France. And I was going to tell you about it. I brought you the rest of my reminiscences, or whatever you want to call them. It's taken me time to write them all down, and then I sat on it all for a while." There was no apology in her tone. "He had piles of books by his sofa while he was living with me."

"Kate described the same thing—I mean about the piles of books. I don't think she ever saw that portrait in one of them, though, or she would have told me." Then I realized that I'd reported on Kate directly to Mary for the first time. I told myself silently not to do it again.

Mary raised her eyebrows. "I can imagine what Kate lived with. I *have* imagined it, many times."

"She lived with Robert," I pointed out.

"Yes, exactly." The brightness was gone now, or had slipped behind a cloud, and she fiddled with her wineglass.

"I'll take you tomorrow to see the painting," I added, to cheer her.

"Take me?" She smiled. "Don't you think I know where the Met is?"

"Of course." I had forgotten for a moment that she was young enough to offend. "I mean that we can go look at it together."

"I'd like that. That's what I came for."

"Only for that?" I immediately regretted it; I hadn't meant to sound arch or flirtatious. My conversation with my father came back to me, unbidden: *Recently abandoned women can be complicated / And she's not only complicated but independent, unusual, beautiful / Of course.*

"You know, I assumed that portrait was what took him to France without me, that it was there and he'd gone to see it again."

I kept my face calm. "He went to France? While he was with you?"

"Yes. He got on a plane and went to another country without telling me. He never explained why he'd kept it a secret." Her face was tight, and she drew her hair back from it with both hands. "I told him I was angry that he'd spent money on a trip alone when he hadn't seemed to have enough to help much with my rent or food, but I was really angrier about the fact that he'd kept it secret from me. That made me realize that he was treating me just as he had treated Kate, being secretive. And it was as if it had never occurred to him to invite me along either. Our biggest fight was about that, although we pretended it was about painting, and when he came back from his trip, we lasted for only a few days and then he moved out."

There were tears gathering in Mary's eyes now, the first I'd seen since the night she'd cried on my sofa. So help me, if I'd been outside Robert's door at that moment, I would have walked in and punched him instead of sitting down in the armchair. She wiped her eyes. Neither of us had drawn breath in a couple of minutes, I think. "Mary, may I ask—did you tell him to leave? Or did he walk out on you?"

"I told him to leave. I was afraid that if I didn't, he might do it on his own, and then I would lose the rest of my self-respect as well."

I had waited a long time to ask these questions. "Did you know that Robert had a package of old letters on him when he attacked that painting? Letters between Béatrice de Clerval and Olivier Vignot, who painted the portrait?"

She sat frozen for a moment, then nodded. "I didn't know they were also from Olivier Vignot."

"You saw the letters?"

"Yes, a little. I'll tell you more later."

I had to leave it there. She was looking directly into my eyes; her face was clear, devoid of hatred. I thought that perhaps what I was seeing, naked in front of me, was what her love for Robert had represented to her. I'd never known anyone as striking as this girl, who stared obliquely at the paint on a museum canvas, ate like a well-bred man, and stroked her hair back like a nymph. The one exception might have been a woman I knew only from old letters and from paintings—Olivier Vignot's and Robert Oliver's. But I could understand why Robert might have loved the living woman in the midst of loving the dead one, to the best of his ability.

I wanted to tell her how sorry I was for the pain her words encompassed, but I didn't know how to say it without sounding patronizing, so I concentrated instead on sitting there, regarding her as gently as I could. Besides, I knew from the way she was finishing her coffee and rummaging for her jacket that our meal was over. But there was a last problem for this evening, and I had to think how to address it. "I've checked at the front desk, and they have extra rooms available. I'd be happy—"

"No, no." She was putting a couple of bills under her plate, sliding out of the booth already. "I have a friend on Twenty-eighth who's expecting me already—I called her earlier. I'll come by, say, nine o'clock tomorrow morning."

"Yes, please do. We can have coffee and go uptown."

"Perfect. And these are for you." She thrust a hand into her bag and gave me a thick envelope—hard and bulky this time, as if it contained a book as well as papers.

She had herself gathered together now, and I hastened to my feet. She was hard to keep up with, this young woman. I would have called her prickly if she hadn't been so graceful, or if she weren't smiling a little now. To my surprise, she put one hand on my arm to steady herself, then reached over to kiss me on the cheek; she was almost my height. Her lips were warm and soft.

When I reached my room, it was still early; I had the evening ahead of me. I'd thought about getting in touch with my one old friend in the city—Alan Glickman, a high-school buddy with whom I'd managed to keep up, mostly thanks to our calling each other a couple of times a year. I enjoyed his keen sense of humor, but I hadn't managed even to phone him ahead, and he was probably already busy. Besides, Mary's package rested on the edge of the bed. Walking out and leaving it here for even a few hours would be like leaving a person behind.

I sat down and opened it and drew out thc pile of typed sheets and a thin paperback filled with color reproductions. I lay down across the bed with Mary's pages. The door was locked and the shades were drawn, but I felt the room full of a presence, a longing through which I could have passed my hand.

Chapter 61

Mary

Frank cornered me at breakfast. "Ready?" he said, balancing a tray that held two bowls of cornflakes, a plate of eggs and bacon, and three glasses of orange juice. We were serving ourselves this morning—democracy. I had found a sunny corner and was on my second cup of coffee and a fried egg, and Robert Oliver was nowhere in sight. Perhaps he didn't eat breakfast.

"Ready for what?" I said.

"For the first day." He put his tray down without asking if I wanted company.

"Help yourself," I said. "I was just wishing for some companionship in this beautiful, lonely spot."

He smiled, apparently pleased with my feistiness; why had I thought sarcasm would work? His hair was crafted into a couple of spiky tufts at the front, and he wore graying jeans and a sweatshirt and frayed basketball sneakers, a red-and-blue bead necklace. He bent from a lithe waist and flexed his shoulders over the cornflakes. He was perfect in his immature way, and he knew it. I pictured him at sixty-five, gaunt and stringy-armed, with bunions and probably a wrinkled tattoo somewhere.

"The first day is going to be long," he said. "That's why I asked if you're ready for this. I hear Oliver's going to work us out there for hours and hours. He's intense."

I tried to get back to my coffee. "It's a landscape-painting class, not football practice."

"Oh, I don't know." Frank was mashing his way through his breakfast. "I've heard about this guy. He never stops. He made his name as a portrait painter, but he's really into landscapes right now. He's outdoors all day long, like an animal."

"Or like Monet," I said, and immediately regretted it. Frank was looking away from me as if I'd begun picking my nose.

"Monet?" he murmured, and I heard the disdain, the puzzlement, through his mouthful of breakfast. We finished our eggs in not-quite-friendly silence.

The hillside where Robert Oliver set us our first landscape exercise commanded a view of ocean and rocky islands; it was part of a state park, and I wondered how he'd known to come exactly here, to this tremendous setting. Robert drove his easel legs into the ground. We all gathered around, holding our gear or dropping it on the grass, watching while he demonstrated a sketch, showed us how to focus on form first, without considering yet what the forms represented, and then made suggestions about color. We would need a grayish ground, he said, to reproduce the bright cold light all around us, but also some warmer brown tones under the tree trunks, grass, even the water.

His presentation in the classroom that morning had been minimal: "You're all accomplished, working artists, and I don't see the need to talk a lot—let's just get out in the field and find out what happens, and we can discuss composition later, when we've got some pictures to take a look at." I'd been glad, after that, to escape to the out-of-doors. We'd driven to this area, then walked up through the woods from the parking lot, carrying our gear. The conference had provided sandwiches and apples; we hoped it wouldn't rain later in the day.

I was remembering a lot about Robert Oliver now, standing close enough to see his demonstration but not so close as to seem eager; I recognized that passionate insistence on form, the way his voice deepened to conviction when he told us to ignore everything except the geometry of the scene until we got it right, the way he stood back, weight on his heels, examining his work every few minutes, then leaned into it again. Robert made some sort of contact with everyone, I noticed; more than ever, he had that easy, disheveled gift for hospitality, as if wherever he taught was a dining room instead of a classroom, and we were all eating at his table. It was irresistible, and the other students seemed drawn in by him at once, crowding trustingly around his canvas. He pointed out some views and the shapes they might form on a canvas, then roughed in the forms of the view he'd chosen and laid on color, much of it burnt umber, a deep-brown wash.

There were enough level places on the hillside for six people to set up easels and find easy footing, and we all spent some time hunting for views. It was hard to go wrong, actually—hard to choose which of 180 degrees of natural splendor to paint. I finally settled on a long vista of firs creeping down to the beach and water, with the bulk of Isle des Roches in the far right and a flat horizon of water meeting the sky to the left. It wasn't quite balanced; I moved my easel a few degrees and caught a frame of evergreens by the beach at far left, to give my canvas extra interest on that side.

Once I'd chosen my spot, Frank planted his easel enthusiastically near mine, as if I'd invited him and would be honored by his company. Some of the other students seemed quite pleasant; they were my age or older, mainly women, which made Frank look like a precocious child. Two of the women, who said they already knew each other from a conference in Santa Fe, had engaged me in friendly talk in the van. I watched them putting easels into the lower reaches of the hillside, conferring with each other about their palettes. There was also a very shy elderly man whom Frank told me in a whisper had exhibited at Williams College the year before; he set up near us and began to sketch with paint rather than pencils.

Frank had not only shoved the legs of his easel into the ground near mine but also pointed it more or less in the same direction; I noted with annoyance that we'd be doing very similar views, which put our skills into direct competition. At least he was immediately absorbed and probably wouldn't bother me; he already had his palette set up with a few basic colors and was using graphite to outline the distant mass of the island and the edge of the shore in the foreground. He was quick, sure, and his lean back moved under its shirt in graceful rhythm.

I looked away and began to prepare my palette: green, burnt umber, a soft blue with some gray to it, a squeeze of white and one of black. I was already wishing I'd replaced two of my brushes before the conference; they were superb ones, but I'd had them so long that they'd lost some hairs. My teaching job didn't cover much in the way of expensive painting supplies, once I'd paid rent and groceries, and DC wasn't cheap, although I'd found an apartment in a neighborhood Muzzy never would have approved of and fortunately never came to see. I wouldn't have dreamed of asking her for money either, after disappointing her in her career choice for me. ("But lots of people with degrees in art become lawyers these days, don't they, darling? And you've always been such an arguer.") I renewed my vow, as I did daily: I would keep trying to build enough of a portfolio, participate in enough shows, amass enough excellent references, to apply for a real teaching job. I glared at Frank, since he wasn't looking. Perhaps Robert Oliver could help me somehow, if I did well in this workshop.

I checked, covertly, and discovered that Robert was painting with absorption, too. I couldn't see his canvas from where I stood, but it was large and he'd begun to fill it with long strokes.

The color of the water changed from hour to hour, of course, making it difficult to catch, and the peak of Isle des Roches proved a challenge; my version of it was a little too soft, like custard or whipped cream rather than pale rock, the village at its lowest shore smudgy at best. Robert painted for a long time, down the slope from us, and I wondered if he'd ever come up to see our work, and dreaded that.

At last we broke for lunch, Robert stretching, joining his great hands inside out high above his head and the rest of us imitating, in one way or another, looking up, putting down brushes, raising our arms. I knew we'd eat quickly, and when Robert sat down in a sunny spot farther down the hill and drew his lunch out of a big canvas bag, we all followed, huddling around him with our own sandwiches. He gave me a smile; had he been glancing around for me a second before? Frank began to talk with the two friendly women about the success of his recent show in Savannah, and Robert leaned across to ask how my landscape was shaping up. "Very poorly," I said, which for some reason made him grin. "I mean," I said, encouraged, "have you ever had that dessert called Floating Island?" He laughed and promised he'd come take a look at it.

Chapter 62

Mary

When lunch was over, Robert left us and strolled off into the woods—to pee, I realized eventually, something I managed myself as soon as the three men were all safely at work again; I had a bit of tissue in my pocket, which I buried under the damp leaves and lichen-covered branches. After lunch we started new canvases to accommodate the change in light, and then painted for hours more. I began to realize that Frank's assessment of Robert's dedication to nature was an accurate one. He didn't come over to look at anyone's work after all, and I was relieved as well as a little disappointed. My legs and back ached, and I began to see plates of dinner in front of me rather than the textures of water and firs.

Finally, just before four o'clock, Robert circulated slowly among us, making suggestions, listening to problems, calling us together once to ask what we thought about the differences between morning and afternoon light in that landscape, commenting that painting a cliff was no different than painting an eyelid—we had to remember that light revealed form no matter what the object. He finally stopped by my easel, and stood examining the canvas with his arms folded. "The trees are very good," he said. "Really very good. Look, if you put a darker shadow on this side of the island—do you mind?" I shook my head, and he borrowed a brush. "Don't be afraid to make a shadow darker if you need contrast," he murmured, and I saw my island swell into geological reality under his hand. And didn't mind his improving my work. "There. I won't mess with it any more—I want to let you get on with it." He touched my arm with his big fingers and left me, and I worked deeply, almost blindly, until the sun began to sink enough to interfere with true visibility.

"I'm hungry," Frank hissed, leaning over into my space. "This guy is a crazy man. Aren't you starving? Cool trees," he added. "You must like trees."

I tried to make some sense of his words but couldn't, couldn't even say, "What?" I was completely stiff, chilled under my sweatshirt and the cotton scarf I'd wrapped around my neck as the ocean breeze grew cooler; I hadn't painted this hard in a long, long time, although I worked almost every day, around the edges of my job. I had one other thing to ask Robert, now that I'd concentrated so deeply on my shadows and needed to add some flecks of white to the whole scene, to brighten it. Should I wait and add the white tomorrow, in something closer to the light with which we'd begun, or do it now—quickly, from memory?

I made my way down the slope to Robert's easel, where he was beginning to clean his brushes and scrape his palette. He stopped every few seconds to look back at his canvas and out at the view. It occurred to me that he'd forgotten for a while to teach us anything, and I felt a pang of sympathy; he, too, had been absorbed, beyond consciousness, in the movement of brush and hand, fingers, wrist. We could learn just from being near that kind of obsession, I thought. I stood in front of his work. He made it seem easy, this viewing of basic forms and blocking them in, adding color, touching them with light—the trees, the water, the rocks, the narrow beach below. The surface wasn't finished; he, like us, would probably be working on this same canvas at least another whole afternoon, if there was time. The forms would expand later to full reality; the details of branch, leaf, and wave would be touched in here and there.

But one section of his canvas was beautifully complete. I wondered why he had finished it ahead of the rest: the rugged beach and pale rocks stretching out into the ocean, the soft colors of stone and reddish seaweed. We were at some height from the edge of the water, and he'd caught that sense of looking down, or aslant, at the two distant figures walking hand in hand along the shore, the smaller bent over as if to pluck something from a tidal pool, the taller upright. They were just clear enough, close enough, so that I could see the woman's long skirts pulled back in the wind, the child's bonnet hanging by its blue ribbons, two people companionably alone where there had been no one but a painting class on the hill above all afternoon. I found myself staring at them, then at him; Robert touched the woman's minuscule shoe with a brush, as if polishing its toe, then wiped the sable hairs again. I'd forgotten what my question had been—something about the changing light.

He turned to me with a smile, as if he'd known I was there and had even known who I was. "Have you had a good afternoon?"

"Very good," I said. His relaxed manner made me feel it would be silly to ask him why he'd put two fictional figures into the summer scene before us. He was known for his nineteenth-century references, and he had every right, as Robert Oliver, to stick whatever he wanted into a lesson in landscape. I hoped someone else would ask him instead.

Then I hoped something different: that I would someday know him well enough to ask him anything. He glanced at me, the friendly, distant expression I remembered from college—a puzzle, a cipher of a face. Where his shirt collar parted over his chest, I saw tufts of silvered dark hair. I wanted to reach out and touch that hair, to see if age had softened it or made it wiry—which? He had rolled his sleeves almost to the elbow. Now he stood in his familiar tall-man's pose, his arms crossed, hands holding up his bare elbows, his legs braced against the hill's slant. "It's a hell of a view," he said companionably. "And I guess we should clear out for dinner now." It *was* a hell of a view, I could have pointed out, but it didn't include any figures in long dresses skirting the tide. No shore could have been more strikingly empty—a landscape without people, which had been the point of the exercise, hadn't it?

CHAPTER 63

1879

At the end of March, her painting of the golden-haired maid is accepted for the Salon, under the name Marie Rivière. Olivier comes to tell them the news in person. He and Yves and Papa drink her health around the dining table from their best crystal, while she bites back the smile on her lips. She tries not to look at Olivier and succeeds; already she is growing accustomed to seeing all these loves gathered around one table. She cannot sleep that night for happiness, a complicated joy that seems to rob her of some of the original exhilaration of the painting. Olivier tells her in his next letter that this is a natural reaction. He says that she feels exposed as well as jubilant, and that she must simply go on painting, like any artist.

She begins a new canvas, this one of the swans in the Bois de Boulogne; Yves finds time to accompany her on Saturdays so that she need never walk or paint alone. Sometimes Olivier goes with her instead, helps her mix colors, and once he paints her sitting on a bench near the water, a little portrait of her from the lace at her throat to the top of her bonnet, which is pushed back to show her wide gaze. He says it is the best portrait of his career. He marks it in bold strokes on the back, *Portrait of Béatrice de Clerval, 1879,* and signs a corner.

One night when Olivier is not there, Gilbert and Armand Thomas come to dinner again. Gilbert, the older brother, is a handsome man with calculated manners, good company in a drawing room. Armand is quieter, as elegantly dressed as Gilbert but with a certain listless tendency. They complement each other, Armand setting off Gilbert's intensity, and Gilbert making Armand's silence seem refined rather than dull. Gilbert has special access to the juried works of the Salon now being hung; when the other guests have left and the four of them linger together in the drawing room, he claims to have seen Olivier Vignot's submission, the young man under the tree, as well as the mysterious work Monsieur Vignot has submitted on behalf of an unknown painter, a Madame or Mademoiselle Rivière. Curious, how the picture reminds him of something. Annoying, too, that Vignot refuses to reveal Madame Rivière's identity; surely it isn't her real name.

Gilbert turns to Yves when he speaks, then to Béatrice. His large, handsome head inclines to one side as he asks them if they know this painter—perhaps young and timid. How brave of an unknown woman to submit work to the Salon! Yves shakes his head, and Béatrice turns away; Yves has never been good at hiding things. Gilbert adds that it is a pity none of them has more information, and that Monsieur Vignot is so secretive. He has always believed there is more to Olivier Vignot than meets the eye; he has a long history—as a painter. The room is pleasant, as always, the furniture upholstered in new colors, Papa's great andirons, the light from the fire and the fine candles catching Béatrice's painting of her garden, framed in gold across the room. Gilbert's tone is measured, his manner respectful and cultivated; he glances at the painting and at her, and straightens his perfect cuffs. For the first time since she gave Olivier permission to submit her work, Béatrice feels alarmed. But what harm could it really cause for Gilbert Thomas to discover her identity, since the piece has been accepted?

He seems to be driving at something deeper, and now she is really uneasy. Perhaps it is a compliment, a graceful hint that he might be able to sell her work if she is willing to continue the ruse. She might be willing to continue it but is not willing to ask him what he means. Just as she has felt Olivier's goodness, his idealism, from his first evening by this fireside, she senses something out of place in Gilbert Thomas, something loose and hard that rattles around inside him. She wishes he would leave but cannot explain to herself why. Yves finds him clever; he has bought a painting from him, a lovely image from the rather radical Degas, a little dancer standing with hands on hips, watching her fellow dancers at the barre. Béatrice turns the conversation to this purchase, and Gilbert responds enthusiastically, joined by Armand—that Degas will be a great one, they are sure of it, he has been a good investment already.

She is relieved when they depart, Gilbert kissing and pressing her hand and asking Yves to remember them to his uncle.

CHAPTER 64

Mary

I wish I could report that Robert Oliver and I became dignified friends from that moment, that from then on he was a mentor and wise voice and active proponent of my painting, that he helped my career along and I admired his in turn, and it was all very conscientious until he died at eighty-three, leaving me two of his paintings in his will. But none of this was the case, and Robert is still very much alive, with all of our actual strange history done and behind us. I don't know how much of it he remembers now; if I had to guess, I'd say not all, not none, but some. My guess is that he remembers some of me, some of us together, and the rest rolled off him like topsoil in a flash flood. If he'd remembered everything, absorbed it right down into his pores, as I did, I wouldn't be explaining all this to his psychiatrist, or any psychiatrist, and maybe he wouldn't be insane. Insane—is that the word? He was insane before, in the sense that he wasn't like other people, and that was why I loved him.

The evening after our first landscape excursion, I sat next to Robert at dinner and of course Frank sat next to me with his shirt unbuttoned. I wanted to tell him to button it up and get over it. Robert talked a good deal with a faculty member on his other side, a woman in her seventies, a grande dame of found art, but every now and then he glanced around and smiled at me, usually absently and once with a directness that shocked me until I realized he was turning it equally on Frank—it seemed that he'd liked Frank's treatment of water and horizon better than he'd liked mine. If Frank thought he was going to outpaint me in front of Robert, he was dead wrong, I promised myself, listening to Frank help himself right across me to gobs of Robert's attention. When Frank had finished his prolonged brag in the form of technical questions, Robert turned to me again; I was right by his jawbone, after all. He touched my shoulder. "You're very quiet," he said, smiling.

"Frank's very noisy," I said in a low voice. I had meant to say it louder, to give Frank a little piece of my mind, but it came out low and harsh, as if meant only for Robert Oliver's ear. He looked down at me—as I said, Robert looks down at almost everyone. I'm sorry to use this cliché, but our eyes met. Our eyes met, and they met for the first time in our acquaintance, which after all had been interrupted by a hiatus of many years.

"He's just getting started on his career," he observed, which made me feel a little better. "Why don't you tell me something about how things are with you? Did you go to art school?"

"Yes," I said. I had to lean very close so that he could hear me; there was soft black hair in the opening of his ear.

"Too bad," he said, loud-soft in return.

"It wasn't so awful," I confessed. "I secretly enjoyed it."

He turned so that I could see him directly again. I felt that it was dangerous for me to see him that way, that he was much more vivid than a person ought to be. He was laughing, his teeth large and strong-looking but yellowing—middle age. It was wonderful that he didn't seem to care about anything, or even to know that his teeth were yellow. Frank would be whitening his a couple of times a month before he was thirty. The world was full of Franks, when it should be full of Robert Olivers.

"I enjoyed some of mine, too," he was saying. "It gave me something to be angry about."

I risked a shrug. "Why should art make anyone angry? I don't care what anyone else does."

I was imitating him, his own uncaring, but it seemed to strike him as unusual. He frowned. "Maybe you're right. Anyway, you get over that stage, don't you?" It was shared experience, not a real question.

"Yes," I said, daring myself to look him in the eye again. It wasn't hard, once I'd done it a time or two.

"You've gotten over it young," he said soberly.

"I'm not so young." I hadn't meant to sound aggressive, but he gazed at me even more attentively. His eyes strayed down my neck, flicked over my breasts—the masculine registering of female presence, automatic, feral. I wished he hadn't betrayed that look; it was impersonal. It made me wonder about his wife. Now, as at Barnett, he wore his wide gold band, so I had to assume he was still married. But his face was gentle when he spoke again. "Your work shows a lot of understanding."

Then he turned away, tugged somehow by the other people around us, and talked with the table in general, so that I didn't find out, at least then, what kind of understanding he had in mind. I concentrated on my food; I couldn't hear in all that noise anyway. After some of this, he turned to me, and there was that quietness between us again, that waiting. "What are you doing now?"

I decided to tell the truth. "Well, working two dull jobs in DC. Going to Philadelphia every three months to see my aging mother. Painting at night."

"Painting at night," he said. "Have you had a show?"

"Not a solo or even a joint one," I said slowly. "I guess I could have created some opportunity—somehow, maybe at school, but the teaching keeps me so busy that I can't think straight about that. Or maybe I don't feel quite ready. I just go on painting whenever I can."

"You should have a show. There's usually a way, with work like yours."

I wished he'd elaborate on "like yours," but I didn't look that gift horse in the mouth, especially since he'd already characterized my one landscape as having "understanding." I told myself not to fall for anything, although I knew from years before that Robert Oliver did not hand out empty praise, and I knew instinctively that even if he had looked me over, a reflex, he wouldn't use praise to get anywhere with me. He was simply too dedicated to the truth about painting; you could see it in every line of his face and shoulders, hear it in his voice. It was the most reliable thing about him, I realized much later, that unvarnished praise or dismissal; it was, like his glance at my body, impersonal. There was a chilliness to him, a cold eye under his warm-colored skin and smile, a quality I trusted because I trusted it in myself. He could be relied upon to dismiss you with a shrug, to shrug off your work if he didn't think it was good. There was no effort in this, no struggle in him not to compromise for personal reasons. Face-to-face with work, painting, his own or other people's, he was not personal.

Dessert was bowls of fresh strawberries. I went to get a cup of black tea with cream, which I knew would keep me awake, but I felt too excited by the whole setting to think about sleep anyway. Possibly I could stay up and paint. There were studios open all night, not too far from the dormitory stables—garages that had probably once housed the estate's first Model Ts and were now equipped with big skylights. I could stay there and paint, perhaps produce a few more versions of that landscape from the first, unfinished one. And then, shamelessly, I could say to Robert Oliver at breakfast, or on our next hillside, "I'm a little tired. Oh, I painted until three this morning." Or maybe he would be out roaming the dark and would stroll by and see me in the garage window, working hard; he would wander in and touch my shoulder with a smile and tell me that the painting showed "understanding." That was all I wanted—his attention, and briefly, and almost but not quite innocently.

As I finished my tea, Robert was rising from the table, full height, his hips in their worn trousers at the level of my head; he was saying good night to everyone. He probably had more important things to do, like his own work. To my disgust, Frank followed him away from the table, his chiseled profile swiveling this way and that, talking Robert's ear off. At least that would keep Frank from following me instead, pulling his shirt aside a little farther or asking me if I wanted to take a walk in the woods. I felt a twinge of loneliness at this, deserted by not one but two men, and tried to gather my independence around me again, the romance of *all by myself*. I would go paint after all, not to keep Frank away or to draw Robert Oliver to me, but to paint. I was here to use my time well, to restart my sputtering engines, to savor my precious bit of vacation, damn all men.

That was why Robert did find me in the garage, so late that the other two or three people working here and there in the big musty space had already packed up and left, so late that I was woozy, seeing green instead of blue, putting in some yellow too quickly, scraping it off, telling myself to stop. I had reworked my landscape from the afternoon on a fresh canvas brought from my bed stall, with several differences. I had remembered the daisies in the grass, which I hadn't gotten to in daylight, and put them in on the surface of the hill, trying to make them float, although they sank instead. And there was another difference, too. When Robert came in and shut the side door behind him, I was already so tired of contemplating these changes that I saw him as a manifestation of my vision at dinner, my wish that he would appear here. I'd actually forgotten about him, although he had somehow filled my thoughts at the same time. I had been unaware, so that now I looked at him through blindness.

He stood in front of me, smiling a little, arms crossed. "You're still up. Working on your future show?"

I stood, staring. He was unreal, ringed with haze in the dangling ceiling lights. I thought in spite of myself that he was like an archangel in one of those medieval triptychs, larger than humanity, his hair longish, curly, his head ringed with gold, his huge wings folded out of the way for convenience while he delivered some celestial message. His faded, golden clothes, the dark brightness of his hair, the olive of his eyes, would all go with wings, and if Robert had had wings, they would have been immense. I felt outside the bounds of history and convention, at the rocky edge of a world that was too human to be real, or too real to be actually human: I felt only myself, the painting on my easel, which I no longer wanted him to see, and this big man with curly hair standing six feet away.

"Are you an angel?" I said. Immediately it felt false, silly.

But he scratched under his chin, which was growing dark stubble, and laughed. "Hardly. Did I startle you?"

I shook my head. "You looked radiant for a moment, as if you ought to be in cloth of gold."

He had the grace to appear confused, or perhaps he really was. "I'd make a bad angel by anyone's standards."

I forced myself to laugh. "I must be very tired, then."

"May I see?" He stepped toward my easel rather than exactly toward me. It was too late; I couldn't say no. He had already come around behind me, and I tried not to turn to watch his face, but I couldn't help watching, too. He stood looking at my landscape, and then his profile grew serious. He unfolded his arms, and they dropped to his sides. "Why did you put them in?"

He pointed at the two figures walking along my revised shore, the woman in her long skirts and the little girl beside her.

"I don't know," I faltered. "I liked what you'd done."

"Didn't you think they might belong to me?"

I asked myself whether there was something close to dangerous in his tone; his question was a little bizarre, but I felt mainly my own foolishness, and the foolish tears rising but still hidden under my chagrin. Was he going to actually chastise me? I rallied. "Does anything belong to one artist?"

His face was dark but also reflective, interested in my question. I was a little younger then; I did not understand how people can simply *appear* to be interested in something other than themselves. Finally he said, "No, I suppose you're right. I suppose I just feel possessive of the images I've lived with for a long time."

All of a sudden I was back on that campus, so many years before; it was, weirdly, the same conversation, and I was asking him the identity of the woman in his canvases, and he was about to say, "If I just knew who she was!"

Instead, I touched his arm—presumptuously, maybe. "Do you know, I think we talked about this once before."

He frowned. "Did we?"

"Yes, on the lawn at Barnett, when I was a student there and you had exhibited that portrait of a woman in front of a mirror."

"And you are wondering if this is the same woman?"

"Yes, I am wondering that."

The light in the big open studio was harsh and bare; my body hummed with the late hour and the proximity of this strange man who had only increased in attractiveness with the elapsed years. I could hardly believe the fact that he had survived the passing of time in my own life to return to it. In fact, he was frowning at me. "Why do you want to know?"

I hesitated. There were many things I could have said, but in the rawness of that time and place, the unreality that seemed to have no future and no consequences, I said what was least thought-out, closest to my heart. "I have the feeling," I said slowly, "that if I knew why you were still painting the same thing after so many years, then I would know you. I would know who you are."

My words fell deep into the room, and I heard their starkness and thought I should feel embarrassed but didn't. Robert Oliver was frozen there, fixed on me, as if he had been listening all along and wanted to know my reaction to the point he was going to make. But instead of making a point, he stood there, silent—I even felt defiantly tall next to him, tall enough to reach his chin—and at last instead of speaking he touched my hair with his fingers. He drew a long strand of it over my shoulder and smoothed it with just his fingertips, not really touching me.

I remembered with a jolt that this was Muzzy's gesture; I thought of my mother's hands, now so much older, picking up a lock of my hair when I was a teenager, telling me how glossy and straight and smooth it was, and letting it drop tenderly. It was her gentlest gesture, in fact, a silent apology for all the requirements, the molding against which I'd argued until I'd worn us both to resentment. I stood as still as I could, afraid I might begin to tremble visibly, hoping Robert would not touch me further because that could cause me to shake in front of him. He raised both hands and stroked my hair back, arranging it behind my shoulders, as if he wanted it that way for a portrait. I saw that his face was thoughtful, sad, full of wonder. Then he dropped his hands and stood there for a moment longer, as if he wanted to say something. And then he turned and walked away. His back was big and deliberate, his opening and closing of the door slow, polite; there was no farewell.

When he was out of sight, I cleaned my brushes, put my easel in the corner, turned out the glaring bulbs, and left the building. The night smelled dewy, dense. The stars were still thick—stars that didn't exist in DC, apparently. In the dark, I put my hands to my hair and pulled it forward so that it fell to my breastbone, then lifted it up and kissed it where his hand had been.

Chapter 65

1879

On a fine spring day, at last, they visit the Salon. She and Olivier and Yves go together, although she and Olivier will return another day alone, her gloved hand tucked under his arm, to see their two paintings, hanging in different rooms. They have been there other years, but this is the first time—of two, as it will turn out—that Béatrice is looking for her own painting among the hundreds that crowd the walls. The ritual of attendance is familiar to her, but today it is all different; in the thronged halls, every person she sees may have seen her painting, glancing at it indifferently, gazing at it sympathetically, or frowning at its ineptitude. The crowds are no longer a blur of fashionable clothing but individuals, each capable of passing judgment.

This, she thinks, is what it means to be a public painter, to be on display. She is glad, now, not to have used her own name. Ministers of government have probably walked past her painting; perhaps so have Monsieur Manet and her old teacher, Lamelle. She wears her new dress and hat, both pearl gray, the dress edged with a thin line of crimson, the small flat hat tipped forward above her forehead, with long red streamers down the back. Her hair is coiled tightly under it, her waist tightly corseted, the back of her skirt caught up in a series of tight cascades, its hem trailing behind her. She sees the admiration in Olivier's eyes, the younger man gazing out of them.

She is thankful that Yves has paused to view a painting, his hat held in two hands behind him.

It has been a glorious afternoon, but that night the evil dream returns; she is at the barricade. She has arrived too late, and Olivier's wife bleeds in her arms. She will not write to Olivier about it, but Yves has heard her groans. A few nights later he tells her firmly that she must see a doctor—she is nervous, pale. The doctor prescribes tea, a beefsteak every two days, and a glass of red wine at lunch. When the nightmare recurs a few more times, Yves tells her he has made plans for her to take a holiday on the Norman coast they love.

They are sitting in her small boudoir, where she has been resting all evening with a book; Esmé has built up the fire. Yves says he must insist; there is no point in her wearing herself down further with household cares when she is not well. She can see from the concern in his face, the lines under his eyes, that he will not take no for an answer; this is the determination, the will, the love of order that has made him so successful in his career and brought him through hard times in the city again and again. She has forgotten, lately, to search his face for the person she has known and admired for years; his firm gray eyes, his air of neat prosperity, his surprisingly kind mouth, his thick brown beard. She has not noticed in some time what a young face it is; perhaps it is simply that he is in the prime of life, his life and hers—he is six years older than she. She closes her book and asks him, "How can you leave your work?"

Yves brushes the knees of his suit; he has not stopped to change for dinner, and the dust of the city is still on his clothes. Her blue-and-white chairs are a little too small for him. "I will not be able to come," he says regretfully. "I wouldn't mind a bit of a rest myself, but it would be terribly difficult for me to leave now, with the new offices going in. I have asked Olivier to take you."

She steels herself not to speak for a moment, but she is dismayed. Is this what life has in store for her? She considers telling Yves that his uncle's history is the cause of her nervous state, but she will not betray the trust Olivier has placed in her. Besides, Yves could never understand how one person's love could give another person nightmares. At last she says, "Will that not greatly inconvenience him?"

"Oh, he was hesitant at first, but I pressed him hard, and he knows how grateful I shall be if you can get the color back in your face."

It hovers between them that they might yet conceive a child, and also that Yves is constantly busy or tired and they have not made love in several months. She wonders if he is proposing some kind of fresh start, but wants to make her well first.

"I'm sorry if you're disappointed, my dear, but I simply can't leave at the moment." He folds his hands over his knee; his face is anxious. "It will do you good, and you needn't stay for more than a couple of weeks if you find it dull."

"What about Papa?"

He shakes his head. "He and I will get along fine. The servants can see to us."

Her fate seems to open out in front of her. She sees again the body behind the barricade, Olivier, his hair not yet white, kneeling over it, crushed by grief. She will go halfway to meet them, if this is what life requires. Before this, she has not understood love, despite the best efforts of the businessman sitting opposite her. She composes herself for the worst, smiles at him. If it's to be done, she'll at least be thorough. "Very well, darling. I will go. But I shall leave Esmé here to tend to you and Papa."

"Nonsense. We can manage, and you must have her to look after you."

"Olivier can look after me," she says bravely. "Papa depends on Esmé nearly as much as he does on me."

"Are you certain, my dear? I don't want you making sacrifices when you're not yourself."

"Of course I'm certain," she says firmly. Now that the journey is inevitable, she feels exuberant, as if she no longer needs to watch where she sets her feet. "I shall enjoy the independence—you know how Esmé fusses over one—and I shall worry far less, knowing Papa is being well tended."

He nods. She can see that the doctor has told him she must have whatever she wants, must rest; a woman's health can be undermined all too rapidly, and particularly that of a woman in her childbearing years. He will have the doctor examine her again, no doubt, before she leaves, pay the unreasonable fees, allow himself to be reassured. She feels a wave of affection for this steady, anxious man. He might have blamed her painting, she realizes, or the suspense of her having submitted to the Salon, but he has not said a word about those things. She gets up, pushing her feet back into her slippers, and crosses the room to kiss him on the forehead. If she is ever herself again, he will have the benefit of it. The full benefit.

Paris
May 1879

My dear,

I am sorry indeed that Yves will not accompany us to Étretat, but I trust you will not mind putting yourself in my respectful care. I have procured the tickets, as you requested, and will come in a hansom for you at seven in the morning on Thursday. Write me ahead to let me know what I can bring you in the way of painting supplies; that, I am certain, will be better medicine than anything else I can do for you.

Olivier Vignot

CHAPTER 66

Mary

At breakfast the second morning, I braced myself to avoid Robert's eyes if I met them, but to my relief he wasn't there, and even Frank seemed to have found someone else to talk with. I hunched over my coffee and toast, stupefied from painting and a lack of sleep, reluctant for the day to begin. I had twisted my hair up out of the way and put on a faded khaki shirt with paint on the hem, Muzzy's least favorite. The hot coffee helped steady my nerves; after all, it was nonsense for me to think about this man, this unavailable, strange, famous stranger, and I planned not to. The morning was depressingly clear, perfect for a landscape excursion; when nine o'clock came, I was in the van again. Robert drove, and one of the older women consulted a map for him. Frank was nudging me from the neighboring seat, and it was as if the night before had never happened.

This time we painted at the edge of a lake with a run-down cottage on the other side and a lacework of white birches around its shores. Robert cautioned us humorously not to put in any moose. Or women in long dresses, I could have added through my headache. I set my easel as far away from his as I could without allying myself with Frank. I certainly didn't want Robert Oliver to think I was pursuing him, and my one gratification was that he studiously avoided looking at me the entire afternoon and did not even come by to critique my painting, which was a disaster in any case. That meant that last night's conversation was still in his bloodstream, too; otherwise he would be bantering with me, his old student. I couldn't remember what I knew about trees, or shadows, or anything else; I seemed to be painting a muddy ditch in which I could see only my own shape looming, stirring the water, something familiar but ominous.

We ate lunch in a huddle at two picnic tables (I did not sit at Robert's), and at the end of the day we gathered around Robert's canvas—how did he make water seem actually alive like that?—and he talked about the shapes of the shoreline and the color choice he'd made for the distant blue hills. The challenge of this scene was its monochromatic nature, blue hills, blue lake, blue sky, and the temptation to overdo the white of the birches by contrast. But if we looked hard, Robert said, we would realize that there was incredible variety in those muted shades. Frank stood rubbing a finger behind one ear, listening with an air of respect-but-I-could-tell-you-something-more that made me want to slap him; what made him think he knew more than Robert Oliver?

Dinner was worse; Robert came into the crowded dining hall after I did and seemed to choose a seat as far away from me as possible after letting his eyes slide across my table. Later the bonfire was lit in the dark yard, and people drank beers and talked and laughed with a new level of abandon, as if friendships had solidified already. And what had I solidified? I had hung around with Frank the Perfect, or gone back to my room by myself, or thought about and avoided our genius teacher, when I could have been making friends. I considered seeking out one of the women I liked in our landscape class, bringing over a beer, and settling on a garden bench to hear about her life at home, where she'd gone to school and where she'd had a group show, what her husband did—but I felt weary before I'd even started. I scanned the crowd for Robert's curly head and found it; he was towering above a group that contained a couple of my classmates, although I was pleased to see that this time Frank wasn't glued to his side. I collected my sweatshirt and slouched off toward the stables, my bed, and my book—Isaac Newton would be better company than all these people having too good a time together, and once I'd gotten more than three hours' sleep I'd be decent company myself.

The stables were deserted, the rows of little bedroom doors closed, except for mine, which I'd apparently left open—that was careless, although my wallet was in my jeans pocket and I wasn't worried about the rest of my things. Nobody seemed to lock up much here anyway. I went in, numb, and gave a little screech in spite of myself; Frank sat on the edge of my bed, wearing a clean white shirt open to the waist, jeans, and a necklace of heavy brown beads that was actually rather like mine. He had a sketchbook in his hand; he was rubbing his thumb on a fresh drawing, blurring lines. His tan was breathtaking, his muscled ribs contracted a little as he leaned forward over the page; he rubbed with concentration for a second more and then looked up and smiled. I tried not to actually put my hands on my hips. "What do you think you're doing here?"

He put the sketch down and grinned at me. "Oh, come off it. You've been avoiding me for days."

"I could call the organizers and have you evicted."

He settled his face into more seemly attention. "But you won't. You've noticed me as much as I've noticed you. Stop blowing me off."

"I haven't been blowing you off. I believe the word is 'ignoring.' I've been ignoring you, and maybe you're not used to that."

"Do you think I don't know I'm a spoiled brat?" He put his

bristly blond head to one side and regarded me. "How about you?" His smile was contagious, to my dismay. I folded my arms. "Are you one, too?"

"If you weren't a spoiled brat, you certainly wouldn't be here in this totally inappropriate manner."

"Come on," he said again. "You don't think about appropriate and inappropriate like that. I'm not here to jump your snotty bones anyway. I've just thought all along we could be friends, and I thought you might talk with me if we were alone and you didn't have to show off to other people."

I didn't know where to begin taking him apart. "Show off? I've never seen anyone more concerned with image than you seem to be, young man."

"Oh, now we see your true colors. An anti-snob. That's better. After all, you went to art school yourself, and I know where. Not bad." He smiled and showed me his sketchbook. "Hey—I've been trying to do a self-portrait in your mirror. I was just touching it up. Do I look like a show-off?"

I glanced at the drawing in spite of myself. It was wistful, quiet, a thoughtful face I wouldn't have associated with what I'd seen of Frank. It was good, too.

"Very poor shading," I said. "And the mouth is too big."

"Big is good."

"Get off my bed, mister," I said.

"Come over here and kiss me first."

I should have slapped him, but I began to laugh. "I'm old enough to be your mother."

"Not true," he said. He put his sketchbook down on the bed, stood up—he was exactly my height and width and shape—and put a hand on either side of me, against the wall, a gesture he had surely learned from Hollywood. "You are young and beautiful and you should stop being so cranky and have some fun. This is an *art* colony."

"I should have you kicked out of this *art* colony, you child."

"Let's see, you would be—what, eight years older than I am? Five? So dignified." He put one hand on my face and began to stroke my cheek, so that a flame leapt from my shoulder to my hairline. "Do you like to pretend you're self-sufficient, or do you really enjoy sleeping alone in this stall?"

"Men are not allowed in here anyway," I said, removing his hand, which went right back to its gentle work around my temple and down my jawbone. I began to long in spite of myself to put that fine, dexterous young hand elsewhere, to feel it everywhere.

"That's only on paper." He leaned in, but slowly, as if to hypnotize me, a successful enterprise. His breath had a pleasant, fresh smell. He stayed there until I kissed him first, humiliating myself but hungry, and then his lips met mine thoroughly, with a restrained strength that made my stomach flip. I might have ended up spending the night against that silky chest if he hadn't put his hand to my hair and lifted a strand of it. "Gorgeous," he said.

I slipped out from under his tanned arm. "You are, too, little boy, but forget it."

He laughed with surprising good nature. "All right. Let me know if you change your mind. You don't have to be this lonely if you don't want to. We can just have a few of those good conversations you insist on avoiding."

"Just leave, please. Jesus. Enough."

He picked up his sketchbook and went out as quietly as Robert Oliver had from the studio the night before, even closing the door respectfully behind him, as if to show me the maturity I had underestimated in him. When I was sure he'd left the building, I threw myself down on my bed and wiped my mouth on the back of my sleeve and even cried a little, but fiercely.

Chapter 67

1879

By the time their train arrives at the coast, it is night and they have fallen silent; she is weary, her veil spotted with a little soot that makes her feel there is something wrong with her eyesight. At Fécamp they prepare to leave the train for a hansom cab to Étretat. Olivier collects their smaller bags from the shelf in the compartment where they have talked all day—the trunks will follow—and it seems to her when he stands up that he is stiff, that his body under his well-cut traveling suit is indubitably old, that he has no business touching her elbow when he speaks with her, not because he isn't Yves but because he isn't young. But he sits down again and takes her hand. They are both wearing gloves. "I am holding your hand," he tells her, "because I can, and because it is the most beautiful one in the world."

She can't say anything to equal that, and the train is shivering, stopping. Instead she pulls herself free and peels off her glove, then returns her hand to his. He lifts it up to examine it, and in the dim compartment light she sees it objectively, noticing as always that the fingers are too long, the whole hand too big for the small wrist, that there is blue paint around the ends of her first and second fingers. She thinks he will kiss it, but he only bows his head, as if pondering something private, and lets her go. Then he stands, agile, picks up their bags, and invites her politely to leave the compartment ahead of him.

The conductor helps her down into the night, which smells like coal and damp fields. The monstrous train behind them is still groaning, steam from the engine white against dark rows of houses, the shapes of engineers and passengers vague. In their cab, Olivier settles her carefully on a seat beside him; the horses pull forward, and she wonders for the hundredth time why she has consented to such a journey. Is it because Yves insisted or because Olivier wanted her to come with him? Or is it because she herself wanted to and was too weak to talk Yves out of it, too curious?

Étretat, when they arrive, is a blur of gas lamps and cobbled streets. Olivier offers a hand for her to alight, and she pulls her cloak around her, stretches discreetly—she is stiff herself, from traveling. The wind smells of salt water; somewhere out there is the Channel, making its lonely sound. Étretat has the injured air of a resort caught off-season. She knows that melody, knows this town from previous visits, but tonight it seems to her a new place, a wilderness, the edge of the world. Now Olivier is giving some orders about their things. When she allows herself a glance at his profile, she finds him distant, sad. What decades have brought him here? Did he visit this coast long ago with his wife? Can she ask him such a thing? Under the streetlamps, his face looks lined, his lips elegant, sensitive, wrinkled. In the first-floor windows of one of the tall, chimneyed houses across from the station, someone has lit candles; she can see a shape moving around inside, perhaps a woman straightening up a room before going to bed. She wonders what the life in that house is like and why she herself inhabits a different one, in Paris; she thinks how easily fate might have accomplished such a trade.

Olivier does everything gracefully, a man long used to his own skin—accustomed, also, to having his own quiet way.

Watching, she realizes with a sudden lurch of her insides that unless she tells him some kind of no, she will eventually find herself lying naked in his arms here, in this town. It is a shocking thought, but once it presents itself she can't turn away. She will have to find the strength to form that word, "*non.*" *Non*—there is no such word between them, only this strange openness of spirit. He is closer to death than she is; he doesn't have time to wait for answers, and she is far too moved by his desire. The inevitability of it catches tightly in her rib cage.

"You must be tired, my dear," he is saying. "Shall we go straight to the hotel? I'm certain they will give us a little supper."

"Will our rooms be nice?" It comes out more starkly than she intends, because she means something else.

He looks at her, surprised, mild, amused. "Yes, they both are very nice, and I believe there is a sitting room for you as well." She feels a wave of shame. Of course; Yves has sent them here together. Olivier has the grace not to smile. "You will want to sleep late, I hope, and we can meet to paint tomorrow in the late morning, if you'd like. We shall see how the weather is—fine, I think, by the feel of this air."

The man has moved up the street already with their luggage in a wheeled cart, their bags and boxes, her leather-strapped trunk. She and her husband's uncle are alone at the edge of another world, bounded by only the dark salt water, a place where she knows no one but him. She suddenly wants to laugh.

Instead, she sets down the bag with her precious painting supplies in it and raises her veil; she steps close to him, her hands touching his shoulders. His eyes are alert in the light of the gas lamp. If he is surprised by her upturned face, her rashness, he hides it at once. She surprises herself in turn by accepting his kiss without reservation, feeling in it his forty years' experience, seeing the edge of his cheekbone. His mouth is warm and moving. She is one in a line of loves, but she is the only one at this moment, and she will be the last. The unforgettable, the one he takes with him to the end.

Chapter 68

Mary

The third day was the surprising one. I could never describe all of the five hundred days I more or less spent with Robert Oliver, but the first days of loving someone are vivid; you remember them in detail because they represent all the others. They even explain why a particular love doesn't work out.

On the third morning of the conference, I found myself eating breakfast at the same table as a couple of women faculty members who seemed not to notice my presence at the other end, which made it fortunate that I'd brought my book. One of them was a woman of about sixty whom I vaguely recognized as a teacher of printmaking at the retreat, and the other was perhaps forty-five, a painting instructor with short bleached hair who began by declaring that she wasn't finding the caliber of the painting students as high as last year's. *Well, I'll be reading my book, then, ma'am,* I thought. My eggs were runny, not the way I like them.

"I'm not sure why that is." She took a big swallow of coffee, and the other woman nodded. "I hope the great Robert Oliver isn't disappointed, that's all."

"I'm sure he'll survive. He teaches at a small college now, right?"

"Well, that's true—I think it's Greenhill, in North Carolina. In all fairness, a very good department, but hardly what he would find at a real school. I mean, at an art program."

"His students seem to like him," observed the printmaker mildly; she clearly hadn't associated the egg-picking reader at her own table with Robert's group. I kept my head down. It's not that other people's idiocy makes me shy; it simply makes me want to walk away.

"Of course they do." The bleached woman pushed her coffee cup around. "He's made the cover of *ARTnews,* he has work all over the place, and he's hip enough not to care and to go on teaching in the middle of nowhere. It doesn't hurt that he's six two and looks like Jupiter."

Poseidon, in fact, I corrected silently, cutting my bacon. *Or Neptune. You have no idea.*

"His female students run after him constantly, I'm sure," said the printmaker.

"Naturally." Her companion seemed pleased by this opening. "And you hear things, but who knows what's true. He seems to me kind of oblivious, which is refreshing. Or he might be one of those men who just really don't notice anyone but themselves in the end. I think he has a youngish family, too. But you never know. The older I get, the more I think men in their forties are a complete mystery, usually an unpleasant one."

I wondered what age she liked better. I could, for example, introduce her to the enterprising Frank.

The printmaker sighed. "I know. I was married for twenty-one years—*was*—and I still don't think I understood anything about my ex-husband."

"Do you want to take some extra coffee with you?" asked the spiky woman, and they left together without glancing my way. I noticed as they walked off how graceful the younger woman was—lovely, actually, dressed in svelte black with a red belt, trimmer at forty-five than most women were at twenty. Maybe she would take up the Robert Oliver challenge herself, and they could compare their coverage in *ARTnews*. Except that Robert would never be interested in that kind of competition, I decided; he would scratch his head and fold his arms and think about something else. I wondered if my picture of him as incorruptible was correct; was he simply oblivious, as the woman had said? He hadn't been quite oblivious to me two nights before, and yet nothing much had happened between us. I drank my tea in a rush and went back to the stables to get my gear. If he wasn't oblivious, it proved that I was probably unmemorable.

Robert collected us near the vans again, but this time he said we would walk instead of driving. To my surprise he led us out the path through the woods that I'd taken to the water the first day, and we set up our easels on the rocky beach where I'd seen him first dive into the cold tide and then emerge from it. He smiled around the group, not excluding me, and gave us some directions about the angle of the light and the way we could expect it to change. We would do one canvas for morning, right here, take a lunch break back at the camp, and then do a second canvas for afternoon. That clinched it for me; if he could return to this spot and teach a landscape class here, he was truly oblivious, and to me in particular. I felt a kind of sad relief; I had been not only wrong, unethical, but also silly to believe he'd felt what I had. I could have cried for a moment, watching Robert move among his students, giving us a hint here and there about positioning our easels; at the same time, I felt my freedom begin to flood back, the romance of myself, the loneliness. I had been right to value that, and right to laugh Frank out of my room as well.

I tied back my hair and set up facing the longest promontory into the ocean, where I could catch a big stand of firs with their roots on Atlantic rock. I knew right away that this would be a good canvas, a good morning; my hand moved easily through sketching the forms and my eyes were immediately filled with the underlying grays, browns, the green of firs that appeared black in the distance. Even Robert's presence, his moving off to set his own easel in plain sight, his bending and stooping in his yellow cotton shirt—none of that could interrupt me for very long. I painted hard until we broke for a snack, and when I looked up from cleaning my brushes, Robert was smiling at me from the middle of the group in an ordinary way that confirmed my conclusions. I began to speak to him, to say something about the view and its challenges, but he had already turned to talk with someone else.

We painted until lunchtime, and began again at one o'clock with fresh canvases. My morning's picture, propped against a tree to dry, had pleased me more than any I'd done in months; I promised myself I'd come back to finish it at the right time of day, maybe the morning everyone left the conference, which was only two more days away. I wished Robert had come over to see it, but he hadn't checked anyone's paintings today. In the afternoon, we worked in our silent spread, planting easels here and there; Robert went off to the edge of the woods with his, but he returned as the light began to deepen into late afternoon, talked with us a little about the view, and took us back to camp. I was less pleased with my second canvas, but he walked by and praised it a little, commented on everyone equally, then brought us together for a final critique. It had been a good couple of sessions, a pleasant workmanlike day, I thought, and I looked forward to the evening, to making myself drink a beer with a fellow painter or two, then going off to bed to sleep soundly.

Chapter 69

Mary

I managed to have my beer early, over dinner, and then I sat near the fire for a while with two men taking the watercolor class. Their discussion of the relative merits of oils and watercolor for landscape painting was interesting and kept me there longer than I'd intended to stay. At last I excused myself and brushed off the seat of my jeans, preparatory to heading for my neatly made bed. Frank was talking with someone else by the fire, someone young and pretty, so I didn't have to worry about finding him sitting in front of my mirror again. I took a long detour around him anyway, and that was what put me at the edge of the yard, the deep dark where the firelight didn't reach.

A man was standing there, almost in the woods, a tall man rubbing his eyes with his hands, then rubbing his head, as if weary and distracted, and he was looking toward the trees instead of back at the fire with its crowd of festive figures. After a few minutes he began to walk into the woods, along the path I already thought of as ours, and I followed him, knowing that I shouldn't. There was just enough twilight to show his stride ahead of me and assure me that he wasn't aware of being followed. I told myself a couple of times to turn back, to give him his privacy. He was going toward the shore where we'd worked that day; probably he wanted to see some of the forms we'd painted there, even if they would be half visible now, and if he'd left the camp alone, he probably didn't want company.

At the edge of the woods I stopped and watched him go on down the stones of the beach, which clinked together under his feet. The slop of the ocean was audible; the sheen of water stretched darkly to an even darker horizon. Stars were coming out, but the sky was still blue—sapphire—rather than black, and Robert's shirt pale, his form moving along the edge of the water now. He stood still, then stooped to pick something up, flung his arm back with the childhood gesture of baseball-in-hand, and hurled it away from land—a stone. It was a quick, furious gesture: anger, maybe despair, release. I watched him without moving, half frightened by his emotion. Then he crouched down, a strange gesture for such a large person, again a child's gesture, and seemed to put his head in his hands.

I wondered for a moment if he was tired, irritated (as I was myself) by the lack of sleep and the endless necessity of being with other people at the conference, or if he might even be crying, although I couldn't imagine what someone like Robert Oliver would have to cry about. Now he was sitting down on the beach—it would be damp, I thought, hard and slippery—and he stayed there on and on, his head in his hands. The waves came forward smoothly, unfurling white half visible in the dark. I stood watching and he simply sat there, his shoulders and back glimmering. In the end, I always act from the heart, even if I also value reason and tradition. I wish I could explain why, but I don't know. I started down the beach, hearing the stones rattle under my feet, once almost tripping.

He didn't turn around until I was very close, and even then I couldn't see his expression. But he saw me, whether or not he recognized me in the first moment, and he stood up—started up. At that moment I finally felt shame and real apprehension at having invaded his solitude. We stood looking at each other.

And I could see his face now; it was dark, troubled, and my presence hadn't cleared it. "What are you doing here?" he said flatly.

I moved my lips but no voice came out. Instead, I reached over and took his hand, which was very large, very warm, and closed automatically over mine. "You should go back, Mary," he said with (I thought) a quiver in his voice. It gratified me that he had used my name, and so naturally.

"I know I should," I said. "But I saw you and I felt worried about you."

"Don't worry about me," he said, and his hand closed more tightly over my hand, as if saying it made him worry about me in return.

"Are you all right?"

"No," he said softly, "but that doesn't matter."

"Of course it matters. It always matters if a person is all right or not." *Idiot,* I told myself, but there was the problem of his huge hand over mine.

"Do you think artists are really supposed to be all right?" He smiled, and I thought he might even begin to laugh at me.

"Everyone is supposed to be," I said staunchly, and I knew that I was indeed an idiot and that was my destiny and I didn't mind it.

He dropped my hand and turned to the ocean. "Have you ever had this feeling that the lives people lived in the past are still real?"

This was weird and out of context enough to give me a chill. I very much wanted him to be all right despite his strange assertion, so I thought about Isaac Newton. Then I thought about how often Robert Oliver painted historical or pseudo-historical figures, even those distant people I had seen in his landscape our first full day here, and realized that this must be a natural question for him. "Certainly."

"I mean," he continued, as if talking to the edge of the water, "when you see a painting that was painted by someone who's been dead for a long time, you know without a doubt that that person really lived."

"I think about that sometimes, too," I admitted, although his observation didn't fit my first theory about him, that he was simply interested in adding historical figures to his canvases. "Do you mean somebody in particular?"

He didn't answer, but after a moment he put his arm around me as I stood beside him, then stroked my hair down my back, a continuation of his gesture of two nights earlier. He was stranger than I'd thought, this man—it was not simply eccentricity but genuine oddness, a sort of complete focus on the world of his own thoughts, a disconnect. My sister, Martha, would have given him a peck on the cheek and walked back up the beach, I'm sure, and so would any sensible person I know. But there is another meaning to *sensible*—Muzzy made us take years of French. He stroked my hair. I raised my hand to take his hand, and then I drew it to my face and kissed it in the dark.

Kissing someone's hand is more a man's gesture than a woman's, or a gesture of respect—for royalty, for a bishop, for the dying. And I did mean it respectfully; I meant that I was awed and thrilled by his presence, as well as a little afraid of it. He turned toward me and pulled me in, one of his arms crooked gently around my neck, and ran his other hand over my face as if wiping dust from it, and drew me up against him to kiss me. I hadn't been kissed like that, ever, not ever; his mouth had the feel of a completely unself-conscious passion, a longing possibly unconscious even of me, full of the act itself. His hand caught the small of my back and lifted and pressed me against him, and I could feel the self-sufficient warmth of his chest through his worn shirt, the little buttons pressing into me as if to mark my skin.

Then he slowly let me go. "I don't do this," he said, as if drunk. There was no alcohol on his breath, not even the beer I'd had myself. He put his hands on my face and kissed me again, quickly, and this time I felt he knew exactly who I was. "Please go back."

"All right." I, whom Muzzy had called willful, whom my high-school teachers had considered a little sullen and my art-school instructors had found trying, turned obediently away and walked, stumbling, up the dark beach.

Chapter 70

1879

Her room in their boardinghouse overlooks the water; his, she knows, is on the same floor at the other end of the corridor, so that it must have a view back into the town. Her furniture is simple, an assortment of old pieces. A polished shell sits on the dressing table. Lace curtains veil the night. The innkeeper has lit lamps and a candle for her and left a tray under a cloth: stewed fowl, a salad of leeks, a slice of cold *tarte aux pommes*. She washes in the basin and eats ravenously. The fireplace is dead, perhaps abandoned for the season, or to save fuel. She could request a fire, but that might involve Olivier—she prefers to remember their kiss on the station platform, not see him now, with his weary face.

She takes off her traveling dress and boots, pleased, glad she has not brought her maid. For once, she will do things for herself. Beside the cold fireplace, she removes her corset cover, unlaces her corset, and hangs it temporarily over a chair. She shakes out her chemise and petticoats and slips out of them, pulls the tent of her nightgown over her head, its scent her own, comforting, something from home. She begins to button up the neck, then stops and takes it off again; she spreads it on the bed and sits down in front of the dressing table wearing only pantalets. The chill of the room makes her skin prickle. It has been a year or more since she has sat looking at her body, bare from the waist up. Her skin is younger than she thinks of it; she is twenty-seven. She can't remember when Yves last kissed her nipples—four months, six months? During the long spring she has forgotten to coax him even at the right time of month. She has been distracted. Besides, he is usually traveling, or tired, or perhaps he has all he wants elsewhere.

She puts a hand over the swell of each breast, notes the effect of her rings catching the candlelight. She knows more now about Olivier than about the man she lives with. Olivier's decades of life lie open to her, while Yves is a mystery who shuttles in and out of her house, nodding and admiring. She squeezes hard with both hands. In the mirror, her neck is long, her face pale from the train trip, her eyes too dark, her chin too square, her curls too heavy. Nothing about her should add up to beauty, she thinks, taking the pins out of her hair. She uncoils the heavy knot at the back; she lets it fall over her shoulders and between her breasts, sees herself as Olivier might, and is ravished: self-portrait, nude, a subject she will never paint.

Chapter 71

Mary

Robert and I didn't look at each other the next day; actually, I don't know whether he looked at me or not, because by then the only thing I could think to do was to ignore everything around me except my hand on the brush. I still like the landscapes I did at that conference as much as anything I've painted. They are tense—I mean, full of tension. Even I can feel when I see them now that they have that little bit of mystery every painting needs to be successful, as Robert had once put it to me himself. That final day, I ignored Robert, I ignored Frank, I ignored the people around me at our last three meals, I ignored the dark and the stars and the bonfire and even my own body curled in the white bed in the stables. I slept deeply after my initial exhaustion. I didn't even know if I would see Robert the last morning, and I ignored my conflicting hopes of seeing and not seeing him. Anything else had to be up to him; that was how he had arranged things by not arranging them.

The departure morning of the conference was a busy one; everyone was supposed to clear out by ten o'clock, because a retreat for Jungian psychologists was arriving the next day and the staff had to clean our dining hall and stables to prepare for them. I methodically packed my duffel bag on my bed. At breakfast Frank clapped me on the shoulder, very cheerful; clearly he had gotten good and laid. I shook hands solemnly with him. The two nice women from my painting class gave me their e-mail addresses.

I didn't see Robert anywhere, and this caused me a pang but also that strange relief again, as if I'd narrowly avoided scraping a wall. He had quite possibly left early, since he would have a long drive back to North Carolina. A caravan of artists' cars was pulling out onto the drive, many of them plastered with bumper stickers, a couple of enormous old town cars loaded with equipment, one van painted with Van Gogh swirls and stars, hands waving out the windows, people shouting last good-byes to their workshop mates. I loaded my truck and then thought better of waiting in the line and went for a walk instead, out into the woods in a direction I hadn't yet taken; there were enough cleared trails for forty minutes of browsing without straying far from the estate. I liked the underbrush, with its lichened fir branches and shaggy low bushes, the light filtering from the fields into the forest.

When I emerged, the traffic jam was gone and only three or four cars remained. Robert was loading one of them; I hadn't known that he drove a small blue Honda, although I could have thought to check around for North Carolina plates. His method of packing seemed to be to shove things into the rear storage area without putting most of them into bags or boxes; I could see him jamming in some clothes and books, a folding stool. His easel and wrapped canvases were already carefully stowed, and he seemed to be using the rest of his possessions to pad them. I was planning a silent stroll to my truck when he turned and saw me, and stopped me. "Mary—are you leaving?"

I went over to him; I couldn't help it. "Aren't we all?"

"I'm not." To my surprise, he had a grin on his face, complicit, a teenager sneaking out of the house. He looked refreshed and bright, his hair on end but still glistening damp as if from a shower. "I slept late, and when I woke up I decided to go paint."

"Did you go?"

"No, I mean I'm going now."

"Where are you going?" I had begun somehow to feel jealous, irritated, left out of his secret happiness. But why should it matter?

"There's a great stretch of state park about forty-five minutes south of here, right on the coast. Near Penobscot Bay. I checked it out on the way up."

"Don't you have to drive all the way to North Carolina?"

"Sure." He balled up a gray fleece sweatshirt and used it to brace one leg of his easel. "But I have three days to do it, and I can make it in two if I push hard."

I stood there, uncertain. "Well, have a good time. And a safe trip."

"Don't you want to come?"

"To North Carolina?" I asked stupidly. I had a sudden vision of myself traveling home with him to see his life there, his dark-haired wife—no, that was the lady in the pictures—and two children. I'd heard him tell someone in the group he had two now.

He laughed. "No, no—to paint. Do you have to rush off?"

I wanted less than anything in the world to "rush off." His smile was so warm, so friendly, so ordinary. There couldn't be any danger in it when he put it that way. "No," I said slowly. "I don't have to be back for two days myself, and I can make it in one if I push hard, too." Then I thought it must sound as if I were propositioning him, counting that night into the occasion, when it was probably not what he'd meant, and I felt my face getting warm. But he didn't seem to notice.

*

That was how we spent the day painting together on the beach somewhere south of—well, it doesn't matter; it's my secret, and almost all the Maine coast is picturesque anyway. The cove Robert picked was indeed beautiful—a rocky field crowned with blueberry bushes, summer wildflowers stretching down to low bluffs and piles of driftwood, a beach of smooth rocks in all sizes, the water broken darkly by islands. It was a bright, hot, breezy Atlantic day—that's how I remember it, at least. We braced our easels among the gray and green and slate-blue rocks, and we painted the water and the curves of the land—Robert commented that it was like the southern coast of Norway, which he had seen once just after college. I filed this away in my very small store of knowledge about him.

We didn't talk much, however, that day; mostly we stood a couple of yards apart and worked in silence. My painting went well, despite my divided attention, or perhaps somehow because of it. I gave myself thirty minutes for the first canvas, which was small, working rapidly, holding the brush as lightly as I could, an experiment. The water was deep blue, the sky a nearly colorless brightness, the foam at the edge of the waves ivory, a rich, organic hue. Robert glanced quickly at my canvas when I removed it and set it to dry against a boulder. I found I didn't mind that he said nothing, as if he were no longer teacher but simply company.

I worked my second canvas over more slowly and had finished only some background by the time we stopped for lunch. The dining-hall staff had graciously allowed me to load up on egg sandwiches and fruit. Robert seemed to have no food with him, and I'm not sure what he would have eaten if I hadn't provided his lunch. After we'd finished, I got out my tube of sunscreen and put some on my face and arms; the breeze came in cooling gusts out there, but I could feel I'd already let myself burn. I offered it to Robert, as I had my lunch, but he laughed and refused. "Not all of us are so fair." And then he touched my hair again with one hand, and my cheek, with his fingertips, as if merely admiring, and I smiled but did not respond, and we went back to our work.

As the light began to deepen and fail, the shadows changed on the face of the islands and I began to wonder about the night. We would have to spend it somewhere—not we, but I, and I could make it to Portland if I set out by six or seven, and find a motel there. It had to be cheap, and I had to have time to hunt for cheap. And I was not going to think about Robert Oliver and his plans or—I'd begun to suspect—lack thereof. It was enough, it had to be enough, to have had this day of working more or less at his elbow.

Robert slowed at the canvas; I sensed the fatigue in his brush before he stopped or spoke. "Have you had it?"

"I could stop," I admitted. "Maybe fifteen minutes more, so I can remember some colors and shadows, but I've lost my original light."

After a while he began to clean his brush. "Shall we go eat?"

"Eat what? The rose hips?" I indicated the bluff just behind us. They were gorgeous, larger than any I'd ever seen, rubies against the green of the wild rose hedges. Looking straight up from there, you saw only blue sky. We stood staring together at that triad of colors: the red, the green, the blue, surreally bright.

"Or we could eat seaweed," Robert said. "Don't worry—we'll find something."

Chapter 72

1879

Afternoon, Étretat: the light stretches grandly across the beach, but her painting has not gone well. It is her second attempt at this scene—overturned fishing boats on the shingle. She wants a human figure for it and has finally settled for the effect of two ladies and a gentleman strolling down by the cliffs, city ladies with light-colored parasols who strike a perfect note against the darker, colonnaded arch in the distance. Another painter is present today, too, a bulky man with a brown beard who has set the legs of his easel almost in the tide; she regrets not having chosen him for a subject instead. She and Olivier glance at each other when he passes them on his way to the water's edge, silent company for their silence.

Her sky won't go right today, even when she adds more white and a fine blending of ocher. Olivier leans over to ask her why she is shaking her head. The ocher in the vast, real light touches his bristling hair, his mustache, his pale shirt. She doesn't intend it, but when he bends close she puts one hand to his cheek. He catches and holds her fingers, kisses them with a warmth that courses through her. In sight of the windows of the town, in sight of the heavy back of the stranger painting the cliffs, the ladies under their distant parasols, they kiss each other for an endless moment, their third kiss. This time she feels his mouth insisting, opening hers as Yves would have tried only in the darkness of their bedroom. His tongue is strong and his mouth fresh; she understands then, with her arms around his neck, that his youth really is still inside him and that this mouth is the passage into it, a tunnel for the tide.

He stops just as abruptly. "My dearest." He puts down his brush and walks a few paces away, stones sliding audibly under his boots. He stands looking out to sea, and she sees no melodrama, only his need for a greater distance to collect himself. She follows him anyway and slips her hand into his. His hand is older than his mouth. "No," she says. "It was my fault."

"I love you." An explanation. He is still gazing out toward the horizon. His voice sounds bleak to her.

"And why is that so hopeless?" She watches his profile for a response. In a moment he turns and takes her other hand.

"Be careful what you say, my dear." His face is composed now, gentle, completely his own. "An old man's hope is more fragile than you imagine."

She suppresses the urge to stamp her foot on the loose shingle—that would only make her look childish. "Why do you think I can't understand that?"

He is gripping her hands, still facing her. For once, she likes his disregard of any possible onlookers. "Perhaps you can," he says. He is beginning to smile, his affectionate, grave smile, his teeth yellowed but even. When he smiles she knows where the lines of his face have come from; it solves a mystery every time. She knows now that she loves him, too, not only for who he is but for who he was long before she was born, and because he will someday die with her name on his lips. She puts her arms around him without any invitation, around his lean body, his ribs and waist, under the layers of clothes, and holds him tightly. Her cheek rests on the shoulder of his old jacket, where it fits. His arms go around her completely in return; they are full of living warmth. In that moment, it will later seem to her, all the rest of his brief future is settled, and even the longer reach of hers.

Chapter 73

Mary

The restaurant we found, caravanning a few miles farther south with our cars smelling of fresh paint, was faux Italian of the straw-plaited-bottle variety, red-checked cloths and curtains, a pink rose in a vase on our table. It was a Monday night, and the place was empty except for one other—couple, I almost wrote—and a man dining alone. Robert asked for a candle. "What color would you call that?" he said when the underage waiter had lit it.

"The flame?" I said. I was already learning that often I couldn't understand Robert, couldn't follow his private and sometimes chaotic train of thought. But I liked where it led, usually.

"No. The rose."

"It would be pink if everything else weren't red and white," I guessed.

"Correct." And then he told me the paint he would use for that rose, the brand, the color, the amount of white to be added. We ordered the same lasagna, and he ate with gusto while I picked at mine, hungry but self-conscious. "Tell me something else about yourself."

"You know more about me than I do about you," I demurred. "There's not much to tell anyway—I go to my job, do the best I can for my dozens of students of all ages, come home, and paint. I don't have a—family, and I don't especially want one, I guess. That's it. Very dull story."

He drank the red wine he'd ordered for both of us; I'd hardly touched mine. "That's not dull. You paint with dedication. That's everything."

"Your turn," I said, and made myself eat some lasagna.

He was relaxing now; he put down his fork and leaned back, rolled up a fallen sleeve. His skin was just at the point of fine tracery on the surface, good leather worn for a while. His eyes and hair looked the same color in that light, and there was something alert and a little wild in both. "Well, I am also very boring," he said. "Except that my life is not as well organized, I suppose. I live in a small town, from which I escape occasionally but which I actually like. I teach endless studio courses to mainly untalented or slightly talented undergraduates. I'm fond of them, and they like my classes. And I show my work here and there. I like not being a New York artist anymore, although I miss New York."

I didn't interject that his "here and there" was adding up to a rather extraordinary career. "When did you live in New York?"

"Graduate school and after." Of course; he'd been a rebel at one of the New York schools that had turned down my own portfolio. "I was there for about eight years, total. Got a lot of work done, actually. But Kate, my wife, wasn't very happy in the city, so we moved. I don't regret it. Greenhill has been a good place for her and the children." He said this guilelessly. For a long moment that was like falling from a tree, I wished that someone were sitting in a restaurant far away, saying such matter-of-fact, devoted things about me and the children I didn't want to have.

"How do you make time for your own work?" I thought a change of subject was the best idea.

"I don't sleep much—sometimes. I mean, sometimes I don't need to sleep very much."

"Like Picasso," I said, smiling to show that I didn't mean this seriously.

"Exactly like Picasso," he agreed, also smiling. "I have a studio at home, and that means I can just go upstairs to work at night, instead of going back to school and dealing with a lot of locked doors."

I pictured him hunting through all his pockets for a key.

He finished his wine and poured more, but moderately, I noticed; he must have been planning to drive, and safely. There was no motel attached to our Italian haven. "Anyway," he finished, "we moved out of the college a while ago, and we have a lot more space. That's been good, too, although now the commute to school is twenty minutes by car instead of four minutes on foot."

"Too bad." I ate the rest of my lasagna so that I wouldn't later regret being hungry as well as whatever else I was going to be. I still had Isaac Newton to finish, and he was turning out to be very interesting, more than I might have predicted. Reason versus belief.

Robert ordered dessert, and we talked about favorite painters. I confessed my love of Matisse and speculated aloud about how our jaunty table and curtains and rose could all have ended up coming off Matisse's brush. Robert laughed and didn't confess to being more traditional than that and to having an interest in the Impressionists; it was obvious, perhaps, or his awareness of the critical coverage of his work had made him stop justifying it. His acclaim was growing nicely; he had paid back his instructors and jeering conceptual-artist classmates. I read these things between the lines as he spoke. We talked about books, too; he loved poetry and quoted Yeats and Auden, whom I'd read a little in school, and Czesław Miłosz, whose collected poems I had read through once, long ago, because I'd seen a volume of them on

Robert's desk. He didn't like most novels, and I threatened to send him a long Victorian one like a bomb in the mail, *The Moonstone* or *Middlemarch*. He laughed and promised not to read it. "But you *should* like nineteenth-century literature," I added. "Or at least the French authors, since you love Impressionism."

"I didn't say I love Impressionism," he corrected. "I said I do what I do. For my own reasons. Some of it happens to resemble Impressionism."

He hadn't said that either, but I didn't correct him in turn. I remember he also told me a story of having been on a plane that seemed about to crash. "I was flying back to New York from Greenhill once, while I had that teaching job at your college, actually—at Barnett. And something happened to one of the engines, so the pilot got on the intercom and announced that we might have to make an emergency landing, although we were almost to LaGuardia. The woman sitting next to me got very frightened. She was a middle-aged woman, kind of ordinary. Before that she'd been talking with me about her husband's job or something. When the plane lurched and the seat-belt sign started flashing, she reached out and grabbed me around the neck."

He rolled his napkin into a heavy tube. "I was frightened, too, and I remember thinking that I just wanted to live—it panicked me to have her gripping my neck like that. And—I'm sorry to say this—I pushed her off me. I had always thought I would be naturally brave in a crisis, that I would be someone who pulls other people out of burning wrecks, as an automatic response." He lifted his head, raised his shoulders. "Why am I telling you this? Anyway, when we landed safely a few minutes later, she wouldn't look at me. She was turned away, crying. She wouldn't even let me help her with her bag and wouldn't look at me."

I couldn't think of anything to say, although I felt a piercing sympathy. His expression was dark, heavy; it reminded me of that moment in college when he'd told me about the woman whose face he couldn't forget.

"I could never tell my wife about that." He flattened the napkin with both hands. "She already thinks I don't take good enough care of anybody." Then he smiled. "Look what ridiculous confessions you bring out in me."

I was content.

At last Robert stretched his big arms and insisted on paying the bill, then let me insist on splitting it with him, and we stood up. He excused himself to go to the restroom—I had already been twice, mainly to be alone for a couple of seconds and question myself in the mirror—and the restaurant seemed even emptier without him. Then we went out into the dark parking lot, which smelled like ocean and fried food, fishy, and stood next to my car. "Well, I'm going to start driving," he said, but this time not matter-of-factly, which would have stung more. "I like to drive at night."

"Yes, you've got a long trip, I guess. I'm going to start mine, too." I planned instead to let him pull out ahead of me and drive faster. Then I would hunt for the first decent motel in the first town; it was too late to make Portland, or I was too tired, or too sad. Robert looked ready to drive to Florida by himself.

"This has been lovely." He put his arms slowly around me, and I was struck by the feminine word. He held me for a moment and kissed my cheek, and I was careful not to move. I had to memorize him, after all.

"It has been." Then I released him and unlocked my truck.

"Wait—here's my address and phone number. Let me know if you come south."

Like hell. I didn't have a business card with me, but I found a piece of paper in my glove compartment and wrote my e-mail address and phone on it.

Robert glanced at it. "I don't do email much," he said. "I use it for business, if I have to, but that's about it. Why don't you give me your real address, and I'll send you a drawing sometime?"

I added my real address.

He stroked my hair, as if for the last time. "I guess you understand."

"Oh, yes." I kissed his cheek rapidly. It was sharp-tasting, even very slightly oily, the finest extra-virgin, cold-pressed—the traces of it were on my lips for hours. I got in my truck. I drove away.

His first drawing arrived in my mailbox ten days later. It was just a sketch, whimsical, hasty, on folded paper; it showed a satyrlike figure rising from waves and a maiden sitting on a rock nearby. The note enclosed said that he'd thought about our conversations and enjoyed them, that he was working on a new canvas based on his painting of the beach. I wondered, immediately, if he'd included the figure of the woman and child. He gave a PO box, and he wrote that I should use that address, and that I should send him a better drawing than his, to put him in his place.

CHAPTER 74

Mary

Robert and I wrote to each other for a long time, and those letters are still one of the best things I've ever experienced. It's funny; in this era of email and voice mail and all those things that even I did not grow up with, a plain old paper letter takes on amazing intimacy. I would come home at the end of the day to find one—or none, many days—or a sketch, or both, crammed into an envelope and scrawled with my address in Robert's looping hand. I made a collage of the drawings on the bulletin board above my desk. At home, my office is also my bedroom, or vice versa; I could see all his sketches, a growing exhibition, as I lay in bed with my book at night, or when I woke up in the morning.

Oddly, once I'd pinned up two or three of those sketches, I stopped having that sense one gets of being single and always watching out for someone, for the right person. I began to belong to Robert—I who had never wanted to belong to anything. I guess in the end we belong to what we love. It wasn't that I thought Robert was available or that I had some obligation to be faithful to him; at first it was just the feeling that I wouldn't have wanted any other pair of eyes to see those drawings from my bed. He drew trees, people, houses, me, from memory; he drew himself in a "funk" over his latest project. I still don't know what it meant to him to send me all those images, whether he would have done them anyway and stuffed them into a file drawer or dropped them on his office floor, or whether he did more of them or drew them with fresh inspiration because they were for me.

Once, he sent me part of a poem by Czesław Miłosz, with a note saying that it was one of his favorites. I didn't know whether or not to take it as a declaration from Robert himself, but I kept it in my pocket for several days before I tacked it on my bulletin board:

O my love, where are they, where are they going
The flash of a hand, streak of movement, rustle of
pebbles.
I ask not out of sorrow, but in wonder.

I didn't put his letters up on my bulletin board, however. Those sometimes arrived with the sketches, sometimes on their own, and they were often very brief, a thought, a reflection, an image. I think Robert was—is—a writer at heart, too; if someone had collected in order all those bits and pieces of his writing to me, they would have made a kind of short and impressionistic but very good novel about his daily life and the nature he was constantly trying to paint. I wrote him back every time; I had a rule for myself that I would mirror whatever he did, to keep things balanced, so that if he sent only a sketch, I sent only a sketch in return, and if he sent only a note, I sent only a note in response. If he sent both, my rule went, I could write him a longer letter and illustrate it right on the page.

I don't know if he ever noticed this pattern, and it was one of the things I didn't ask him. It kept me from writing him too often, and we exchanged letters or sketches several times a week once our correspondence was well under way. After our last fight, I made up a whole new rule: I would burn only the letters and keep the sketches, although I removed all but his very first sketch from my bulletin board. The first, the satyr and the maiden, I glued to cardboard, a few weeks after he left, and tinted with watercolor, and then I did a series of three small matching paintings based on it. I might as well have blended the colors with actual tears, they were so painful to work on.

I often imagined the post office box into which he put his hand every few days. I wondered what size the box was, and whether his hand fit or just the fingers; I imagined him feeling blindly inside it like Alice grown too large in Wonderland, groping up the chimney to catch whatever little character it was, a lizard or a mouse. He knew my address, of course, which meant he knew where I lived. And I saw Greenhill College once, as well; about halfway through our correspondence, Robert surprised me by inviting me to come to the opening of a show he was having there, his second since he'd started teaching. He said he was inviting me because of my support of his work and intimated that he couldn't give me a place to stay; I understood from this that he wanted to invite me but wasn't sure he wanted me to come.

I didn't wish to displease him, but I didn't like to displease myself either, so I drove down from DC—as you know, it's only a long day's trip—and stayed at a Motel 6 outside the town. There was a wine-and-cheese reception at the new art gallery on the Greenhill campus. I didn't dare to call Robert, so I sent a note to the PO box several days before I arrived for the opening, which he didn't get until too late.

My hands were trembling when I walked into the reception. I hadn't seen Robert since Maine—and since we'd begun writing each other—and I already regretted having come at all; he might be offended, might think I'd come to disrupt his life in some way, which I honestly hadn't. I just wanted to see him, maybe from a distance, and to see the new paintings whose conception and execution I'd heard about week after week. I had dressed in a very ordinary way, in a black turtleneck and my usual jeans, and I got to the gallery a good half hour after the party started. I saw Robert at once, towering over the crowd in one corner; several guests with wineglasses in their hands seemed to be asking about his paintings. The place was mobbed, not only with students and faculty but also with a lot of elegant people who didn't look as if they belonged to a small rural college. There were probably buyers there, too.

The paintings, whenever you could get a glimpse of them, were riveting; for one thing, they were larger than any work by him I'd seen before, nearly life-sized scenes and portraits, often full-length depictions of the lady I remembered from his canvases at Barnett College, except that now she was not only bigger but also thrust into a terrible scene, holding what looked like the dead body of another, older woman in her arms, grieving over her. I wondered if this was supposed to be her mother. The older woman had a gruesome wound in the middle of her forehead. There were other dead bodies on the ground, I remember, some of them facedown on cobblestones, or with blood on their backs, but they were the bodies of men. The backgrounds were vaguer than the figures: a street of some sort, a wall, piles of rubble or garbage. The images were straight out of the mid-nineteenth century—I thought immediately of Manet's painting of the execution of Emperor Maximilian, the one that looks like Goya, although Robert's images were more detailed and realistic.

It was hard to tell what all this was about; I just know that the power of his fantasy swept over you as soon as you saw those scenes: the woman was as beautiful as ever, even with her face white and the front of her dress stained, but Robert had depicted something horrible. It was all the more horrible because she was lovely, as if he'd felt compelled to see her with blood on her gown, her face stark. I'd gathered from his notes to me that the paintings were fierce and strange, but seeing them in the flesh was completely different, shocking; I had a moment of feeling frightened, as if I'd been corresponding with a murderer. It was very jarring; it disoriented me in the midst of my growing love for Robert. Then I saw the tremendous sculptural quality of the figures, the sense of compassion, the grief that was deeper than the gore, and I knew I was looking at paintings that would last in importance long after we were all gone.

I almost left without greeting Robert at all, partly out of this shock, partly to keep the sense of privacy between us—and partly out of riveting shyness as well, I'll admit. But I'd driven so far that I finally made myself walk over to him when some of his admirers turned away. He saw me pushing through the crowd, and he froze for a moment. Then a startled, joyful expression flashed over his face—how I treasured the remembrance of that look afterward—and he collected himself and came forward to shake hands warmly with me, making it all very proper, making it work, managing to murmur to me first that he was very touched that I had come. I had half forgotten how large he was in person, how strangely handsome, how striking. He took my elbow in his hand; he began at once to introduce me to a shifting circle of people without explaining anything but my name and, in a couple of cases, that I was a painter as well.

Among these people, among these momentary introductions, was his wife, who shook my hand warmly, too, and tried to ask me something kind about myself, to make me welcome, whoever I was. Mercifully, someone else waylaid her a second later. I was stricken by my sudden recognition of her identity, flooded with something I would have called jealousy if I hadn't known how absurd that would be. I liked her instantly and, in spite of myself and forever after, at a distance. She was much smaller than Robert (I had imagined a sort of huntress for him, an Amazon, a larger-than-life Diana)—in fact, she just came up to my shoulder. She was tawny-haired, freckled, like a golden flower with a green-stemmed dress. If she'd been my friend, I would have asked her to let me paint her, just for the pleasure of choosing the colors.

I felt the warmth of her hand in my own for the rest of the evening, after I'd tactfully left early without speaking to Robert again so that he would not have to cope at all with the question of where I was staying and for how long, and also after I had driven a few hours back toward DC, when I lay curled, mute, in a motel bed in southern Virginia, full of having seen him. Having seen them—Robert and his wife.

May 1879
Étretat
To: M. Yves Vignot
Rue de Boulogne, Passy, Paris

Mon cher mari:

I hope this finds you and Papa as well as can be expected. Have you had a great deal of work? Will you be returning to Nice or can you stay at home for some weeks, as you hoped? Is it still raining?

I am getting on perfectly here and have spent the first day painting on the promenade, as the weather is very bright for May, if cool, and am now resting before dinner. Uncle accompanied me. He is working on a large canvas of the water and cliffs. I confess I have done only one thing I like, and it is rather sketchy, at that—a couple of local women with delightful big skirts tucked up and a child wading alongside, but no doubt I will have to try something grander in order to keep up. The landscape is as lovely as I remember from our visit, although it is much changed by the season's difference—the hills are just greening now, and the horizon looks gray-blue, without those fluffy midsummer clouds. Our hotel is quite comfortable, so you should have no worries—it is spotless and well appointed, and I like the relative simplicity. I ate a hearty breakfast this morning—you would approve. The trip did not tire me at all, and I fell pleasantly asleep the minute I reached my room. Uncle has brought with him notes for some articles he is working on when we are not painting, so I shall be able to rest during those times, as you requested. I have also begun reading Thackeray for entertainment. There's no need for you to send anyone to me. I am managing perfectly and am pleased that Esmé cares so tenderly for Papa even while she does other things. Please keep yourself very well—don't go out without your coat unless the weather becomes more springlike there. Know me to be your devoted

Béatrice

Chapter 75

Mary

One morning I realized I hadn't had a letter or a drawing from Robert for five days, which was now a long time for us. His latest sketch had been a self-portrait, humorously caricaturing his own strong features, his hair on end and somehow alive, like Medusa's. Under it he had written: "Oh, Robert Oliver, when will you pull your life together?" It was probably the only time I ever knew him to criticize himself directly, and it startled me a little. But I took it as a reference to one of the "melancholies" he sometimes described offhandedly to me, or as an acknowledgment of the increasingly double life he led through our letters. I took it, in fact, as a kind of compliment, which is the way one wants everything to look in the midst of love, isn't it? But then he didn't send anything for three days, then four, five, and I broke my rule and wrote him a second time, concerned, yearning, trying to be casual about it.

He never got that letter, I'm sure; unless the post office has closed his box and thrown my letter away, it's probably still sitting there, waiting for the hand that never reached in to pull it out. Or perhaps Kate cleared out the box eventually and threw it away. I like to think she didn't read it, if that's the case. The morning after I sent it, my apartment buzzer rang at six thirty. I was still in my bathrobe, my hair wet but combed out, getting ready to go to my drawing class. No one had ever rung my bell at that hour, and I thought immediately about calling the police; that's the nature of the neighborhood I live in. But just to see what was going on, I pressed the button on my speaker and asked who it was.

"Robert," said a voice, a big, deep, strange voice. It sounded tired, even a little hesitant, but I knew it was his. I would have known it in outer space.

"Just a minute," I said. "Wait. Wait just a minute." I could have buzzed him in, but I wanted desperately to go down myself; I couldn't believe it. I threw on the first clothes I could find, grabbed my keys, and ran barefoot to the elevator. On the first floor, I could see him through the glass inner doors. He had a duffel bag over his shoulder; he seemed very weary, more rumpled than ever but also alert, scanning for me through the lobby.

I thought I must be dreaming, but I unlocked the door anyway and ran to him, and he dropped the bag and lifted me up in his arms and crushed me; I felt him burying his face in my shoulder and hair, smelling them. We weren't even kissing in that first moment; I think I was sobbing with relief because his cheek felt the way I'd thought it would, and maybe he was sobbing a little, too. We pulled apart with our hair sticking to each other's faces, tears, sweat glistening on his forehead. He had let his beard grow out for a few days; he looked unshaven, a lumberjack on the sidewalks of a DC neighborhood, one old shirt over another. "What?" I said, because that was all I could manage.

"Well, she threw me out," he admitted, lifting the bag again as if that were proof of his exile. And at my look of shock, I guess: "Not because of you. Something else."

I must have looked more shocked than ever, because he put an arm around my shoulders. "Don't worry. It's all right. It was just about my paintings, and I'll explain it to you later."

"You drove all night," I said.

"Yes, and can I leave my car there?" He pointed to the street, its signs and litter and incomprehensible meters.

"Certainly," I said. "You can, and it will be towed sometime after nine." Then we both began to laugh, and he brushed my hair back again, the gesture I remembered from our encounter at the camp, and kissed me, kissed me, kissed me.

"Is it nine yet?"

"No," I said. "We have more than two hours." We went upstairs with his heavy bag, and I locked the door behind us and called in sick.

Chapter 76

Mary

Robert didn't move in with me; he simply stayed on, with his big heavy bag and the other things he'd brought in his car, the easels and paints and canvases and extra shoes and a bottle of wine he'd picked up for me as an arrival gift. I would no more have dreamed of asking him his plans or telling him to find his own place to live than I would have moved out of the apartment myself. It was a kind of heaven for me, I admit, to wake up with his golden arm spread across my extra pillow, his dark hair in ringlets on my shoulder. I would go to class and then come home without painting at school as I usually did, and we would go back to bed for half the afternoon.

On Saturdays and Sundays we got up around noon and went to the parks to paint, or drove out to Virginia, or visited the National Gallery if it was raining. I remember distinctly that at least once we went through that room in the NGA where *Leda* hangs, and those portraits, and that amazing Manet with the wineglasses; I swear he paid more attention to the Manet than to *Leda,* which didn't seem to interest him—at least that's how he behaved when I was with him there. We read all the plaques, and he commented on Manet's brushwork, then wandered off shaking his head in a way that meant admiration beyond words. After the first week, he told me sternly that I wasn't painting enough and that he thought it was because of him. I'd come home regularly to find a canvas prepared for me, toned in gray or beige. I began to work harder, under his guidance, than I had in a long time, and to push myself to try more complicated subjects.

I painted Robert himself, for example, sitting in his khakis on my kitchen stool, bare to the waist. He taught me how to draw hands better, noticing that I routinely avoided them. He taught me not to disdain flowers and flower arrangements in my still lifes, pointing out how many great painters had considered them an important challenge. Once, he brought home a dead rabbit—I still don't understand where he got it—and a big trout, and we piled up fruits and flowers with them and painted a pair of Baroque still lifes, each in our own kind of imitation, and laughed over them. Afterward he skinned the rabbit and cooked both it and the trout, and they were delicious. He said he had learned to cook from his French mother; he certainly almost never did it, to my knowledge. Often we would open cans of soup and a bottle of wine and leave it at that.

And we read together almost every night, sometimes for hours. He read his favorite Miłosz aloud to me, and poems in French, which he translated for me as he went along. I read him some of the novels I had always loved, Muzzy's collection of classics, Lewis Carroll and Conan Doyle and Robert Louis Stevenson, which he hadn't known growing up. We read to each other clothed or naked, rolled up together in my pale-blue sheets or sprawled in our old sweaters on the floor in front of my sofa. He used my library card to bring home books on Manet, Morisot, Monet, Sisley, Pissarro—he loved Sisley particularly and said he was better than all the rest of them put together. Occasionally he copied effects from their work, on small canvases he reserved for that purpose.

Sometimes Robert fell into a quiet or even sad mood, and when I stroked his arm he would say he missed his children, and even get out his photographs of them, but he never mentioned Kate. I was afraid that he could not or would not stay forever; I also hoped he might eventually find his way out of his marriage and into my life in a more settled sense. I didn't know that he had a new post office box, one in DC, until he mentioned one day that he'd picked up his mail there and read Kate's request for a divorce. He'd sent her a PO address, he said, in case she needed him in an emergency. He told me he'd decided to go home briefly to get through the initial paperwork and see the children. He told me he would stay in a motel or with friends—I think that was his way of making clear to me that he didn't plan to return to Kate. Something in his firmness about never returning to her chilled me; if he could feel that way about her, I knew, he could one day feel that way about me. I would have preferred to see regret in him, some ambivalence—although not enough doubt to take him away from me.

But he seemed oddly certain about leaving Kate, saying that she didn't understand the most important thing about him, without saying what that was. I didn't want to ask, since that would make it look as if I didn't understand either. When he returned from five days in Greenhill, he brought me a biography of Thomas Eakins (he always said my work reminded him of Eakins's, that it was somehow wonderfully American in flavor) and told me with zest about his little adventures on the road, and that the children were well and beautiful and he'd taken lots of pictures of them, and said nothing of Kate. And then he drew me into what I thought of by then as our bedroom and pulled me down onto the bed and made love to me with insistent concentration, as if he had missed me the whole time.

None of this minor paradise prepared me for the gradual shift in his mood. Autumn came on, and with it a dampening of his spirits; it had always been my favorite season, the moment of a fresh start, new school shoes, new students, glorious color. But for Robert it seemed a kind of wilting, an encroaching gloom, the death of summer and of our first happiness. The ginkgo leaves in my neighborhood turned into yellow crepe paper; the chestnuts scattered themselves in our favorite parks. I got out new canvases and tempted him on a midweek trip to Manassas, on my day off from teaching, to the battlefield there. But Robert for once refused to paint; instead, he sat under a tree on a historic hill and brooded, as if he were listening to ghostly sounds of the clash that had occurred there, the carnage. I painted in the field by myself, hoping he would get over it if I left him alone for a while, but that evening he was angry with me about almost nothing, threatened to break a plate, and went out for a long walk alone. I cried a little, in spite of myself—I don't like to do that, you know; it was just too painful to see him in that state, and to feel rejected by him after all our glorious times together.

But it also seemed to me natural that he would suffer an aftershock from his legal separation from Kate—they had another three months to go before the divorce—and from the permanence of his departure from his old life. I knew he must feel under pressure to look for work in DC, although he didn't show any signs of doing that; I had the sense that he had some small independent income or pool of earnings, probably from selling his remarkable paintings, but it surely wouldn't last him forever. I didn't like to ask about his income either, and I had been careful to keep our money separate, although I was paying the rent as I always had, and buying our food. He often brought home a few groceries, wine, or some useful little gift, so I hadn't noticed any great strain, although I'd begun to wonder if I should eventually ask him to split the rent and the utilities with me, since I struggled at the end of each month. I could have gone to Muzzy for help, but she had not been encouraging in her response to my living with a soon-to-be divorced artist, and that stayed my hand. ("I know about love," she said mildly on one visit I paid to her during Robert's sojourn with me. It was before the horrifying spectacle of her tumor, her tracheostomy, her speaking box. "I do, dear, more than you might think. But you're so talented, you know. I've always wanted someone who would take *care* of you a bit.") Now Robert would surely need to pay child support, and I didn't dare ask him the details when he sat glowering on the sofa.

On sunny weekends, his mood would occasionally lift, and I would find myself hopeful, easily forgetting the previous days and convincing myself that these were growing pains in our relationship. I thought, you see, not of marriage, exactly, but of some kind of longer-term life with Robert, a life in which we would commit ourselves, rent an apartment with a studio, combine our strength and resources and plans, go to Italy and Greece on a pseudo-honeymoon so that we could paint there and visit all the great sculpture and painting and landscape I'd longed to see. It was a vague dream, but it had grown while I wasn't looking, like a dragon under my bed, and it had undermined my romance of "all by myself" before I'd realized what was happening. On those remaining happy weekends, we went on short trips, mostly at my insistence, and with picnics packed to save money—the happiest time was to Harpers Ferry, where we stayed at a cheap inn and walked all over the town.

One evening in early December, I came home to find Robert gone, and I didn't hear from him for several days. He returned looking oddly refreshed and said he'd been to visit an old friend in Baltimore, which did seem to be true. Another time he went to New York. After that visit he seemed not refreshed but actually elated, and that evening he was too busy to make love, something that had never happened before, and stood at his easel in the living room making sketches in charcoal. I did the dinner dishes, tamping down my annoyance—did Robert think the dishes did themselves, day after day?—and tried not to watch over the counter that divided my tiny kitchen from my tiny living room while he sketched in a face I hadn't seen since my impulsive trip to Greenhill for his college show: she was very beautiful, with her curling dark hair so like his own, her fine square jaw, her thoughtful smile.

I knew her immediately. In fact, when I saw her I wondered how I could not have noticed her absence all these happy months; I had never questioned Robert's leaving her entirely out of his paintings and drawings in the time he'd been staying with me. He had never even included the distant figures of mother and child I'd seen in some of his earlier landscapes, like the one he'd painted on the shore in Maine during our workshop. Her return that evening had a strange effect on me, a crawling fear like the sense you get when someone has entered a room too quietly and is standing behind you. I told myself it wasn't fear of Robert, but if it wasn't that, what was I afraid of?

Chapter 77

1879

She watches Olivier paint.

They are standing on the beach in the afternoon light, and he has begun a second canvas: one for morning, one for afternoon. He is painting the cliffs and two large gray rowboats the fishermen have pulled far up onshore, their oars stowed inside, the nets and cork floats catching an elusive sun. He sketches first with burnt umber on the primed canvas, and then begins to mass in the cliffs with more umber, with blue, a shadowy gray-green. She wants to suggest that he lighten his palette, as her teacher once told her; she wonders why this scene of shifting lights and sky looks to Olivier so somber underneath. But she believes that neither his work nor his life can change much now. She stands in silence beside him, about to set up her own work, her folding stool and portable wooden easel—delaying, observing. She wears a thin wool dress against the chill in the afternoon's brightness, and over that a heavier wool jacket. The breeze catches at her skirt, the ribbons of her bonnet. She watches him bring the churning water partly to life. But why doesn't he put more light into it?

She turns away and buttons her smock over her clothes, arranges her canvas, unfolding the clever wooden stool. She stands before the easel as he does, instead of sitting, digging her boot heels in among the pebbles. She tries to forget his figure not far away, his silver head bowed over the work, his back upright. Her own canvas is already washed a pale gray; she has chosen this one for afternoon light. She puts in aquamarine, a heavy smudge on her palette, cadmium red for the poppies on the cliffs to the far left and right, her favorite flowers.

Now she gives herself thirty minutes by the watch on her chain, squints, holds the brush as lightly as she can, painting with wrist and forearm, quick strokes. The water is rose-colored, blue-green, the sky nearly colorless, the stones of the beach are rosy and gray, the foam at the edge of the waves is beige. She paints in Olivier's dark-suited form, his white hair, but as if he stands at a great distance, a minor figure on the strand. She touches the cliffs with raw umber, then green, then with the red specks of poppies. There are white flowers as well, and smaller yellow ones—she can see the cliff both up close and far off.

Her thirty minutes are gone.

Olivier turns, as if he understands that her first pass over the canvas is finished. She sees that he is still working slowly across an expanse of water, has not yet reached the boats again or even the cliffs. It will be a careful piece, controlled and even beautiful, and it will take days. He steps near to see her canvas. She stands staring at it with him, feeling his elbow brush her shoulder. She is conscious of her skill, as seen through his eyes, and of the painting's flaws: it is alive, moving, but too rough for even her taste, an experiment that fails. She wants him to be silent, and to her relief he doesn't interrupt the rumble of the waves on the heavy gravel, the wash of stones rolled over and out to sea. Instead he nods, looks down at her. His eyes are permanently reddened, a little loose around the edges. At that moment, she would not trade his presence for anything in the world, simply because he is so much closer to the edge of it than she is. He understands her.

That evening they eat with the other guests, sitting across from each other, passing the dishes of sauce or little mushrooms. The landlady, serving veal to Olivier, says that a gentleman has come by that afternoon to ask if she had a famous painter there, a friend of his from Paris; he left no card. Is Monsieur Vignot famous? she asks. Olivier laughs and shakes his head. Plenty of famous painters have worked in Étretat, but he is hardly one of them, he says. Béatrice drinks a glass of wine and regrets it. They sit in the main parlor, reading, with a mustached English guest who rustles the papers from London and clears his throat over something he sees there. Then she puts her book down and tries to write a second letter to Yves, without much success; her pen seems not to like the paper no matter how many times she dips and blots. The landlady's mandarin clock strikes ten, and Olivier rises to bow to her, smiles affectionately out of his wind-reddened eyes, seems about to kiss her hand but then does not.

When he has gone upstairs, she understands: he will never invite more from her. He will never visit her in private, will never propose that she visit him, will never make another move that a gentleman and relative should not. He will initiate nothing. The kiss in his studio was his first and last, as he promised; her kiss on the station platform was her own responsibility, as was their kiss on the beach. Both took him by surprise. He means this restraint as a gift, she is certain—a proof of his respect, his care. But the result is a cruel dilemma; whatever happens she must effect herself and live with later. Whatever they experience together will spring from her own desire, her comparative youth. She cannot imagine knocking on his door upstairs. He has left her a trail of bread crumbs, like the boy in the fairy tale.

Later, she hardly sleeps, in her white bed, watching the curtains move a little where she has left a window open to the menace of the night air, feeling the town around her, hearing the Channel maul the shale on the strand.

CHAPTER 78

Mary

For weeks after the return of the dark-haired lady to his paintings, Robert was preoccupied, and not only preoccupied but also silent and touchy. He slept long hours and didn't bathe, and I began to feel repelled by his presence in a way I never had before. Sometimes he slept on the sofa. I'd made a date weeks earlier, for my sister and her husband to meet him, and Robert never showed up. I sat in humiliation at a table in a little Provençal place called Lavandou that my sister and I have always loved. I still wouldn't want to go back there now, even if I had money to throw away on fine dining.

The only thing he had energy for was his painting, and the only thing he painted was this woman. I knew better by then than to ask who she was, because this always elicited the vague, almost mystical answers that annoyed me so much. Nothing had changed, I once thought bitterly, since the days when I'd been a student and he'd been purposely mysterious about where he had seen this subject of his work and why he painted her.

I might have gone on believing forever that he had known her in life—face, dark curls, dresses, and all—if I hadn't looked through some of his books while he was out one day buying canvases. It was the first time he'd left the apartment in a while; I took it as a good sign that he'd had the energy to go on an errand and also to plan some new paintings.

After he went out, I found myself hovering around the sofa, which had become a sort of Robert den, so that it even smelled like him. I threw myself down there and breathed in the smell of his hair and clothing, without the inconvenience of his irritable presence. It was littered, like a real den—scraps of paper, drawing supplies, books of poetry, cast-off clothing, and library tomes full of portraiture. Everything was portraiture now, and the dark lady was his only subject. He seemed to have forgotten his old love of landscape, his great skill at still lifes, his natural versatility. I noticed the shades were drawn in my small living room and had been down for days, while I'd been hurrying back and forth to my teaching.

It rushed over me like a proof of my own idiocy that Robert was depressed. What he called his "funks" were just good old garden-variety depression, and perhaps more serious than I'd been willing to contemplate. I knew he kept medications among his things and took them out now and then, but he'd told me they were to help him sleep occasionally after a long night of painting, and I never saw him take anything regularly. On the other hand, he never did anything at all regularly. I sat grieving over the transformation of my bright little apartment, mourning that loss so that I would not have to think about the transformation of my soul mate.

Then I began to clean up, putting all of Robert's mess into a basket, stacking the books neatly by the bed, folding the blankets, plumping the sofa cushions, taking the dirty glasses and cereal bowls to the kitchen. And I had a sudden vision of myself, a tall, clean, competent person clearing up someone else's dishes from the rug. I think I knew in that moment that we were doomed, not because of Robert's idiosyncrasies but because of my own sense of self. I watched him shrink a little, felt my heart contract. I raised the shades and wiped the coffee table and brought a vase of flowers from the kitchen into the renewed sunlight.

I could have left the situation there, you know, left it at the normal must-we-break-up level. I sat on the sofa a little longer, feeling myself reclaiming something, sad, frightened. But because I was sitting there, I began to turn through Robert's books. The top three were library books on Rembrandt, and there was another on Leonardo da Vinci—Robert's taste seemed to be wandering a little from the nineteenth century. Underneath was a heavy book on Cubism, which I hadn't seen him open at all.

And near those were two books on the Impressionists, one about their portraits of one another—I flipped through the familiar images—and one, less predictably, a slim, illustrated paperback about the women of the Impressionist world, running from Berthe Morisot's crucial role in the first Impressionist exhibition up into the early twentieth century and lesser-known, later female painters of the movement. I felt a flicker of respect for Robert's having such a book—it was his, not a library volume, I saw when I opened it—and a sense of wonder at its being worn with use; he had read it thoroughly, referred to it often, even smudged it a little with paint.

I enclose a copy of this volume, which I tracked down myself for you over the last month, since he took his away with him. Turn to page forty-nine, and you will see what I saw as I flipped through it—a portrait of Robert's lady and a seascape from the coast of Normandy by the lady herself. Béatrice de Clerval, I learned, was a highly gifted painter who had given up art in her late twenties; the short biographical text blamed this desertion on her having become a mother, which she'd done at the dangerously ripe age of twenty-nine, in an era when women of her class were encouraged to concentrate solely on family life.

The reproduction of the portrait was in color, and her face was unmistakable to me; I even knew her ruffled neckline of pale yellow on pale green, the bow on her bonnet, the exact soft carmine in her cheeks and lips, the expression of mingled wariness and joy. According to the text, she had been very promising as a young artist, studying from the age of seventeen until her midtwenties with the academy instructor Georges Lamelle, had exhibited a painting just once at the Salon, under the false name of Marie Rivière, and died of influenza in 1910; her daughter, Aude, a journalist in Paris before the Second World War, died in 1966. Béatrice de Clerval's husband was a noted civil servant, establishing the modern postal offices of four or five French cities. She was an acquaintance of the Manets, the Morisots, the photographer Nadar, and Mallarmé. Work by Clerval can now be found in the Musée d'Orsay, the Musée de Maintenon, the Yale University Art Gallery, the University of Michigan, and several private collections, notable among them that of Pedro Caillet of Acapulco.

Well, you will see all that in the book, but I want to try to explain the effect this set of images and the biography that accompanied them had on my feelings. You'd think that knowing your partner is obsessed with a long-ago glimpse of a living woman, someone he's seen only once or twice, would make you uneasy; but you expect an artist, a fellow artist, to be obsessed with some image or other. Learning that Robert was obsessed with a woman whom he'd never seen alive caused me much greater unease—it was a shock, in fact. You can't be jealous of someone who's dead, and yet the fact that she had once been alive at all gave me a feeling perilously close to jealousy, and then the fact that she was long dead was somehow grotesque, as if I'd caught him in some vague act of necrophilia.

No, that's wrong. The living often still love the dead; we'd never criticize a widower for loving his wife's memory or even being rather obsessed with her. But someone Robert had never known, could not have known, someone who had died more than forty years before his own birth—it was stomach turning. That's too strong a description, I suppose. But I felt queasy. It was too strange for me. I had never thought he might be crazy when he'd been painting a living face over and over; but now that I knew it was the face of a long-dead woman, I wondered if there was something really wrong with him.

I read the biographical note several times to be sure I hadn't missed anything. Perhaps not much was known about Béatrice de Clerval, or maybe her retreat from painting into domesticity had bored all the art historians. She seemed to have lived decades after that without doing anything of note, until she died. A retrospective of her work had been held in the 1980s at a museum in Paris whose name I didn't recognize, the pictures probably borrowed from private collections, put up and taken down again before I'd even applied to college. I looked at her portrait again. There was the wistful smile, the dimple in the left cheek near the mouth. Even from the glossy page, her eyes followed mine.

When I couldn't stand this any longer, I closed the book and put it back in the stack. Then I got it out again and wrote down the title and author, the publication information, some of the facts it contained about Clerval, and replaced it carefully, hiding my notes in my desk. I went into our bedroom and made up the bed and lay down on it. After a while, I went into the kitchen and cleaned that up, too, and made a meal out of whatever I could find in my cabinets. It had been a long time since I'd really cooked something. I loved Robert, and he would have the best possible treatment, care that would help him to get better; he had told me that he still had health insurance. When he came home, he looked pleased and we ate together by candlelight and made love on the living-room rug (he didn't seem to notice that I'd cleaned up the sofa), and he took a picture of me wrapped in a blanket. I didn't say anything about the book or the portraits.

Things were a little better that week, at least on the surface, until Robert told me that he was going to Greenhill again. He had to see the lawyer with Kate, he said, and to settle some financial matters, and he would be gone a week. I was disappointed, but I thought it might be best for his mood to get more of that work behind him, so I simply kissed him goodbye and let him go. He was flying; his plane left while I was teaching and I couldn't drive him to the airport. He did stay away only a week, showing up one evening very tired and smelling odd, like travel, a dirty but also somehow exotic smell. He slept for two days.

On the third day, he left the apartment to run some errands, and I went through all his things, shamelessly—or rather, with shame but determined to know more. He hadn't unpacked his bag yet, and in it I found receipts in French, some that said "Paris," a hotel, restaurants, De Gaulle Airport. There was a crumpled ticket for Air France in one of his jacket pockets, along with his passport, which I had never seen before. Most people have terrifying-looking passport photos; Robert's was gorgeous. Among his clothes I found a package wrapped in brown paper, and inside that a bundle of letters tied with ribbon, very old letters, apparently in French. I had never seen them before. I wondered if they might have to do with his mother, if they might be old family letters, or if he had gotten them in France. When I saw the signature on the first one, I sat there for a long nightmare moment, and then I folded them up again and put the package back into his luggage.

And then I had to decide what to say to him. *Why did you go to France?* That was only slightly less important than *Why did you not tell me you were going to France, or even take me with you?* But I couldn't bring myself to ask; it would have hurt my pride, and by that time my pride was very sore, as Muzzy would have said. Instead, we quarreled, or I quarreled with him, I picked a fight with him about a painting, a still life we'd both worked on, and I threw him out, but he went willingly enough. I cried to my sister, I vowed never to take him back if he showed up again, I tried to get over him, and that's an end to it. But I worried when he didn't get in touch with me at all. I didn't know for a long time that he had gone from me to the National Gallery—or just months later—and tried to hurt a painting. That was not like him. In no way was that like him.

Chapter 79

Marlow

Mary rejoined me at my hotel for breakfast, meeting me in the half-empty restaurant. It was a quieter meal than dinner had been the night before; the first flush of her excitement was gone, and I noticed again those violet smudges, shadows on snow, under her eyes. Her eyes themselves looked dark this morning, clouded. She had a few freckles on her nose that I hadn't registered before, tiny shavings, completely unlike Kate's. "Did you have a bad night?" I asked, at the risk of courting one of her stern glances.

"Yes," she said. "I was thinking about how much I've told you about Robert, so many private things, and how you were sitting there in your hotel room thinking about it all."

"How did you know I was thinking about it?" I passed her a plate of toast.

"I would have been," she said simply.

"Well, I was. I think about this constantly. You are remarkable to let me see so much of him, and your doing that will help me more than anything has, to help Robert." I paused, feeling my way while she let her toast get cold. "And I see why you waited for him for a long time, when he was unavailable."

"Unattainable," she corrected.

"And why you love him."

"Loved him, not love him."

I hadn't hoped for this much, and I focused on my eggs

Benedict so that I wouldn't have to meet her eyes. In fact, we finished our breakfast mainly in silence, but after a while the silence became comfortable.

At the Met, she stood looking at *Portrait of Béatrice de Clerval,* 1879, the picture she'd first encountered in a book Robert had left next to her sofa. "You know, I think Robert came back here and found her again," she said.

I was watching her profile; it was the second time, I remembered sharply, that we'd been in a museum together. "He did?"

"Well, he traveled to New York at least once while he lived with me, as I wrote to you, and he came back strangely excited."

"Mary, do you want to go see Robert? I could take you when we get back to Washington. On Monday, if you'd like." I hadn't meant to say it right away.

"Do you mean that you want me to find out more for you by asking him myself?" She stood straight and stiff, examining Béatrice's face one more time without looking at me.

It shocked me. "No, no—I wouldn't ask that of you. You've already helped me see him in a new way. I only meant that I don't want to keep you from him if you need to see him yourself."

She turned. Then she came closer, as if for protection, with Béatrice de Clerval watching us; in fact, she suddenly slipped one hand into mine. "No," she said. "I don't want to see him. Thank you." She took her hand away and walked around looking at the Degas ballerinas, and the nudes drying off with their big towels. After a few minutes she came back to me. "Shall we go?"

Outside, it was a bright, soft summer day, warm rather than hot. I bought each of us a hot dog with mustard at one of the stands on the street. ("How do you know I'm not a vegetarian?" said Mary, although we'd already had two other meals together.) We wandered into Central Park and ate on a bench, cleaning our hands with paper napkins. Mary unexpectedly wiped the mustard off my hands as well as hers, and I thought what a lovely mother of young children she might have made, but naturally I didn't say it. I spread out my fingers.

"My hand looks much older than yours, doesn't it?"

"Why shouldn't it? It *is* somewhat older than mine. Twenty years, if you were born in 1947."

"I won't ask how you know that."

"No need to, Sherlock."

I sat watching her. The shade from oaks and beeches dappled her face and short-sleeved white blouse, the fine skin of her throat. "How beautiful you are."

"Please don't say that," she said, looking down at her lap.

"I meant it only as a compliment, a respectful one. You're like a painting."

"That's idiotic." She crumpled up the napkins and aimed them into a wastebasket next to our bench. "No woman actually wants to be a painting." But when she turned back to me, our eyes met across the strange sound of what each of us had just said. She glanced away first. "Have you ever been married?"

"No."

"Why not?"

"Oh, a lot of medical school, and then I didn't meet the right person."

She crossed her legs in their jeans. "Well, have you ever been in love?"

"Several times."

"Recently?"

"No." I considered. "Maybe yes. Almost yes."

She raised her eyebrows until they disappeared under her short bangs. "Make up your mind."

"I'm trying to," I said as evenly as I could. It was like conversing with a wild deer, some animal that could start up and spring away. I stretched one arm across the back of the bench without touching her, and looked out into the park, the bends of gravel path, boulders, green hills under patrician trees, the people walking and biking along a nearby route. Her kiss caught me by surprise; at first I understood only that her face was very close. She was gentle, hesitating. I sat up slowly and put my hands on her temples and kissed her back, also gently, careful not to startle her further, my heart pounding. My old heart.

I knew that in a minute she would draw away, then lean against me and begin to sob without making a sound, that I would hold her until she was finished, that we would soon part with a more passionate kiss for our separate journeys home, and that she would then say something like, *I'm sorry, Andrew—I'm not ready for this*. But I had the long patience of my profession on my side, and I already understood certain things about her: she loved to go out to Virginia for the day to paint, as I did; she needed to eat often; she wanted to feel in control of her decisions. *Madame,* I said to her, but silently, *I observe that your heart is broken. Allow me to repair it for you.*

Chapter 80

1879

She can't stop thinking about her own body. Surely she should think a little of Olivier's, which has lived in so many interesting ways. Instead, she considers the bug bite on the inside of her right wrist, scratches it, shows it companionably to him as they paint on the beach the second morning. They gaze together at the white forearm, where she has rolled back the sleeve of her linen smock. Her wrist, with that tiny red mark, the long hand and its rings—she regards them herself, as he must, with desire. They are working at their easels on the beach; she has set down her brushes, but Olivier still holds a small one wet with dark-blue paint.

They stand looking at the curve of her arm, and then she raises it slowly toward him, toward his face. When it is so close that he can't mistake her meaning, he presses his lips to the skin. She shivers, more from the sight than from sensation. He lowers her arm gently and their eyes meet. She can't think of any words to fit this situation. His face is reddened against his white hair, from emotion or from the Channel wind. Does he feel embarrassment? It is the sort of thing she might ask him at an intimate moment she won't yet let herself picture.

Chapter 81

Marlow

Sometime after this, I tried the experiment of staying in Robert's room with him in silence for an hour; I brought a sketch pad with me and sat in my chair with it, drawing him as he sat drawing Béatrice de Clerval. I wanted to tell him that I knew who she was, but, as usual, caution stayed my hand. After all, I might need to learn more about her before I did that, or about him. After a first look of annoyance at my presence and a second glare that showed me he'd registered the fact that he was the subject of my drawing, Robert ignored me, but a faint sense of companionship crept into the room, if I wasn't simply imagining that. There was no sound but the scratching of our respective pencils, and it was peaceful.

The escape of drawing in the middle of the morning gave the day a kind of harmony I rarely experience at Goldengrove. Robert's face, in profile, was very interesting; and the fact that he didn't show anger or get up and move away or otherwise disrupt my work pleased and rather surprised me. It was possible he had withdrawn further and simply didn't care, but I felt he was actually tolerating my gesture. When I had finished the effort, I put the pencil in my jacket pocket and tore the drawing out of my book, laying it silently on the end of his bed. It wasn't half bad, I thought, although of course it lacked the brilliant expressiveness of his portraits. He didn't look up as I left, but when I checked a couple of days later, I saw that he had taped my gift up in his gallery, although not in a place of prominence.

As if she'd somehow known about my hour with Robert, Mary called that very evening. "I want to ask you something."

"Anything. That's only fair."

"I want to read the letters. Béatrice's and Olivier's."

I hesitated for only a moment. "Of course. I'll make you a copy of the translations I have so far, and the rest as I get them."

"Thank you."

"How've you been?"

"I'm fine," she said. "Working, I mean painting, since my semester is over now."

"Would you like to go out to Virginia to paint this weekend? Just for an afternoon? It's supposed to be springlike, and I was thinking of going. I can bring you the letters then."

She was silent for a beat. "Yes, I think I'd like that."

"I wanted to call you before this. You've stayed away."

"Yes, I know. I'm sorry." She did sound sorry, genuinely so.

"It's quite all right. I can imagine what a hard time you've had this last year."

"You mean, you can imagine it as a professional?"

I sighed in spite of myself. "No, as your friend."

"Thank you," she said, and I thought I heard the choke of tears in her voice. "I could use a friend."

"I could, too, actually." It was more than I would have said to anyone six months earlier, and I knew it.

"Saturday or Sunday?"

"Let's say Saturday but watch the weather."

"Andrew?" Her voice was gentle, and on the edge of smiling.

"What?"

"Nothing. Thank you."

"Thank you, instead," I demurred. "I'm glad you want to go."

On Saturday she wore a thick red jacket, her hair twisted up and pinned with two sticks, and we painted together much of the day. Later, in the unseasonably warm sun, we picnicked and talked. There was color in her face, and when I leaned over the blanket to kiss her, she put her arms around my neck and pulled me close—no tears this time, although we only kissed. We ate dinner outside the city, and I dropped her off at her apartment on a litter-strewn block in Northeast. She had the copy of the letters in her bag. She didn't invite me up, but she came back from her front door to kiss me again before going inside.

Chapter 82

1879

To: Yves Vignot
Passy, Paris

Mon cher mari,

I hope this finds you well and that Papa is mending. Thank you for the kind note. Papa's troubles worry me—I wish I were there to care for him myself. Warm compresses on his chest usually help, but I suspect Esmé has already tried those. Please send him my fond greetings.

For myself, I cannot say I'm finding it dull here, although Étretat is quiet before the season. I have completed one canvas, if you can call it complete, as well as a pastel and two sketches. Uncle is helpful, making suggestions about color—of course, our handling of the brush is so very different that there I always have to strike out on my own. I thoroughly respect his knowledge, however. Now he is talking with me about my doing a much bigger canvas, one with an ambitious subject, which I could submit to the Salon jury next year, although Mme Rivière would be its author. I do not know if I want such a large undertaking, however.

Having slept well the last two nights, I am quite refreshed.

She puts down her pen and looks around the wallpapered bedroom. The first night she has slept from pure exhaustion, and the third she has spent half awake, thinking of Olivier's firm, dry lips approaching her arm—the sensitive shape of the older man's mouth and the pale stretch of her own skin.

She knows the correct thing: she should tell Olivier that she feels unwell here—nerves, she can call it, the eternal excuse—and that they must return home at once. But that is the reason Yves has sent her here to begin with. Even if she could muster this act, Olivier will see through it. She is blooming in the fresh wind from the Channel, with the expanses of water and sky coursing through her, a relief after stifling Paris. She loves working on the shore, wrapped in her warm cloak. She loves his company, his conversation, the hours they spend reading together in the evenings. He has made the world larger for her than she had ever thought possible.

Instead she blots the last word of her letter and considers the loop of the "d" in "*dormi.*" If she claims that she must go back, Olivier will know that she is lying; he will think she is fleeing. It will hurt him. She cannot do that; she owes him trust in return for his vulnerability, his putting his hand in hers when it might be the last time he touches any woman. Especially when she could assail him from the vantage point of her youth.

She goes to the window and unlatches it. From above the street, she has an oblique view of the gray-beige expanse of beach and the grayer water. A breeze stirs the curtains, rifles the skirts of her morning dress where it lies, bent double, over a chair. She tries to think about Yves, but when she shuts her eyes, she sees an annoying caricature, like a political cartoon in one of his newspapers. Yves in hat and coat, his head enormous, out of proportion, holding a walking stick under one arm, putting on his gloves before kissing her goodbye. It is easier to picture Olivier: he is standing with her on the beach, upright and tall, subtle, with his silver hair, rosy lined face, watering blue eyes, his well-cut, well-worn brown suit, his craftsman's hands and square-tipped, slightly swollen fingers around the brush. The image makes her sad in a way she does not feel when he is actually with her.

But she can't sustain even this vision long; it is replaced by the street itself, the brick fronts and elaborate trim on a row of new shops blocking half her view of the beach. What lingers there for her is a question. How many nights can she pass in this suspended state? In the afternoon they will go somewhere in the bright expanse of beach to paint, return to their rooms to dress for dinner, share their public meal again, sit in the overfurnished hotel parlor and talk about their reading. She will feel she is already in his arms, in spirit; shouldn't that be enough? And then she will retire to her room and begin her nightly vigil.

The other question she asks herself, elbows propped on the sill, is still more difficult. Does she want him? Nothing in the stretch of shore, the upturned boats, hints at an answer. She closes the window, her lips pursed. Life will decide, and perhaps has already decided—a weak answer, but there is no other, and it is time for them to go paint.

Chapter 83

Marlow

One evening I came home to a letter—a very hospitable letter, to my surprise—from Pedro Caillet. After I'd read it, I surprised myself in turn by going to the phone and calling a travel agent.

Dear Dr. Marlow:

Thank you for your note of two weeks past. You probably know more than I do about Béatrice de Clerval, but I would be happy to assist you. Please come to talk with me between March 16 and March 23, if that is possible. Afterward I will be traveling to Rome and cannot be your host. In answer to your other question, I have not heard of an American painter researching the work of Clerval; such a person has never contacted me.

With warmest wishes,

P. Caillet

Then I called Mary. "How about Acapulco, week after next?"

Her voice was thick, as if she'd been sleeping, although it was late afternoon. "What? You sound like a—I don't know what. A personal ad?"

"Are you asleep? Do you know what time it is?"

"Don't harass me, Andrew. It's my day off, and I painted until very late."

"Until when?"

"Till four thirty."

"Oh, you honest-to God artists. I was at Goldengrove at seven this morning. Now, would you like to go to Acapulco?"

"Are you serious?"

"Yes. Not for vacation. I have research to do there."

"Does your research have to do with Robert, by chance?"

"No. It has to do with Béatrice de Clerval."

She laughed. It warmed me, to hear her laugh so soon after she'd uttered Robert's name. Perhaps she really was getting over him. "I had a dream about you last night."

"About me?" My heart jumped, ridiculously.

"Yes. A very sweet one. I dreamed that I learned you were the inventor of lavender."

"What? The color or the plant?"

"The scent, I think. It's my favorite."

"Thank you. What did you do, in your dream, when you found this out?"

"Never mind."

"Are you going to make me beg?"

"All right—no. I kissed you, in thanks. On the cheek. That was all."

"So, do you want to come to Acapulco?"

She laughed again, apparently well awake. "Of course I want to go to Acapulco. But you know I can't afford it."

"I can," I said softly. "I've been saving for years because my parents told me to." And then I had no one to spend it on, I didn't add. "We could schedule it for your spring break. Isn't it the same week? Isn't that a sign?"

There was a hush between us on the phone, like the moment you pause to listen in the woods. I listened; I heard her breathing, the way you hear (after the first silence, after stilling and settling yourself) birds in the canopy of branches or a squirrel rustling in dead leaves six feet away.

"Well," she said slowly. I thought I detected in her voice years of saving because her mother had told her to also, but with almost nothing to save, her years of painting her way through each small bit of time or cash she could put aside for a few days or weeks or months, the fear and pride that kept her from borrowing, her mother's probably modest onetime gift to her out of the remains of her upbringing, the dedication that kept Mary from quitting her teaching, the students who had no idea how her bank account trembled on the verge of emptiness after she paid for her rent, heat, food—the whole constellation of miseries that I had avoided by going to medical school. Since then, I had done only ten paintings that I liked at all. Monet had painted sixty views of Étretat alone in the 1860s, many of them masterpieces; I had seen the dozens of canvases stacked along Mary's studio walls, the hundreds of prints and drawings on her shelves. I wondered how many of them she still liked.

"Well," she said again, but with more light in her voice, "let me think about it." I could imagine her stirring in a bed I had never seen; she would be sitting up now to hold the receiver, maybe wearing one of her loose white shirts and pushing her hair aside. "But there is another problem if I go with you."

"Let me save you the trouble of saying it. You don't have to sleep with me if you accept my invitation," I said, feeling at once that it had come out more starkly than I'd intended. "I'll find a way for us to stay separately."

I could hear her breath drawn in as if she were on the verge of a gasp, or a laugh. "Oh, no. The problem is that I might *want* to sleep with you there, but I wouldn't want you to think it was a thank-you card for paying my way."

"Well," I said. "What can a fellow say?"

"Nothing." Mary was almost laughing, I felt sure. "Don't say anything, please."

*

But at the airport two weeks later, after a rare Washington snowstorm, we were quiet and constrained with each other. I began to wonder if this adventure had been a good idea or would prove an embarrassment on both sides. We had arranged to find each other at the gate, which was filled with students who could have been Mary's sitting in impatient rows, already dressed in summer clothes, although planes outside the window rolled past heaps of dirty snow. Mary met me with a canvas satchel over one shoulder and her portable easel in her hand, and leaned forward to kiss my cheek, but awkwardly. She had coiled her hair up in the back and was wearing a long navy sweater over a black skirt. Against the background of squirming teenagers in their shorts and brightly colored shirts, she looked like some sect of laysister leaving the convent for a field trip. It occurred to me that I hadn't even thought to bring my painting kit. What was wrong with me? I would only be able to watch her paint.

We chatted in a desultory way on the plane, as if we'd been traveling together for years, and then she fell asleep, sitting straight up in her seat at first but drooping gradually toward me, her smooth head touching my shoulder: *I painted until very late*. I'd thought that we would talk intensely on our first real trip together, but instead she was sleeping almost against me, pulling herself back from time to time without waking, as if she feared this creeping domesticity between us. My shoulder came alive under her nodding head. I carefully took out a new book on borderline-personality-disorder treatment, which I'd been trying for some time to get to—my professional reading had begun to suffer under the weight of my research on Robert and Béatrice—but I couldn't take in the words for more than a sentence at a time; after that, they unraveled.

And then that bad moment that always forced itself on me sooner or later: I imagined her head on Robert Oliver's shoulder, his naked shoulder—had she been telling me the truth when she'd said she didn't love Robert anymore? After all, he might get well under my care, or at least better. Or was the truth more complicated? What if I didn't feel like helping him anymore, given what might happen if he went back to a functional life? I turned another page. In the light through the clouds outside, Mary's hair was pale chestnut, golden on the surface under the feeble airplane reading light, and darker when she rolled away from the window; it shone like carved wood. I raised a finger and, with infinite lightness, stroked the part on the top of her head; she stirred and muttered something, still asleep. Her eyelashes were roseate, and they lay on pale skin. There was a small mole near the corner of her left eye. I thought about Kate's galaxy of freckles, about my mother's emaciated face and huge, still-compassionate gaze before she died. When I turned a page again, Mary sat up, hugged her sweater around her, and wedged herself against the window, fleeing me. Still asleep.

Chapter 84

1879

She goes to the wardrobe and chooses between two day dresses, blue or soft brown, finally deciding on the brown, with warm stockings and sturdy shoes. She pins up her hair and takes her long cloak, her bonnet lined with crimson silk, and her old gloves. He is waiting for her in the street. She smiles at him without restraint, happy in his pleasure. Perhaps nothing matters but this odd joy they give each other. He carries their two easels, and she insists on taking the bags. His is a battered leather *musette de chasse* he has had since he was twenty-eight—one of the many things she knows about him now.

When they reach the shore, they put their equipment in a neat pile under the seawall and set off for a short walk without having to discuss it. The wind is strong but warmer today, with a smell of grasses; the poppies and daisies are out in great profusion. She takes his hand whenever she needs help over a rough spot on the path. They climb up the eastern bluffs to a plateau midway above the Channel, where they can look down the beach to the more dramatic arches and pillars at the other end. She is afraid of heights and stays back from the edge, but he peers over and reports the spray splashing high today, dramatic, wetting the cliff below.

They are completely alone, and the setting is so splendid that she feels nothing else matters, certainly nothing as small as the two of them; even her yearning for children, that sore spot under her rib, has no significance for a few moments. She cannot remember the shape of guilt or its purposes. His closeness is her comfort, the small human note in a sublime landscape. When he comes back to her, she leans against him. He keeps her shoulders nestled against the breast of his painting jacket, his arms folded around her as if to hold her back from the cliff's edge. Simple relief floods her, then pleasure, then desire. The wind pulls hard at them. He kisses the side of her neck below her bonnet, the edge of her pinned-up hair; perhaps because she cannot see him, she forgets to measure the years between them.

This is what it might be like with the lights blown out, the two of them together without any barrier, darkness hiding their differences. The thought makes a vein of heat run through her toward the rock under their feet. He must sense it; he holds her against him. She knows the heavy curve of her skirts, the bulk of petticoats, feels what he must feel, and inside of that their strange belonging to each other, sea and horizon, their holding on to each other in the middle of immensity. They stand like this for so long that she loses track of the passing of her life. When the wind begins to chill them, they make their way back down to the beach without speaking and set up their easels.

CHAPTER 85

Marlow

The streets of Acapulco seemed dreamlike to me; I felt only disbelief that in my fifty-two years I'd never before made it south of the border. The long, divided highway into town was familiar as a film, with its mixture of concrete and steel under construction, ramshackle two-story houses decorated with bougainvillea and rusting auto parts, bright-colored little restaurants and huge date palms, also rusty-looking, waving in the wind. The taxi driver spoke broken English to us, pointing out the old city, where we would go tomorrow for my appointment with Caillet.

I had booked us a room in a resort hotel that John Garcia had told me was the world's best place for a honeymoon—he'd been there for his. He'd said this with no ribbing, no humor, no curiosity in his voice when I'd called to ask his advice and told him I'd fallen in love. I didn't tell him who she was, of course; that would have to come later, with explanations. "That's good news, Andrew" was all he said; behind it I heard probable past conversations with his wife: *Marlow's not getting any younger—is he ever going to find anyone, poor guy?* And behind that the self-congratulation of the long-married, the still-married. But he hadn't said anything more, except to give me the name of the hotel, La Reina. I thanked him silently as I watched Mary walk into the lobby, which was open on all sides to views of palms crowding in, the ocean beyond, warm wind sweeping through it. The wind smelled soft and tropical and impossible for me to identify, like ripe fruit of a sort I hadn't eaten before. She had removed her long nun's sweater and stood there in a thin blouse, her skirt catching the breeze, her head tipped back to see up to the roof of the enormous courtyard, the pyramidal rows of balconies draped with vines.

"It's like the Hanging Gardens of Babylon," she said, glancing sideways. I wanted to come up behind her and put my arms comfortably around her waist and hold her against me, but I felt she wouldn't like this familiarity in a new place, a strange place, where we were alone among strangers. Instead I looked up at the skylight with her. Then we went to the long black marble counter and got two keys to one room—with a moment of hesitation, during which she seemed to comprehend, then accept, my having taken her at her word. We went silently up in the elevator together. It was glass, and the courtyard rushed away at our feet until we were near the top. I thought, not for the last time, how inappropriate it was to stay in this kind of hotel in a country so desperately poor that millions of its people were pounding at our own nation's doors in hope of finding a living wage. But it was not for me, I told myself; this was for Mary, who turned the heat in her apartment down to fifty-five degrees at night in order to lower the heating bill.

Our room was large and simple, full of elegant design: Mary walked around touching the lantern of square translucent marble, the soft stucco of the walls. The bed—I turned away—was broad and made up with a spread of beige linen. Our single large window looked across to other balconies with similar vines and black wooden chairs, down the dizzying well of the central court. I wondered if I should have gotten a room with an ocean view, despite the extra expense—had that been stingy of me, given the cost I'd already incurred? Mary turned to me, smiling, diffident, embarrassed; I guessed that she didn't want to seem to thank me for conjuring all this luxury, and yet wanted to say something. "Do you like it?" I asked, to put myself in the wrong instead.

She laughed. "I do. You are impossible, but I do love it. I feel as if I'm going to have a good rest here."

"I'll make sure of it." I put my arms around her and kissed her forehead, and she kissed me on the mouth, then drew away and busied herself with her luggage. We didn't touch each other again until we'd strolled out together to the beach, where she took my hand, with her shoes in her other hand, and we waded through the incoming tide. The water was astoundingly warm, like tea left in a pot. The beach was edged with towering palms and filled with little thatched huts and people speaking English and Spanish, playing radios and running after their tanned children. The sun splashed over everything, an unquenchable joy. I hadn't waded into an ocean in several years—six or seven, actually, I thought with a sudden shock—and I hadn't seen the Pacific since I was twenty-two. Mary tucked her skirt up a little, so that her thin knees and long shins glistened bare in the water, and rolled up the sleeves of her blouse. I felt her trembling next to me in the wind, or perhaps simply vibrating with it. "Do you want to come with me tomorrow?" I called over the huge sound of the waves.

"To see what's his name? Caillet?" She waded into a finger of tide. "Do you want me to?"

"Unless you'd like to stay and paint."

"I can paint the rest of the time," she said reasonably.

As we walked back to the hotel gardens, I saw that the entrance to the beach was patrolled by a guard with an M16 slung over his uniform.

*

We had our lunch on the veranda outside the lobby. Mary got up once or twice to look at the artificial lagoon and waterfall outside, where a couple of live flamingos waded—owned by the hotel? Wild? We drank tequila in small, thick glasses, raising them in a toast but saying nothing, toasting nothing but our own presences there. We ate seviche, guacamole, tortillas, the taste of lime and cilantro lingering in my mouth like a promise. I wasn't a complete stranger to this feeling creeping over me from the warm wind, the rustling palms, the breath of the Pacific; it was a childhood belief in jungle and ocean, *Treasure Island* and *Peter Pan*—yes, that was what these resorts were supposed to evoke—a magical, safe version of the tropics. And the place evoked in me something else, too, a sense of the long voyage of a book, my favorite, *Lord Jim,* for example, and the breath of the Far East to the far west of us. *Mistah Kurtz—he dead.* But wasn't that a different Conrad novel? *Heart of Darkness*. T. S. Eliot quoting. Gauguin coming out of a hut after sex to get back to his paints. The cycle of the year casual because no one had to wear much clothing. The heat.

"We'll need to leave for Caillet's at about nine," I said to distract myself from the first softening wave of tequila in my head and the edge of Mary's face as she tucked a strand of hair into place behind one ear. "He asked me to come in the morning before it gets hot. He lives in the old part of the city, on the bay. It should be an adventure, just seeing his place, whatever it's like."

"Does he paint?"

"Yes—he's a critic and a collector, but I think he must be above all a painter, from the interview I read."

When we returned to our room, I felt the release of the new place and the fatigue of our early-morning travel taking over.

I half hoped Mary would throw herself down on the bed next to me and we would sleep together and gradually reach across the awkwardness between us, but she picked up her easel and bag. "Don't go far," I said in spite of myself, remembering the guard at the gate. Then I regretted speaking; I felt not that she was young and wouldn't understand me but that I was old and might appear to be directing or reprimanding her.

But she didn't bristle. "I know. I'll set up in the garden next to the lobby. On the right side as you're facing the beach, if you need to find me." Her gentleness surprised me, and when I lay down on the bed—I couldn't bring myself even to remove my shirt first, with her there—she bent over and kissed me the way we'd kissed that afternoon on my picnic blanket, with all the longing stored up and dictated against previously. My response was profound, but I lay still, willing myself to let her walk out of the room, since she wanted to. She turned at the door and smiled again—relaxed, affectionate, as if she felt safe with me.

Then she was gone. The sleep I drifted into was a tangle of trees and sunlight, a pulsating surf somewhere beyond my eyelids. The light was fading when my alarm went off; I thought for a moment I'd missed an appointment, probably with Robert Oliver, and sat up in a panic. Fear caught at my chest, but no—Robert was alive and at least partly well, as far as I knew, and Goldengrove had the phone number at the hotel. I went to the window and slid back the heavy drapes, then the sheer ones, and saw people walking far below in the lobby, where a few lamps had been turned on.

Another panic: where was Mary? I'd been asleep only two hours, but it seemed to me too long to have left her anywhere unattended; I found my beach shoes and slid them on. In the gardens the palms were turning noisily inside out, every frond in a stir, the wind up and soaring in from the ocean, too strong now not to be a little menacing, waves breaking wildly in sight of the hotel. Mary was exactly where she'd promised to be, touching the canvas, stepping back to see it, suspending her brush for a moment. She stood with her weight on one hip, then shifted easily, but I could see in her that kind of hurry that comes with losing your light at the end of a landscape session—the race, the way the shadow comes more and more rapidly toward you, the longing to turn back the day or to brush that creeping shadow off your canvas.

A moment later, she noticed me and turned. "No more light."

I stood behind her. "It's wonderful." I meant it. Her scene of soft, rough colors—the blue of the sea with the colorless sheen of evening already on its surface—was really accomplished, but I saw something poignant in it as well. I don't know what gives a landscape pathos sometimes, but those are the canvases you stand in front of longer, whatever their technical skill. She'd caught the last throb of a perfect day, perfect because it was ending. I didn't know how to tell her all this, or whether she'd want more words, so I stayed quiet and watched the edge of her face as she studied her work.

"It's not too bad," she said finally, and began to clean her palette with a knife, scraping the shavings into a little box. I held the wet canvas while she closed up her easel and put everything away.

"Are you hungry? We ought to make it an early night, since we've got a big day tomorrow." I felt at once the awkwardness of this; it might sound like I was hurrying her to bed, and patronizing her at the same time.

To my surprise, she whirled in the dimness, caught me and kissed me hard, avoiding the canvas and laughing. "Would you just stop worrying? Stop *worrying*."

I laughed, too—relieved, a little shamed. "Do my best."

CHAPTER 86

1879

In the parlor that evening, she sits close to him instead of across the room. Her hands cannot concentrate on the embroidery; she leaves it unattended in her lap and watches him. Olivier is reading, his neatly brushed head bent over his book. The ottoman he has chosen is too short for his long legs. He has changed into dinner clothes, but she still sees his threadbare suit covered with the coarse smock. He glances up and offers with a smile to read aloud. She accepts. It is *Le Rouge et le Noir;* she has already read it twice, once to herself and once to Papa, and has been moved, and often annoyed, by the hapless Julien. Now, she is not able to listen.

Instead she watches his lips, feeling her own dullness, her sad inability to follow the words. After a few minutes he puts the volume down. "You are not paying any attention at all, my dear."

"No, I'm afraid not."

"I'm sure the fault is not with Stendhal, so that leaves me. Have I done anything wrong? Well, I have, I know."

"What nonsense." It is as close to an outburst as she would know how to make in this polite room, with the other guests nearby. "Stop it."

He looks narrowly at her. "I shall stop, then."

"Please excuse me." She lowers her voice, picks at the lace

on the front of her skirt. "It's just that you have no idea what effect you do have on me."

"The effect of annoying you, perhaps?" But the confidence in his smile compels her. He knows perfectly well he has caught her attention. "Here, let me read you something else." He fishes among the cast-off volumes on their landlady's shelves. "Something elevating, *Les mythes grecs*."

She settles herself more deeply, making each stitch count, but his first choice is mischievous. "'*Leda and the Swan*. Leda was a maiden of rare beauty, and she drew from afar the admiration of mighty Zeus. He swept down upon her in the form of a swan . . .'"

Olivier looks up at her over the book. "Poor Zeus. He couldn't help himself."

"Poor Leda," she corrects him demurely; peace has been restored. She cuts the thread with her stork scissors. "It was not her fault."

"Do you suppose Zeus enjoyed being a swan, apart from his courtship of Leda?" Olivier has propped the book open over his knee. "Never mind—he probably enjoyed anything he undertook, except perhaps disciplining the other gods when that was necessary."

"Oh, I don't know," she proposes, for the pleasure of discussion; why is it always such a pleasure, with him? "Maybe he wished he could visit lovely Leda in the form of a human being, or even that he could simply be a human being for a few hours, to have an ordinary life."

"No, no." Olivier takes up the book, puts it down once again. "I'm afraid I must disagree—think of the joy of his being a swan, soaring over the landscape, discovering her."

"Yes, I suppose so."

"It would make a marvelous painting, wouldn't it? Just the sort of thing the Salon jury would welcome." He is silent for a moment. "The subject has been handled before, of course. But what if it were done in a fresh way, in a new style—an old subject, but painted for our era, more naturally?"

"Indeed—why don't you try?" She puts down the scissors and looks at him. His enthusiasm, his presence, floods her with love; it pools inside her throat, behind her eyes, spills over her as she adjusts her embroidery across her lap.

"No," he says. "It could be done only by a bolder painter than I, someone with a great feel for swans but also with a fearless brush. You, for example."

She seizes her work again, her needle, the silk. "Nonsense. How could I paint such a thing?"

"With my help," he says.

"Oh no." She almost calls him "dearest," bites back the words. "I've never done such a canvas, so complicated, and it would require a model for Leda, of course, and a setting."

"You could paint most of it out of doors." His eyes are fixed on her. "Why not in your garden? That would make it new and fresh. You could draw a swan from the Bois de Boulogne—you already have, and so well. And you could use your maid as a model, the way you did before."

"It's such a—I don't know. It's a strong subject for me—for a woman. How could Madame Rivière ever submit it?"

"That would be her struggle, not yours." He is in earnest, but he smiles, faintly, his eyes brighter than before. "Would you be afraid, if I were there to help? Could you not take a risk? Be courageous? Aren't there things greater than public censure, things that ought to be attempted and cherished?"

The moment has come; his challenge, her panic, her longing, all rise up in her rib cage. "If you were there to help me?"

"Yes. Would you be afraid?"

She makes herself look at him. She is drowning. He will guess that she wants him, she does want him, even if she tries to avoid uttering the words. "No," she says slowly. "If you were there to help, I would not. I don't think I could be really afraid of anything. If you were there with me."

He holds her gaze, and she loves the fact that he does not smile; there is no triumph, nothing she can attribute to vanity. If anything, he seems on the verge of tears. "Then I would help you," he says, so softly that she can hardly hear it.

She says nothing, at the edge of tears herself.

He regards her for a long minute, then picks up the book. "Do you want to hear the story of Leda?"

Chapter 87

Marlow

We ate dinner at a table near the lobby bar, at the open edge of the building, where we could hear the pounding of the waves barely out of sight and see the fronds of coconut palms streaming past. The afternoon's breeze had certainly become a wind, tossing and rustling them so that the noise was as persistent as the sound of the ocean, and I thought again of *Lord Jim*. I asked Mary what she was reading, and she described a contemporary novel I hadn't heard of, a translation of a young Vietnamese author. My attention wandered from her words to her eyes, strangely hooded in the flicker of our candle, and to her narrow cheekbone. The waiters at the bar were climbing on a stool to light torches in a pair of stone bowls high above the glasses and bottles, so that the bar looked like a sacrificial altar—some designer's dramatic effect, Mayan or Aztec.

I saw that Mary's attention had wandered, too, although she hadn't stopped telling me about the boat people in the novel, and I noticed that there was only one other couple having dinner nearby, and three children teasing a scarlet macaw that preened on a perch a few yards away. Tourists came in and out of the wind: a man in a wheelchair with a younger woman pushing it and bending over him to say something, a glossy-haired family strolling around, looking at the flat turquoise fountains, the irritable bird.

Watching all this, I felt divided down my center, half of me riveted by Mary's presence—the pale hair on her arms and the even finer down, nearly invisible, along her cheek in the candlelight—and half mesmerized by the newness of this place, its smells and echoing spaces, the people passing through . . . on their way to what pleasures? I had seldom been in a place constructed completely for pleasure; my parents hadn't really believed in such experiences, or in spending money on them, and my adult life had revolved almost entirely around work, with the occasional edifying trip or painting excursion. This was different, first of all because of the softness of the wind, the luxury of every surface, the smells of salt and palm, but also because of the absence of ancient architecture or national park, something to study or explore, a justification; it was entirely a place for relaxation.

"This is all to worship the ocean, isn't it?" Mary said, and I realized she'd interrupted her description of her reading to finish my own thought. I couldn't speak; my throat swelled. It was a mere coincidence, our convergent thoughts, but I wanted to lunge across the table and kiss her, almost to weep—and for what? For the people I knew who were no longer alive and were missing this, maybe, or for everyone who was not me at that moment, not my most fortunate self, with all I seemed to have to look forward to.

I nodded, indicating what I hoped was judicious agreement, and we ate in silence. For a few minutes, the flavors of guava and salsa and the delicate fish took up my attention, but I was still watching her, or letting her watch me. I saw myself, as if there were a mirror on the other side of the bar, a little past my prime—my shoulders broad but slightly stooped, my hair still thick but also beginning to gray, the lines from the well of my nose to the corners of my mouth deepened by the dim light, my middle (under the linen napkin) as trim as I could keep it. I'd lived companionably, undemandingly, with this body for a long time, asking of it only that it take me to and from work, that it get some exercise several times a week. I dressed it and washed it, fed it, made it swallow vitamins. In an hour or two I would put it in Mary's hands if she still wanted me to do that.

A shiver went over me when I thought of this, first of pleasure: her fingers on my neck, between my legs, my hands on her breasts, which I knew only by their shadowy outline in her blouse. Then a shiver of shame: my years exposed under a bedside light, my long absence from love, my sudden possible failure, her disappointment. I had to force the thought of Kate out of my mind, and the thought of Robert, lying on top of each of them, Kate and Mary. What was I doing here, with a second of his women? But she was something different for me now; she was herself. How could I not have been there with her? "Oh God," I said aloud.

Mary glanced up at me with her fork to her lips, startled, her sheet of hair slipping forward over one shoulder.

"Nothing," I said. She, calm, unquestioning, drank water. I silently blessed her for not being the sort of woman who demands of you constantly, "What are you thinking?" Then it occurred to me that I was highly paid to ask people exactly that question all day—I smiled in spite of myself. She was watching me, clearly puzzled, but didn't speak. She was, I felt with a wave of affection, a person who did not even want to know everything. She carried her own sphere around her, her beautiful diffidence.

After dinner we went upstairs together without speaking, as if words had been swept away from us; I couldn't bring myself to look at her during the seconds it took me to unlock the door of our room. I wondered if I should wait in the hall while she used the room or the bathroom, and then decided that it would be more awkward to ask if she'd like me to stay outside than it would to go in with her. So I followed her into our shared space and lay down fully dressed on the bed with a leftover *Washington Post* while she took a shower behind the closed bathroom door. When she came out, she was wearing one of the bathrobes provided by the hotel, white and thick, with the fan of her wet hair across it. Her face and neck were flushed. We both stayed very still, staring at each other. "I'll take a shower, too," I said, trying to fold my newspaper and then trying to set it normally on the bed.

"All right," she agreed. Her voice was tight and distant. *She regrets this,* I thought. *She regrets having agreed to come, putting herself into this situation with me. She feels trapped now.* And I felt suddenly harsh—too bad; we were both there and we had to go through with it, make the best of it. I got up without attempting to speak to her again and took off my shoes and socks; my feet looked dismally skinny against the pale carpet. I got my toilet kit out of my suitcase while she moved to the corner of the room to let me pass into the bathroom. Why had I ever thought this would work? I shut the door quietly behind me. The man in the mirror probably had one other thing wrong with him: he was not Robert Oliver. Well, Robert could go to hell, too. I took off my clothes, forcing myself not to look away from the patch of silver moss between my breasts. At least I had kept my shape, my running muscles, but she would never feel them now. No need, after all, to go through with anything. There was no reversing Mary's history. I had been foolish to think of trying.

I washed myself under the beating shower with water so hot it hurt, soaping my genitals, although she probably wouldn't be touching them. I shaved my middle-aged chin carefully in the mirror and put on the second hotel bathrobe. ("If you love our robe, you can take one home! Ask of the hotel shop in the lobby"—and then a heart-stopping price in pesos.) I brushed my teeth and combed my toweled hair. It was also not possible late in life to let anyone else in, not in a serious way; that was clear. I began to wonder how either of us would get any sleep after not making love. I might still be able to request a single room for myself—I would leave the double bed to her and take my suitcase with me, let her rest in privacy and comfort. I hoped we could settle this division of rooms, and whatever it meant, without a quarrel, with dignity and civility. I would tell her at the right point that I'd certainly understand if she chose to leave Acapulco early. When I had arranged this with myself and gripped one of my hands into a fist for a second or two, to still my breathing, I was able to open the bathroom door with regret only at leaving my steamy haven to begin such a conversation.

To my surprise, the room was dark. For a moment, I thought she must have settled the matter herself by moving to another room, and then I saw a form glimmering white in one corner—she was sitting on the edge of the bed, just out of reach of the light from the bathroom. Her hair was as dark as the room, and the lines of her naked body were blurred. I turned out the bathroom light with frozen fingers and took two steps toward her before I thought to remove my own bathrobe. I dropped it over the desk chair, or where I thought the chair was, and reached her in a few hesitant steps. Even then, I wasn't sure enough to put my hands out toward her, but I felt her rise to meet me, so that the warmth of her breath came close to my mouth and the warmth of her skin was against me. I had been chilled, I realized. I had been chilled for years. Her hands came down like two birds on my cold, bare shoulders. Then she was slowly filling all the other deficits—my speechless mouth, the hollow space in my breast, my empty hands.

*

I first began to draw human anatomy in a course with George Bo, at the Art League School—over a long period, I took that course twice and then one on painting the human body, because I realized that the portraits I was trying to paint would never improve unless I learned the muscles under the face, neck, arms, hands. In class, we did draw muscles, endlessly, but over them we finally put skin—over those long, smooth lines, over the muscles that make us walk and bend and reach, we drew skin. There is so much that even an observant person doesn't know about the body, so much hidden inside all of us.

I wondered, when I began to study anatomy as an artist, years after I'd studied it for medicine, if this new perspective would make flesh clinical for me once again. It didn't, of course. Knowing the muscles that cause the dimple on each side of the base of the spine has not diminished my wish to caress that dimple, and the same is true for the way the spine itself makes an exquisite long division of the back. I can draw the muscles that give the waist its supple bend to each side, although I don't need them in most of my portraits, because I like to show my subjects from the breastbone up, to concentrate on shoulders and face. But I know that bone well, too, and the muscles that radiate from it, and the smooth hook and curl of the collarbone, and the smooth flesh in between. When I need to, I can draw correctly the ripple in the strong supporting thigh, the long reach from knee to buttock, the firm swell toward the inside of the leg. The painter shows muscles through skin, through clothing, but he or she depicts something else as well, something both elusive and immutable: the warmth of the body, its heat and pulsing reality, life. And, by extension, its movements, its soft sounds, the tide of feeling that rises and floods us when we are loved enough to forget ourselves.

*

Sometime close to morning, Mary put her head against my neck and slept; and I, cradling all of her in my previously empty arms, slept instantly, too, with my cheek against her hair.

Chapter 88

1879

That evening, in her candlelit room, she stares at a book until late, unseeing, uncomprehending. When the clock downstairs strikes midnight, she brushes out her hair and hangs her clothes on the hooks in the wardrobe. She pulls on her second nightgown—the best one, with its tiny ruffles at throat and wrists, its million tucks covering her breasts—and ties her dressing gown over it. She washes her face and hands in the basin, puts on her silent and gold-embroidered slippers, takes her key, and blows out the candle. She kneels by the bed and says a short prayer, a memorial to the grace she is leaving, asking in advance for forgiveness. Perversely, it is Zeus she sees when her eyes are closed.

Her door does not creak. When she tries his at the end of the hall, she finds it unlocked, which makes her heart pound from certainty; she closes it behind her with infinite quiet and locks it. He has been reading, too, in the chair by his curtained window, one candle on the desk. His face is old, with a sudden look of skull in the frugal light, and she fights an urge to turn back to her room. Then his eyes meet hers, and they are sober, soft. He is wearing a scarlet dressing gown she has never seen. He closes his book, blows out the candle, and rises to open the curtains a little; she understands that now they can see each other at least vaguely in the gaslight seeping off the street, without being observed from outside. She has not moved. He comes to her, putting his hands gently on her shoulders. He searches for her gaze in the dimness. "My dearest," he whispers. Then her name.

He kisses her mouth, beginning at one corner. Through her fright and doubt, a vista opens, a road in sunlight, someplace he must have walked years before she knew him, possibly years before she was born, a road leading out under sycamores. He kisses her lips, a fraction at a time. She puts her hands on his shoulders in return, and his bones are knobby under the silk, the mechanics of a well-built clock, a branch on a stately tree. He is drinking from her mouth, tasting the youth in it, telling into the hollow inside her the things love has taught him decades before this, dropping a tiny stone into the well.

When she is panting, he stands straight, unbuttons her nightgown from the topmost pearl, and slips his cupping, tender hand inside it, brushes it back over her shoulders, lets it fall around her to the floor. For a moment she fears this is merely another anatomy lesson for him, man of the world, old master of the brush, friend of models. But then he touches her mouth with one hand and reaches slowly down with the other, and she catches the shine, the tracks of salt water on his face. He is the one shedding a skin, not she; he is the one she will comfort in her arms until almost morning.

Chapter 89

Marlow

Caillet lived in a house overlooking the Bay of Acapulco, on a terraced street high above the sweep of water. It was one of a neighborhood of elegant adobe houses crowded among oleanders, and of stucco walls ornamented with bougainvillea. The bell was answered by a man with a mustache and a white coat like a waiter's. Inside Caillet's gate, another man, this one in brown shirt and trousers, was carefully watering the grass and an orange tree. There were birds in the branches and roses climbing the shutters of the house. Mary, standing beside me in her long skirt and pale blouse, was looking around—at the colors, I knew—alert as a cat, her hand unabashedly in mine. I'd called Caillet this morning to be certain he was expecting me, and added that I hoped he wouldn't mind if I brought along my painter friend, to which he assented gravely. His voice on the phone was mellow and deep, with an accent I thought might be French.

Now the door among the flowers opened, and a man came out to greet us—Caillet himself, I thought immediately. He was not tall, but his presence was distinct. He wore a black Nehru jacket over a deep-blue shirt, and he held a burning cigar in one hand, so that the smoke rose around him in the doorway. His hair was white and thick, brushy, his skin brick-colored, as if the Mexican sun had made him mysteriously ill over the years. Up close, his smile was genuine, his dark eyes faded. We shook hands. "Good morning," he said in that same baritone, and kissed Mary's hand, but matter-of-factly. Then he held the door for us.

The interior of the house was very cool—air-conditioned and with thick walls. Caillet led us from the low-ceilinged hall through brightly painted doorways and into a large, spreading room with columns. There I found myself gazing around in astonishment at paintings whose quality leapt out from every wall. The furniture was modern and unobtrusive, incidental, but those paintings hung four or five in a row, from waist-level to ceiling, a kaleidoscope. They spanned a wide range of styles and eras, from a few canvases that looked like seventeenth-century Dutch or Flemish to abstract forms and a disturbing portrait I felt sure was an Alice Neel. But the dominant theme was Impressionism: sunny fields, gardens, poplars, water. It was as if we'd stepped across a threshold dividing Mexico from France, into a different light. Of course, some of the paintings around us could have been from nineteenth-century England or California, but at first glance I felt we were seeing Caillet's heritage, places he himself might have known and wandered through; perhaps that was one reason he'd collected these images.

I heard a movement from Mary; she had turned away and was standing in front of a large canvas next to the door where we'd entered. It showed a winter scene, snow, the bank of a river, bushes gold under the creamy weight, the surface of water frozen to a silver patina with pale olive patches of open water, the familiar strokes and layers, white that was not white, gold, lavender, the heavy black name and date in the lower right-hand corner. A Monet.

I looked around at Caillet, who stood calmly next to his minimalist sofa, smoke from his cigar drifting (shockingly) across all these treasures. "Yes," he said, although I hadn't asked. "I bought it in Paris in nineteen fifty-four." His accent was harsh, the voice under it rich and gentle. "It was very expensive, even then. But I do not regret it even one minute." He gestured for us to sit down with him on the pale-gray linen. There was a glass table in their midst, which held some blooming prickly plant and a book of paintings: *Antoine et Pedro Caillet: Une Rétrospective Double.* The glossy cover showed two vertical paintings, deeply different from each other in form and color but reproduced side by side in a forced diptych; I recognized in them the styles of some of the abstract paintings in the room. I yearned to pick the book up and turn through it but didn't want to presume, and now the man in the white jacket was bringing in a tray laden with glasses and pitchers—ice, limes, orange juice, a bottle of sparkling water, a spray of white flowers.

Caillet mixed the refreshments for us himself. He had begun to seem to me almost as silent as Robert Oliver, but he handed a spray of flowers to Mary—"For you to paint, young lady." I expected her to bristle, as she would have had I said such a thing to her. She smiled instead, and caressed the flowers in her dark-draped lap. Caillet tapped cigar ash into a glass bowl on the glass table. He waited while his man closed the shutters on one side of the room, extinguishing half the paintings. Finally, he turned to us and spoke.

"You would like to know about Béatrice de Clerval. Yes, I owned some of her early work and—as you may have read—she had only early work. It is believed that she stopped painting at the age of twenty-eight. You know that Monet painted until he was eighty-six and Renoir until he was seventy-nine. Picasso, of course, worked until he died at ninety-one." He gestured to a set of four bullfights behind him. "Artists keep working, for the most part. So you see that Clerval was a strange case, but then women were not so encouraged. She was very, very gifted. She could have been one of the great ones. She was only a little younger than the first Impressionists—eleven years younger than Monet, for example. Think of that." He mashed the stub of his cigar in the glass dish. His nails looked manicured; I had never seen such a perfect hand on an old man, and certainly not on a painter. "She would have been a major artist, like Morisot and Cassatt, if she had not blocked her own way." He settled back again.

"You said you owned some of her work. Do you no longer have it?" I couldn't help looking around the cavernous room. Mary was scanning it, too.

"Oh, I have some. I sold most of it in nineteen thirty-six and nineteen thirty-seven to pay off my debts." Caillet smoothed his hair back over the top of his head. He did not appear to regret this decision in any way. "I bought her paintings from Henri Robinson—who is still alive, by the way. In Paris. We have not kept in touch, but I saw his name in a magazine article very recently. He is still writing about literature and furniture and philosophy. Philosophy and bric-a-brac." I thought he would have snorted if he had been the sort of man to snort.

"Who is Henri Robinson?" I asked.

Caillet regarded me for a moment, then dropped his gaze to the Christmas cactus, or whatever it was, between us. "He is a fine critic and art collector, and he was the lover of Aude de Clerval until she died. Béatrice's daughter. She left him what was surely Béatrice's greatest painting, *The Swan Thieves*."

I nodded, hoping he would continue, although I hadn't seen any mention of this work in the material I'd read so far. But Caillet seemed to have fallen into that profound silence again. After a moment, he began to fish in his inner jacket pocket and finally drew out another cigar, this one small and slender, like a child of the first one. A little more searching produced a silver lighter, and his beautifully manicured old hands went through the whole ritual, lighting, cupping. He drew on it, and smoke curled away from him.

"Did you know Aude de Clerval yourself?" I asked at last. I was beginning to wonder if we would get more than the most rudimentary information from this elegant man.

He leaned back again, propping one arm up with the other hand. "Yes," he said. "Yes, I knew her. She took my lover from me."

A very long silence followed this meditative statement, during which Caillet smoked slowly and Mary and I, of one accord, did not look at each other. I thought about what to say that would not jeopardize our search and at last fell back on my office manner. "That must have been very difficult for you."

Caillet smiled. "Oh, at the time it was difficult, but that was because I was young and I thought that it mattered. In any case, I liked Aude de Clerval. She was a wonderful woman, in her way, and I believe she made my friend happy. And she also made it possible for him to buy about half my collection, and that made it possible for me and for my brother"—he indicated the museum catalog on the table—"to paint. So life arranges things. Aude wanted to have the works by her mother that I had bought, especially *The Swan Thieves*. I owned that one only a short time—it came from the sale of the estate of Armand Thomas, the younger brother, in Paris."

Caillet tapped his cigarillo in the ashtray. "Aude thought that was her mother's greatest painting and also her last, although I'm not sure. Everybody was happy, you might say. But Aude died in nineteen sixty-six, so Henri has had to live for years without her. Apparently, Henri and I are both cursed with very long life. He is even older than I, poor man. And Aude was twenty-two years older than he. The queer and the old lady—they were an interesting pair. The heart does not go backward. Only the mind." He seemed lost in this for so long that I began to wonder if he was a user of substances other than the tobacco and the tequila, or if he had simply lapsed into the silences of living alone.

Mary broke his reverie this time, and her question surprised me. "Did Aude talk about her mother?"

Caillet glanced at her, his ruddy face alert, remembering. "Yes, sometimes. I will tell you what I remember, which is not very much. I knew her for only a little time, because after Henri fell in love with her, I left Paris and came here, to Acapulco. I grew up here, you know. My father was a mostly French engineer and my mother was Mexican, a schoolteacher. I remember that Aude said one day that her mother had been a great artist all of her life. 'No one stops being an artist,' she said to us. And I argued with her that a painter who stops painting is no longer a painter. It is the act of painting that matters. Yes, we were sitting in a café in the rue Pigalle. Another time she told us that her mother had been her closest friend in life, and Henri actually looked hurt. She was not a painter herself, Aude, and she collected only her mother's work. She guarded *The Swan Thieves* jealously after she bought it from me, a tradition poor Henri has continued, I assume, since it has never appeared anywhere and has never been written about, to the best of my knowledge. I think Henri wanted Aude because she was so complete, so finished, so *parfaite*. She needed no one. He was part English, too—his father's parents—always a little the outsider, and Aude was absolutely, totally French. And he wanted maybe to show to her that she could have one last friend in life. They went through the war together in terrible deprivation. He was faithful to her until the end. She died slowly."

Caillet tapped his cigarillo and pointed it to the ceiling in one raised hand. Clearly he could speak at length once he got going. "Aude was not exactly the beauty her mother had been, to judge by the little Olivier Vignot portrait—I mean, Béatrice de Clerval was a beauty. But Aude was tall, with a very interesting face—what they call in French 'jolie laide,' ugly one moment and mesmerizing the next. I painted her myself one time, soon after I met her. Henri kept that one. I do not paint portraits often, and I do not trust self-portraits." He turned to Mary. "Do you paint self-portraits, madame?"

"No," she said.

Caillet regarded her a moment longer, one cheek resting on his hand, as if she might be an emissary from a tribe he had once studied. Then he smiled again, and his face was so transformed by indulgent kindness that I found myself thinking irrelevantly what a sweet grandfather he might have made—assuming, of course, that he actually wasn't one. "You came to see the paintings of Béatrice de Clerval, not a too-talkative old Mexican. Let me show them to you."

CHAPTER 90

Marlow

We got to our feet at once, but Caillet did not take us directly to Béatrice's work. Instead, he gave us a tour, the lingering tour of the collector who loves his paintings and introduces them as if they are people. There was a small canvas by Sisley, dated 1894—which he'd bought in Arles, he said, for nothing, because he had been the first to authenticate it. There were two canvases by Mary Cassatt, of women reading, and a pastel landscape on brown paper by Berthe Morisot, five strokes of green, four of blue, a dash of yellow. Mary liked that one best: "It's so simple. And perfect." And there was an Impressionist landscape of such beauty that we both paused in front of it—a castle rising out of heavy greenery, palms, golden light.

"That is Majorca." Caillet pointed with a blunt finger. "My mother's mother lived there, and I used to visit her when I was a child. Her name was Elaine Gurevich. She did not live in the castle, naturally, but we took walks there. It is her painting—she was my first teacher. She adored music, books, art. I would sleep in her bed, and if I woke up at four in the morning she was always reading, with the light on. I loved her more than almost anyone." He turned away. "If only she had painted more. I always felt I was painting for her, a little."

There were twentieth-century works as well—de Kooning and a small Klee and the abstractions of Pedro Caillet himself, and his brother's. Pedro's work was surprisingly colorful and lively, while Antoine's tended to lines of silver and white.

"My brother is dead," Caillet said flatly. "He died in Mexico City six years ago. He was my greatest friend—we worked together for thirty years. I am more proud of Antoine's work than of my own. He was a deep, reflective person, a marvelous person. His labor inspired me. I am traveling to Rome for an exhibition of his work. That will be my final trip." He smoothed his hair. "When Antoine died, I decided to stop painting. It was cleaner that way, not to go on and on. Sometimes it is better for an artist not to last too long. That means I am no longer a painter. I buried my last painting with him. You know that Renoir had to have his paintbrush tied onto his hand at the end? And Dufy."

This explained the immaculate fingernails, I thought, the perfect blue-and-black clothes, the lack of studio smells. I wished I could ask him what he did with his time now, but the house, as exquisite as its owner, made the answer plain: nothing. He had the air of a man waiting thoughtfully for an appointment, the patient who arrives early in the waiting room and hasn't brought a book or newspaper but disdains to pick up any of those glossy magazines. Doing nothing was apparently a full-time job for Pedro Caillet; he could afford it, and his paintings kept him silent company. It struck me that he had asked us nothing about ourselves, except whether Mary painted self-portraits; he didn't seem to want to know why we were interested in his old friends. He had freed himself even from curiosity.

Now Caillet moved from his cave of a living room through the yellow-and-red doorway to the dining room. Here we saw something different: treasures of Mexican folk art. There was a long green table set around with blue chairs, with a perforated-tin lamp in the shape of a bird hanging over it, and an ancient wooden sideboard, all apparently waiting for no dinner guests. One wall was decorated with an embroidered tapestry, magenta and emerald and orange people and animals going about their business on a black background. The opposite wall displayed (incongruously, I thought) three Impressionist paintings and a more realist portrait in pencil, a woman's head, which looked twentieth-century. Caillet raised a hand as if to greet them all. "Aude particularly wanted these three oils," he remarked, "so I declined to sell them to her. Otherwise, I was very polite, and I sold her all the others, my whole collection—which was not large, perhaps twelve pieces, since Béatrice did not paint that much."

The paintings were remarkable, even at first glance, evidence of a quietly splendid Impressionist talent. One of them showed a golden-haired girl before a mirror. A maid, shadowy background presence, was bringing her clothes to her, or perhaps taking something out of the room, or perhaps simply watching her; there was something furtive about the more distant figure glimpsed in the mirror, ghostlike. The effect was lovely, sensual, unsettling. I was seeing my first Béatrice de Clerval in the flesh, and in every one of her few works I've seen since then, there was an unease of this sort. In the corner was a strong mark in black, which looked decorative, like a Chinese character, until you deciphered the letters: *BdC,* a signature.

The largest oil showed a man sitting on a bench in the shade of roughly painted flowering bushes. I thought of the garden in Béatrice's letters and took a step backward to see it in focus, moving carefully so as not to bump the blue chairs. The man wore a hat and an open jacket with a cravat at his neck. He was reading a book. In the foreground were brilliantly vivid flowers, scarlet and yellow and pink, blazing against the green, while the man was a blurred figure, relaxed and stable but far less important to the composition, I thought. Had Béatrice de

Clerval found her husband so much less definite a character than her garden, or had she simply shrouded their intimacy in vagueness?

Caillet, on the other side of the table, confirmed some of my guesses. "That one is Béatrice's husband, Yves Vignot, as confirmed by their daughter, Aude. You may know that Aude changed her name from Aude Vignot to Aude de Clerval after her mother died—fanatic loyalty, I suppose, or perhaps she sensed her mother's achievement as an artist and wanted a little of her glory. She was too proud of her mother."

He walked to one end of the dining hall and stood there, contemplating a ceramic duck studded with unlit candles that sat on a perforated-tin cabinet. Mary and I turned to study the third Béatrice de Clerval painting, which showed a pond in a park, its flat surface ruffled by wind that threw the reflections of the arching trees overhead into confusion. This skillful scene was brightened by a flower garden at one end of the pond and the shapes of birds on the water, including a swan just raising its wings for flight. It was a stunning piece of work; I thought to myself that—to my eye, at least—the handling of light on the water approached Monet's. Why would anyone with such a gift ever stop painting? The form of the swan, swiftly brushed in, was the essence of flight, of sudden, free movement. Mary said, "She must have watched a lot of swans."

"It's completely alive," I agreed. I turned to Caillet, who had propped himself against the back of a chair and was watching us. "Where was this painted, do you know?"

"Aude told me when she asked me to sell it to her that it was the Bois de Boulogne, near their home in Passy. Her mother painted it in June eighteen eighty, just before she stopped painting. She called it *The Last Swan*—that's what's written on the back, in any case. It is really fine, isn't it? Henri would almost have killed to buy it back for Aude. He wrote me three times about it when she was dying. The third time was an angry letter, by the standards of Henri."

He waved a hand as if that emotion had been dismissed for all the ages to come. "I believe this was the final painting that Béatrice de Clerval made, although I cannot prove that. But that would explain the title—it is her last swan—and the fact that I have never been able to find anything about a painting with a later date. Henri, of course, thinks that his painting is the last one—the one called *The Swan Thieves*. He is very strange about it. It is true that there was not a later one in the first exhibition of her work in the nineteen eighties—it was at the Musée de Maintenon, in Paris. You know about that show? I loaned this large canvas to them for it. In the end, it does not matter," he added, leaning slowly forward with his hands on the back of a chair. "It is a superb painting, one of the best in my collection. It will stay here until I die."

He didn't add what might happen to it after that, and I decided not to ask him. I pointed instead to the portrait sketch. "Who is this?" It was not quite a professional piece of work—a depiction of a woman with wavy short hair like that of a movie star from the 1930s, a little clumsy in execution but also expressive around the eyes, which were full of life, and the thin, sensitive mouth. She seemed to look rather than speak, as if she'd resolved not to say anything, then or later, and it increased the intensity of her gaze. She wasn't a pretty woman, exactly, but there was something handsome and even arresting about her; she had refused, boldly, to be pretty.

Caillet put his head to one side. "That is Aude," he said. "She gave me that portrait while we were still friends, and I have kept it in her honor. I thought she might have liked to have it hanging here with her mother's paintings. I am sure she likes that, wherever she is now."

"Who did it?" The sketch said "1936" in one corner.

"Henri. It was six years after they met. The year before I left. He was thirty-four and I was twenty-four and Aude was fifty-six. So I have his portrait of Aude, and he has mine—a nice symmetry. As I told you, she wasn't beautiful, although he was."

He turned away, as if the conversation had come to its logical conclusion, and if he wanted it to, it had. I rapidly pictured them all: he had left for Mexico just before the war, then, escaping not only love troubles but also the coming disaster in Europe. He had been ten years younger than Henri, and to an artist in his twenties, Aude must have seemed ancient at fifty-six (only four years more than my current age, I realized with a pang). But the woman in the sketch did not look ancient, and she did not look like Béatrice de Clerval, if the Vignot portrait was to be trusted. Not in the least, unless you counted the glow of the eyes. Where and how had Aude and Henri gotten through the war? They had both survived it. "So Henri Robinson is still alive?" I couldn't help saying as we followed Caillet back to his gallery living room.

"He was alive last year," Caillet said without turning around. "He sent me a note on his ninety-seventh birthday. Turning ninety-seven makes one remember all one's former amours, I suppose."

When we reached the sofas again, he did not make his gracious gesture for us to sit down but remained standing in the middle of the room. I realized that he must be eighty-eight himself, if I was calculating all this correctly. It hardly seemed possible. He stood in front of us, graceful, upright, his dark-red skin smooth, his white hair thick and brushed neatly back, his black suit with its unusual cut well-pressed, a man perfectly preserved, as if he had stumbled on the gift of eternal life and had wearied politely even of that. "I am tired now," he said, although he looked as if he could have stood there all day.

"You've been very kind," I told him at once. "Please forgive my asking you one more thing. With your permission, I'd like to write to Henri Robinson for some further information about Béatrice de Clerval's work. Do you have an address you'd be willing to share with me?"

"Of course," he said, folding his arms, the first sign of impatience I'd seen. "I shall find the information for you." He turned and went out of the room, and we heard him calling someone in a controlled, low voice. After a moment he returned with an ancient address book, bound in leather, and the man who had brought us the tray of drinks. There was a little negotiation between them, and the man wrote something out for me while Caillet watched.

I thanked them both—it was an address in Paris, with an apartment number. Caillet checked it over my shoulder. "You may give him my best wishes—from one old Frenchman to another." He smiled then, as if viewing something familiar from a great distance, and I felt guilt at having asked a favor so personal.

He turned to Mary. "Goodbye, my dear. It is nice to see a beautiful woman again." She gave him her hand, and he kissed it respectfully, without warmth. "Goodbye, *mon ami*." He shook hands with me—his grip was strong and dry, as before. "We probably will not meet again, but I wish you the best of luck with your research."

He walked us in silence to his front door and held it open; there was no sign of the servant now. "Goodbye, goodbye," he repeated, but so gently we could hardly hear him. I turned on the walk and waved to him once, where he stood framed by his roses and bougainvillea, impossibly upright, handsome, embalmed, alone. Mary waved, too, and shook her head without speaking. He did not wave back.

*

That night, as we made love for the second time ever—swimming into the current with more confidence, old lovers overnight—I found Mary's cheeks wet with tears.

"What is it, my darling?"

"Just—today."

"Caillet?" I guessed.

"Henri Robinson," she said. "Caring for so many years for the old woman he loved." And she ran her hand down my shoulder.

CHAPTER 91

1879

She comes in to breakfast a little late but fresh, washed, only her eyes heavy. Her body is entirely new, unrecognizable to her, her hair done in the simple style she uses when Esmé is not there. Her soul tugs inside her. Perhaps that is the reality of sin, to know the shape of the soul and feel it chafing inside the body. But her heart, shamefully, is light, and that makes the morning seem fair—the sea outside the windows is a giant mirror; the muslin of her skirts feels pleasant against her hands. She asks the innkeeper for news of Olivier, disingenuously, trying to look right at her. The old lady says that monsieur has gone out early for his walk and left an envelope for Béatrice on the front hall table. When she goes to see, the note is not there; perhaps he has removed it himself to give to her. She must ask him later.

The woman puts hot coffee and rolls before her, with a tart of jam; this thick, elderly person in a blue dress, bent at shoulders and waist, is Olivier's age. She feels a kind of indignity on behalf of the old lady, whom Olivier could properly marry and make happy. Then she thinks of a little passage from the night, something, a particular caress that must have lasted two or three minutes at most but that has stayed like a presence on her skin. She asks humbly if there is more butter and hears the woman's "*oui*" spoken on the in-breath, and the pressure of a warm, impersonal hand on her shoulder. Béatrice wonders why she feels guiltier about this stranger, with her apron and her air of contentment, than about Yves, the overworked and now betrayed husband. But it is true. She does.

And then he is there—Yves Vignot. It is one of the two strangest moments of her life. He comes into the dining room like a hallucination, peeling off his gloves, his hat and walking stick already somewhere at the entrance—now she remembers having heard the front door open and shut. The small hotel is full of him, he is everywhere, a blur of neat dark jacket, bearded smile, his *"Eh, bien!"* He has counted on surprising her, but the surprise that fills her is almost faintness. For a moment, the pleasant provincial room, a little raw and new, merges with their rooms in Passy, as if her delight, her guilt, have summoned him to her side, or her to his.

"But I've really startled you!" He throws down his gloves and comes to kiss her, and she manages to rise in time. "I'm sorry, my dear. I should have known better." His face is all regret. "And you're still a little unwell—how could I have thought to surprise you?" His kiss on her cheek is warm, as if he knows this will restore her.

"What a lovely shock," she manages to say. "How did you get away?"

"I told them my beloved wife was ill and that I needed to see to her—oh, I didn't advertise any dangerous illness, but the supervisor was sympathetic enough, and as everyone else answers to me . . ." He smiles.

She can think of nothing to say that won't come out with a quaver or sound like a lie. Fortunately, he is full of the pleasure of seeing her and of the adventure of his trip, so that by the time they sit down again to her cold coffee, he has already concluded that she looks better than expected, and that the train line is better than he remembered, and that he is thoroughly pleased at being away from the office. After he has washed his hands and had two cups of coffee and a large portion of bread, butter, and jam tart, he asks to see her rooms. He has already booked a room for himself; he won't infringe on her little kingdom, he adds with a squeeze to her shoulder. He is so large, so dignified yet cheerful, his beard thick and well-trimmed. He is, she thinks, so young.

On the way upstairs he puts his arm around her waist. He has missed her, he says, even more than expected. Not that he'd thought he wouldn't miss her, but he missed her even more than that. His joy makes her want to weep. She has forgotten how safe his arm feels, how sturdy; now she remembers, from the touch of it. In her bedroom he shuts the door behind them and admires all her arrangements with the lightheartedness of a vacationer: the shells she has collected for the dressing table, the small polished desk where she sketches if the weather is bad. She explains each of these things for as long as possible. He stands smiling at her through all of it.

"You look wonderfully healthy, now that I get a better view. You have real roses in your cheeks."

"Well, I have been out painting nearly every morning and afternoon." She will show him her canvases next.

"I hope Olivier goes with you," he says a little sternly.

"Of course he does." She finds her canvas of boats from the first sessions and hands it to him. "In fact, he has encouraged me to work every day, as long as I'm warmly dressed. I always remember to dress myself warmly."

"This is beautiful." He holds the painting up for a moment, and she thinks with a pang how encouraging he has always been, long before Olivier came along. Then he sets it down, careful, understanding that it is still not dry, and takes her hands. "And you are radiant."

"I'm a little tired still," she says, "but thank you."

"On the contrary, you're blushing—there's your old self

indeed." He imprisons her hands in both his own, firm now, and kisses her lingeringly. His lips are second nature to her, and frightening. He gathers her face in his hands and kisses her again, then takes off his coat, murmuring something about not having yet bathed. He locks the door and draws the curtains. Travel, the release from work, have made him young again, he says—or she thinks this is what he says, because she hears it from behind the curtain of her hair, the pins loosened out of it, and then again during his gentle unbuttoning, unbuckling, unhooking, his drawing a line down her body on the bed, taking her in his slow, matter-of-fact way, her long-accustomed response, the gap between them closing with a fiery familiarity in spite of the images behind her eyelids. It has been months since he has approached her, and she realizes now that he has probably been holding back out of concern for her health. How could she have thought otherwise?

At last, he sleeps against her shoulder for a few minutes, a tired, surprisingly young man with a growing bank account, a man who has escaped his life briefly and taken a train to be near her again.

Dear Monsieur Robinson:

Please excuse a note from a stranger. I am a psychiatrist working in Washington, DC; recently, I have been involved in the treatment of a distinguished American artist. His case is rather unusual, and some of it revolves around an obsession with the French Impressionist painter Béatrice de Clerval. I understand that you had both a personal and a professional connection with her and that you are a collector of her work, including the canvas known as The Swan Thieves.

Would you allow me to call on you at home in Paris for an hour or so in the next month? I would be very grateful if you could assist me with a little further information about her life and work. It could be of great importance to me in caring for my gifted patient. Please let me know at your earliest convenience.

Sincerely yours,
Andrew Marlow, MD

Chapter 92

Marlow

Partly to distract myself from my visions and partly to see what he was doing, I went to visit Robert one time too many. I'd been in that morning, a Friday. When I returned to his room in the afternoon, I found him standing at the easel I had given him. It had been a long week for me, and I'd been sleeping poorly. I wished Mary would visit more often; I always seemed to rest well in her arms. As usual, I thought of her when I entered Robert's room. I wondered, in fact, how he could look at me and not see the secrets I was keeping, and it reminded me how little I really knew about him. I could not hear his life through those well-washed old clothes, his frayed yellow shirt and paint-stained trousers, or even through the warm color of his face and arms below the rolled sleeves, the curl of his hair with its threads of silver. I could not even know him through the reddened, weary eyes he turned on me. Not knowing enough, how could I release him? And if I released him, how would I ever stop wondering about his love for a woman dead since 1910?

He was painting her today—no surprise there—and I sat down in the armchair to watch. He didn't turn his easel away. I assumed that was a kind of pride, like his silence. She was faceless; he was still roughing in the rose color of her gown, the black sofa on which she sat. Part of his skill was this ability to paint without a model, I realized. Had that been one of her gifts to him?

Suddenly it was too much for me. I jumped out of my chair and took a step forward. He painted, arm raised, brush moving, ignoring me. "Robert!"

He said nothing, but he turned his eyes toward me for a split second, then went back to the canvas. I'm reasonably tall, reasonably fit, as I've said, although I don't have anything like Robert's imposing casual presence. I wondered what it would be like to punch him. Kate surely must have wanted to. And Mary. I could say, *I did it for her. You can talk to anybody you want.* "Robert, look at me."

He lowered his brush, giving me the patient, amused face I remember consciously turning on my parents as a teenager. I didn't have any teenagers of my own, but this attention, which should have counted for something, made me angrier than any outburst on his part ever could have. He seemed to wait for the tiresome interruption to pass, so that he could paint again.

I cleared my throat, steadying myself. "Robert, do you understand my desire to help you? Would you like to lead a normal life again—a life out there?" I waved at the window, but I knew I'd already lost this round with the word "normal."

He turned back to the easel.

"I want to help you, but I can't possibly do so unless you participate. I have gone to some trouble for you, you know, and if you are well enough to paint, you are surely well enough to speak."

His face was gentle but closed now.

I waited. Could anything be worse than yelling at a patient? (Sleeping with his former lover, perhaps?) I felt my voice begin to rise in spite of myself. What angered me most was my sense that he knew I did not simply want to help him for his own sake.

"Damn you, Robert," I said quietly instead of shouting, but my voice shook. It came over me that in all my years of training and practice, I had never behaved this way with anyone.

Never. I was still looking at him as I left the room. I wasn't afraid he would lunge at me or throw something—I was the one at risk of that myself. I wished later I hadn't kept an eye on him at that moment, because it forced me to see the change in his expression; he didn't return my glance, but he raised his face toward the canvas, and it wore a faint smile. Triumph: a paltry victory, but probably the only kind he had these days.

Chapter 93

1879

Yves stays half a week, walking the beach with a hand on Olivier's shoulder, kissing Béatrice on the back of her neck when she bends to pin up her hair. He is having a veritable holiday—in private he calls it a honeymoon. He loves the view of the Channel; it *rests* him enormously. But he must go back, to his regret, and he apologizes for having to leave them so soon. She does not dare look at Olivier the entire time Yves is there, except to pass salt or bread at the table. It is intolerable, and yet there are moments when she glances at herself in the mirror, or sees them strolling together, and feels surrounded by love, beloved by both, as if this is the right thing. They take a hansom with Yves to the station in Fécamp; Olivier demurs, but Yves insists that he must come along so that Béatrice will not have to ride back alone. The train exhales loudly; the wheels begin their husky motion. Yves leans out the window and waves, his hat in his hand.

They ride back to the hotel and sit on the veranda, talking about ordinary matters. They paint on the beach and eat their dinner—an old couple now that the third guest is gone. By some mutual consent, she does not visit Olivier's room again, nor does he visit hers. Every wall between them has fallen already, and she does not long for a repetition. It is enough to have this silent memory in their midst. The moment that he—or the moment that she—or the way his tears of surprise and pleasure fell onto her face. She had thought he would belong to her forever after such a transgression, but it is equally the other way around.

In the train back to Paris, when they are alone, he holds her hand like a bird in his large glove, and kisses it before she alights to claim her luggage. They speak very little. She knows, without asking, that he will come to dinner the next day. Together they will tell Papa almost all about their vacation. They will begin work together on their great painting. She will remember him, his long smooth body, his silvery hair, the young man in love inside him, until the day she herself dies. He will always be near her, a spirit of the Channel.

CHAPTER 94

Marlow

Henri Robinson's reply came as a shock.

Monsieur le Docteur:

Thank you for your letter. I think your patient must be a man named Robert Oliver. He came to see me in Paris nearly ten years ago, and again more recently, and I have good reason to believe that he took something valuable from my apartment on his second visit. I cannot pretend to want to assist him, but if you can bring some light to this matter I will be happy to see you myself. I will consider allowing you to view The Swan Thieves. *Please be aware that it is not for sale. Shall we say during the first week of April, any morning, if that suits you?*

Respectfully yours,
Henri Robinson

CHAPTER 95

Marlow

I wished devoutly that I could take Mary to Paris with me, but she had to teach. From the way she declined, I knew that she wouldn't have come even if I'd arranged the trip to fall during her next vacation; it was too big a gift for her to accept from me after Acapulco. Once had been a pleasure, but twice would be a debt. I found a book on the Musée d'Orsay, which I knew she'd longed to see, and she turned the leaves over slowly.

Still, she shook her head, standing in my kitchen, her long hair catching the light. A decisive shake: no. It was less a rejection than quiet self-knowledge on her part. She was making breakfast for us as we talked, a surprising gesture of domesticity. It was the fourth time she'd stayed over at my apartment—I could still count those nights. When she departed, even earlier than I—for her university studio or classroom, or for the café where she liked to draw on lighter workdays—I left the bed unmade behind me and closed the door to the bedroom, to hold her scent. Now she flipped over four eggs and some bacon and set them in front of me with a grin. "I can't go to France with you, but I can cook you an egg, this once. Don't get any ideas, though."

I poured coffee. "If you go to France with me, you can have those nice hard-boiled eggs in little cups with your bread and jam, and much better coffee than this."

"*Merci*. You know the answer."

"Yes. But what will you say when I ask you to marry me, if I can't even get you onto a plane to France?"

She froze. I had uttered it casually, almost not knowing I was going to, but now I understood I'd been planning it for weeks. She was playing with her fork. My obstacle, I thought, too late, took the form of Robert Oliver, lounging somewhere behind me. No need to ask her what held her gaze, no point in pointing out that there was no one there, or that the Robert she'd known had been replaced by a lethargic man sketching on an institutional bed. Had Robert ever asked her to marry him, even jokingly? The answer, I thought, was written in the lines around her mouth, her eyes, the droop of her hair.

Then she laughed—"If I've gotten this far without marriage, Doctor, I don't need it now"—and surprised me, in that way she had of knowing things I hadn't thought someone of her generation would, with a line from Cole Porter: "'For husbands are a boring lot and only give you bother.'"

"*Kiss Me, Kate,*" I said promptly, slapping the table. "You're too young to get married without your mother's permission anyway. And I'm no cradle robber, no Humbert Humbert, no—"

She laughed and flicked a drop of orange juice at me. "Cease the flattery." She picked up her fork again and cut into her eggs. "When you're eighty, buddy, I'll be—"

"Older than I am now, but look how young that is. 'Come on and kiss me, Kate!'" I cried, and she laughed more naturally and came around the table to sit in my lap. But there was a strange echo in the room, the name, Robert's Kate. We felt it together without a word. Perhaps to silence it, Mary kissed me hard. Then I gave her my last piece of bacon, and we finished breakfast like that, Mary on my lap, keeping out bad spirits by huddling together.

*

I had a great deal to do before I traveled, and it took me much of the morning, the day before I flew to Paris, to get through my paperwork. I saw Robert at noon and sat with him in the usual silence; I had no intention of telling him yet that I had decided to visit Henri Robinson. He would probably notice my absence, but I was willing to let him wonder where I was, since he wouldn't be willing to ask anyone.

There was something else I had to take care of, too. Around four o'clock I went back to Robert's room, when I knew he was painting on the lawn. His door was open, to my relief, so that I didn't have quite the sense of breaking and entering that I might otherwise have felt, although I did look over my shoulder at the corridor a couple of times. I found the letters on the top shelf of the cabinet, a neat package. There was pleasure in having the originals in my hand again, as if I'd missed them without knowing it—the worn paper, the brown ink, Béatrice's elegant penmanship. Robert might well be upset when he discovered they were missing, and he would guess who had taken them again. There was no help for that. I put them in my briefcase and went quietly out.

Mary spent the night at my apartment. I woke once to find her awake, too, and staring at me in the half dark. I put a hand to her face. "Why aren't you asleep?"

She sighed and turned to kiss my fingers. "I have been. Then something startled me. Then I started thinking about you in France."

I pulled her silky head to my neck. "What?"

"I feel jealous, I think."

"You know I invited you."

"Not that. I didn't want to come. But in a way, you're going to see *her,* aren't you?"

"Don't forget that I am not—"

"You are not Robert. I know. But you can't imagine what it was like, living with them."

I struggled up onto my elbow to see into her face. "Them? What are you talking about?"

"With Robert and Béatrice." Her voice was sharp and clear, not fuzzed with sleep. "I think that's something I could say only to a psychiatrist."

"And that's something I could hear only from the love of my life." I saw the glint of her teeth in the dark; I caught her face and kissed her. "Stop it, my darling, and go to sleep."

"Please just let her die properly, the poor woman."

"I will."

She found the place for her forehead on my shoulder, and I arranged her hair around her in a wide shawl before she slept again. This time I lay awake myself. I thought of Robert, sleeping, or not sleeping, at Goldengrove, the bed a little small for his massive frame. Why had he gone to France those two times? Had it been because he wondered, as I did, whose hand had painted *Leda*? Had he found an answer? Maybe it really would have been too strong a subject for a woman, in a Catholic country in 1879. If Robert believed his Mistress Melancholy had done the painting herself, why would he have attacked it? Had he been jealous of the swan for some reason I couldn't fathom? I thought of getting up, dressing, taking my car keys, and driving to Goldengrove. I knew the alarm codes, the front desk procedures, the night staff. I would go silently to Robert's room, knock on the door, open it, and shake him awake. Startled out of sleep, he would speak. *I took a knife with me to the museum. I attacked her because . . .*

I put my face against Mary's hair and waited for the urge to pass.

Chapter 96

Marlow

De Gaulle Airport was noisier than I remembered, and somehow larger, more bleakly institutional. Three years after this, arriving on a delayed honeymoon, I would see the same terminal cleared by police and hear the explosion from a safe vantage behind some shops: they were detonating a suitcase left unattended in the middle of one of the great halls. The noise went through our nerves, an echo of the bomb that turned out not to be inside. But in 2000, nerves were quieter and I was alone.

I took a cab to the hotel Zoe had recommended: my room there was little more than a concrete box, one window looking down the central building shaft, my bed hard and creaky; but it was steps away from the Gare de Lyon and just up the street from a bistro with the requisite awning, which the manager rolled up in the mornings by means of a large crank. I dropped my bags and went there for the first of many meals, this one satisfying beyond belief after the plane flight, the coffee steaming and strong, with plenty of milk. Then I returned to my box of a room and slept through even the caffeine for a drugged hour. When I woke, the day seemed half gone. I showered under hot water, groaning with the pleasure of it; I shaved, walked around the city a little with a pocket guidebook.

Henri lived in Montmartre, but I wouldn't visit him until

tomorrow morning anyway. A few minutes after leaving the hotel, I glimpsed the domes of Sacré-Coeur against the sky. I remembered landmarks from my previous visit, a good twelve or thirteen years earlier. The guidebook reminded me that the dreamlike white church had been built as a symbol of government power, after the decapitation of the Paris Commune. I couldn't bring myself to sightsee, however, and I wandered instead; the book stayed in my pocket most of the rest of the day, except once when I lost my way far from the hotel, along the Seine, looking at bookstalls. It was damp weather, somewhere between warm and cool, sunlight breaking through now and then to make the water shine. I wished I had not stayed away so long, when all this was a mere plane ride from Washington. On a stairway leading down to the surface of the river, I spread my handkerchief over the slimy stone and sat sketching the boat—a restaurant edged with pots of flowers—moored on the other side.

I was also eager to see the Béatrice de Clerval paintings at the Musée d'Orsay before closing time; those at the Musée de Maintenon could wait until tomorrow, after my visit to Henri Robinson. I followed the river to the Musée d'Orsay; I had missed it when I was last in Paris, and it had been newly open then. I won't try to describe the effect of the huge glass-roofed hall, its array of sculpture, the splendid ghost of a train station that had once served Béatrice de Clerval's generation and others. It was stunning—I lingered there for several hours.

I went first to Manet and the heady sensation of standing in front of *Olympia,* meeting her challenging gaze. Then I stumbled on a beautiful surprise—a Pissarro canvas showing a house in Louveciennes in winter. I didn't remember ever having seen this anywhere, the reddish house and sinuous trees laden with snow, the snow underfoot, the woman and little girl hand in hand and bundled up against the cold. I thought of Béatrice and her daughter, but this painting was dated 1872, years before Aude's birth. There were other winter scenes in the gallery, too—Monet and Sisley, more Pissarro, *effets d'hiver,* snow and carts and fences, trees and more snow. I saw heavy skies above the church towers of their adopted villages—Louveciennes, Marly-le-Roi, and others—and over the parks in Paris. Like Béatrice, they had loved their gardens in winter.

With Sisley and Pissarro, I found two Béatrice de Clervals, one a portrait of a golden-haired girl sewing—she must have been the maid described in the letters. The other was a painting of a swan floating pensively on brown water, an everyday swan, not divine. Béatrice had practiced that form with rigor, I thought, perhaps in preparation for the painting I would see tomorrow at Henri Robinson's. I found a landscape by Olivier Vignot, a bucolic scene, cows grazing, a field, a row of poplars, lazy fertile clouds. Perhaps Béatrice had respected his work more than I'd imagined; it was a skillful painting, although hardly innovative. The plaque dated it to 1854. Béatrice, I thought, had been three years old at the time.

When I'd finished my tour, I found a steak and *frites* for dinner and went back to the hotel. There, despite my efforts to read a chapter from an excellent history of the Franco-Prussian War, I slept for thirteen hours, waking the next morning at a reasonable time and to the equally reasonable explanation that I was no longer a young traveler.

Chapter 97

Marlow

Henri Robinson's street in Montmartre was steep—not narrow but picturesque anyway, with wrought-iron balconies. I found the address and stood in the street for a few minutes before ringing—the bell sounded audibly, although his apartment sat on the second level of the building. I made my way up; the stairs were dark and dusty, and I wondered how a man of ninety-eight could negotiate them. The only door on the second floor opened before I could touch it; an old woman stood there, a woman in a brown dress, heavy stockings and shoes. For a weird moment, I thought I was looking at Aude de Clerval. The woman wore an apron and a quick smile, and she used a few words I didn't understand to show me into the sitting room. Aude, had she lived until now, would have been 120.

Henri Robinson held court in a jungle—plants filled the space, in orderly profusion. The room was sunny, at least on the street side, the light filtering in between bands of rose-colored silk. The walls were a soft pale jade, as were a pair of closed doors. There were paintings everywhere, not in the kind of careful display I'd seen at the home of his old friend Caillet, but crowded into every available space. Near Henri's chair was a head in oils that I thought must be Aude de Clerval, a long-faced, blue-eyed, aging woman with a coiffure from the 1940s or '50s. I wondered if that was the portrait of her Pedro Caillet claimed to have painted; I saw no signature. There were also some little pieces that might have been by Seurat—pointillist work anyway—and a host of paintings from between the wars. I didn't see anything that looked like the work of Béatrice de Clerval, and no sign of a painting that might be called *The Swan Thieves*. The niches and shelves that did not sag with books displayed a collection of celadon ceramics, which could have been Korean, and old. Perhaps I could ask him about them later.

Henri Robinson sat in an armchair nearly as worn as himself. When I entered, he got up slowly, despite my attempts at protest, my clumsy few words of French, and extended a transparent hand. He was a little shorter than I, skeletal in frame but able to stand upright once he straightened. He wore a striped dress shirt, dark trousers, and a red cardigan with gold buttons. His remaining wisps of hair were combed back, his nose as transparent as his hands, his cheeks chafed red, his eyes brown but fading behind glasses. It would have been a striking face in youth, dark-eyed and with high cheekbones, a fine, straight nose. His hands and arms trembled, but his handshake was decisive. It went through me like a chill that I was touching a hand that had caressed Béatrice's daughter, whose own hand Béatrice had once no doubt held and stroked.

"Good morning," he said in accented but clear English. "Please come in and sit down." The blue-veined hand again, pointing to a chair. "Too many newspapers." His smile showed teeth startlingly young and orderly—dentures. I cleared the papers from a second chair and waited until he'd lowered himself on skinny arms into his own seat.

"Monsieur Robinson, thank you for seeing me."

"It is a pleasure," he said. "Although, as I told you, the name of the man you mentioned is not a favorite with me."

"Robert Oliver is ill," I told him. "I suspect he was ill when he took these from you, because his condition is a cyclical one, and chronic. But I know it must have been upsetting to you." I drew the letters carefully from the inside pocket of my jacket; I had enclosed them in a folded envelope, from which I removed them before placing the bundle in his hands.

He looked down in astonishment, then at me.

"They are yours?" I asked.

"Yes," he said. His face worked a little, his nose reddening and twitching, his voice breaking, as if the ghost of tears had invaded him for a moment. "They belonged, in fact, to Aude de Clerval, with whom I lived for more than twenty-five years. Her mother gave them to Aude when she was dying."

I thought of Béatrice, not young and earnest but middle-aged, perhaps white-haired, wracked by illness, consumed in what should have been her prime. She had died in her late fifties. My age, more or less, and I didn't even have a daughter to take leave of.

I nodded soberly to show my sympathy for the outrage he had endured. Henri Robinson's eyesight seemed sharp enough through the gold-rimmed glasses. "My patient—Robert Oliver—probably didn't realize the hurt he might cause by this theft. I can't ask you to forgive him, but perhaps you can understand. He was in love with Béatrice de Clerval."

"I know that," the old man said rather sharply. "I, too, know about obsession, if that is what you mean."

"I've read the letters, I should tell you. I had them translated. And I don't see how anyone could avoid loving her."

"She was apparently very sweet, *tendre*. You know that I loved her also, through her daughter. But how did you come to be interested in her, Dr. Marlow?"

He had remembered my name.

"Because of Robert Oliver." I described Robert's arrest, my struggles to get to know him during his first weeks with me, the face he sketched and later painted in place of any speech, my need to understand the vision that drove him. Henri Robinson listened with his hands together, sweatered shoulders hunched, simian and absorbed. Now and then he blinked but said nothing. I went on to tell him, with a strange feeling of relief, about my interviewing Kate, about Robert's paintings of Béatrice, about Mary and the story Robert had told her of encountering Béatrice's face in a crowd. I did not mention that I had been to see Pedro Caillet. I could deliver his greetings later, if that seemed right.

He listened in silence. I thought of my father—a young man, complete with car and girlfriend, by contrast with Henri Robinson. Robinson, like my father, would guess a great deal even if I didn't tell him everything. I spoke slowly and clearly, wondering a little about the extent of his English, and ashamed that I wasn't even attempting to air my rusty French. He seemed to understand me, in all senses. When I'd finished, he tapped his fingers against the bundle of letters that lay in his lap. "Dr. Marlow," he said, "I am deeply grateful to you for returning these. I understood that Robert Oliver must have stolen them—it was after his second visit that I could not find them. You know, he kept them for years."

I remembered crouching on the office floor at Kate's, reading a word: *Étretat*.

"Yes. Well, I suppose he did not tell you that either, if he does not talk anymore." Henri Robinson arranged his bony knees in front of him. "He came here the first time in the early nineties, after he read in an article about my relation to Aude de Clerval. He wrote me, and I was so touched by his enthusiasm and his evident seriousness about art that I consented to let him visit me. We talked quite a lot—yes, he was certainly speaking then. And he listened well. He was very interesting, in fact."

"Can you tell me what you talked about, Monsieur Robinson?"

"Yes, I can." He put a hand on each armrest. There was something remarkably strong about this man, with his fine nose and chin, his cobweb hair. "I have never forgotten the moment when he walked into my apartment. As you know, he is very tall, Robert Oliver, a real presence, like an opera singer. I could not help but feel a little intimidated—he was a complete stranger, and I was alone at that time. But he was charming. He sat in the chair, I think where you are sitting now, and we talked first about painting and then about my collection, which I had given to the Musée de Maintenon, except for one piece. He had gone to see it the same afternoon, and he was very impressed."

I said, "I haven't been to the Maintenon yet, but I plan to."

"In any case, we sat here and we talked, and finally he asked me if I could tell him what I knew about Béatrice de Clerval. I told him a little about her life and work, and he said that he knew much of that already from his research. He wanted to know how Aude spoke about her mother. I could see clearly that he loved Béatrice's paintings, if 'loved' is the correct word. There was something very warm in him—I felt . . . drawn to him, in fact."

Henri coughed. "So I began to tell him what I remembered from Aude—that her mother had been gentle and lively, always a lover of art but completely dedicated to her, Aude. She said that her mother never painted or sketched in all the years that Aude knew her. Never. And that she never talked about her painting with regret—she would laugh if Aude asked her about it, and say that her daughter was her happiest work and she no longer needed anything else. When she was a teenager, Aude began to draw and paint a little, and her mother was always helpful, enthusiastic, but she would never join her. Aude told me once that she begged her mother to sketch with her, and her mother said, 'I have done my last drawings, dear, and they are waiting for you.' And she refused to explain what she meant and why she did not draw anymore. It always troubled Aude."

Henri Robinson turned toward me, his dark eyes glossy with a sheen like soap on water, which might have been cataracts or might have been the reflection of his glasses. "Dr. Marlow, I am an old man, and I loved Aude de Clerval very much. She has never left me. And Robert Oliver seemed deeply interested in her story and in the story of Béatrice de Clerval, so I read him the letters. I read them to him. In retrospect, I think Aude would have wanted me to. She and I read them aloud to each other once or twice, and she said she thought they were for people who could appreciate their story. That is why I have never published them or written about them."

"You read the letters to Robert?"

"Well, I know now that I certainly should not have, but I thought he needed to hear them because he was so interested. A mistake."

I imagined Robert, propped forward on big elbows, listening while the frail man in the other chair read out Béatrice's words, and Olivier's. "Did he understand them?"

"You mean the language? Oh, I gave him a translation when he needed it. And his French is quite good, you know. Or do you mean the content of the letters? I do not know what he understood about that."

"What was his reaction?"

"When I came to the end, I saw that his face was very—how do you say?—grim. I thought he might cry. Then he said a strange thing, but to himself. 'They lived, didn't they?' And I said yes, that when one reads old letters one understands that people in the past really did live, and it is very touching. I myself was moved by reading them aloud to this stranger. But he said no, no—he meant that they had really lived, but he had not." Henri Robinson shook his head, his eyes on me. "Then I began to think he was a little odd. But I am accustomed to artists, you know. Aude was terribly strange about her history and her mother's paintings—it was a thing I liked in her." He was silent. "Before we said good-bye, Robert told me the letters had helped him to know better what Béatrice would have wanted him to paint. He said he would dedicate himself to painting her life, to her memory and her honor. He talked like a man in love with the dead, as you say—I know what that means, Doctor. I sympathize."

I had a sense, watching him, of the restless person he had once been, the highly intelligent person he still was; twenty years before, he would have been wandering around the room as he talked with me, touching the spines of his books, adjusting a painting, picking a dead leaf off a plant. Perhaps Aude had been as calm and poised as the two portraits of her I'd seen—an intense woman, full of dignity. I thought of them together, the energetic, alluring young man who might have filled her with a sense of activity, and the confident, rather aloof woman whom he had made a vocation of adoring. "Did Robert say anything else?"

Robinson shrugged. "Nothing that I can remember. But my memory is not what it was. He left soon after that. He thanked me very politely and told me that his visit to me would always be part of his art. I did not expect to see him ever again."

"But there was a second time?"

"That was a surprise and a much shorter visit, within the last two years, I think. He did not write to me before he came, so I did not know he was in Paris. One day the bell rang, and Yvonne went to answer it and brought Oliver in. I was astonished. He said he was in Paris to get background for his work, and he had decided to come see me. I was having more problems by then—I could not walk well and could not remember things sometimes. You know that I reached ninety-eight this year?"

I nodded. "Yes—congratulations."

"It is an accident, Dr. Marlow, not an honor. In any case, Robert came in, and we talked. Once, I had to get up to go to the bathroom, and he helped me walk there because Yvonne was talking on the telephone in the kitchen. He was very strong. But you see I remember all that because about a week after he left, I wanted to look at the letters, and they were gone."

"Where did you keep them?" I tried to ask it casually.

"In that drawer." He pointed with white fingers to a cabinet across the room. "You can look in it if you want. It is still empty except for one thing." He closed a hand over the letters in his lap. "Now I will be able to put them back. I knew it had to be Oliver, because I have few visitors and Yvonne would never touch them—she knows how I feel about them. You see, I gave away all the paintings, all of Béatrice's paintings, some years ago. All except for *The Swan Thieves*. They are at the Musée de Maintenon. I know I could die at any time. Aude wanted us to keep them for ourselves, but also to protect them, so I made the best decision I could. *The Swan Thieves* is different. I am still waiting to know for certain what to do with it. For a few minutes during the first visit of Robert Oliver, I thought I might even give it to him someday. Thank God I did not. The letters were all I had from Aude's love for her mother. They are precious to me."

I felt rather than saw the old man's rage, couched in these delicate terms. "And did you try to get them back?"

"Of course. I wrote to Oliver at the address he had left me

the first time, but my letter was returned after a month. Someone wrote on it that there was no person of that name at the address."

Kate, perhaps, in a rage herself. "And you never heard from him again?"

"I did. This made it worse, I think. He sent me a note. It is for now the only item in that drawer."

Chapter 98

Marlow

With Henri Robinson's eyes on me, I rose and went slowly to the cabinet he had indicated. It seemed unreal to me that I was in this overstuffed apartment with a man nearly a century old, rummaging again through the past of a patient who had not only assaulted a work of art but also stolen private papers, as it turned out. And yet I couldn't quite bring myself to condemn Robert. Jet lag swept over me; I thought of Mary's arms and wanted suddenly to go home to her. Then I remembered that she wasn't at my home but at hers. What did four nights and one breakfast mean to someone young and free? I opened the drawer with weakening fingers.

Inside was an envelope dated before Robert's attack on *Leda:* no return address, a Washington postmark, international postage. Inside that, a folded slip of notepaper.

Dear Mr. Robinson,

Please forgive my borrowing your letters. I WILL get them back to you sooner or later, but I am working on some major paintings, and I must read them every day. They are wonderful letters, full of her, and I hope you agree with this. I have no excuse for myself, but maybe in the end they are safer with me. I remembered enough from them to do a series of paintings already that I think are my best so far, but I NEED TO BE ABLE *to read them every single day. Sometimes I get up and read them at night. My new series, an important one, will show the world that Béatrice de Clerval was one of the great women of her time and one of the great artists of the nineteenth century. She stopped painting too young. I must continue for her. Someone must avenge her, since she might have continued to paint for decades if she had not been cruelly prevented. And by what? You and I know that she was a genius. You can understand how I have come to love and admire her. Perhaps you know what it is like not to be able to paint when you want to, even if you are not a painter yourself.*

Thank you for your help and for the use of her words, and please forgive my decision. I will make it up to you a thousand times over.

Yours,

Robert Oliver

I cannot describe how this letter made my heart sink. It was the first time I'd heard Robert speak at length in his own voice, at least the voice of that moment. The repetitions in it, the irrationality, the fantasies about the importance of his mission, all indicated mania. The self-centered theft of another person's treasure saddened me as much as its significance seemed to elude him; at the same time I understood this as the loss of contact with reality that had culminated in his assaulting *Leda*. I started to put the letter back, but Henri Robinson stopped me with a gesture. "Keep it, if you like."

"Sad and shocking," I said, but I put it inside my jacket. "We must try to remember that Robert Oliver is a psychiatric patient, and that the letters have indeed come back to you. But I can't, and shouldn't, defend him."

"I am glad that you have returned my letters," he said simply. "They are very private. For the sake of Aude, I would never publish them. I was afraid Robert Oliver would do that."

"Perhaps in that case you should destroy them," I suggested, although I could hardly bear the thought myself. "They may one day be of too much interest to some art historian."

"I will think about that." He folded his hands together with interlaced fingers.

Don't think too long, I wanted to tell him.

"I'm so sorry." He looked up at me. "I have completely forgotten my manners. Would you like some coffee? Some tea, perhaps?"

"Thank you, no. You're very kind, and I won't keep you much longer." I sat opposite him again. "Could I ask you one more favor without trespassing on your hospitality?" I hesitated. "Could I see *The Swan Thieves*?"

He looked at me gravely, as if considering everything we had already said. Had he given me any inaccurate or invented information? I would never know. He put steepled fingers to his chin. "I did not show it to Robert Oliver, and I am glad now that I did not."

This took me by surprise. "Didn't he ask to see it?"

"I think he did not know I owned it. It is not well known. It is private information, in fact." Then his head snapped up. "How did *you* know? How did you know I have it?"

I would have to say what I should have said earlier, and I feared it might open old wounds. "Monsieur Robinson," I said, "I wanted to tell you before, but was uncertain—I went to see Pedro Caillet in Mexico. He was very kind to me, as you've been, and that was how I learned about you. He sent you warm greetings."

"Ah, Pedro and his greetings." But he smiled almost impishly. There was friendship still between these men, with their stale, long-forgiven rivalry across an ocean. "So he told you that he sold Aude *The Swan Thieves,* and you believed him?"

It was my turn to stare. "Yes. That's what he said."

"I think he really believes that, poor old cat. In fact, he tried to buy it from Aude himself. They both considered it extraordinaire. Aude bought it from the estate of Armand Thomas, a gallery owner in Paris. It had never been exhibited, which is strange, and it has not been exhibited since then either. Aude would never have sold it to Pedro, or anyone else, because her mother told her it was the only important thing she had ever painted. I do not know how Armand Thomas got it." He closed his hands over the letters in his lap. "*The Swan Thieves* was one of the only paintings that remained from the failure of the Thomas business—Armand's older brother, Gilbert, was a good painter, but not a good businessman. They appear in Béatrice's and Olivier's letters, you know. I have always felt they must have been rather mercenary types. Certainly not great friends of painters, like Durand-Ruel. They also made far less money in the end. They did not have his taste."

"Yes, I've seen two of Gilbert's paintings in the National Gallery," I said. "Including, of course, *Leda*, the one Robert attacked."

Henri Robinson nodded. "You may go in to see *The Swan Thieves*. I think I will stay here. I see it several times a day." He gestured toward a closed door at the end of the sitting room.

I went to the door. Beyond it was a small bedroom, apparently Robinson's own, judging from the prescription bottles on the bureau and bedside table. The double bed wore a green damask spread. Matching drapes hung at the single window, and again there were shelves of books. The sunlight was dim here, and I turned on the light, feeling Henri's gaze but not wanting to close a door between us. At first I thought there was a window above the head of the bed, looking into a garden, and then I thought there was a painting of a swan there. But I saw at once that it was a mirror, hung to reflect the one painting in the room, on the opposite wall.

*

I have to stop here, to catch my breath. *The Swan Thieves* is not easily put into words. I had expected the beauty in it; I had not expected the evil. It was a largish canvas, about four feet by three, rendered in the bright palette of the Impressionists. It showed two men in rough clothes, brown-haired, one with strangely red lips. They were moving stealthily toward the viewer, and toward a swan that rose in alarm out of the reeds. A reversal, I thought, of Leda's fright: now the swan was victim, not victor. Béatrice had painted the bird with hasty, living strokes that made its very wing tips seem real; it was a blur, hastening up out of its nest, a suggestion of lily pads and gray water beneath, a curve of white breast, gray around its numb dark eye, a panic of failed flight, the water churning under a yellow-and-black foot. The thieves were too near already, and the larger man's hands were about to close over the swan's straining neck; the smaller man looked ready to heave himself forward and catch the body.

The contrast between the swan's grace and the coarseness of the two men shone clearly through the rapid brushwork. I had studied the face of the larger man before, in the National Gallery; it was the face of an art dealer counting coins, too eager now, intent on his quarry. If this was Gilbert Thomas, of course, the other man must be his brother. I had seldom seen such skill in a painting, nor such desperation. Perhaps she had given herself thirty minutes, perhaps thirty days. She had thought deeply about this image and then produced it with speed and passion. And after that, if Henri was correct, she had set down her brush and never picked it up again.

I must have stood rooted there a long time, staring, because I felt a sudden fatigue wash over me—the hopelessness of imagining other lives. This woman had painted a swan, it had meant something to her, and none of us would ever know what. Nor would it matter, beyond the vehemence of this work. She was gone and we were here, and someday we would all be gone, too, but she had left a painting.

Then I thought of Robert. He had never stood in front of this image and puzzled over its passionate misery. Or had he? How long had Henri Robinson, old and independent, been safely out of the way? I'd seen just one bathroom so far, near the entrance to the apartment, and there was none here, off the bedroom—the apartment was old, eccentric. Would Robert have stopped at opening a closed door? No—he had surely seen *The Swan Thieves;* why else would he have returned to Washington in a rage that would shortly after overflow in the National Gallery? I thought of his portrait of Béatrice in Greenhill, her smile, her hand clasping a silk robe over her breast. Robert had wanted to see her happy. *The Swan Thieves* was full of threat and entrapment—and perhaps revenge as well. Probably Robert understood her grief in a way that I, thank God, never could. He had not needed to look at this painting to understand it.

I remembered Robinson, then, pinioned in his chair, and went back into the salon. I knew I would never see *The Swan Thieves* again. I had spent five minutes with it, and it had changed the look of the world.

"Ah, you are impressed." He made an openhanded gesture: approval.

"Yes."

"Do you think it is her greatest work?"

"You would know better than I."

"I am tired now," Henri said—as Caillet had said to me and Mary, I suddenly remembered. "But I would like you to come back tomorrow, after you have seen my collection at the Maintenon. Then you can tell me if I have kept the best one for myself."

I went quickly to take his hand. "I'm sorry I've stayed so

long. And I would be honored to come back. What time tomorrow?"

"I take my nap at three o'clock. Come in the morning."

"I can't thank you enough."

We shook hands and he smiled—those artificially perfect teeth again. "I enjoyed our talk. Perhaps I will decide to forgive Robert Oliver after all."

Chapter 99

Marlow

The Musée de Maintenon was in Passy, near the Bois de Boulogne and perhaps near Béatrice de Clerval's family home, although I had no idea how to find that and had forgotten to ask Henri. Probably it wouldn't be a museum anyway; I doubted her brief career would have warranted a plaque. I took the metro and then walked a few blocks, crossing a park full of children in bright-colored jackets swarming over swings and modernist climbing structures. The museum itself was a tall, cream-colored, nineteenth-century building with heavily decorated plaster ceilings. I wandered around the first floor and through a gallery of works by Manet, Renoir, Degas, few of which I'd seen before, then into a smaller room that housed the Robinson gift, paintings by Béatrice de Clerval.

She had been more prolific than I'd realized, and she'd begun painting young; the earliest piece in the collection dated from her eighteenth year, when she had still been living in her parents' home and studying with Georges Lamelle. It was a lively effort, although without the skill of her later paintings. She had worked hard—as hard in her way as Robert Oliver had in his obsession. I'd imagined her as a wife, the young mistress of a household, and even as a lover; but I had forgotten about the strong workaday painter she must have been in order to complete all these pictures and to grow in technique from year to year. There were portraits of her sister, sometimes with a baby in her arms, and there were glorious flowers, perhaps from Béatrice's own garden. There were small sketches in graphite and a couple of watercolors of gardens and the coast. There was a cheerful portrait of Yves Vignot as a newly married man.

I turned away with reluctance. The third floor of the Musée de Maintenon was lined with enormous Monet canvases from Giverny, mainly of water lilies, most of them from very late in his career, executed almost abstractly. I had never understood before how many water lilies he had actually managed to paint—acres of them, spread all over Paris now. I bought a handful of postcards, some of them gifts for Mary's studio walls, and left the museum to stroll in the Bois de Boulogne. There was a boat with a canopy pulling up to the shore of a little lake there, as if expressly to ferry me across; it went to an island with a grand house on it. I paid and stepped in, followed by a French family with two small children, all dressed for a special occasion. The smaller girl stole a look at me and returned my smile before hiding her face in her mother's lap.

The house turned out to be a restaurant, with shaded outdoor tables, blooming wisteria, frightening prices. I had coffee and a pastry and let the sun on the water lull me. No swans, I realized, although they would have been there in Béatrice's day. I pictured Béatrice and Olivier by the water with their easels, his quiet coaching, her attempts to catch the swan rising out of the reeds. Rising in flight or landing? And had I re-created their conversations too freely, in imagination?

In spite of my rest on the island, I was bone-weary by the time I reached the Gare de Lyon. The bistro near the hotel was open, and the waiter seemed to consider me an old friend already, exploding the myth that all Parisians mistreat foreigners. He smiled as if he understood what my day had been like and how badly I needed a glass of red wine; when I left, he smiled again and held the door for me and returned my "Au revoir, monsieur" as if I had been dining there for years.

I'd meant to find a place to call Mary with my new phone card, but on my return to the hotel I fell into bed and slept like the dead, without pretending to read first. Henri and Béatrice crowded my sleep; I woke with a start that had some connection to Aude de Clerval's face. Robert was waiting, and I was supposed to call him, not Mary. I woke and slept, and overslept.

Chapter 100

It is an early morning in June of 1892, and the two people waiting on a provincial train platform wear the conscious, alert look of travelers who have been up since before dawn, neatly dressed and standing aloof from the stirring of the village. The taller one is a woman in her prime, the other a girl of eleven or twelve with a basket on one arm. The woman is dressed in black and wears her black bonnet tied firmly under her chin. The veil makes her see the world as sooty, and she longs to push it up, to replenish for herself the colors of the ocher station and the field across the track: gold-green grasses and the first poppies of the summer, which show cadmium even through her twilit netting. But she keeps her hands firmly on her purse, her veil over her face. Their village is strictly conventional, at least for women, and she is a lady among villagers.

She turns to her companion. "Didn't you want to bring our book?" The last few nights they have been reading from a translation of *Great Expectations*.

"*Non, maman.* But I have my embroidery to finish."

The woman reaches out a hand cased in fine black lace to touch the girl's cheek where it curves down to a mouth that matches her own. "In time for Papa's birthday, after all?"

"If it turns out well enough." The girl checks in her basket, as if her project is alive and needs constant care.

"It will." For a moment the woman is flooded with a sense of rushing time, which has caused this flower, her beauty, to grow tall and articulate overnight. She can still feel her daughter's robust baby legs in her arms, pushing upright in her lap. The memory can be summoned at a moment's notice, and she summons it often: mingled pleasure and regret. But she doesn't regret for a moment standing here, a woman alone in her heart, past forty, a woman with a doting husband waiting in Paris, a woman mature and sheathed in mourning. In the last year, they have lost the kind blind man who had the place of a father in her heart. Now there is a different cause for sadness as well.

But she feels also the course of a life advancing as it should: a child's growth, a death that brings relief as well as loss, the dressmaker sewing something a little more fashionable than what she'd worn when her mother died years ago—skirts have changed again since then. The child has all this ahead of her, with her basket of embroidery, her birthday dreams, her love of her papa before any other man. Béatrice has not dressed her daughter in unrelieved black; instead, the girl wears a white dress with gray collar and cuffs, a black sash around the pretty waist that is still thin but will soon be shapely. She takes the child's hand and kisses it through her veil, surprising them both.

The train to Paris is seldom late; this morning it comes a little early, a distant rumble interrupting the kiss, and they both arrange themselves to wait. The child always imagines the train crashing into the village itself, smashing houses, piling up old stones and raising clouds of dust, overturning chicken coops and wrecking the market stalls—a world *bouleversé* like one of the prints in her book of nursery rhymes, old ladies holding their aprons up and running away on the wooden sabots that seem an extension of their big feet. A comic disaster, and then the dust settling and everything coming to rights in an instant as people like Maman climb quietly into the train. Maman does everything quietly, with dignity—she reads quietly to herself, she turns your head quietly a little more to the right when you sit for her to braid your hair, she touches your cheek quietly.

Maman also has sudden moments that Aude recognizes in herself but has no way of knowing yet as the moments of youth that never leave us—the surprising kiss of the hand, a laughing embrace of Papa's head and hat as he sits reading his paper on the garden bench. She looks beautiful even dressed in mourning, as they now are for Aude's grandfather and more recently for the death of Papa's uncle in faraway Algeria, where he went to live years ago. Or she will catch Maman standing at the back window watching the rain fall over the meadow, and see the rare sadness in her eyes. Their house in the village is at the edge of all the others, so that you can leave the garden directly for the fields; there is a line of darker woods beyond those fields where Aude may not go except with one of her parents.

In the train, once the conductor has stowed their luggage, Aude settles herself in imitation of her mother. Her composure is brief; after a moment she jumps up again to look out the window at a pair of horses driven by her favorite coachman, Pierre le Triste, who comes daily with packages, deliveries for the small shops in the village center, sometimes for Maman herself. They know him well after all these years; Papa bought their village house the year she was born, the perfect, rounded date called 1880. Aude cannot remember a time when they didn't come to the village, just between Louveciennes and Marly-le-Roi, the train steaming through three times a week, the brief visits and long summers here with her mother and sometimes both her parents. Pierre has gotten down from his perch and seems to be conferring with the conductor outside about a package and a letter; his face is wreathed in smiles—the overflow of jollity that has earned him his affectionately ironic nickname. Through the window she can hear his voice but misses the words.

"What is it, darling?" Her mother is taking off gloves and cloak, arranging her bag and Aude's basket, their small picnic.

"It's Pierre." The conductor sees her and waves, and Pierre waves back and comes up beside the train, motioning with his big arms for her to lower the window and take a package and letter. Her mother stands to receive them and gives the package to Aude, nodding to let her know she may open it at once. It is from Papa in Paris, a delayed but welcome gift; they will see him tonight, but he has sent Aude a little ivory shawl with daisies in the corners. She folds it contentedly and drapes it across her lap. Maman has taken a jet pin from her hair and is opening her letter, which is also from Papa, although another envelope falls out of it, one with unfamiliar stamps and a shaky handwriting Aude has never seen before. Maman snatches it up and opens it with trembling care; she seems to have forgotten the new shawl. She unfolds the single page, reads it and folds it again, unfolds it and reads it, puts it slowly back in the envelope and lays it on the black silk of her lap. She leans back, puts her veil down; but Aude sees her close her eyes, sees her mouth turn upside down and quiver the way one's mouth does when one resolves not to cry. Aude drops her eyes and strokes the shawl and its daisies; what could make Maman feel this way? Should she try to comfort her, say something?

Maman is very still, and Aude looks out the window for answers, but there is only Pierre in his boots and big jacket, unloading a case of wine, which a boy trundles away in a handcart. The conductor waves goodbye to Pierre, and the train whistle screams once, twice. Nothing is wrong in the village, which has come to life everywhere.

"Maman?" she tries in a small voice.

The dark eyes behind the veil open, glittering with tears, as Aude has feared.

"Yes, my love?"

"Is something—is it bad news?"

Maman looks at her for a long time, and then she says, her voice a little unsteady, "No, not news. Just a letter from an old friend that took a long time to reach me."

"Is it from Uncle Olivier?"

Maman catches her breath, then lets it out.

"Why, it is, yes. How did you guess that, my darling?"

"Oh, because he died, I suppose, and that's very sad."

"Yes, very sad." Maman folds her hands over the envelope.

"And did he write you about Algeria and the desert?"

"Yes," she says.

"But it came too late?"

"Nothing is ever really too late," Maman says, but her words trip over a sob. This is alarming; Aude wishes the journey were over and Papa there with them. She has never seen Maman cry before. Maman smiles more than almost anyone she knows, except for Pierre le Triste. She smiles especially when she looks at Aude.

"Did you and Papa love him very much?"

"Yes, very much. And so did your grandfather."

"I wish I remembered him."

"I wish you did, too." Maman seems to have collected herself now; she pats the seat beside her, and Aude moves gratefully close, bringing her new shawl along.

"Would I have loved Uncle Olivier, too?"

"Oh yes," says Maman. "And he would have loved you. You are like him, I think."

Aude loves to be like people. “In what way?”

“Oh, full of life and curiosity, good with your hands.” Maman is silent for a second; she looks at Aude in that way Aude welcomes and cringes under, the straight, straight gaze, bottomless dark. Then she speaks. “You have his eyes, my love.”

“I do?”

“He was a painter.”

“Like you. As good as you were?”

“Oh, much better,” she says, stroking the letter. “He had more experience of life to put in his paintings, which is very important, although I didn’t know that at the time.”

“Will you save his letter?” Aude knows better than to ask to see it, although she would enjoy reading about the desert.

“Perhaps. With other letters. All the letters I have been able to keep. Some of them will be yours when you are an old lady.”

“How will I get them then?”

Maman puts her veil up and smiles, pats Aude’s cheek with her gloveless fingers. “I will give them to you myself. Or I will be sure to tell you where to find them.”

“Do you like my shawl from Papa?” Aude spreads it over her white muslin skirts and Maman’s heavy black silk.

“Very much,” Maman says. She smoothes the shawl so that it covers her letter and its big strange stamps. “And the daisies are almost as pretty as the ones you stitch. But not quite, because yours always look alive.”

CHAPTER 101

Marlow

Robinson greeted me cordially on my return to his sitting room. He did not try to stand up, but he was neatly turned out in gray flannel slacks, a black turtleneck, and a navy jacket, as if we were going out to lunch rather than planning to sit immobilized in his salon. I could hear the rattle of pans in the kitchen, to which Yvonne had retreated, and I smelled onions, butter frying. To my delight, he asked me at once to promise I would stay for lunch. I reported on the Musée de Maintenon. He made me try to recite the name of each canvas he'd given the museum. "Not bad company for our Béatrice," he said, smiling.

"No—Monet, Renoir, Vuillard, Pissarro . . ."

"She will be appreciated more in the new century."

It was hard to believe in a new century at all, here in this apartment where the same books and paintings had sat for perhaps fifty years and even the plants seemed to have been alive as long as Mary. "Paris celebrated pretty well, didn't she? The millennium?"

He smiled. "Aude remembered New Year's Eve of nineteen hundred, you know. She was almost twenty." And he himself had not yet been born. He had missed the century of Aude's childhood.

"Could I ask you one more thing, if that wouldn't be

inappropriate? It might help me in my treatment of Robert, assuming you can find it in you to be so generous."

He shrugged without objecting—a gentleman's reluctant pardon.

"I wonder what you believe yourself about the reasons Béatrice de Clerval stopped painting. Robert Oliver is very intelligent, and he must have thought deeply about this. But do you have your own theories?"

"I do not deal in theories, Doctor. I lived with Aude de Clerval. She confided everything to me." He straightened a little. "She was a great woman, like her mother, and this question troubled her. As a psychiatrist, you can see that she must have felt to blame for the end of her mother's career. Not every woman gives up everything for her child, but Aude knew her mother had, and it weighed on her all her life. As I told you, she tried to paint and draw herself, but she had no gift for it. And she never wrote anything personal about her mother or about her own life—she was a strict journalist, very professional, very brave. During the war, she covered Paris for la Résistance—another story. But she sometimes talked to me about her mother."

I waited in a silence as deep as any I'd known with Robert. At last the old man spoke again.

"It is a mystery, your coming here, and Robert before you. I am not accustomed to talking with strangers. But I will tell you something I have told no one else, certainly not Robert Oliver. When Aude was dying, she gave me this package of letters you have so kindly returned to me. With them was a note from her mother to Aude. She asked me to read the note and then to burn it, which I did. And she gave the rest of the letters into my keeping. Aude had never shown me these things before. I felt hurt, you understand, that she had not, because I had thought that we shared everything. The note to Aude from her mother said two things. One was that she loved her, Aude, more than anything in the world because she had been the child of her greatest love. And, second, that she was leaving evidence of that love with her servant, Esmé."

"Yes—I remember the name from her letters."

"You read the letters?"

I was startled. Then I realized he had been serious when he said he sometimes forgot things. "Yes—as I said, I felt I should read them for the sake of my patient."

"Ah. Well, it doesn't matter now." He patted sharp fingers on the arm of his chair; I thought I could see a worn spot under them.

"You said Béatrice left something with Esmé?"

"I suppose she did, but Esmé died, you know, soon after Béatrice. She had a sudden illness, and perhaps she simply did not manage to give to Aude whatever it was, from her mother. Aude always said that Esmé died of a broken heart."

"Béatrice must have been a kind mistress."

"If she was at all like her daughter, then she was a wonderful presence." His face was growing sad.

"And Aude never knew what this proof of love was?"

"No, we never knew. Aude wanted so much to know. I searched for information on Esmé, and discovered from a municipal record that her full name was Esmé Renard, and that she was born in, I think, 1859. But I could not find anything else. Aude's parents bought a house in the village from which Esmé came, but it was sold when Yves died. I do not even remember the name of it."

"Then she was born eight years after Béatrice," I pointed out.

He shifted in his seat and shaded his eyes as if to see me more clearly. "You know so much about Béatrice," he said, with wonder in his voice. "Do you love her, too, like Robert Oliver?"

"I have a good memory for numbers." I was beginning to think I should leave the old man before he tired again.

"In any case, I found nothing. Just before Aude died, she said her mother had been the loveliest person in the world, except"—he cleared a catch in his throat—"except for me. So perhaps she did not need to know more."

"Surely it was enough," I said, to comfort him.

"Would you like to see her portrait? Béatrice?"

"Yes, of course. I've seen the Olivier Vignot piece in the Metropolitan Museum."

"A good portrait. But I have a photograph, which is very rare—Aude said her mother did not like to be photographed. Aude would never let anyone publish it. I keep it in my album." He pushed himself up very slowly, before I could protest, and took a cane from the side of the chair. I offered my arm; he accepted, grudgingly, and we went across the room to a bookcase, where he pointed his cane. I took out the heavy leather album he'd indicated—worn bald in spots, but still embossed with a gilt rectangle on the cover. I opened it on a nearby table. Inside were family photos from several eras, and I wished I could ask to see them all: small children staring straight ahead in frilly dresses, nineteenth-century brides like white peacocks, gentlemanly brothers or friends in top hats and frock coats, hands on one another's shoulders. I wondered if Yves might be among them, perhaps that dark-bearded, bulky-shouldered man with the smile, or Aude, a little girl in a wide-skirted dress and buttoned boots. Even if they were there, or if any one of them was Olivier Vignot himself, Henri Robinson was skipping past them on his mission, and I didn't dare interrupt his fragile mind or hands. At last he stopped. "This is Béatrice," he said.

I would have known her anywhere; still, it was eerie to see her face from life. She was standing alone, one hand on a studio pedestal and the other holding back her skirt—the stiffest of poses, and yet her figure was full of energy. I knew the intensely dark eyes, the shape of her jaw, the slender neck, the abundance of curly hair swept up from her ears. She wore a long dark dress with a sort of shawl flaring around her shoulders. The sleeves of the dress were large at the top and narrowed to the wrists; her waist was small and tight, and her skirts trimmed at the bottom with a wide border of some lighter color, a cleverly geometric pattern. The lady of fashion, I thought: an artist in dress if not in practice.

The picture was professionally dated, 1895, and bore the name and street address of a Paris photographer's studio. Something veiled was pulling at me, a reminder, a figure from elsewhere, a melancholy I couldn't shake. For a long moment I thought that my memory was not much better than Henri Robinson's—far worse, in fact. Then I turned to him. "Monsieur, do you have a book of the works of—" What was it? Where was it? "I'm looking for a painting—I mean, a book of paintings by Sisley, if you happen to have one."

"Sisley?" He frowned as if I'd asked for a drink he didn't keep on hand. "I suppose I have something. It would be in that section." He jammed his cane in the air again, steadying himself on my arm. "Those are Impressionists, beginning with the original six."

I went to his shelves and began to look, slowly, and found nothing. There was a book on Impressionist landscapes, and this had Sisley in the index, but not what I was searching for. At last I found a volume of winter scenes.

"That is new." Henri Robinson was looking at it with surprising sharpness. "Robert Oliver gave it to me when he came the second time."

I held the volume—an expensive present. "Did you show him Béatrice's photograph?"

He thought for a moment. "I don't think so. I would remember that. Besides, if I had, he might have stolen that, too."

I had to admit it was a possibility. The Sisley painting was there, to my relief, as I remembered it from the National Gallery: a woman walking away down a high-walled village lane, snow under her feet, the bleakly dark branches of trees, a winter sunset. It was a stunning work, even in reproduction. The woman's dress swinging around her as she walked, the sense of urgency in her figure, the short dark cloak, the unusual blue border around the bottom of her skirt. I held the book up to Henri Robinson. "Does this look familiar to you?"

He examined it for long seconds, and then he shook his head. "Do you really think there is a connection?"

I brought the album over and rested the pictures side by side. The skirt was certainly the same. "Could this dress have been a popular model?"

Henri Robinson held my arm with tight fingers, and I thought again of my father. "I don't think that is possible. A lady would have her dresses made especially for her by a seamstress, at that time."

I was reading the text under the painting. Alfred Sisley had painted it four years before his death, in Grémière, just west of his own village, Moret-sur-Loing. "May I sit and think for a moment?" I asked. "May I see your letters just for a second?"

Henri Robinson let me help him back to his chair and handed me the letters more reluctantly. No, I couldn't read the French well enough, the script. I would have to go through my own copy, Zoe's translation, back at the hotel room. I wished now I'd brought it with me—the obvious thing to do. Mary would have figured this out by now, I felt sure, with her jaunty, disrespectful "That's it, Sherlock." I handed them back in frustration. "Monsieur, I would like to call you this evening. May

I? I'm thinking about what this connection between the photograph and Sisley's painting could mean."

"I will think, too," he told me kindly. "I doubt it can mean very much, even if the dress is similar, and when you are my age you will see that ultimately it does not matter. Now Yvonne is expecting us for lunch."

We sat across from each other at a polished dining room table, behind another closed green door. That room, too, was lined with paintings and with framed photographs of Paris between the wars, limpid, heartbreaking images: the river, the Eiffel Tower, people in dark coats and hats, a city I would never know. The chicken stewed with onions was delicious; Yvonne came out to ask how the meal tasted and stayed to drink half a glass of wine with us, wiping her brow with the back of one hand.

After lunch, Henri seemed so weary that I took my cue and prepared to leave, reminding him I would call. "And you must come to say goodbye," he told me. I helped him to his chair and sat with him a moment longer. When I got up to go, he tried to rise again, but I stopped him and shook his hand instead. He suddenly seemed to fall asleep. I rose quietly to my feet.

As I reached his sitting-room door, he called after me. "Did I mention to you that Aude was the child of Zeus?" His eyes shone, the young man looking out of the dazed old face. I should have known, I thought, that he would be the one to tell me aloud what I had thought for so long.

"Yes. Thank you, monsieur."

When I left him, his chin had sunk into his hands.

Chapter 102

Marlow

In the narrow hotel room, I lay down with Zoe's translation and located the passage:

I am a little tired today myself, and can't settle down to anything but letter writing, although my painting went well yesterday because I have found a good model, Esmé, another of my maids; she once told me, shyly, when I asked her whether she knows your own beloved Louveciennes, that hers is the very next village, called Grémière. Yves says I shouldn't torment the servants by making them sit for me, but where else could I find such a patient model?

In the store next to the hotel, I was able to buy a phone card for the equivalent of twenty dollars—lots of conversation time to the United States—and a road map of France. I'd noticed several phone booths in the Gare de Lyon, across the street, and I strolled up there with the file of letters in my hand, feeling that tremendous building hovering above me, its external sculptures eaten by acid rain. I wished for a moment that I could walk inside and board a steam train, hear it whistle and gasp, ride it out of the station into some world Béatrice would have recognized. But there were only three sleek, space-age TGVs pulled up to the near end of the rail, and the interior echoed with unintelligible departure announcements.

I sat down on the first empty bench I could find and opened

my map. Louveciennes was west of Paris, if you followed the Seine and the footsteps of the Impressionists; I'd seen several scenes from Louveciennes at the Musée d'Orsay the day I arrived, including one by Sisley himself. I found Moret-sur-Loing, where he had died. Nearby, a speck—Grémière. I shut myself into one of the phone booths and called Mary. It was afternoon at home, but she would be back by now, painting or getting ready for her evening class. To my relief, she answered after the second ring.

"Andrew? Are you all right?"

"Of course. I'm in the Gare de Lyon. It's marvelous." From where I stood I could look up through the glass and see the murals above Le Train Bleu, once the Buffet de la Gare de Lyon, the most fashionable station restaurant of Béatrice's era, or Aude's, at least. It was still serving dinner after a century. I wished acutely that Mary were with me.

"I knew you'd call."

"How are you?"

"Oh, painting," she said. "Watercolors. I'm tired of my still life right now. We ought to go on a landscape excursion when you get back."

"Absolutely. You plan it."

"Is everything all right?"

"Yes, although I'm calling about a problem. Not a practical problem, exactly—more like a puzzle for Holmes."

"I can be your Watson, then," she said, laughing.

"No—you're my Holmes. Here's the question. Alfred Sisley painted a village landscape in 1895. It shows a woman walking away down a road, wearing a dark dress with a special design around the bottom, sort of a Greek geometrical pattern. I saw it at the National Gallery, so maybe you know it."

"I don't remember that one."

"I think she's wearing Béatrice de Clerval's dress."

"What? How on earth do you know that?"

"Henri Robinson has a photograph of her in it. He's fabulous, by the way. And you were right about the letters. Robert got them in France. He took them from Henri, I'm very sorry to say."

She was silent for a moment. "And you returned them?"

"Of course. Henri is very happy to have them back."

I thought she must be brooding over Robert and his multiplying crimes, but then she said, "Even if you're sure it's the same dress, what does that matter? Maybe they knew each other and she posed for him."

"The village where he painted her is called Grémière, which was where her maid came from. Henri told me that, when Béatrice's daughter, Aude, was dying, she told Henri—if you follow me—that Béatrice gave her maid something important, some proof of her love for Aude. Aude could never figure out what it was."

"Do you want me to go to Grémière with you?"

"I wish you could. Is that what I should do?"

"I don't see how you could find anything in a whole village, and after so much time. Maybe one of them is buried there?"

"Possibly Esmé—I don't know. I suppose the Vignots would be buried in Paris."

"Yes."

"Am I doing this for Robert?" I wanted to hear her voice again, reassuring, warm, mocking.

"Don't be silly, Andrew. You're doing it for yourself—as you know perfectly well."

"And a little for you."

"And a little for me." She was silent along that endless Atlantic cable. Or was it satellite these days? It occurred to me that I should call my father while I was at it.

"Well, I'll take a quick trip up there, since it's close to Paris.

It can't be too hard to drive to that area. I wish I could go to Étretat, too."

"Maybe we'll go there together someday, depending." Her voice sounded tight now, and she cleared her throat. "I was going to wait, but may I talk with you about something?"

"Yes, of course."

"It's a little hard for me to know where to start, because," she said, "I found out yesterday that I'm pregnant."

I stood squeezing the receiver in my hand, conscious for a moment only of bodily sensation, a seismic registration of difference. "And it's—"

"It's certain."

I had meant something different. "And it's—" The door that opened in my mind at that moment seemed to hold a looming figure, although my phone booth stayed firmly shut.

"It's yours, if that's what you want to know."

"I—"

"It can't be Robert's." I could hear her resolution over the phone, her determination to tell me all this straight, the long fingers holding the receiver on the other side of an ocean. "Remember, I haven't seen Robert in months and months, or wanted to. You know full well I've never been to see him. And there is no one else. Only you. I was taking precautions, as you know, but there's a rate of failure with almost anything. I've never been pregnant before. In my life. I've always been so careful."

"But I—"

An impatient laugh. "Aren't you going to say something about it? Happiness? Horror? Disappointment?"

"Give me a moment, please."

I leaned against the inside of the booth, put my forehead on the glass, not caring what other heads had touched it in the last twenty-four hours. Then I began to cry. It had been years since

I'd cried; once, a moment of hot and angry tears after a favorite patient had committed suicide—but, most important, years before that, when I'd sat at my mother's side, holding her warm, soft, dead hand and realizing after long minutes that she could not hear me anymore, so that she wouldn't mind my giving way, even if I had promised to prop up my father. Besides, it was he who had propped me up. We were both familiar with death, from our work; but he had comforted the bereaved all his life.

"Andrew?" Mary's voice was searching over the line, anxious, hurt. "Are you that upset? You don't have to pretend—"

I rubbed my shirtsleeve over my face, catching my nose with the cuff links. "Then you won't mind marrying me?"

This time her laugh was familiar, if choked, the contagious mirth I had noticed in Robert Oliver. Had I noticed it myself? He had never laughed with me; I must have been thinking of someone else's description. I heard her grappling with her voice to steady it. "I won't mind, Andrew. I didn't think I'd ever feel like marrying anyone, but you aren't anyone. And it's not because of the baby."

At the moment I heard that phrase—the baby—my life divided itself in two, mitosis of love. One half was not even quite present yet; but those two small words, over the phone, had carved out another world for me, or doubled the one I knew.

Chapter 103

Marlow

When I had blown my nose and walked around the station for a few minutes, I dialed the number Henri had given me. "I'm going to rent a car and go out to Grémière tomorrow morning. Would you like to come along?"

"I have been thinking about this, Andrew, and I don't believe you can learn anything, but perhaps it will be a satisfaction for you to go." I took a keen pleasure in hearing him use my first name.

"Then could you come, if that doesn't sound mad? I would make it as easy for you as possible."

He sighed. "I do not often leave the house now, except to go to the doctor. I would make you slow."

"I don't mind going slowly." I refrained from telling him about my father, who still drove and saw parishioners and went for walks. He was almost ten years younger—by that point a lifetime, in terms of agility.

"Ah." He was thinking over the phone. "I suppose the worst thing that can happen is that the trip will kill me. Then you can bring my body back to Paris and bury me next to Aude de Clerval. To die of fatigue in a beautiful village would not be the worst fate." I didn't know what to say, but he was chuckling, and I laughed, too. I wished I could tell him my news. It was dreadful that Mary couldn't meet this man, who might have been her grandfather, or even her great-grandfather, similar to her in his long thin legs and sly sense of humor.

"May I get you at nine tomorrow?"

"Yes. I will not sleep all night." He hung up.

Driving in Paris is a nightmare for the foreigner. Only Béatrice could have persuaded me to do it, and I had a sense of simply closing my eyes—and sometimes opening them wider than ever before—to survive the swerving traffic, the unfamiliar signs, and the one-way streets. I was in a sweat by the time I found Henri's building, and relieved to be able to park there, if illegally and with my blinkers on, for the twenty minutes it took me and Yvonne to help him down the stairs. If I'd been Robert Oliver, I would have been able to simply pick Henri up and carry him down, but I didn't dare suggest such a thing. He settled in the front seat, and his housekeeper put a folded wheelchair and an extra blanket in the trunk, to my further relief—we would be able to navigate at least some of the village safely.

We made it alive out of one of the main boulevards, Henri directing me with surprisingly good memory, and then through suburbs, a glimpse of the wide Seine, winding roads, woods, the first villages. Just west of Paris, the terrain grew more rugged; I had never been to this area. It was a mix of steep hills and slate roofs, mellowed churches and patrician trees, fences laden with the first wave of roses. I rolled down a window in the fresh air, and Henri looked steadily around him, silent, waxen-faced, sometimes smiling.

"Thank you," he said once.

We turned off the main road at Louveciennes and drove slowly through the town, so that Henri could show me where great painters had lived and worked. "This town was nearly destroyed in the Prussian invasion. Pissarro had a house here.

He had to run away, with his family, and the Prussian soldiers who lived in it used his paintings as carpets. The town butchers used them for aprons. He lost more than a hundred paintings, years of work." He cleared his throat, coughed. "*Salauds.*"

Beyond Louveciennes, the road dipped far down; we passed the gates of a small château, a flash of gray stone and big trees. The next town was Grémière, and it was so tiny that I nearly missed the turn. I caught the sign as we entered the square, which was really just an expanse of cobblestones in front of a church. The church was very old, probably Norman, squat and heavy-towered, the beasts across the portal worn away by wind. I parked nearby, observed by a couple of old women with sensible rubber boots and shopping bags, and got the wheelchair and then Henri out of the car.

There was no need to hurry, because we didn't know why we were there. Henri seemed to enjoy our leisurely coffee in the one local café, where I parked his chair by a table outside and spread the blanket over his knees. It was a cool morning, but springlike in the sun; the chestnuts were blooming along a stretch of road to the right, towers of pink and white. I got the hang of pushing the chair—my father would probably need one of these someday—and we went down the first walled lane to see if it was the right one. I steered around a broken cobblestone. My father would, in all likelihood, live to see his grandchild.

Henri had insisted on bringing the Sisley book; after a few tries we decided that one of these walled lanes matched the painting, and I took some photos. Cedars and plane trees hung over the wall, and at the end was a house, the one Béatrice—if it were she—was walking toward in the painting. The house had blue shutters and geraniums in pots by the front door; it was tidily restored, and perhaps the owners lived in Paris. I rang the bell in vain, with Henri sitting in his chair on the front walk. "No use," I said.

"No use," he echoed.

We went to the store and asked the grocer about a family named Renard, but he shrugged pleasantly and went on weighing sausages. We went into the church, finding a way around the steps. The interior was cold, unlit, a cavern. Henri shivered and asked me to take him into the aisle, where he sat for a while with bowed head—revisiting his spirits, I thought. Next we went into the *mairie* to see if there were any records of Esmé Renard or her family. The lady behind the front desk was glad to help; she had clearly seen no one all morning and had tired of her typing, and when another official came out—I never entirely understood who he was, although in such a small place he could have been the mayor himself—they looked up some documents for us. They had files on the history of the village, and also a birth-and-death log that had originally been in the church but was now stored in a fireproof metal box. No Renards; perhaps they had not owned their home themselves but only rented it?

And then we were thanking them and leaving the building. In the entry, Henri signaled for us to stop and reached back to take my hand. "It does not matter," he said kindly. "Many things are never explained, you know. It is not really a bad thing."

"You said that yesterday, and I'm sure you're right," I said, and squeezed his hand gently; it was like a collection of warm sticks. What he said was true—my heart was already racing toward something else. He patted my arm.

It took me a moment to get the chair aimed toward the exit. When I looked up, it was there, the sketch. It hung, framed, on the old plaster wall of the entry, a bold fragment in graphite on paper: a swan, but not the victim of the painting I'd seen the day before; this one was rushing to land rather than struggling upward. Beneath it lay a human form, a graceful leg, a bit of drapery. I carefully engaged the brake on Henri's chair and took a step closer. The swan, the maiden's calf, the lovely foot, and the initials marked in one corner, hasty but recognizable, as I'd seen them against flowers and grass and near the foot of a heavy-booted thief. It was a familiar signature, more like a Chinese character than a set of Latin letters, her characteristic mark. She had made that mark a finite, too-short number of times and then stopped painting forever. The door to the office behind us was shut, and I carefully took the little frame off the wall and put it in Henri's lap, holding it so that he could not drop it by accident. He adjusted his glasses, looked closely. "Ah, *mon Dieu,*" he said.

"Let's go back in." We stared our fill and I rehung it on the wall, my fingers shaking. "They will know something about this, or someone will."

We reversed our direction and returned to the office, where Henri asked in French for information on the drawing in the entry. The young mayor—or whoever he was—was again pleased to help us. They had several drawings like that one in a drawer—he had not been here when they had been found, in a house under restoration, but his predecessor had liked that one and had it framed. We asked to see them, and after some searching he found an envelope and handed it to us. He had a phone call to attend to in his office, but we were welcome to sit there under the secretary's eye and examine the drawings, if we liked.

I opened the envelope and handed the sketches to Henri one by one. They were studies, mostly on a heavy brown paper—wings, bushes, the swan's head and neck, the figure of the girl on the grass, a hand up close and digging into the earth. With them was a thick sheet of paper, which I unfolded and gave to Henri.

"It is a letter," he said. "Just sitting here, a letter."

I nodded, and he read, stumbling, translating for me, sometimes stopping when his voice broke.

September 1879

My beautiful one,

I am writing you from what feels like the greatest possible distance, in the greatest possible agony. I fear I am separated from you forever, and it is killing me. I write you in haste from my studio, to which you must not return. Come to the house instead. I do not know how to begin. After you left this afternoon, I continued my work on the figure; it was giving me trouble and I stayed longer than I intended. At about five, when the light began to fail, a knock came; I thought it might be Esmé, returning with my shawl. Instead it was Gilbert Thomas, whom you know. He came in bowing and shut the door. I was surprised but assumed he had heard that Yves had given me a studio.

He said he had stopped first at the house and learned that I was only a few steps away. He was polite—he said he had wanted for some time to talk with me about my career, that, as I knew, his gallery was a great success and needed only new painters to make it even greater, that he had long admired my skill, etc. Bowing again, with his hat in front of him. Then he stepped up and studied our painting and asked if I had painted it by myself, with no assistance—here he gave a delicate gesture, acknowledging my condition, although I was still wearing my smock. I did not want to explain that I would finish soon and begin my confinement; I had no wish to embarrass him or myself, or mention your helping me, so I said nothing. He looked closely at the surface of the painting and said it was extraordinary and that I had blossomed under my mentor's tutelage. I began to feel uncomfortable, although he could not have known we have worked together. He asked what price I might put on it, and I said I did not intend to sell it until it had been judged by the Salon, and even then might want to keep it. Smiling pleasantly, he asked what price I might put on my reputation or that of my child.

I pretended to clean my brush in order to have a moment to think, then inquired as calmly as I could what he meant. He said I must be planning to submit the painting under the name Marie Rivière once again—that was no secret to him, who looked at the work of painters every day. But neither Marie nor I would value her reputation less than that of a painting. He of course was open-minded about women's painting. In fact, on his trip to Étretat in late May, he had seen a woman working en plein air, on the beach and cliffs, properly chaperoned by an older relative, and he had a note that she might have missed. He took it out of his pocket, held it up for me to read, and drew it away when I reached for it. I saw immediately that it was one you wrote me that morning, with a broken seal. I had never seen it before, but it was your hand, addressed to me, your words about us, about our night—he put it back in his jacket.

He said that it was wonderful how women were beginning to enter the profession, and my paintings could compete with those of any others he'd seen. But a woman may change her mind about painting after she becomes a mother, and certainly about any public scandal. Money was not sufficient reward for this superb painting, but if I would finish it to the best of my ability, he would honor it by putting his own name in the corner of it. The honor would be all his, actually, as it was already magnificent, a perfect combination of old and new, classical and natural painting—the girl was especially fine, young and rendered beautifully enough to attract anyone—and he would be happy to do the same for any future paintings, with the understanding that I would be spared any unpleasantness. He rambled on as if he had simply been commenting on the fittings of the studio or some interesting color I was using.

I couldn't look at him, nor speak. If you had been there, I fear you might have killed him, or he you. I wish indeed that he were dead, but he is not, and I have no doubt he is in earnest. Money cannot change his mind. Even if I deliver the painting to him when it is finished, he will not give us any peace. You must leave, my dearest. It is appalling, especially as the friendship that is the joy of my life and has brought my brush all this new skill is now completely pure. Tell me what to do and know that my heart will go with you whatever you decide, but spare Yves, only that, please, my love. I cannot have mercy on myself or you. Come to the house once and bring me all my letters, and I will think about what to do with them. And I will never paint for this monster after I finish, or if I do it will be only once, to record his infamy.

B.

Henri looked up at me from his chair.

"My God," I said. "We have to tell them. What they have here. And these drawings."

"No," he said. He tried to put it all back in the envelope, then indicated that I should help him. I obeyed, but slowly. He shook his head. "If they know something, there is no need for them to know more. It is better for them not to know. And if they know nothing, that is best of all."

"But no one understands—" I stopped.

"Yes—you do. You know all you need to. And I do, also. If only Aude were here. She would say the same thing." I thought he might cry, as he nearly had over the letters, but his face shone. "Take me out to the sunshine."

Chapter 104

Marlow

On the plane to Dulles, a blanket over my knees, I imagined Olivier's last letter—burned, perhaps, in the grate of her Paris bedroom.

1891

My darling,

I know the risk I take in writing you, but you will forgive an old artist's need to say goodbye to a comrade. I will seal this with care, trusting that no one but you will break it open. You never write, but I feel your presence in every one of my days in this alien, bleak, beautiful place—yes, I have tried to paint it, although heaven knows what will ever become of my canvases. Yves told me in his latest letter, about eight months ago, that you have not painted at all and that you dedicate yourself to your daughter, who has blue eyes, an open nature, a keen mind. How lovely and bright she must indeed be if you have transferred that gift to your care of her. But how could you, my love, put away your genius? You might have enjoyed it in private at the least. Now that I have been in Africa a decade and Thomas is dead, neither of us could be a threat to your reputation anymore. He kept the best of your work for his own glory; could you not take revenge by going on to do even better? But you are a stubborn woman, as I remember, or at least a purposeful one.

Never mind; I see at eighty what I could not even at seventy, that one forgives almost everything in the end except oneself. Now I forgive even myself, however, either because I am weak in character or because anyone would have fallen as I did at your feet, or perhaps simply because I do not have long to live—four months, six months. I do not mind, particularly. Everything you gave me cast a long light back down my years and doubled their illumination. I cannot complain after having had so much.

But I did not pick up my pen today to tax your patience with philosophy—rather to tell you that you will have the wish you whispered to me, at a moment I recall with the sharpest feelings, your request that I should die with your name on my lips. I shall. I'm sure there's no need to tell you that, and this may never even fall into your hand—the post from here is uncertain at best. But it will reach your ears somehow, that murmured name.

Now, my dearest love, think of me with all the pardon you can muster, and may the gods shower you with happiness until you are far older than this old wreck. Blessings upon your little daughter and Yves, lucky in your safekeeping. Give her a story or two about me when she is grown. I am leaving my money to Aude—yes, Yves has told me her name and he will hold my savings for her in the account in Paris. Use a small part of it to take her to Étretat someday. You know that it, with all the villages and cliffs and walks around, is a painter's paradise, should you ever pick up a brush again. I kiss your hand, my love.

Olivier Vignot

CHAPTER 105

Marlow

The morning of my return to Goldengrove was equally sunny; I seemed to have brought spring back with me from France. I had also brought Mary's ring, a nineteenth-century setting, rubies and gold, that had cost me more than my whole previous six months' expenses put together. The staff was glad to see me, and I got through the first onslaught of messages and paperwork on a single cup of coffee. Their notes, and those of Dr. Crown, in whose care I had left Robert, were reassuringly positive; Robert had still not spoken, but he had been busy and cheerful, had seemed engaged in the common meals, had smiled at patients and staff.

Then I checked on my other patients, two of whom were new. One of these was a young girl, released from suicide watch at a DC hospital and determined to get well enough to cause her family no more pain. She told me that watching her mother weep in fear over her had changed her mind about many things. The other newcomer was an elderly woman; I doubted she was in fit physical condition to be here, but I would confer with her family about her. She offered me her leaf-thin hand for a moment, and I held it. Then I took my briefcase and went to Robert.

He sat on the bed, a sketch pad on his knees and his eyes vague. I went right up to him and put my hand on his shoulder. "Robert, may I talk with you for a few minutes?"

He rose. I read the anger in his face, the surprise, something like hurt. I wondered if he would have to speak now—*You took my letters*. Maybe he would say *Damn you,* bitterly, as I had said to him. But he simply stood there.

"May I sit down?"

He made no motion, so I sat in my usual place, the armchair, a sort of home, a familiar spot. It felt strangely comfortable to me today.

"Robert, I went to France. I went to see Henri Robinson."

The effect was immediate; his head jerked around and he dropped his sketchbook to the floor.

"Henri has forgiven you, I think. I returned the letters to him. I'm sorry I had to take them without asking you. I was afraid you would not consent."

Again, an immediate surge of affect; he stepped forward and I got to my feet, feeling safer that way. I had left the door open, as always. Looking at him, however, I saw that he was not hostile, only startled.

"He's glad to have them back. Then I went with him to a village that is mentioned in the letters. I don't know whether you'll remember—Grémière, where Béatrice's maid came from."

His gaze was fixed on me, his face pale, his hands dangling at his sides.

"There was no evidence of the maid's family there, but I went because Henri told me that Béatrice had put something in that village that would show the truth about her love for her daughter. We found a drawing—a series of studies, actually, with her initials."

I took my own sketches from my briefcase and was acutely aware, for a moment, of my lack of skill. I handed them silently to him. "Béatrice de Clerval, not Gilbert Thomas. You guessed that?"

He held my sketches in his hands. It was the first time he'd ever taken anything I'd tried to give to him directly.

"There was a letter with these studies. I've brought you a copy of that, so that you can read it for yourself. Henri has translated it for me, too. It is from Béatrice to Olivier, and it proves that Thomas blackmailed her and claimed one of her greatest works as his own. You guessed that, too, I think."

I gave him the folded sheets. He stood holding them, gazing. Then he put one hand over his face and stayed that way for several seconds, interminable time. When he uncovered his eyes, he was looking directly at me. "Thank you," he said. I hadn't known, or hadn't remembered, how pleasant that voice was, resonant and rather deep, a fitting voice.

"There is something I simply can't understand." I stayed by him, conscious of his eyes first on me, then on the sketch. "If you suspected that *Leda* was Béatrice's work, why did you want to injure it?"

"I didn't."

"But you went in there with a knife, on purpose."

He smiled, or almost. "I tried to stab him, not her. But I was also not in my right mind."

Then I saw: the portrait of Gilbert Thomas counting his coins. Robert had come into the gallery alone. Yes—and he had taken the knife from his pocket, opened it rapidly, lunged as the guard who had just come in lunged for him in turn. And he had scraped the frame of the scene that hung next to the Gilbert Thomas self-portrait. I wondered what would have happened to Robert inside, to his already fragile state, if he had damaged *Leda,* his love. One of his loves. I touched his shoulder. "And are you in your right mind now?"

He was serious, a man taking an oath. "I have been for quite a while. I believe so."

"Some of this could happen to you again, you know, with

or without Béatrice. You will need to see a psychiatrist and perhaps a therapist, and to keep up your meds. Maybe forever, to be safe."

He nodded. His face was open, attentive.

"I can recommend another psychiatrist if you don't stay in the area. And you can always call me. Think hard about this, first. You've been here a long time."

Robert smiled. "So have you."

I had to smile with him. "I'd like to see you again tomorrow. I'll be in early, and you can sign the releases then, if you feel ready. I'll let the staff know—you can make any phone calls you need to today." This last part was the hardest for me to say; there was one person whose life I didn't want him to touch again.

"I'd like to see my children," he told me in a soft voice. "But I'll call them later, when I can get myself settled somewhere. Soon." He was standing in the middle of the room, his arms crossed, his eyes bright. I left him, then—he returned my handshake warmly, if a little absently—and went to my other duties.

I did manage to get to Goldengrove very early the next morning, since I was still on Paris time. Robert must have been watching for me; he came to my office door as I was organizing for the day. He had already showered and shaved and dressed neatly in the clothes I'd first seen him in, and his hair glistened with damp. He looked like a man awake after a hundred years' sleep. The staff had apparently given him some large bags for his possessions, which he had propped up in the hall. I could still feel Mary's arms around my neck, see the ring on her hand as she slept. He had not called her, and I now understood, beyond a doubt, that she did not want him to. I would have to decide whether to let Kate know about his release, too, of course.

Robert smiled. "I'm ready."

"Are you sure?" I asked him.

"I'll call you if I get into a bad situation."

"*Before* you get into a bad situation." I gave him my phone numbers and his papers.

"All right." He took the forms and read through them, signed without hesitation, returned my pen.

"Do you need a ride somewhere? Or can I call you a cab?"

"No. I'd like to walk a little first." He was very tall, lingering in the doorway to my office.

"You know, I broke every goddamned rule for you." I wanted him to hear it, or perhaps I just wanted to say it aloud.

He actually laughed. "I know that."

We stood looking at each other, and then Robert Oliver put his arms around me and embraced me for a moment. I had never had any brother, or a father large enough to crush me, or a friend of this magnitude. "Thank you for your trouble," he said.

Thank you for your life, I wanted to tell him, but I didn't. I meant, *Thank you for mine.*

I let him go alone, although I would have liked to walk him out, to smell the early morning that was his again, the flowering trees on the old drive in front of the building. He strode directly up the hall to the main door, and I saw him open it and step out, take his bags, close the door behind him.

I went to his room instead. It was empty, apart from his painting supplies; he'd piled those neatly on one shelf. The easel stood in the middle of the floor with a finished painting of Béatrice on it, unsmiling but radiant. That would be for Mary, and I found that I didn't mind the idea of delivering it. He had taken his other paintings with him.

I know now that I guessed right, that day. Robert would go somewhere new and paint: landscapes, still lifes, living people with quirks and attractions, with the ability to grow old—pieces that more than ever would grace collections and hang in museums. I couldn't quite foresee, of course, that his rise to lasting recognition would be my only message from him, perhaps ever, and the only one I needed. I would follow his paintings of his children as they grew, of the new women in his life, of the unfamiliar pastures and beaches where he set his easel. Robert had been right—I had gone to some trouble, although not entirely on his behalf. In payment, I'd kept something for myself: those long minutes in Paris, in front of a painting the world may never see. I have had my large rewards, my joys, but the small ones are as sweet as any.

1895

Almost night. The light is hopeless now; dark branches merge with one another and with the deepening sky. I imagine him putting away his things, scraping his palette. He is cleaning brushes near the lantern when she walks by again, close to his windows this time, returning with a hasty step from her errand. He cannot make out much of the face inside her hood; she must be looking at the ground, at the ice, the puddles freezing over, the patches of snow and mud. Then she glances up and he sees that her eyes are dark, as he'd hoped; he catches their glow—not a young face, despite her lithe body, but one he might have fallen in love with if his heart were younger, one he would like even now to paint. Her gaze catches the light from his window and she bends her head again, picking her way in shoes too good for this trampled road. He notices that her hands hang empty at her sides, as if she has left behind whatever they cradled—a gift, food for a sick elder, mending for the village seamstress, he guesses, or even a baby. No; it is too cold a night for a baby.

He doesn't know this village as well as his own; Moret-sur-Loing, where he will die in about four years, is to the west. An end he is aware of already. The pain in his well-wrapped throat is not enough to dim his curiosity, and he gently opens the door and looks after her. A carriage waits at the near end of the lane, before the church; fine horses, lanterns lit and hung high. He can see the sweep of her dark, ornamented skirts as she climbs in; she pulls the door shut with a black-gloved hand, as if to prevent the driver from getting down and delaying them further. The horses strain, their phantom breath visible in the air; the carriage creaks forward.

Then they are gone and the village is quiet, as usual at this hour, sinking into night. He locks the door and calls his servant from the back room for a little supper. Tomorrow he must go home to his wife and studio, waiting just up the river, and send a note to the friend who so kindly lends him this place every winter. A short drive back in the morning, and then more painting, for all the time left to him. Meanwhile, the fire has begun to throw shadows around the room and the kettle on the hob is boiling. He surveys his afternoon's landscape; the trees are quite good, and the strange woman's silhouette makes a mark of distinction on a rural road, gives it some mystery. He has added his name and two numbers to the lower left corner. Enough for now, although he will touch up her clothing tomorrow, and fix the light on those windows in the farthest house, at the end of the lane, where old Renard is mending harnesses. The paint is setting already on his new work. In six months it will be dry. He will hang it in his studio; he will take it down some sunny morning and send it to Paris.

Acknowledgments

Thanks to:
Amy Williams, agent and friend extraordinaire; Reagan Arthur, beloved editor-friend, Michael Pietsch, who lifted this book with his skill, and other much-admired colleagues at Little, Brown and Company.

Also:
Georgi H. Kostov for his wonderful reading and for the freedom to go and learn. Eleanor Johnson for her loving assistance with research in Paris and Normandy; Dr. David Johnson for his belief in this project and for a rest in the Auvergne; Jessica Honigberg for showing me a painter's mind and hands; Dr. Victoria Johnson for a renewed love of France; my Dutch uncle, Paul Howard Johnson, for his unflagging support and encouragement over four decades; Laura E. Wolfson, sister writer, for her reading and our thirty years of excursions to museums; Nicholas Delbanco, cherished mentor, for his reading and for discussions of Monet and Sisley; Julian Popov, fellow novelist, for his critiques: *благодаря;* Janet Shaw for her reading and for years of sheltering wings; Dr. Richard T. Arndt for his help with all things French: *merci mille fois;* Heather Ewing for her reading and her hospitality in Manhattan; Jeremiah Chamberlin for his fearless help with revisions and for cutting down on the driving; Karen Outen, Travis Holland,

Natalie Bakopoulos, Mike Hinken, Paul Barron, Raymond McDaniel, Alex Miller, Josip Novakovich, Keith Taylor, Theodora Dimova, and Emil Andreev for readings/endless camaraderie in the craft; Peter Matthiessen, Eileen Pollack, Peter Ho Davies, and others for outstanding tutelage; Kate Dwyer, Myron Gauger, Lee Lancaster, John O'Brien, and Ilya Pérdigo Kerrigan for fragments; Iván Mozo and Larisa Curiel for hospitality in Mexico and advice on the Acapulco settings; Joel Honigberg for his thoughts on the Impressionists, which helped to spark this story; Antonia Hodgson, Chandler Gordon, Vania Tomova, Svetlozar Zhelev, and Milena Deleva for treasured friendship, publishing, translation, tales of art, and literary camaraderie; the Hopwood Program at the University of Michigan, the Ann Arbor Book Festival, the Apollonia Festival of Arts in Bulgaria, the MFA program at the University of North Carolina at Wilmington, and the American University in Bulgaria for hosting public readings of passages from this work; Rick Weaver for allowing me to observe his painting class at the Art League in Alexandria; Dr. Toma Tomov for information about the psychiatric profession, Dr. Monica Starkman for the same and for her invaluable help with the editing of this book; Dr. John Merriman, Dr. Michèle Hanoosh, and Dr. Katherine Ibbett for help with French history and sources; Anna K. Reimann, Elizabeth Sheldon, and Alice Daniel for all their moral support; Guy Livingston for twenty-five years of brotherhood in the arts; Charles E. Waddell for his *excellent* suggestion; Dr. Mary Anderson for wise counsel; Andrea Renzenbrink, Willow Arlen, Frances Dahl, Kristy Garvey, Emily Rolka, and Julio and Diana Szabo for outstanding help with my household at various periods during the writing of this book; Anthony Lord, Dr. Virginia McKinley, Mary Parker, Josephine Schaeffer, and Eleanor Waddell Stephens — beloved introductions to France and the

French language. Other family, friends, students, and institutions I cannot even begin to list.

Finally, I am indebted to Joseph Conrad and his great portrait, *Lord Jim;* may the author's spirit enjoy and forgive the heartfelt homage I've paid in these pages.

THE HISTORIAN

Elizabeth Kostova

Late one night, exploring her father's library, a young woman finds an ancient book and a cache of yellowing letters addressed ominously to 'My dear and unfortunate successor'. Her discovery plunges her into a world she never dreamed of – a labyrinth where the secrets of her father's past and her mother's mysterious fate connect to an evil hidden in the depths of history.

From the archive libraries of Oxford to Istanbul and Budapest, and into the depths of Eastern Europe, *The Historian* is a captivating tale that is almost unbearably suspenseful – and utterly unforgettable.

978-0-7515-3728-4

Other bestselling titles available by mail

☐ The Historian — Elizabeth Kostyova — £6.99

The prices shown above are correct at time of going to press. However, the publishers reserve the right to increase prices on covers from those previously advertised, without further notice.

sphere

Please allow for postage and packing: **Free UK delivery.**
Europe: add 25% of retail price; Rest of World: 45% of retail price.

To order any of the above or any other Sphere titles, please call our credit card orderline or fill in this coupon and send/fax it to:

Sphere, PO Box 121, Kettering, Northants NN14 4ZQ
Fax: 01832 733076 Tel: 01832 737526
Email: aspenhouse@FSBDial.co.uk

☐ I enclose a UK bank cheque made payable to Sphere for £ . . . .
☐ Please charge £ . . . . . . to my Visa/Delta/Maestro

☐☐☐☐☐☐☐☐☐☐☐☐☐☐☐☐

Expiry Date ☐☐☐☐   Maestro Issue No. ☐☐

NAME (BLOCK LETTERS please) . . . .

ADDRESS . . . .

. . . .

. . . .

Postcode . . . . Telephone . . . .

Signature . . . .

Please allow 28 days for delivery within the UK. Offer subject to price and availability.